Out of Odessa and Into Ideation

by Eric Bragg

Out of Odessa and Into Ideation

by Eric Bragg

OYSTER
MOON
PRESS

BERKELEY, CALIFORNIA

Out of Odessa and Into Ideation
by Eric Bragg

Front cover illustration:
"Licking You with My Thoughts, and Thinking of You with My Tongue"
by Eric Bragg.

"The Sassy Sky Diva..." was originally published @ www. surrealcoconut.com.

"Spider" was originally published in *The Somnambulist Footprints:
A Collection of Surrealist Tales*, Oyster Moon Press, 2008.

"Out of Odessa and Into Ideation" was originally published in
What Will Be: Almanac of the International Surrealist Movement. Brumes Blondes, 2014.

ISBN: 978-0-578-19564-3

Additional copies of this book can be ordered from LuLu:
http://www.lulu.com

Oyster Moon Press is a non-profit, surrealist publishing co-op located in
Berkeley, California.

http://www.oystermoonpress.com

This book is dedicated to all of the self-righteous parents of the world, especially those emotionally stunted, highly insecure but seemingly normal individuals whose cowardice and narcissistic, predatory psychopathology compel them to violently invade the privacy of others, while at the same time hypocritically pretending to be morally upright citizens. You know who you are.

Contents:

The Broken Mountain
(2002)

1

Paper cutouts from the totem pole flutter in the wind, representing a laughable cross-section of an airplane's fuselage. The riveted cutouts shed the paper spines like a confused buffalo, but the swinging pendulums occupy the windows of the centralized room that was put there by the hands of plumbing that understood the eruption of a manicured summer lawn on the rings of twisted house limbs. Planet fears are reduced to equations, and so the watchdog of the ultraviolet remedies creates a parody of transferring shotguns to alcoves, and vice versa. Surely this preemptive gesture captured a wink of the yesteryears through the immortalization of the totem pole of tissue paper?

The broken windows of the cutouts cannot hold back the incoming fog as it turns lakes into death traps for the unwary. These geological creations represent desecrated easter eggs that have been influenced by the tectonics of alien DNA that is pressed between ancient, well-preserved rock strata in haunted museums.

If these special eggs have their corresponding forms secretly grinning from within the fickle angles and voids of the totemic cutout representatives, then these poetically lacerated bodies had shared intimate moments with exchanged living room lamp stories between the fluttery eyes of rubbery, ghoulish species. This exchange had somehow been represented in the forms of these corrupted eggs with their imprinted alien DNA and stratified museum layers. Over-ripe fruits couldn't have picked a better time to drop, and so when the collection of glass eggs began to be peeled, layer by layer, the ringing of female telephones commenced, creating the illusion of vast networks of cattail-lined country roads that led in all directions, especially toward hills where citrus trees opened their orange blossoms, giving light to gristled trees with artificial anthropomorphism. These particular orange growers were representative of a broadly occurring belt of freshly flowing life, and when the silk umbrellas were left by the door, an unidentified portrait of a very famous petty, provincial bureaucratic functionary was hung on a dim wall. The hanging of the picture must have created a few wind currents, and so the resulting meow from the umbrella rack created a wind sculpture that was so rare it could have only lasted for a fraction of a second, and yet its highly cherished and wholesomely desiderated harmonics spoke of an infection that was as easy to transmit as it was figuratively bottled in a perfume factory, where all employees involved wear highly ornate toe-rings that end up touching the ground with tactile hairiness which can sometimes mimic the nocturnal lurchings of wild canines and other such beasts.

When the windy paper cutouts of totemic proportions were finally implemented in the most recent years as identification cards, the personalities of feet became apparent. It was as if noticing feet moving on a twilit country road lined with perfect rows of fresh cattails would diversify the file folders of ancient and future civilizations, at least as how the walking feet knew it. If that didn't work, then elephants could butt their heads against oak trees to shake them for honey-dripping acorns with perfect smiley faces on each one. This latter strategy, although perhaps a little severe, could in time produce many lengths of cheery colored lightbulbs with black, overlaid snowflake designs on each tiny bulb. Were these the sorts of times when the rubbery arms of trans-dimensional fish-cats would sympathetically emulate the cheery, colorful snowflake bulbs that contained a coded message? The trans-dimensional fish-cat arms were alien, and so their spider web of knowledge led to an arms race of mathematics, coding for geometrical sounds that could woo any candy-perfume obstacle in the way arteries move blood. The resulting pyramid of stone steps resembled a fallen and thoroughly collapsed bird's nest. The abandoned feathers contained within resembled an extremely attractive magazine rack, and thus the perfume of all the rooms etched the forms of reticulating fossilized lizards onto the stone walls of the inner-pyramid tomb. Once etched, the lizard images are used as barcodes to transport various descriptive social reports to various islands located near the equator. The perfumed blood is smeared around eyes, and so verminiferous night wolves forage for sleeping bodies in the dark hours.

2

The minute hands of the wrist watches deceptively jump back and forth, due to the peculiar stimulation received by the internal mechanics, spilling black machine oil onto the floor. The wristwatches still continue to function, however.

Suddenly, a hot mountain begins to cleave down the length of its side, enabling a finely cobbled stream to arise. The water from this stream was about as pure as a cognizant potato, and this relay was translated into an alien language, leading to the arrival of silly tourists eager to sink their numerous armpits into the cool, effervescent stream water. The creation of this infant mountain stream was the result of a vastly rending division, leaving behind a downward trail of orange blossoms that get caught in the flow of the water, almost a geoactive cascade of teardrop magnitude, using newspapers as nesting material for a time-corroded industrial, seafaring vessel. The empty compartments of this floating, metal box contain the memories of fish, and so the cascade of orange blossoms has a new holistic library with which it can edify itself during moments of growth, like when primal humans made comfortable bedroom sandals from cool, broad leaves that were harvested from mildly fragrant trees. A ray of hope shoots through the sandaled keyhole that masks the glass gate of a door that stood upon the orange tree thresholds of mountains frequently patrolled by metamorphic squid-people whose panting breath evokes a twigged country road perplexed by perfect rows of fertile cattails, evoking the satin honey of a beehive that resided within a crevice that overlooked the fresh, cobbled stream.

When cats lick their whiskers, their glassy, colorful eyes canvas a pyramid of precariously arranged marbles of colored glass, strange moons which orbited their feline brains and within which contained legions of the sultry squid-people. These squid people managed to abandon their produce trucks from the weekend and bring light to the abandoned buildings on the neglected town's outskirts. Their magical presence brought kisses to the tops of fluid dreams, and their prehensile grappling limbs brought a glimpse of home from underneath mossy, jeweled rocks that contain the defenestrated satellites that remain vigilant, even under adverse horseshoe conditions, when spiders will substitute for metallic units of social worth.

The growing memories of the traveling, wayward squid-people create a gypsy lumber yard where certain kinds of ornamental wooden cabinets are forged from the organic pith left behind as driftwood by the twilit orange-blossom stream. The fresh, moist, organic odors of the wood insert the words of seconds into the randomly occurring stones from the stream, and the wooden forms of the hands of the forest become sentient. This catastrophic awakening hurls tectonic tremors down the old country roads, and the resulting nightfall releases a minute for every time that the moon is round, shining its healthy golden light on the dimly perceived sleeping forms of the living. Mortals shear great globules of clay from the sides of the mountains, but only in their dim dreams generated by biochemical electricity. On the diagonal hills of the moonlit midnight, the squid-people emerge from their farm-like lairs, pull the twigs from their oral apertures, and greet the golden moonlight with their childlike eyes wide-open in hungry awe as they regard the glorious beginning of their period of foraging activity. Although somewhat unknown were the objects of their foraging; only could their predictable cackles from unseen mouths provoke the alien intelligence of the moment.

The nocturnal country roads beckoned to the squid-people, but they maintained their woodsy indifference to it, within the purpose of achieving their telepathic link to the irregular architecture that spoke of ancient, long-dead picnics where festive checkered blankets had captured flying saucers and other extraterrestrial manifestations of corrupted instructions from a society that no longer existed. The dark, gray moths hugged the walls and then understood their place next to the underground pools of the leisure sectors of the neglected city. Only there had the gray, pulsating wall-moths decided to erect their center of operations. The squid-people nevertheless managed to keep their link with the gothic picnic architecture. The moment ended pleasantly, and the relics of a past ice age were placed in large vaults of subterranean ice fields that hadn't seen the light of the surface for many eons. The squid-people were prolific in the reproductive kind of way, and succeeded in populating the abandoned city, bringing back a velvet life to the structures of awakening shadows of dawn. This bold colonization effort transformed the squid-people, and they gave up farming for the temporal manufacture of a special variety of robotically synthesized squid flowers. These amazing and gregarious colonization events led to a new kind of settlement that was secluded within the folds of a thick forest lacerated with self-assured cat-tailed roads that moved great convoys of red maple-leaves as they infiltrated the moment like a self-expanding star nucleus.

In the aftermath of the ancient picnic, the corroded forms of dead harps littered the roadsides of the dead city, but the squid-people ignored them, having no use for them, and refusing to remove their ancient, musical skeletons that mimicked the hollow shapes of metallic butterflies. Despite these wholesome distractions, the squid people never ended their twilit romances, and they shared great passions in the way two clouds can become married despite the occasional whirling discharges of electricity and the booming thunder that can grip the forms of ancient lizards of unknown, indifferent identities, creating a rushing force of history, magnetizing electrified spinal columns of the sleepy squid-people as they gently and contentedly shut their eyes at the advent of a solar day that might bleach the sensitive spots on their nocturnal skins, and so they all found the appropriate bedrooms and slept.

3

Aching tweeters and woofers drown out the virus of boats and other vehicles displaced by a bilingual wind that burns the highways. Flirts in the sky; flirts in the ocean. It is only after candles are used to create a repetitive spare tire that the sparrows emerge from the socketed hollows in the deathly trees. The fear of tall places unsettles the sparrows, and their implanted memories carry the dreams of watermelon telepathy and the balustraded indifference of royal red carpets pocked with fossilized chewing gum. Mountain streams could have moved faster.

A balanced letter from a shaky trapeze falls into a mailbox, and this arrival bears claws in the same way a displaced crustacean does. The confusion of the mailboxes with the sporadic and highly unpredictable mail-delivery system does little to inspire confidence. Somehow, the walls sense this deficiency, and begin to rebel, pushing forward their bricks in the attempt at collapsing the Babylonian skyscraper. These sorts of zero gravity theatrics mimic the arc of exploding fireworks when they are released over midnight rivers on their troubled courses towards coffee shops. These coastal coffee shops resemble a stopped train when perceived from far distances, but their saxophone music is imprinted on all of those past bricks that choke the old subterranean passageways that represent ancient service hallways that used to subtly connect old buildings of great importance.

A missing ocean wind spreads salty sea fumes through the cracks in the outer windows, creating ephemeral spiderwebs indicating the presence of undercover agents hiding inside of sugary cereal boxes. The ocean wind supplies the webs with fresh bloodsalt, and these uncertain feeding behaviors dismiss the rains beginning to blow through from up the street.

Confusion on the piano staircase. Rattlesnake doors that were burnt onto hands were the model for the new year. These messages were etched onto tree stumps made of bronze, and these monuments sometimes caused disbelieving ears to close when doldrums of roses had been located within the favorite local rattlesnake den, when vipers hibernated in darkness with their eggs.

The wolf at the head of the cave left behind a sponge anvil as a peace offering, and initiated a hunting strategy that led to a rabbit barbecue. The anvil remained at the mouth of the cave, and its spongy flesh absorbed water from the air. When the snakes awoke much later, each of them moistened their fangs through puncturing the sponge anvil. It was a good way for them to wake up, and yet they developed a concern that perhaps they were losing precious venom to the sponge.

4

Red maple leaves moved through the night air in a gust, thankful for the end of a day that involved those ever-sinister wolves and mailboxes. The fall of night was mercifully indigo, sporting a full moon that somehow stimulated the flight-patterns of the red maple leaves as they streamed great distances through the air, always being drawn to unfamiliar destinations, like pre-industrial film processing plants.

Usually the indifferent squid-people would shun places like the processing plants. These nocturnal people enjoyed their new colonization successes, and their society evolved as the young, Martian palm trees grew, producing an infinite supply of fresh dates. Under these circumstances, the squid-people would never starve, so their optimism was in a healthy state, seeking the newest solutions to the newest questions. The tiles in one of their gardens rustled with the oscillation of opposing colors, and this fluctuation caused many distortions on the readily available civil maps, indicating a radius of linear uncertainty around the tiled garden of squid-people architecture.

Somehow, the welcomed reflective eyes of cats shone through the darkness, and the squid-people of the twilight performed rituals with painted chicken bones, sending out a steady pulse of information to the bright cat eyes beaming through the telepathic flannel darkness. The passage of the cat eyes did much to bring harmony to the random color oscillations that were occurring within the agitated squid garden. Here, many things were continually reborn, but continually reabsorbed. This theoretical factory of the squid-people was clearly labeled in their own terminology, and the information that the squid-people derived from the outlying garden became a wealthy knowledge-reserve, and thus highly protected at all hours by the administrators of that society.

Walnut manuals were removed from alcoves located on each side of the garden entrance, and weak candles were lit ceremoniously, so that the elders could read to their children of squid-people lore and other culturally significant documents which would better instruct them in the ways of their society. After this brief cycle of learning, the walnut manuals were replaced in their alcoves, and boxes of trick mirrors were allowed inside the garden walls so that much sunlight would be captured during the morning hours when the squid-people would be preparing for bed.

The trick mirrors did their job in sunlight absorption, and much light was captured while the beautiful squid-people slept. Simultaneously, wooden decoy ducks were brought into town, submerged in liquid nitrogen. The nitrogen trucks dumped their frozen, wooden cargo, and the boredom of over-permed armpit hair occupied their troubled thoughts as their finely carved wooden bodies began to thaw. Before these thawing wooden decoy ducks were placed many carefully sliced wedges of toothpaste sushi, and upon being doused with generous dollops of hydrocortisone, the wedges of toothpaste sushi came to life and abruptly addressed the thawing decoys:

"As you can see, there are many different ways to be rolled up, and since we were born as sushi, we will die as sushi, also."

The decoys responded: "Yes, we understand that logic, but we nevertheless are offended by the way you gave us the phone number of our local, petty bureaucrat without the area code. Now we will be unable to attend her very important prison parties. Despite that, however, we still believe in your inner toothpaste goodness, so we will perhaps forgive you over time. Meanwhile, why don't you roll on over here so that you might better sit atop our thawing heads?"

The magnetic effects of this touching conversation brought in the tide, which dragged several dunes of sand with it. The new beach landscape had an odd relationship with the decaying urban architecture, forcing open peeling doors and depositing sand in areas where people used to tread daily. The deflated corpses of purple jellyfish were observable, and a wandering troupe of inquisitive cats played pattycake with them. Despite the apparently innocent intrusion of the beach biome into the skeletal remains of the city, there could be heard the sinister and highly unnatural sounds of thumping beneath the ground. A lion could only imagine what manner of insanity lurked beneath the barren urban beaches, with the sticky, dehydrating purple jellyfish.

Within the twitch of an eyestalk, the arms of all squid-people became intimate shards of stained glass, of a splotched color assignment ranging from blood red to the most emotional of ambers. A woman with a newspaper managed to surrender a smile to the encroaching weather section, and the news of forthcoming urban storms sent erotic shivers and tremors all along her finely toned limbs, encouraging the appearance of latent mollusk suction cups. In a dead town where bodies of stained glass were the new hope for the future, the urban beach with its lapping saltwater encroached on everything, even the toothpaste sushi that was still growing above and below the sea cobbles. In response to the incessant ebb and flow of the unnatural tide, the squid-woman left her cave and searched for lost pieces of stinky ambergris technology, which she believed would provide her with eventual extracts. Needless to say, these powerful extracts would give her a new face, and transform her ephemeral physiology into something more human, or so the elder mice believed, as they studied her efforts at the unabashed reclamation of the unknown ambergris technology. Even though there were fossilized gambling devices embedded in the insecure urban beach sand, the squid-woman paid no heed, and pulled many reeking ambergris fragments from the yowling vortex of indifference.

As fast as a nauseating subterrene vault releases its foul monsters, the squid-people hid underneath eyeball-shaped boulders as the unnatural, subterranean thumping grew in pitch. Squid-women wrapped their bodies in colorful, aeronautical kites, while the squid-men bound themselves with thick, nutritious belts of olive-green kelp. Although the squid-people were unable to understand their own impulsive behaviors, they nonetheless opined that such gestures would help ward off mysterious dangers that reeked of salt and the raw perfume technology. Ancient vomit had never been more sacred.

Faster than a tongue can circumscribe a cognizant clitoris, the high tide besieged the old city that had been layered with sand and occupied by the gypsy-like squid-people. Life histories were created via the crack of thunder, and the clarity of water faucets presented itself. In fact, some of the squid-women felt compelled to remove a few water faucets that had gently appeared on the sides of their majestic craniums, and this action resembled a spasmodic, fluttering saxophone that jerkily moved from note to note. The Excalibur of the moment cut through the turbid fog that made the loveliest of things frustratingly inaccessible. The wolves howled at the moon, but the squid-people danced, heedless of the terrestrial warning. There was present some kind of warning klaxon, but the frugal beauties with adorable button noses etched their arching shadows onto the crumbling concrete walls. It was as if a beauty tornado appeared and blew all of the festive party lights from their sockets. Despite these heart-throbbing shenanigans, the erotic, highly tessellated garden of the squid-people allowed for the materialization of legless cobalt blue streaks within the atmosphere of Neptune.

During the soft interim of night, the furtive glances of albinoid creatures broke free from their non-sentient plastic shackles, and the birthing tubs which had nourished them for so long became a smoldering pile of old, pungent socks. The lethal foot-odor really wasn't all that bad, but the irregular street lamps needed more convincing than just a highly ephemeral wink. The laughter of the moment teetered on the edge, and what was once a flatulent politician now transmuted to higher levels of abnormal indignation mixed with narcissistic friendliness, of the same caliber as the uncertainty of bedtime honeycombs. The rocks in the wall ceased to glow.

5

Thumping eyelids of pre-bubonic greed. Callous insurrections following along the front lines of electrified puddles. An ignominious existence rustled between blind eyeballs of the drunk, clacking lights around which nocturnal beach beauties cruise with agonizing vigilance. These saline moths spew forth from the long-lost yowling feline vortex, of so many odd years ago, full of fur and timidity.

The aether of a Wisconsin cheese factory might be a burden to some, but as long as the sand is washed from the ears and asses of hyperbolic cows, then all should be fine in the end or at least as some appropriate songs indicate. Loose gestures of nothing perpetrate magic tricks of rabbits, silk handkerchiefs and confetti flowers. These instances of arboreal looseness spill across the udders of compromised farms nestled deep within the eye-caves of trolls who monitor the highway paths, and the troll-like deliberations regarding the safest traveling paths are made known in the form of blood-stained atlases. Can you hear the naughty x-mas music seeping in from the artificial wall polymers that seal within the dead faces of the timebomb? Could these best regards wail out loud with the communication of seagulls? Is it really time again to commence another session of smores, trust-falls, and other instant, waterproof friendships? When would the sun rise over the earwax forest again? Darkness abounds.

These questions were fabulously ignored and repressed within the corpses of female chicken salad and other sprout bouquets. Can we touch that, and perhaps take it with us to the hair salon? So we continue to enroll ourselves within the sad archives of dim, card houses put before us by forces which might have been understandable yet which were mentally denied at all costs, in the same way biological octopus subjects must exercise their curiosity by tampering with their experimental equipment. But the mice would still refuse to return to their holes!

As grains of sand go trick-or-treating in the early morning hours, the timebelts of seaweed become irretractable. They eventually litter the immediate cosmos with stomach-turning, self-generated visions of an ultimate subjective failure that resulted from a well-cultivated fear of money and other linear systems of value-establishment that would suck the eyeballs from fish skulls with the greatest of ease. This tribal mask embodied the last gateway or hurdle to the wonders of girly-world, a porcelain bathtub lined with bleached sand dollars and other such earthly refuse. The peeping ravens perched on the edge of the tub squinted their orange eyes and couldn't help but recall the bedtime memories of indigo honeycombs and all the other places that frustrated, self-righteous parents wished that they could have visited when they were not dutifully transmitting conformist culture to the next generation of well-behaved people (and with all psychotherapy notwithstanding). This incendiary matchstick taught very few lessons not already known throughout the saline cosmos of emotional bricks that would ultimately be used to construct burning houses. Time still marched on, but the springs in the clocks ached and marveled at an untouched life that was systematically shunned by the dogs of internal chaos, to which some occasionally referred to as the self-doubting trauma hounds. Hypnotic bullets with computer chips replaced the regular tortilla fare, and young women put variously organized flying saucers into their uncertain pockets, continuing a life-long hike down abandoned country roads where newly formed mountain steam cleavage reigned supreme. If only the deluge had happened two nebulous "days" before. The clocks refused to die.

6

While the forest was to eventually recede like a thinning hairline, the bathtub still held muddy water, reminiscent of golden days, when every false cobble within the naked mountain streams still contained perfect ingots of gold. These temporally inaccessible treasures kept many awake in their beds at night, but only the soft cats blinked their eyes and looked to the full moon for guidance.

The beacon of the moon shone very yellow that night, and appeared to radiate streams of an unnatural magnetism, leading all parties involved, including the squid-people, to dream of a temporarily inaccessible migration of warmly diaphanous red leaves, perhaps ripped from an unwary tree. This faraway, fateful passage of the swarming red leaves could have easily been compared to an unknown, trans-galactic flow of blood from an unknown source. Nevertheless, all creatures on the side of the cracked mountain had the dream, and they tried in vain to remember the outcome of the red swarm but couldn't remember. All that was seen moving from the yellow moonstruck sands was the dull reflection of the moon itself, and nothing more.

The sands caved in, due to some minor geological event, and the hourglasses of lost phone calls added a mechanistic rhythm to an otherwise desolate urban oblivion, thoroughly ignored by the sleepers.

From behind a rock, a mysterious woman appeared, who seemed to float barely centimeters off the ground, rather than walk. She was cautiously joined by some kind of being that almost resembled a painted, furry puppet, but the low light could barely reveal the eye-movements. The strange woman pulled an abnormal ingot of ice from her sleeve and held it to the moonlight for the puppet creature to see. Upon opening her mouth to speak, the pair of night-dwellers was abducted by a large, night butterfly that somehow managed to live its life only at night. The forms of the woman with the alien ice-cube and the furry, painted puppet were compressed and then injected into the dark wings of the night-butterfly, which then flew away, first in the direction of the sensuous yellow moon, whose frozen, faraway tectonics glared down into the yawning stream-chasm of the broken mountain.

This particularly odd variety of a pseudo-extraterrestrial abduction actually happened quite often enough, and yet somehow most inhabitants usually ended up turning a blind eye. Nevertheless, the odd butterfly abductions began to occur in higher and higher numbers, silencing entire monuments of ancient, civilized integrity with a confusing plethora of intruding emotions that could have only been cast from an optic cantaloupe with tiger-stripes that had been deftly cleft into two separated lobes. The seeping juice of the mutilated cantaloupe was the key that came in two parts. In the same way a naval destroyer annihilated the civilized leviathan, the split cerebral cantaloupe became the dominant pattern of imagery on the wings of the night butterfly who carried the compressed and inextricably entwined forms of the furry puppet and the levitating woman with the curious, transformative ingots of ice *[and who also happened to have a crush on her butterfly man - the editor]*. Ultraviolet explosions abounded, further splintering any unstable archetypes.

The seismic activity of the night abductions revealed many endearing currents, which, although misleading, always released laughter from trees and trapped bones from the cooked hides of large, unidentified fish. Would the marbled eggs nestled in the abandoned swimming pools crack prematurely? Could sharp fish ultimately boomerang from these dead pools only to shatter all of those lovely diamonds of time? Could these obscure butterfly truths be suppressed forever by the dominant order of the present? The obscure lights in the tunnel could only grasp at predicting the coming roar of the train.

Beneath the surface of an outlying oceanic tide-pool, the long-buried plastic legs of Martian mannequins were eroded by a fleet of starfish carrying mirrors, creating odd confrontations between dreams within dreams, altering the popular currents of cosmic self-awareness. The threat of the uncovered mannequins was real, and yet there was the faintest suggestion that more mannequins were forthcoming, possibly from places farther away than Mars. Nevertheless, these tide-pool mannequins currently appeared harmless, in a state of suspended animation, and their only friends were the hapless starfish who silently glided over their legs like a fragrant shadow.

These peculiar, perhaps erotically motivated starfish had a great many legs, and apparently it took having great legs to know great legs. Despite that, the ultimate purpose of the starfish remained unknown, and their water vascular system appeared to be working in a state of overtime. After interacting with the dormant, partially buried mannequin legs, the army of purple starfish retreated into the abandoned den of a once polka-dotted abalone retreat, exchanging gossip in the darkness, and knitting loosely fitting sweaters made of a silky, resilient seaweed. Oddly enough, the highly vocal purple starfish knew of no permanent residence, and their nomadic existence was highly difficult to predict. Their primary method of communication was achieved through their contact with legs, whether hewn of flesh and blood, or even the most resilient of Martian, commercial plastics.

Suddenly, a meteorite crashed into the shallow water nearby, causing the temperature of the saline water to rise a few degrees. The alien materials within the meteorite slowly leached into the water, and the purple starfish withdrew towards the back of the endless polka-dotted abalone cave-retreat, shunning the poisoned light that would seep for miles and miles through the local ocean. In so doing, the falling of the meteorite facilitated a relaxing afternoon for the half-buried Martian mannequin legs, enabling them to stay submerged in peace, devoid of the alien communication of the erotically motivated purple starfish. The leaching compounds from the alien meteorite closely resembled the discerning chirping of magic, yellow birds, and the resulting diffusion evoked the colorless spread of a pungent, braided sunset. If only the nearby lobster traps hadn't cancelled their subscription to *Medieval Pantyhose, Inc.*

7

From the New Jersey slopes to the bread-winning deserts of the colossal Outback, troops of flaccid iguanas traveled to places where unsanctioned tattoo parlors were thriving. These special iguanas could skip over oceans, and breathlessly traverse even the grandest of canyons that periodically arose within the rather small confines of the New Jersey territory. As they hopped across violent ocean waves, unaware of the thriving squids down below, their sunburned limbs became transparent, displaying the glowing, crimson bones beneath. Although they splotched and leapt from wave to wave, they still minded their solar exposure, and from time to time would awkwardly smear sunscreen on their vulnerable flesh de vez en cuando. So while catching rays and code-switching, the iguanas directed their charged phalanx in the direction of various appealing landmasses that bespoke of temperate environments, excluding the oily shores of New Jersey.

The hemispherical arcing of the lizards over the waves confused the avian bypassers-by, but they paid no heed, and focused on their transoceanic quest for the shores of enlightened chemistry. When these shores were attained, they rested awhile on beaches of onyx sand, exploring the washed beds for sand dollars and other exotic skeletal remains of sacrificed seafood. With the scanning ritual complete, the tired iguanas secured their resting positions within the concealed folds of bovine salt-licks, and so managed to avoid the annoying, passing troupes of boy scouts who could find ways to manufacture achievement patches even if the last utilitarian activity on the planet had been exhausted by the ravaging scourges of walking organic bioweapons that lacked charm but who wore attractive scarabs over their modified larynxes. But the sunburned iguanas paid no heed.

Once in their pumice dens, amid the reek of newly released sulfuric fumes, the iguanas crystallized their cherry-red bones, reposing in the shadows of spiderwebs and other festive but proteinaceous lampoons. These activities carried on for possibly several hours, and when these kinetic meditations were complete, the iguanas slept, and dreamed.

8

After the completion of another holy mandate, the pope sat back in his wicker, vatican chair, lifted his left leg and released a malevolent, creaking fart. He then proceeded to pull a moist, green booger from his right nostril, sighing and lamenting the spiritual emptiness of a world that had seen through the pretensions of an obsolete religious code. He used the booger as a bookmark in his income tax files and had dubious thoughts about boiled potatoes covered with pubic hair and an invitation to bless a private game of collegiate croquet.

Meanwhile, mythic ages evolved, and non-human soul-hunters stalked the confines of every New Orleans piano-room available to the public. Pretty medallions were impressed into dried foreheads. The sodomy of reticulated sea urchins became available, and soup-pots were stirred with the utmost care so as to allow the proper stewing of bats' wings, horseshoes and simplistic, four-digited extremities within the rich broth. This combinatorial goulash couldn't have lasted forever, but the ugly weather had the strange tendency to push hail through even the most vigilant of religious smokescreens.

The probably pagan stew came from a very old recipe, from shadowed, half-forgotten human ancestors whose vague impressions of self-awareness stretched back several, uncountable millennia, to the time when crude vocabularies clearly resembled regurgitated alphabet soups with certain letters missing from the language code. The ancientness of the rich, brothy message was unthinkable, yet its disturbing presence could be seen, even in the oldest photographs. In part, these older photographs of ancient alphabet soup-vomit added to the contemporary feeling of the omission of truth, or at least part of the terrestrial truths, with peculiar, selective absences of some of the more revealing and more important letters. Furthermore, these omitted soup letters directly corresponded to the crude phonemes of language, and so the scholastic pursuits of ancient vomit wisdom became the rave, engaging young minds as well as older ones, leading them closer and closer to their true poetic roots, and likewise, further and further away from grossly soiled tax booklets.

The peculiar linguistic transmission inexplicably assumed the form of the cryptic alphabet soup, for whatever reason, and the uncountable volumes of mnemonic wealth passed over tongues, as well as from mouth to mouth by literary lovers from all over the world. Perhaps confusing to the Sunday schoolboy novice, the ancient soup language contrarily served better than the most ancient of tell-tale photographs in elucidating where various nouns were many years ago, and what verbs they were executing in their lonely, twilit hours. Various limbs might have been severed over the long, dark years, but the nefarious head was never found, and so was immune to the tragic effects of ignorant decapitation by the clutchings of genetically advanced brutes wearing superstitious pajamas in their midnight hours of fear and anti-redemption.

The eidetic corpses of these thoughts surfaced from time to time in fragmented form, enabling only the wariest to clutch the bits and pieces of forgotten memories and forgotten lives thrown by the wayside like the smutty husks of diseased corn that some mortal princesses used for their pleasures when their pre-industrial economics were in a state of dental robustness.

Somehow, through a bizarre occurrence of some bizarre, transversal subway relocation, a linear world of varied train cars bled through the metal and plastic, touching an odd countrycide composed of dusty stucco houses and faded plastic flowers. Strangely furred sleepy puppet animals with heightened senses of smell turned the train cars from the valley into drab, olive-colored filing sheds, replete with bad lighting to counteract the sad, horizontally shaped windows. It was also possible that molluscan snakes inhabited the anomalous corridors of the converted trains, but the thick layers of dust covering every surface therein bespoke of bygone congregations of contortion artists. These human-pretzel artists could even throw salt in the direction of the inner train tracks of the lush mountainside, practically dropping crystalline meteors into the backyards of the squid-people, who had been sitting outside in the dark, sipping on lemon water and listening to ominous music while painting their invertebrate toenails.

Although the night had fallen like a red velvet curtain several hours before, the floating lemons in the ice-water of the squid-people suggested at least one solid month of pure sunlight, and this prophecy caused some to rejoice but others to quake with pre-industrial fear. However, the coming of the sunlit month wouldn't happen for several hours, and this time-delay created futuristic ruins of the bedrooms of alien parents, displaying collapsed mattresses and flea-ridden bearskin rugs. With the destruction of the bedrooms came many disturbing tectonic activities, including the disruption of retirement terraces and other examples of echinodermatic accomplishments.

All of a sudden, many poisonous copies of the local newspaper were hurled from the retirement balconies, sending a painful splinter into the smelly foot of ceaseless time, and this lurching march of the eons experienced a temporary standstill. This painful pause caused some to procure long strands of kelp which were used as naughty head bands by intelligent derelicts who begged for alms during the day but studied the distant offspring of neo-quantum mechanics in order to explain how pregnant emotions could travel through the voids of coiled sleep.

Although the poisonous newspapers were later collected and

burned by the displaced, retired people, the memories of world events remained, exposing the lies in the face of a tearful amnesia reinforced with eyeshadow and a cherry-red lipstick.

9

It couldn't have been more than a year that transpired after a magnetic foot massage, but the memory of the liquid moment was more than any lantern snail could bear. Ignorant, conservative minds moved through predictable patterns of behavior, following a strict code of blind mediocrity. Although the cruelty of the illiterate bled through their every exposed form and fiber, their idiocy was the more salient quality, and they all banded close together, like a cooperative pack of foraging rats. Cowardice is most effective when implemented at the collective level.

Despite the social cowardice, every new day broke through the night sky in the same way yolks are removed from shattered eggshells. With every passing day, the memories of life in the cowardly idiotville receded like a sullenly burst zit, abandoned to the ruptured fate of a white-sanded beach. Such mnemonic pleasures are ill obtained, but well worth the thunderstorms endured through the process of immortalizing them. Volumes of such interactions were created, and were nimbly stored within the creased folds of greasy neocortices who harbored dominant philosophies of dishonesty and who monopolized the majority of the prevalent cultural platforms of emotional communication. Although these turbulent nightmares persisted for many centuries, eventually they were to be swept away by azure currents of eagle blood.

The rudely spilled blood from the eagles created a blue storm that was self-protective and which also brought much ozone to the area, via lightning discharges that woke all of the local tabby cats. The incurring storm was unprecedented, yet its worst effects were gauged from the movement of sand dunes through the immediate mountain areas. Despite that minor obstacle, the squid-people peeped out through the dilapidated, drapeless apertures once called windows, and surveyed the minimal damage to their inherited apartment complexes. The dying blue storm winds receded with low, mocking whistles, and the dissipated blue mists revealed the moon, forever full and timelessly cold. Despite the storm, the wind chimes in the oddly tiled inner garden remained silent, but evidence of smashed acoustic guitar pieces was visible all along its leading path. The instruments were apparently unsalvageable, so the squid-people took the pieces and pickled them in garlicky brine, creating a rustic variety of fermented vegetables whose recipe was inscribed on a centralized town monument. Such was the creation of guitar pickles. Even though the squid-folk were constantly berated by two-dimensional owls, they persisted in their pickling efforts, creating poetry from the corroded fronds of popped guitar strings.

On one particularly peaceful evening, one of the more important squid-princesses appeared wearing a paranoid owl kimono. This particular wrap, bearing the furtive markings of camouflaged owls, kept the squid-princess from catching cold as well as highly undesirable desiccation. The graceful princess obtained a geomorphic rock from the recently forged stream, and crushed it open with her deft fingers. Inside of the rock was an artificial hollow made by unknown limbs, which contained tiny plates of finely etched platinum. The symbols on the plates vaguely resembled the schematic representations of organic farm tractors, but their unclear outlines and lack of any recognizable writing made their origin unidentifiable, leading to several nocturnal temper tantrums in the more religious quarters of the squid-people colony. The actual squid-princess who accidentally found the peculiar artifacts cried herself to sleep that night, having dreams of pasteurized cheese-processing plants and other phantasmagoric domestic avalanches.

Within the turbulent dreams, the squid-princess could feel the illuminating darkness move across the hyperactive, cycling retinas, and half-empty forms of dead, shattered parakeets glided through her aimlessly grasping fingers. There was indeed a non-linear entranceway to a moss-covered, choking traveler's inn, but apparently the doorway was blocked by a creeping octopus whose feathery eyebrows could catch the attention of even the most reticent of untalkative birdcages. What could be more pleasant than a Wednesday dehumanization event available for all vulnerable kittens?

Life carried on at a reprehensible pace, and the arms of the future became a sorry resource to sunken ships that choked on the riches of brine. Faster than a corrupt, corporate yes-man could sell his soul to a stock option, the death-cries of dishonest human-made systems rang out like fangs into the isolated skies of dawn. The seizure of sleep was a collapsed eyebrow rake. A true sense of well-being was an erection of lead-packed walls in search of projectile tangerine pulp. The tears from the squeezed citrus seared the bamboo floors with the acid of bloody bile—truly a pot of floating elephant liver stewing in a frozen regime of ocean saline. The outer, peripheral surge of a deviant oak-tree skeleton.

Magnificent hands of death carved out Japanese pumpkins from the inside, ejecting seeds through the loft created by candle fire. Reaching for the carved pumpkins, a troupe of carnivorous baboons grunted with frustration because their raised knuckles came to simulate the confusion of doddering waterslides. Never again would sightly coconuts adorn menstruating wallpaper of the king's court.

The baboon troupe touched themselves all over and entered a church, noticing the floating eyeballs in the horse trough of holy water provided to all equine pilgrims who happened along from the dusty, music-box trails. As if a shady American Western movie could be watched in reverse, dead images removed their 3-D glasses and laughed at mirroring interpersonal images of space stations being overrun by spilled coffee and green slime monsters. The corridors of memory supported these valentine's day messages, and a mysterious woman from the land of pure, speculatory chemistry honored the landscape with her lively eyes that hid behind sexy glasses and the random swath of blond hair. The mnemonic corridors flashed her button nose, and the ache of the new millennium silently passed down the hall, diligently checking on each room with a gorgeous shadow that could only obliterate the annoying skylights of rudely disrupted afternoon naps. These distant memories were closer than the mysterious tattoo of a metallic parakeet dropping in mid-flight. Confusing to the cortical center of real feeling, perhaps, but nevertheless worth the emotive vulnerabilities. Who could trade that wondrous shadow for a silly and rather shallow subjective vanity mirror? How could overcrowded people ever come to the conclusion that life was simply an erotic xerox machine? The divergences of the later centuries was perplexing, and although the presence of those disturbing paint-by-numbers affairs were ready (always available) for the taking at any moment, there was something special about the core spirit which was invulnerable to the phobias of mass lynchings and fratricidal cultural selection.

Despite the labyrinths of various mental confinements, the wrinkling of flesh was the best timepiece ever invented, and it was discovered to be quite the ancient weapon as well. Images of stolen life graced the silver screen, yet the deflated buoys that were mired on the lonely beaches served as an irradiated message of denial, like an octopod rip-tide that wore a seaweed skirt of suction cups.

10

Life's disappointments and smokescreen impossibilities became a hollow plaster-of-paris bust containing hidden birds' nests. With the assemblage of many of these lifelike statues within a cozy study room punctured with sinister bull's eye stained glass windows of canine beauty, the birds' nests within the statues began to release harmonic frequencies, forming cracks in the outlines of the human statues. The ego-dissolve of the moment was a terrifying prospect, leading to genealogical irrigations of an otherwise barren soil that hadn't produced fresh legumes for many seasons in hell, possibly Rimbaud's. This briar-patch of soil contained all of the earthworms that any ravenous child could desire, with all of the accompanying shotgun shell casings as well. This message-in-a-bottle of retro earthworms was sufficient to induce a vomitous chirping of grasshopper vermin, enabling the female insects to remove their baseball hats and to perch within the confines of prismatic ribcages. The constant battles of birth and rebirth became salient, especially within socially defined storage bins that are laughable when they aren't terrifying. So much for an earthly swarming gambit.

Regardless of the negative feedback deficiency, the corroded busts managed to release their troubled birds' nests. These next constructions fell from their newly exposed alcoves utterly released into a mysterious environment that was as hostile as it was beautiful. Imagine the landscape with its mouth and ears completely excised, and this vision was the current situation of the strange birds' nests from the hollow places. Common folk celebrated life-and-death events, but the end result was the same, creating a bloody smear of squashed mosquito limbs and thirsty, insentient mouth parts embedded into a christmas skin that could send frosty chills to the depths of any oversized, beating heart. The emergency switch on the carpet vacuum was bared by lost dogs, leading to an odd and unprecedented triumph of carnivorous teeth over the summits of persnickety mountaintops. Whatever happened to the highly desired heroine when her sideways glance was unavailable for slicing through obnoxious layers of partially solidified horse glue? Would this terrible situation last forever, or would the fields become dominated by apricot refugees who could enter the dragon at any moment, at any time?

The darkness of the wolves dropped a training brassiere into a laundry bin, and the soap opera of flowers gripped many frozen nations writhing in the throes of cowardly, corporate greed, sparking a prickly sweat that rudely bristled along clueless spines in the hours before waking and dying. Silly boxes are welded shut, and the landscape sadly changes with empty guitars that communicate an empty state of mind induced by a war waged because of the diseased concept of money. Orange and red cockatoos send warning feathers to the obscene heights of deadly ocean waves, creating a genealogical tattoo that is secretly imprinted on the inner surfaces of primate crania, in the same way that some specialized and highly lethal weapons are forged devoid of identifying serial numbers. Such are the terrible secrets of an outspoken, phocine prostate gland.

Could life ever return to a state of normalignancy? Such a question begged for myopic scrutiny. Car batteries became damp, and the close-calls with the forces of nature had a counterintuitive fomentation of bile-lust that resulted, clearly displaying a cause and effect relationship that scared away birthing rodents who built salt bridges with matchsticks. These inhuman statues were very thin and were partially covered by a wallpaper composed of labile, conglomerated paper cutouts that could raise the troubled forms of sunken balsa-wood ships that licked up the streams of laser salt melt-downs that presented a diabolical alternative to those troublesome easter bunny marshmallows sprayed with carcinogenic food coloring with which naïve children daily comb their hair.

The weakness of the formless, agonizing moment coaxes the phocine prostate glands to release their spectacular cargo, serving to momentarily distract wayward purple starfish from the legs of mortal people as well as of evil mannequins abandoned more than a thousand years ago. While academic professors play with themselves and write stuffy books, the orbits of planets enter yet one more economic precession, attracting greedy glances and eager faces of astronomers who strive to own the manufactured identities of distant stars. Of course, celestial knowledge is best, but the cranky ownership of who was first to see which faraway object had the tendency to transform the heavens into a sacred, scholastic buttplug that would be accessible to all academics. The sadness of silent theaters revealed the latent provincialism.

A lifetime of stolen identities will walk across your confused consciousness when you seek external purposes for internal being. Crazy parties, disreputable lies, and dried orange peels all serve to raise your eyelids when you walk away from a centripetal vortex of sensual plasma which you deny with your silly spectacles of bottle cap bending and callous boredom displays. Despite your callous, microwavable hot pockets, a window of love can be seen forming above the hemisphere of your current position, laughing at your ears as well as your velvet jokes. The impossibilities of your doubting lips couldn't even kill your intrinsic desire, even with a rotting vat of oxidized capitalist piss, with the stench of nitrogen breakdown entirely evident. Your sunday school is dead.

11

It was ironic that the plunging mists of winter would be the catalytic sparks that would melt the ice castles that you lived in, that you held in your hand, that you were. You seemed to have taken your icebergs with you, when you left. How far away did you drift? How could your sensual body interchangeably convert between multiple realities? You couldn't have over-obsessed over your history tomes like others did, did you? Were cheap, rainforest hamburgers really your undoing, your true Achilles' clitoris? Your icy presence will be missed.

In the meantime, confused, drifting, frozen fossils drop to the bottoms of Jovian lunar oceans, sparking imaginative desires for the beckoning, distant shores of Europa. The faraway laughter comes from somewhere upwind of a familiar, lonely corner of the terrestrial solar system. These future memories travel with the same speed as that of a pregnant bear in search of a corner hotdog 'n honey stand. Even though displaced baseball game tickets are ruthlessly scalped on hairless piers, the incoming tide of Alaskan crabs marches forth like a conflagration of rabid scorpions in search of herbal pillows and graveyard puppet shows. Perhaps the young bearcubs will learn how to perform a scissor kick, but in the event that they do not, the mother bear will teach her obscure offspring how to use C4 to terrorize raunchy flower shops.

These young bears unfortunately count certain unwholesome zealots as their pregnant role models: literal-minded christians who terrorize abortion clinic doctors. Let's make lots of babies for whom we care nothing about! After all, Jesus would approve!

In the backwash of a constipated time corridor, Jesus Christ of Nazareth applied a soothing ointment to his hemorrhoids and began to read a book about how human swarming and over-population was a good thing. Eventually the son of gODD became bored with the ignorant, pathetic musings of mortals, and decided to move to the Ursa Major star system, where he licked aphrodisiacal honey from the armpits of aliens. Interestingly enough, his annoying holy hemorrhoids disappeared upon his extra-solar relocation. Perhaps the stress of an over-populated planet with carbon-based life was too great for those who first created that stress. Go forth and multiply!

The downfall of Martian cowboys occurred when their lightboxes (or brain-lanterns, really) were taken to sea upon a barque made of brittle sandalwood, creating a perfumed shadow of female death which created a ticklishly cephalopod imbalance, multiplying the surface area of perfect smiles. The stretch of a perfect kiss is a honey marmalade that rebounds throughout the spongy planet of carnicidal rainforest hamburger existence. The morning marmalade kiss bespeaks feisty red hair that exists in perfect submersibles that travel many, many miles below the cold ocean currents. Although frozen nipples and sumptuous breasts might be stimulatorily exacerbated by a cool wind, this strange passage from sunset to sunrise comes bearing a pink flower between its teeth, in the form of an airline captain whose cordless phone was smashed by a careless barracuda. The fall of the careless barracuda is an odd, black flight recorder that was ejected in the same way stringed instruments are prized for their saltiness in Japan.

Meanwhile, lizard crustaceans smear raw horse liver over their eyes to simulate eyeshadow, and which raise the sunken parts of naval destroyers lost in battle. The recovered bones from the ships might be encrusted sea lichens and other smelly vermin, but when dried and licked, they can make quite an orchestra of rusted musical instruments. The depths to which these sea instruments are subjected can be occasionally daunting and perhaps overwhelming to some, but this ancient orchestra can orbit the world in the same way moon rocks are displayed next to concrete slag in the more naïve sections of post-industrial cities where people wear post-modern underwear. When might the red forest leaves adhere to the sleeping foreheads to create well-packed dreams of fruit cornucopias exploding from obsolete gramophone devices mysteriously left in the far corners of groggy hotel clinics where patients are locked into their rooms by six-legged animals who carry wicker baskets full of guava pulp around with them, apparently trying to spread a little joy and some cerebral seafood? In two days, Jesus probably wouldn't have minded.

The sun set in a worthless, haphazard manner, tending to strip youth of their self-confidence, making them excellent economic targets. This confusion charade cast its phoniness through the layers of translucent mud and cracked clay revealing the shell outlines of daring lantern snails. The passage of the snails over dark foreheads had nothing tangible to offer, but only promises. Possibly very unsatisfying, but promises were always better than ugly, indifferent silence. At least with paper promises, no matter how thin, there will always be hope.

For those who did have hope, it served much better than the acceptance of pulpit death, and of all the foot serpents that writhed between toes and made a joke out of recorded history. While mobilized social forces always dominated the immediate moment, the tiger toes of their existence were always hounded by acrid crania that could peel away the bleeding bones of their useless feet, confirming an empty destiny that could create laughter within the throats of the innocent, in the same way marching sardines could knock over the sand castles of the classical era. The passage of the classical dead was a gruesome debacle in the impoverished world of men, but apparently the blind heroes weren't even worth their weight in rancid cattle-feed. The show went down the mossy, disheveled path, regardless, and silver key rings were removed from lonely, trans-dimensional pockets.

The keys were hidden, and the old nature trails that lacerated the mountains were reinforced with stolen redwood lumber. School buses full of children of all ages were driven in, and these naïve youth were instructed to colonize the hills that had up until recently been populated by the plastic cephalopod squid-people. Self-doubt and superstitious fears began to show their abundance like fresh mountain flora. Although it was uncertain where exactly the squid-people went, not a trace of their passage was registerable except for a hastily abandoned garden of sanctified proportions, showing dazzling but lonely fountains and oddly alternating and contrasting colored tiles.

But the school buses continued to arrive, and long queues of variously aged children were led into the refurbished mountains, constantly avoiding the electrical cords that randomly crossed the trails that caused some of the unobservant youngsters to trip and then chip their teeth. Rigid schedules were imposed, and the kids moved across the chiseled mountains in well-behaved lines. The noon sun rose overhead, and all clueless humans exasperatedly wiped the summer sweat from their young brows.

Like automatons, the variously aged children mindlessly traversed the altered mountain trails, all noting the exact same features, landmarks, and points of interest in predictable, repetitive frequencies. All the while, an unrecognized pressure system blew in a storm of blood-red autumn leaves, with each leaf vaguely resembling a twitching, outstretched claw.

The swarming of carrion flies could be heard at an indiscriminate distance away, possibly a few miles upwind of the now heavily populated mountain. The diseased nature of unplayed piano keys sent a hungry signal to evil trees that perched within the dirty footholds of the broken mountain.

The pre-programmed calls of monkey mating-love induce the transformation of the red, airborne leaves into a swarm of highly paranoid fruit-bats who then swoop down upon the naïve child-tourists. Hominid limbs are torn from meaty sockets, and the highly paranoid fruit-bats have their first meal of bloody flesh, school supplies, and overwritten, academic gradebooks. This toxic procession could not be averted, as love dies easily in a place where mutual swarming occurs.

A few hours later, when the sacrificial child skeletons are licked clean of the last remaining traces of blood and gristle, the meat-bats look into a chasm of what once was, and shine their beleaguering eyesight in the direction of an advancing northerly wind, blowing clear the stench of fossilized civilization, with a swimming collective psyche moving away in a slow breeze. After a few hours of gentle wind, no trace of civilized life remains on the country mountain, and the broken hills reseal themselves.

The Mayumi Pumpkin Operation
(2003)

1

Under the dawn of a burnt sky, oblong bipeds crossed over rusted train rails in a lurching frenzy that could only make one wonder what was chasing them. The passage of the trains was long gone, but the fall of leaves suggested the movement of large objects through an urban center where a conspiracy against love was in effect. The forces that motivated the oblong bipeds were unapparent, but the fear experienced by the hunted had an odor that was undeniable. Throughout this process of flight, the cobbles that paved the street each exhaled a gasp that spoke of fragmented galaxies careening through the cosmos in painful, unexpected trajectories, creating a private laboratory that was mercilessly conducted in plain view. Parents hid underground, hoarding large crates and observing the flow of water through basements that had been filled to capacity, while their offspring learned of future obligations in mosquito-bitten fragments.

The flight of the oblong bipeds was heard below in the cellars, and the nervous parents fidgeted with their storage crates, while also nervously monitoring unreliable electronic instruments that had an annoying habit of breaking when least expected, especially when dried, flattened fish were found in the mailbox, along with cut-out samples of bizarre, obsequious furniture upholstery. These informational missives were as aggressive as non-biting flies, but the knowledge record was lost by the time young children were able to push chlorine gas into their nostrils, heavily influenced by Canadian loggers who had emptied burning contact lenses into a Mesopotamian body of water presided over by pantheric cats when they became interested in chasing dragonflies. The data was never lost, but it was secretly hoarded and obfuscated by the rulers of the land so that the naïve youth would have difficulties grasping it when needed. The fleeing bipeds moved so quickly that they had no time to perceive their loud footfalls that rattled on the metal streets, and so immature galaxies appeared between their eyes, creating dense thickets of trees from their minds and half-shadowed automobiles from the buttons on their imperfect jackets.

This new day promised much terror and meaningless revelations for the fleeing, oblong bipeds. Sinister, pristine palm trees were used as ornamentation in a way that made sleepy, tired residents indifferently marvel from their wealthy balconies, perhaps with only distant, passing memories of family gatherings within a world glutted with optic slime. The mysteries of the past created a frontline of submerged lobster traps, evoking the love of forgotten pyramids and uncertain knuckles as they rapped on the door of a dimly lit hovel, where the passing moan of feline banshees created a Bermuda's triangle in the center of the pyramid territory. Invisible and imperturbable claws reached into unwary souls and unlatched the restraints on survival instincts, causing them to emerge and then sadly dissolve into a state of blind saturation. From where would hope arrive? Would a swish of Mayumi's hot, black cape remove the perspiration of dark, inner discoveries? Why had Mayumi's panther-prints dotted the sandy beach trails that led to the unforgiving apartment?

The dissolution of identities caused great confusion in the lonely, hungry night. Aimless prostitutes drifted through the apartment beach complex, but refrained from making crude propositions, out of fear of the panther entity called Mayumi who presided over the greatly appreciated feline informants with her silken cape and her cutting eyes. Although once mortal like the fallen, red autumn leaves, the Mayumi Panther had somehow learned to harness her acute hearing which led her to understand the turnings of silent, lonely planets that in turn allowed her to bask in the altered solar radiation that did great things for her timeless, tender skin. For a creature who began life in a strictly feline capacity, that special feline informant known as the Mayumi Panther with her silently swishing, deadly black cape ultimately became more than the sum of her darkly adorable parts. She hiked through dead forests, babbling cities, foul social establishments, and yet her off-worldly youthful but immensely vast temperament enabled her to kill her foes with a flick of her prehensile tail. The Mayumi Panther was a lost moon of Jupiter who could scratch oceans with her claws, producing velvet flowers that emerged only at dawn.

In the end, the highly revered yet taxed feline informant entered a brief state of reprieve, totally overwhelmed by the situation regarding the capitalist conspiracy against love, and so she instead went to the beach to collect her thoughts. Although the highly annoying identity loss on the part of her comrades and acquaintances represented a peculiar form of disablement, it was, in the last analysis, not permanently crippling. Based on this assumption, Mayumi, the dark feline informant with the terrible black cape devised the plan of releasing into the wild a terrifying collection of animal-shaped statuettes in the shape of Easter Island megaliths, with toothless, grimacing faces. Although the exact purpose of these animal megaliths was undetermined, the hope was placed that these artificial creatures could act in tandem to release Mayumi's friends from a hundred chilling years of subjective inactivity. Could these dark fossilizations actually happen to any unwary feline derivatives in an unpredictable manner and through a priori unidentifiable means? Apparently so.

Meanwhile, on an economically stratified submarine that had just plunged beneath a turbulent surface, the drone inhabitants living on the lower decks scratched their nails across the rust-covered walls, wondering when a breach might occur. The oasis of colored buttons assailed their ears, but they paid no heed and instead minded their monotonous tasks, gossiping about meaningless rituals and the occasional keyholes found within the wings of ravens. These mundane predicaments were fought over by some, but in the end, the blind adhesion to gross materialism yielded nothing but heartless and spiritually vacuous consumerism.

On one particular day (or maybe night) the labor submarine stalled in its course due to an unknown obstruction that prevented the massive vehicle's movement through the dark, sorrowful water. Perhaps a giant squid or a vasectomied sperm whale? In keeping with the custom of withholding information from those who have no social power of any sort, the personnel who controlled the course of the submarine had no information whatsoever to share with those who actually operated and maintained the internal, rusting environment. Needless to say, morale had disintegrated many generations before the advent of these economically profitable deep-sea vehicles, but nobody knew the difference, nor perhaps even wanted their children to know. The pounding din on the lower, outer hull was disturbing, and nameless people scrambled their employee numbers, confusing the management software as to where exactly the worker bees were at any given time. Some of the dull-eyed folks initiated a mutiny by storming the upper, cushy decks where dwelled clean-smelling creatures who orbited mindlessly around x-mas trees and treaded upon well-vacuumed floors covered with green billiards flock. All the while, the revolting drones marveled at the external vehicular monitors, seeing for the first time a barrage of what appeared to be giant strands of viscous seaweed wrapping around the poorly maintained hull, possibly capable of crushing the manufactured travesty.

This mentally castrating reality was real, but many chose to invest their identifications in bogus real estate domains that served blistering optic sties to the naïve public. Perhaps a conspiracy, but definitely an insidious one. The universe on this day was a swirling vortex of lethal swords that caused people to become clumsy and to bump into walls. These corporeal frustrations were merely the ugly result of unconsciously orchestrated unsound breeding methods – the callous upbringing of revolting blind sheep.

The much-awaited relief finally arrived with the pulsating renaissance of a liquid glass opening that revealed the inner stars and galaxies of a purposefully obfuscated universe. This radiant starburst revealed the inner heart of the indifferent universe, capable of silencing politicians as well as literary critic-slugs, alike. While the galactic sheep slept, platinum anthills were forged, creating a one-inch Godzilla that could erupt from the stomachs of radiant starfish at any time. Although the concept of "home" was illusory, there was more "home" to be found in a three-toed set of footsteps than in the average stocking-stuffed gingerbread house, where the excessive sugars and starches trap the unwary into a ballet of conformist convulsions, all applauded by the highly approving televisions. The vines of the future wrapped around the profane approving televisions and sunk young, hydrolytic tendrils into the oppressive television plastics, ultimately releasing a flood of ravens who could play the piano in large and lonely houses. The comforts of home.

A blind confusion settled in with the fog, and a city nestled within a rocky cliff created origami submarines that floated like lilies instead of sinking to the bottom of a sea of mucus. To be inside of or external to the seas of cliff-hanging mucus; that was the question. Regardless of the mortal confusions of cliff-hanging mucus, the earth was still wracked by firefly earthquakes. This result opened up the brain of a nearby snail that had been clinging vertically to one of the cliff-rocks. The revealed brain shone through the dense, electrified air, yielding the same colored wavelengths as when argon gas is mercilessly ionized within the confines of an experimental glass tube.

Luckily for the rotting metal submarine, with its wretchedly divided crew and its decaying mechanical architecture, the badly abused vehicle reached the port of the mucus city safe and sound, with barely a scratch from the invading seaweed that had dared threaten it only during the final stages of its lachrymal journey.

With the sub securely moored to the outlying docks, the ship's officers led the worker-prisoners (with their switched identities) to new and terrifyingly exciting assignments, allowing each one to carry misplaced identities to different locales and different worlds. On the farthest dock, a red tabby finished smoothing down the hair between its ears with smart, little paws. The cat blinked and then looked the other way, but not without first noticing shavings of glittering, purple metal that shook free from the grimy overalls of the worker-prisoners. The cat etched beautiful hieroglyphs into the weathered, wooden dock with its claws, capturing vistas of recorded history that might be forgotten on the eternal scale, but which would probably serve as a terrible signpost of hidden beauty on the small-scale of terrestrial evolution. Even if a pear tree is mutilated by a dark, relentless tornado, its memory still has a chance of persisting in the short term.

After finishing with the hieroglyphic notations on the seedy dock, the red feline informant moved to a safer location, away from rusted submarines and crashing waves. The weather changed that evening, giving a disturbing illusion of clarity marked by clouds carrying perfect convoy formations of callous newsprint, with an over-emphasis on the weather section in relation so the news and classifieds sections. It was as if the sky was self-aware, but this nausea passed with every flickering smile. As if the geometry of this alienated seaside town could have been all wrong, the faceless silhouettes of unknown people passed in and among the snowy trees, keeping young minds awake at night, fully preoccupied with the anonymity of dead worlds where unwary minds slept under the passing cosmos. Only the mythical feline informants knew of this at the present millennia. Immediately, thunderstorms began to fall like the claws of silky, black cats who can free-fall several meters without breaking a bone. This explosion of the elements rested as sleepy teardrops within the tired eyes of a herd of neonatal pachyderms. The infantile elephants grasped at appropriate connections to the distant sea-dock, but to no avail. However, despite the apparent disconnections, the baby elephants still caught floating glimpses of houses expressed in a lonely hieroglyphic notation, promoting a sensual laughter that could have only come from a safe, dark forest of cat-trees.

2

Poisoned water drips from a lead tap, suggesting an age-old catastrophe that occurred many years ago, when the hung strings of negative puppets had not been reduced to such a highly shortened length. What's more: the variety of refracted sunlight successfully transmits images of fear up from the bottom of a lonely well where the nuggets of a strong, purple metal are sought for their construction paper. The fear of repetition prevents the completion of any daily, loving chore, causing deaf badgers to hide in their dens where the shirt music cannot reach them. During this exchange of curtain shrouds, the passage of archaic automobile shadows creates a cultural mantra that ripples through all layers of society, initiating a bracketed wave that pushes nimble thunderstorms through the troubled pores of sweat glands. The disturbing train passes through a town in a state of collective denial.

The preservation of giant redwood trees becomes foreshadowed by the calls of certain different species of vulture, and the mouths of invaders are soiled by remnants of fast-decaying entrails from clueless targets. The dead-ends of life couldn't have been more interesting than any isolated, highly dysfunctional potato farm.

These odd potato farms took the raw lumber from giant redwoods and used it to make anthropological beach signals that had odd designs on spelling the word *Abalone* backwards so that the self-justification of shiny umbrellas could be measured. The incoming coffins made entirely of redwood lumber opened their varnished doors to reveal the internally sleeping forms of sniveling vultures with rotten flesh residues apparent on their dirty beaks. The animosities within the starchy confines of the highly dysfunctional potato arm conducted a cycloptic measurement of its own ulna to understand the sorrows of videogame tennis elbow.

Suddenly, excessively positive and overly optimistic music blares through the invisible trumpets of the future, effectively solidifying the potato farm antics within ingots of lead. This representation of the evolution of these aardvark categories is a remembrance of brains on the half-shell, complemented by touching elevator music. The best part about the elevator music is that it is highly repetitive, playing the same strains over and over. A lot of people like that. This music is truly a gesture meant to honor the human psyche. Anyway, the dysfunctional potato farm is highly renowned for its clandestine musical releases, and these innervations of dangerous music carry the weight of approval of a burst carbuncle. The jettisoned musical sounds revere the highly thin atmosphere on Mars, and the mannequins shed their purple velvet robes to revel in the frigidity of mind-control. It is only when cubed potato spots arrive in Phred-Ex boxes that the panic of the mannequins begins, quickly escalating to unprecedented proportions, and ultimately causing them to look to Earth in a way a derelict craves salty oysters from the Gulf of Mexico.

The whirling confusion of the blemished sasquatch caused blood vessels in the wall to burst, releasing a delicious flow of blood that would entice any caring taster of multicolored parachutes. The distracted mannequins immediately remained motionless, oblivious to dangerous baskets of colored marbles. These colored fragments of glass slag were very dangerous and were more powerful than any top-secret poison or aphrodisiac. The glass became crushed by the years, and eventually melted. Some nearby, curious scientist broke open a never-before-seen stratum of sedimentary rock, revealing a historical perspective that had been considered impossible, at least up until that day: inside of the rock stratum were the preserved remains of toothbrushes. The minerals within the rock had replaced the decaying plastic, creating a fossil of such disturbing proportions that the scientists ran into their private quarters and hid underneath the beds. These terrified professionals had peculiar dreams of involuntary, alien tooth loss, and their bodies awoke in the middle of the night drenched in sweat and speaking in circular linguistic pathways that were incomprehensible to the bed-ridden ears. The aged scientists then rolled up their sleeves and began to create sandcastles from the microscopic bones of spiders whose kitchen utensils were thrown over a leather couch like a pair of unappreciated legs.

These discarded jellyfish washed up on a distant beach, in a way similar to the frozen planets as they are habitually discovered around terrible stars in desolate areas. The legends of words built up around the rusted streetlights, and a fast-flying robin settled upon infested boughs of mercurial cleaning brushes obtained from broken thermometers. It had been once hypothesized that the unavoidable presence of the various toothbrushes and cleaning brushes within the rocks of pianoland could be attributed to a nearby cosmos of tactile damnation or deprivation of monkey castles that contained many pumpkin storage sheds and other garden implements.

The, uh, building structures in the gardens were confusing to the eyes. Several trap-doors were arranged around the periphery of each storage shed, and it appeared that the pumpkins had begun to rot, with fibrous orange secretions oozing from under the doorways.

Simultaneously, strange people in schools learn about the capitalist way of life, making interesting display items with crayons and colored paper. The simplified, developmental, neocortical cris-crossing of bared lips castrated all of the clocks and reinforced the unpleasant, illusory concept of the impotent linearity of future life, when existence was deluged with materialism smeared with rotten squid liver. Tainted water drips from the fountain and a bursting storage locker full of confiscated toys and books pops open the badly abused lock. First and foremost, an entire series of leather-bound manuals detailing the psychic physiology of the mysterious clade of Mayumi Panther spills forth, staining the grubby floor with forbidden knowledge. Apparently, the Mayumi Panthers originated from a failed homunculus experiment in a secret foot therapy laboratory in the international space station. These highly vocal felines returned to Earth in seed form, promptly rehydrating themselves when the seed was spilled upon blood-spattered tiles in the middleschool girls' room. These panthers selected only the purest of themselves to be their leader, and this one panther forever after bore the name of Mayumi. The wallpaper began to peel whenever Mayumi looked at it. The school elevator doors began to blister with the threat of a hoary meltdown whenever Mayumi looked at them. The Mayumi Panthers and their leader submitted to a mental scan, hence the creation of the psychic physiological manuals.

These cryptically detailed manuals were instantly seized when the higher school authorities cowed to political pressure and obsequiously performed moral somersaults upon being stabbed in the groin with an electrified hatpin. Although the forbidden books were locked away for many years, their diagnostical attributes eventually found protection under the aegis of pink, summertime umbrellas that helped prevent sunburns and unpredictable thunderstorms. This decent into the shadowy whirlpools was reminiscent of past, invertebrate immersions, yet ultimately different because of the freight trucks that would periodically crash through fields of dragonfly lettuce that could bloom in the dark.

The sinister passage of the freight trucks scared the dragonfly lettuce greatly, even causing some of the more naïve specimens to wither and inexplicably jiggle. The now-actualized Mayumi Panthers comforted the tired lettuce heads and had dreamy visions of fire escapes fashioned from the bleached bones of giant blue whales who were killed because of their love of music. Avoiding the blue whale dream vortex at all costs, the Mayumian feline informants adjusted their black, silken capes and crouched vigilantly among the damaged heads of dragonfly lettuce, with the beginning fragments of a party dirge forming on the tips of their red lips, foraging for the royal magma of bees, and the reotaxis of insolent piscine forms of life. Lantern snails erupted from beneath the feet of the momentarily stalled Mayumian felids, and these mucoid creatures carried the mysterious panthers to a great barrier reef that was located in an unsuspecting oasis in the middle of the dysfunctional dragonfly lettuce patch.

The barrier reef was truly a lattice fence made from an incendiary paper that would only catch flame when subjected to the burn of a laser. For now, however, there was no laser activity, and so the paper barrier remained in place. In time, dismantled musical instruments were flung at the barrier, and their decomposing forms were lost in the acrid, volcanic saltwater from which evil, painted coconuts would spring during times of great social upheaval. The blind eyes of bats couldn't even paint a target on the backs of the majestic volcanoes that permanently liberated waves of lava, regardless of whether or not it was snowing.

Perhaps fossilized red eggs could significantly leak from highly incestuous, maternal coat racks, but the green caterpillars of autumn paid no heed and continued to march across the sculpted branches of the coat depository with toxic, spiny impetuousness. In capsaicin-producing gardens, magnetic Tabasco peppers were cultivated in a highly carefree manner, such that the small, piquant yellow fruits were allowed to mature and then used to create spicy reams of an antiquated stationary that was astute as it was proactive on the part of the pepper cultivators who existed simply to serve the greeting card needs of dopamine-deficient religious folks who brushed their teeth with ukuleles and who enjoyed treading upon broken pottery shards. The resulting musical teeth and the lacerated feet were proof in the subjective domains of the religious folk that pain was the choicest theme song of life. Praiseworthy songs were sung in reverence of highly cherished pain, and the group acted as one entity, impossibly agreeing about everything.

Suddenly, a massive piano comprised of lead oxide fell upon the miserable hamlet of the religious, pain-revering folk, and their crushed craniums leaked a final squeak of unconscionable incomprehensibility which the green toxic caterpillars, still perched atop the incestuous, maternal coat racks, were able to perceive. Their sonically tweaked toxic spines each heard the final religious squeak and resultingly quivered with trans-dermal, super-cosmic amusement. The Mayumi Panthers looked on impassively and had no vocalizations to make. Their opinions would issue forth from a cracked winter melon much, much later. For now, the dark felids observed and blinked, wondering eternally why some cultural currents persist as long as they do. The upshot of their musings occurred when an abandoned wheelbarrow full of shunted bamboo reeds was firmly perceived next to the fig trees under which the panthers were crouched, listening to the dead of summer with its tear-jerker sunsets and abandoned bamboo replacement reeds. Apparently life could be lonely, but with all of the chopped bamboo reeds in a vegetarian desert, who could really care?

The panthers toppled the wheelbarrow, ultimately pawing and sniffing at the bamboo fragments that were scattered among the fig tree grove that represented an odd cooling of the troubled atmosphere. Knee joints began to ache, and a brisk wind blew in the scent of ozone. Perhaps a storm was coming, but then maybe the emblem of a lunar crescent became apparent from the sign of troubling clouds in the sky? In time, the panther felids discovered how to convert the loose bamboo into majestic grandfather clocks, and these colossal timepieces were erected next to each and every fig tree. Unfortunately, the Mayumi Cats were unsure of how to convert the clocks to a terrestrial-based time system, and the resulting asynchronous and amorphic ticking highlighted the passage of time in mysterious, indeterminate ways. Therefore, time became a confusing yet beautiful non-linear progression, causing hair to stand on end and sometimes even grow backwards. Honeybees were able to create music from normally random buzzings, and the moon would eventually become a wolf-like optic orb sprouting displaced teeth in the throes of utter, disheveled lycanthropy. The Mayumi Panthers stared at the moon in disbelief, twitching their whiskers and straining their ears in order to discern a solid moment out of the timeless chronological chaos that had resulted from the construction of the peculiar, upright clocks.

It was almost as if the clocks were primitive digestive systems, somehow removing unknown elements from the surrounding country air and processing them within the bowels of the peculiarly constructed bamboo plumbing. From this perspective, the clock-stomach was more than the sum of its parts. Mayumi, the dominant or α-panther, took a step forward to scratch an image of a faraway constellation on one of the vertical tubes of one of the more prominent bamboo stomach-clocks. The crudely etched image of the constellation almost resembled a streaking comet with female attributes. Although the star map might have been slightly inaccurate in some places, the overall intensity of the image forced all of the bamboo digestive clocks to point in the direction of the enigmatic comet constellation. This polar reorientation confused the avid felines, and the furry mammals consulted their saline calendars to determine if green Japanese pumpkins were useful accessories to maternal coat racks and other solar manifestations. After the intense consultation, the flabbergasted felids observed the bamboo stomach-clocks beginning to emit continuous streams of unquestionably pure mountain spring water. Although these creatures had a significant aversion to water immersion (as well as water sports), they felt compelled to take bamboo stomach-clock showers, casting their black capes aside and leaping underneath the streams of the anointing clock water.

Faster than chopped liver can be smeared all over a rear-view mirror, the bath-hungry felids allowed their soft, black fur to become sopping wet, a condition usually reserved only during drastic thunderstorms and hotel sauna experiences. The cleansing mineral water relieved blocked pores, and removed all geriatric dandruff. Silver parakeets resting on the upper bamboo branches of the stomach-clock-showers chirped their approval, ignoring the taunting of archaic hotheads whose obsolete prostate glands are now bloated with metastatic cancer. The potato-head gallery (with peanut shell crania) continued to make noise, but the disruption did not overpower the reaffirming music of the sentient silver parakeets with their gray-scale beaks and powdery wings of transdimensional luminescence.

The silver parakeets entered the long, dark hallway, and their cheerful music contrasted with the drafts that intersected in various places, tending to extinguish unguarded candles. The drafty passageway was littered with trampled identification cards of missing people, and upon closer inspection, the transdimensional parakeets noticed that as they moved along the oddly illuminated corridor, the birth dates on the cards varied in descending order, possibly leading to an important date at the end of the walkway, or so surmised the silver parakeets as fields of magnetic glass began to foam around their joints and other appendages, propelling them to hoard spiny, reticulated lipid candles and incubate malformed chess pieces within the embryos of Spring.

3

Organized around a line of intimate luxuries, the product bureau bandaged its knuckles in a sea of adhesive gauze strips of a shady black, preparing for the occurrences of sparrows to arrive through gates of dangerous plasma that were friendly as they were stalked by bowties and other rafters of nucleonic fear. The young troupes of kittens create sumptuous banquets of steamed burdock root for their gods and goddesses, at least those pictured in their history catalogues where past leaders are sold for sightly fees and other knockdown window dressings. This cordial exchange facilitates the passage of mannequins that fight against obscene tides pulled along by the moon. At the crossroads, within the sickly vines of negative merlitons, a beautiful woman reveals ash-covered goose eggs within her picnic basket, and she catapults gosling eyeballs onto a passing train that is one of the express love-liners – a special breed of cargo transport whose various destinations include imposing cities, country watering holes and glacial hibernation caverns. Expensive satellites orbit these final train destinations, and explosive mineral deposits encrust the joints of frayed, world-weary metal, spelling the names of metallic, frosted fence-sitters as they revoke candles from the lees of insectoid mandibles used to carve out orange, internally hairy pumpkins when the moon reveals its bloodshot magma ravines. This thirst for the hairy pumpkins fortunately arrives several times each year, and because of it, fairy-tale visions are discarded in favor of other visions that arrive via magnetic impulses from the frozen moons around Jupiter, at least when those heavenly bodies are unexpectedly flung away from the sun into outer, more permissive orbits. A lucky rabbit's foot painted in orange blood complicates things, and people adorn their intimate eyelashes with tragic saline when they reveal the carnage of posted documents.

Catfish swim among the sunken earlobes. The detritus of long forgotten sounds is revealed again, centuries later, and this unearthing is a rustle of crushed leaves pressed between the wedding rows of abnormal textbooks that were abandoned on lightning-wracked bookshelves when fish-eyes were thought to be grapes, and backyard junk depots were the gardening spots of prenatal treasures. Where is Shangri-La, exactly, and on which continent did the shattered windowpane first break?

The faraway separation of oceanic waves proves to serve as a formidable barrier for the broken glass, preventing the integration of pieces of this supercooled silicon drool from occurring over the ablated sunny parasols of anachronistic divas who brought new meaning to the word "brassiere." The rise and fall of the salty, sultry waves moves these parasol-bearing women in their timeless rowboats, and when nobody else is wearing x-ray glasses; their lift could almost seem calm.

At a DeVille bookstore in New Orleans, subhuman locals enter the shop to buy one postcard apiece. When they leave, the couple that run the store close the gate in order to have a few private moments to themselves, releasing tangible bluebirds from ungrateful roadblocks where literary peanut shells litter the well-vacuumed floor.

The x-ray of the ostrich egg revealed bones of radioactive glass splotched with verminous cat teeth, resembling the carved coconuts of October. Paper trails dot the western continents, releasing the coconut plants from their roots, placing life-size dolls in kitchen refrigerators, mimicking the complaints of grandparents and the surreptitious blossoming of purple artichokes when matters of bile production are relevant. The coarse vegetables are fed to subhuman captives, preventing outbreaks of autumn auto-cannibalism. These touching celebrations of life remind one of an opened tomb of barbequed primate ribs eternally gnawed upon by the regenerating incisors of unknown rodents. It's really nice getting close to people in these special sorts of ways.

The long, wayward gaze through backwards centuries of darkness and conspiracy yielded a corpulent jester who scratched at his red nose and then inverted a crystal ball of red and blue fluids of highly different viscosities and miscibilities. Depending on the angle at which the oblate crystal orb was tilted, the red and blue substances would mix in different ways, in different patterns and different speeds, each time yielding a different, utterly unique conglomerate that radiated an ever-changing and evolving musical score. This music of emitted expression was incapable of making plants grow from seeds in and of itself, but in conjunction with the infernal optic rays of captive solenoidal homunculi, all new seed arrivals could germinate before they descended below the grid of upward sunflower growth. These displaced experimental seeds were implementing a shaky sideways dance that could make the hair of gravity stand on end.

Occasionally, due to the schism of the colored fluids, the jester would lose track of the portable crystal ball, sometimes even for a few hundred years at a time. As a result, the fluids would be unconsciously encouraged to migrate apart from each other, with the red half remaining sequestered at the geographic poles and the blue component becoming disguised as a tearful flock of ravens who would mercilessly perch within the hollows of oak trees, waiting for steel girders of senseless construction to erect themselves in patterns of loose, fermented tea that was used by embryonic giraffes as rancid bathwater. The nefarious tea extract might have also served as a liquid clock, but none could tell for sure. Frustrated ingots of ice merged with iron, falling from the open avian knuckles of the watching ravens, and the jester heeded this foreboding gesture with a fully augmented gag reflex that might portend death as it also measured the blindness of yesterday's moons when they crossed the skies, shedding abnormal light on hungry wretches whose brains were composed of molten glass.

This insistence on the passage of the red and blue spheres created the nasal insistence of a paraplegic Hercules when he creates checkmate moves within the wink of an eye.

Even though the shuddering fear might circumvent tired eyes that have become nascent matchboxes, we are surrounded by the green flames of memorable trees and crop-dusting plights put forth from the worlds of yesterday when mammoths combed their hair with glue and spat out thumbtacks that could harpoon even the furthest of prehensile fishes. The longshoremen perhaps could have avoided the beachward migration of lost submersibles, but the belts of kelp that are sometimes fashioned into headbands promote the merciless iodine leakage that occurs when broken rules spot the bursting cracks in dawning underwater vehicles. It was as if the closed windows blared a nerve-wracking cacophony of deadly, bitter grapefruits, bent on converting small pockets of a nauseatingly small universe over to a written system of hieroglyphic ancientness that could terrify the endless corridors of butterflies.

A blank daruma surfaces among the rubble of a destroyed butterfly nesting ground. This particular daruma is more than embryonic, and reveals a warped, tilting axis of blue stars that reminds all people of the most diverse constellations, and yet the brazen anguish of prenucleated eyeballs is comparable to warm smiles hidden away within piss-stained igloos. Acrid epitaphs rebel against the brain-splattered onyx cliffs, and the resulting, swirling chaos is reflective of fish skeletons of purple transparencies that are offered as gifts to the dark goddesses of a flooded storm cellar where naked feet navigate the geode highways of confusing aural brilliance – perpetual audiosculptures that create an electrical chair on which lightning fish can ascend like thrones. The secret darumas are truly lost marsupials forever in search of hopeful homes, dreaming of the chance meeting of indifferent, preoccupied eyes. Even though some of the best things in life can't be grabbed all at once, it doesn't mean that a limping platypus can't forego a trip to the local rice paper department where edible books assist in the transmission of prenucleated optical knowledge.

The limping platypus bats her eyelashes and extends a trembling paw in the direction of a slippery fish camera. Her extended breastplates reveal hexagonal libraries of piano danger and the underlying heartbeat of invisible pursuit; the negative coat rack that spelled a disturbing alphabet of bullet trains and drooling airports.

The liquid airports were disturbing as they were promiscuous, and their rented elevators rose in distracting ways, pulling up a spray of tie-dyed cranes from a bearskin carpet where a hungry woman reclines in wait of something special. The airport became a folded envelope, bearing an impressive array of skinless fish flashlights. These light receptacles were positioned at every mammalian muscle-joint crated from kiln-fired porcelain bricks. Creative processes yielded an abundance of rancid literature, and this entranceway profusion into the deep gullet of sleeping fish was the metallic lightbulb of the heart you display when you comb your long hair and walk through desolate fields of burdock roots. Your shimmering dress only highlights the eyes, and your smile kills me. If only beautiful women could burn peapods from windowpanes with their florid eyes!

After flyswatters are used to dispel the attack force of vicious bumblebees, a cybernetic honeycomb of safety-lead is spilled across the sonic honey of female foreheads, drawing a universal confusion from a hairy, orange, crushed, witch-like pumpkin that contains the forgotten imprints of feline digits as reaching claws are stretched across punctured venom-producing membranes adored by strong but nebulous snakes. The nebulous snakes thrash to country songs sung by people bearing guitar weapons and trucks of cumbersome lodestones whose magnetic fields attract the burnt wings of remote butterfly breasts that burn up the carpet on an uneventful Saturday night. This type of behavior is airport-unforgettable.

Suddenly rude gameshow executives were mutilated with potato-peelers, and their still-twitching limbs were observed in various corners of the platform stage. Unattached eyelashes became sinister, custom-made pool cues that were used to inflate party balloons and other celebratory trinkets from a netherworld where the neighbors listened to country music performed with a well-tuned but superbly monotonous base guitar. That's what happens when people live in the past, leading to the discovery that the plaster fire hydrant was hollow and contained the honeycombs of vicious, stinging colonial insects. The infinity of a childish wristwatch opens wide, and green lanterns of unusual festivities use maturity to deal with irrational youth, at least when utilitarian babbling reveals a narrow-minded harelip of corduroy blackness and intrusive hairstyles that closely resemble the conformism of shaved tomatoes, or Mamatoes, a.k.a. mammalian tomatoes. In the meantime, the elderly break their finest dishware on the rocks outside, in favor of returning to prehistoric feeding rituals where hominids ate with their hands and tossed their salads between each other's legs, possibly even crushing hair-pies on their excessively hairy and bipedal kneecaps. Because of this rock 'n roll kind of change, the prehistoric diversion rooms took the place of cramped phone booths in the eternal, galactic hierarchy of feline informant, daruma-wish-fulfillment feelings.

This characteristic whirlwind of facial reconstruction was apparently laborious at certain moments, but usually the eyes of the vulture prevailed, promising a long train ride into alien worlds where the leaves on the trees were blue- and red-striped and where the, uh, buildings were manufactured with an extrasolar adhesive made from cattlejoint glue. Perhaps the forest elves hadn't noticed, but the monotonous nightly news had nothing good to say, and the cracks in the wall whispered of the passage of rats, suggesting that a monstrously foul holiday was afoot. The forest elves carried pitchers of fermented tea and corrected the reverse turning of their wristwatches, but the unmetered hours were no longer theirs as they observed their own reverse degeneration, marking an odd return to prehistoric eras where cave-dwelling impulses returned. This creation of athletic saliva ripped strange notes across the board of a harpsichord, and plates of rancid cow's feet were served to visiting diplomats. A descending hailstorm destroyed the arctic roofs.

4

In places of destitute eggshells, unawakened dreams might provide the dragon fingers required to move great sheets of water from one iceberg residence to another. Naked women and girls populate a town of frozen red maple leaves where abnormal artifacts are raised from the dead in order to create mud bricks that are fired in primitive stone ovens. These literal building blocks are blessed with a pungent hibiscus extract and then used to erect a familial architecture that is sensually disturbing as it is wide-eyed in the absorption of orange lights that play on its structures cast by rambunctious UFOs.

The intrusion of the UFOs causes diagrammatic representatives of dehydrated ocean beds to appear on the foreheads of the sleeping women in their frozen, red-leaf maple citadel. These flying saucers exact a certain dragonfly radio station from the metal in the young ladies' tooth fillings, and this supersonic vibration disrupts all games of unknown family checkers that occur when the usual rituals of child-rearing have become decrepit and thoroughly boring. This spectrum of overheated dreams created origami kites that got lost in the orange forest, amid the resurrected crates that bore the insignia of the intransigent lotus root, a peculiar symbol created when people attempted to communicate with the oceanic diamonds encrusted in coastal cliffs. The eyes of the vulture registered the presence of these diamonds, and stuck its feet within a finely built fire-ant hill just to enjoy the exquisite insectoid pain created from migrating ants who lived only to produce more eggs to be given to the orange-lit UFOs with the odd predilection for the noisy dental fillings of sleeping, nude women. Imagine being bound to a dark town of orange UFO intrusions where all objects, edifices and activities of marginal intentions were daily grown as a deposited clamshell would – shiny layer upon layer that could sometimes be construed as an unavoidable limestone castle held together by rickety hinges but controlled by sinister internal muscles with claws and ruptured pumpkins spilling out waves of hairy, orange pulp!

This confusion, traced back to the orange structures of ruptured witch pumpkins, tempt the daring to reach into the dark, moist crevice caves in order to extract even more hairy pulp mounted with profuse arrangements of viable seeds, disrupting the partial eyes of meditating Buddhists when they retire to their nine-year caves to think of ways to exile a sunset inside of a glass ampoule. Hence the formation of the neo-daruma nodules. These new magnetic receptacles containing the sunsets of winter are worn by native elephants whose arthritis is diminished by fireside smear campaigns conducted by narcissistic, self-important men of authority who do not know enough about themselves.

The wait for a picture-perfect moment languishes, and another year passes without the rising of copper submarines. This sense of loss isn't permanent, but for the moment, it is an eternity of tattooed butterflies that escape a pigeon leg-tube that was strapped to a royal lamp-post in a fearful corner of a pumpkin storage cabinet where the secret pumpkin hairs germinate, creating even more opportunities for hands that get caught up within snatch.

Ultimately all fresh pumpkins are destined to shed their ruby slippers, leading to unpredictable contractions of the muscles surrounding their sagittal crests, leading to the delights of gorillas and other mountain-residing fauna who have the label "Samhain" etched onto the soles of their traditional shoes. Even the frogs in Madagascar couldn't compete with the secretion of raw, screaming souls from the closed eyelids of pumpkins, making a stiff break for the border of neighboring cypress territory, where the trees are tall and the memories of fashionable rocks are still meticulously prevalent (barring the occasional earthquake or minor landslide). Within display caverns, monstrous slices of fresh cerebrums are presented like jewels, and locusts burrow within the soft, mealy cerebral flesh, forcing the eruption of red daruma totems through the unstable deserts. All of the numerous left eyes on these multi-daruma totems are filled in with black, while the right ones remain glassy voids, possibly but uncertainly with scratched corneas. Exoskeletal seashells of a purely shimmering love appear, and their unpredictable appearance raised the constructed timbers of a hopeful new lily bud that was to be tied only once into a fragrant knot. The temporally uncertain apparition of this unknown life might have only been a passing cloud, or maybe even an unresponsive, self-absorbed woman climbing the ancient stairs, with bowling ball in hand, but despite these fluctuations in nasal perception, the peculiar strain of love was persistent as it moved through closets, withered catacombs as well as the pillowcases of tomorrow. Old dreams die hard, and their ghosts have tendrils sunk into every facet of an immediate heart that has been implanted into sorrowful dwellings at the edge of a newly resurrected Atlantis long forgotten until recently.

Half-filled daruma totems appeared in the way manta rays sometimes conduct a sweep of Japanese juke boxes with their velvet fins, conforming to the odd morphologies of regurgitated automobiles coated with a raucous epoxy. Human indifference was at its cyclical peak, and the shadows of love only served to mock the half-filled eyes of the present, always mired in the present with glutinous red paint. Unknown catalogues of dripping red hair move through the pumpkin lattice cracks of stonewalled vegetative fruiting bodies, spanking the ignorant and the indifferent beauties who only understand cookies and clocks which seep through the fernlike projections of soft red hair, the true antithesis to the loneliness of Sundays.

The damp air turns crisp when the walls of concrete bunkers seethe with hidden trains of vulgar circuitries and hot air balloons from the underground eyesockets of Madagascar. These seething wall-trains spill their lava from the cobwebbed rooftops, signifying a deluge of futility that can only mark the beginning of an infernal war of the spirit, where outmoded forms are razed with icicles, managing the burnt carbon of frozen seagull skeletons that were once embedded within red glass in a masochistic lamp-post library. The fear of green tightropes might be intimidating to some, but not to the released seagull frames that were zirconium spectacles removed from a sickly cook-light. So amazing to view the external world as a conglomeration of one's own building blocks. Watches made of protein signal the deep freeze.

Voodoo chickens hibernated within blood-soaked ruins, and dreams that never ended wore German shirts and carved pumpkins with unnatural scimitars, equipping bare feet with golden shoes, raising an allergic cloud of dust that would scare away the timid masses from the transport tubes of subhuman lunar rocks.

These subhuman lunar rocks, although perfectly capable of the more than occasional outbursts, were cleft from an unknown stratum of fossilized pumpkin rock, sometimes even bearing the fossilized footprints of Mayumi Panther progenitors, revealing brilliant schists and realistic asbestos aprons and bibs that can shield the Mayumi Panthers from the unbearable lunar heat, when the panthers and the subhuman rock strata awake to find themselves many miles away from earth, golf courses and good ship lollypops. These particular subhuman moon rocks were a gem shop's nightmare, and this intrusive incursion somehow converted glass doorknobs to frozen pedestals of sub-arctic wood, calculating the derived integrals as a function of sagging wooden age rings, converting the furniture-producing trees to non-linear representations of a smiling chaos that drew its wings from espaldic sheathes, radiating a sub-dermal imprint of friendly bellybuttons on which no friendly eyes would gaze. The subhuman lunar dermal rocks were the perfumed consolation prize – a truly new ridge of teeth that could erupt mysteriously from the aural sockets of whale skulls from which all sounds of overheated engines could be heard.

And the magnetic ants scratched their heads and moistened their antennae with formic saliva, munching on fresh limes and dreaming of purple shipwrecks that were revealed from the breathless gulfs of time. Surely a moment of sandy peace could result from this sub-dermal, subhuman connection! Nevertheless, the collective fear of facial ants was disruptive to the thoughtful complexions, and divas with sponge costumes created distant memoirs of distant admirers, forever turning blind eyes of Delphic chaos to the fetid crossword puzzles that lumber over diagonal tennis court thresholds, smiling and kissing the dazzling green lights of day!

But sponge suits and overalls will be shed, and the soft birds of eyes peel away the layers of a baked lie – an apple pie of worms and unattainable, alienated yellow elements that resemble gold but show a sea of broken teeth scattered amid disheveled pyrite gales that release crystallized wind and other electrical manifestations of the elements, only when that beloved smile results from spilled machine oil that represents hard work in an embryonic form. This state of admiration might be ignored, but only at the expense of a fall down a steep galactic incline, pushing immobile birds through a paradise vortex on the edge of the moon as it eclipses your eyes in a moment of deaf hope. Beds were never more superfluous.

The wealth of ravens can be unpredictable, yet when it rains it will drip with teary eyes that refract a kiss into a spectrum of primordial joy, complete with gelatinous chicken bones on a performance carcass where paper airplanes can be simple enough to scare away passive ducks that tuck bamboo poles from the espaldic escutcheons of yahtzee spinal cord winning combinations. Logical arrangements of quantitative shapes could never have been more straightforward. Meanwhile, dead fetuses undergo fermentation, and grandpa changes the television channel.

Powdered makeup residues can be sampled with a radio-tracing cotton swab whose sample is then dissolved in an organic solvent and passed through a jealous chromatography column, creating the unknown indifference of evasive bluebirds. Still, time passes, and dice are spilled, almost missing the center of the soup cauldron that multiplies the wished-for embrace into a dream of a new year, where the see-through implements of x-rays dress up beasts of burden in tuxedoes and regurgitate the gism of Hephaestus into a youthful basin which drops upon the head of a petty and needling Hermione Valvolte. This latest insult cannot be tolerated, and ping-pong explanations create an acoustic sermon in the afterlife of charred coconut shells that were deposited by sentient apes when they perform their daily routines, forever indifferent, forever oblivious to the terribly obvious.

Women bearing construction tools erect houses, and these magnificent foundations are nothing more than stable sliders that lay down unpredictable patterns to challenge the tempting metaphor of time travel, chanting the runes of omniman literature. This construction of easing grimaces sometimes takes itself too seriously, sending old ideas through a decrepit pipeline that motivates the wrath of a limp blackboard eraser.

We shall board the whirlybird, and then cross over to the next mountain where we can shoot the deer, loading crossbows and tying strings on soft fingers to secure dates. There is no other way. Perhaps to some this was a joke, but the sun will set only when the sanctitude of a decarbonated cola is spilled upon a lively and highly gregarious olfactory hand that moves in conjunction with the evening sun. This dawning sunrise will probably get stolen tommorrow, but today, before it is snatched up by cheesy mousetraps of infernal half-truths, there will be a moment of rising explosions, taking flowers to the ceiling and disquieting the pre-elderly in their mongoose tracks, resulting in faunal discombobulation that raises eyebrows as it tickles a vulnerable, self-absorbed armpit while tender sponges are released from the jail-time of exactness. This precision of long-distance love-targeting might be futile, perhaps vain, perhaps stupid, but the moment was golden and then the red birds were singing an unstoppable melodic cacophony while the gigolos pushed inverted roses cut from a cosmic backyard garden where the stars can be seen shining from the bottoms of koi ponds and where avian embraces display abnormally colorful butterflies made of tissue paper. Still, the call goes momentarily unanswered, as if a self-aware ecosystem could drool happiness from the fragrant orchids growing next to your penetrating eyes, always penetrating, always with radiant emotions and smooth whispers of sympathy. From the moment the moon rose, the nocturnal callings of the red birds were endless, releasing one mind-piercing blast after the next, ending a moment of black satin with a powder keg of infinite laughter, and then vice versa. Such moments fall under an unknown category of autumn leaves, and the dry tumbleweeds move across a desolate face like a lost flock of lachrymal droplets born from the cut roses sold by the gigolos. Your moth army lands on my arm and you make me into a wheel of light.

We found you sleepwalking next to the maternal coat racks, which might not be good for your complexion, but then who really knows about that? Raising you from the dead like a massive shipwreck wasn't easy, but with the fertilization of uncertain soils, there might still be growth on dead worlds, places that normal eyes wouldn't understand. And now we are all smiles. In a separate vein, the fertilization of those dead worlds constitutes a titanium-clad burst of laughter, amidst a backdrop of inherited sorrow, forced on every successive generation like a plague, but only until the ugly circuit is broken in all imaginable ways, in the same way impossible motorcycle helmets are converted to toilet bowls, whence come the hordes of marauding invaders on horseback, slashing through the sturdy ribbons of fences and carrying only the most faithful of flashlights. This must be the price to pay for a perfect moment, and yet venus flytraps abound everywhere.

The premeditated mailbox animals are relentless, like the overplayed songs of yesteryear, with fibrillating, caged butterflies metamorphosing into obscene, painted lanterns that might wear six different shoes on each foot on some of the hotter days. Sleepy painted trails forge new melodies from the wing-thumping, caged butterflies, and this mandragoran face can remind the beautiful of certain regenerative shooting ranges where the absconded biscuits are filled with transistors and capacitors, revealing a nightgown of window drapery, bulwarking colossal pillars of tall stone weights. This antechamber of breasts reveals an escaped flock of ravens carrying corn kernels made of gold, clasped tightly in black claws, forever remembering the way home. Sport flags might wither and drop to a mowed lawn, but the shadows of noon are plentiful, and they register their fingerprints, creating the identity designs of the wings for the thumping, caged butterflies that begin to loom over the dusky hills of the rabid hunted twilight that falls upon the reflexive knees of nurses, forever hitting cold-treated lizards over the head with a rubber hammer. The art of conversation could never rescue this polished, silver lock that dangles over the soft, pillow mirror. A fluorescent pineapple is then thrown into a tree-shredder, spattering nearby automobiles with severely disrupted pulp.

The parrots reached out and grabbed the loose cages that housed the thumping, fingerprint butterflies, while erupting feathery mustaches from their beaks which seemed more like tentacles than feathery hair. Suddenly, x-mas socks are pulled off the feet of a green velvet mannequin that had once been very well versed in mannequin etiquette. These pulled socks became perplexing to the peculiar green parrots, but their feathers will change to blue once they have used their squid beaks to release the thumping, fingerprint butterflies from their gluey, rickety cages of suckered calcium ribbons. These shucked oysters really were the whole world found between smooth, secreted carbonate minerals. When the secreted fog of iridescence was lifted, their hieroglyphic messages of religious horseshoes were pressed into the indentations on occipital lobes of skulls, creating loving spectra from pink hearts tossed by the thumping, fingerprint butterflies when they reached the hollowed caves of pumpkin patch nether-reality, descending furtive ladders into long, blackened hovels of silky cobwebs of pure abandonment, serving to amplify the din of people, as they contort and move their translocative steps through the cosmos.

Ever since car batteries were replaced with cologned, buck teeth, the manner in which embroidered sunsets had been revised so that rabbits and turtles alike could destroy expensive lampshades when the choked graveyards erupt adulterated bus tickets with nipple-displaying buses not very far behind. The blurred, dried eyes of the electrocuted octopus released the mousetrap, and the captured skulls of rodents became the transformed houses of lovers, arguing about baseball games as well as the positioning of cologned spring peas in an ambivalent driftwood garden where snails uncurl their shells when spectacular radioactive emissions stimulate the destabilization of calcium carbonate.

This deregulation led to an unregistered burn permit, which ultimately blew sultry smoke into the face of a young, gloved creature who had approached because of the magnetic, noisy lights. The burn permit was the magic flashcard – the feather under the unsuspecting red nose. This concussive percussion sent harmonic visions over the airwaves, in the same way you perpetually address your favorite new song when your arms resume their arboreal conformations and when the kiss of a bronchial snail is a rebirth of museum shoes. The finely-crafted museum shoes are teutonic, and their footsy chainmail is pervasive and ineradicable. This passage of telescopic feelings raises a lost shipwreck everyday, bringing silent kisses of parrot gold to the beaks of lost citizens that missed the first train but managed to forego forgotten newspapers in favor of a time-warp to next week – the unquantifiable unit of time that is as deceptively arbitrary as it anonymously blends in with the street-lacquered woodwork, releasing the formaldehyde smell of naked honeybees when they create petroleum honeycombs that solidify when touched with the whisper of an organic catalyst. These daily cauldrons have high yields, and ultimately make cranky, overseer personalities obsolete. The disloyalty was optional but necessitated by the manufactured beehives. Although the cave skull is reaching now for the escaped pumpkin honey, the unopened vegetable tins are found with square, unnatural can-opener punctures, revealing the unconscionable spent matches and the discarded snowshoes of the dead. Necronomicon panties couldn't have been better absentmindedly flung over the dark, dreaded neighborly fence, and the derangement of suspenseful, close minutes tug at the cheery house lanterns that line the dusty, teutonic driveway and house the once-again caged, thumping fingerprint butterflies, who now tend to the nectar proboscis of each, and thirst for the construction flowers hewn from resilient concrete – smart-concrete, perhaps.

These deadly hills have their calling, but the takeoff of Russian airplanes couldn't crush the forests of amber fossils propped amid the charred ruins of architectural squid bones, essentially representing an impossible choice of spanking happiness within forbidden quadrants of shunned water wells where light switches are unknown or at least deregulated so that the joy of geode rock messages might represent a latent syntax that professes the blocked love from a sweltering beaver dam, thumping the earth with an annoyed tail. The list of grievances goes on.

A magic sneeze from a discarded knapsack on a hiking trail could almost remind one of a good blowjob and also a good night's sleep at a highly esteemed country inn, where road-signs are weathered and where disruptive floods coursed through photosynthetic pathways not very long ago. The purgatory of knowledge is confusing at times, yes, but this remake of a forgotten cardiac diagram performs the initiation of a paper lattice form of symbiotic resistance that only exists to be torn when tarnished leaves fall from icy trees, and when future maidens carry flower baskets down a toad-ridden country road, perfectly situated within the sights of skeletal driftwood and maritime borings created by sedentary crustaceans.

Perhaps the ship wouldn't go down with the weathered lobster traps, and perhaps a cherished pocket watch could become a house in the way a snail secretes a valuable shell of balsa wood artifacts. Nervous zombies trip the lateral eyebeams. Spring flowers of incomprehensibility erupt through the cubed nautilus of Australia's desert driftwood, pulling in the old manuals of demonstrating factories that bled indigo dyes into the sand when an unanticipated thunderstorm ravaged the impossibly icy wastes of chaparral and other coyote pumpkin airplanes. Neurotic party music abounds, though, and conspecific relationships catapult through the open windows of airline observatories, breeding confusion through linguistic differences of tomorrow's chelationary olive trees.

5

A new bridge was crossed when tender footsteps broached the saline waters over the steel decks of marine observatories. A thunderous rain drenched the oil refinery's main pipeline, and a fresh supply of inane questions was asked. Were there any new birds' nests that had erupted from magnetic nodes where Jesus had bartered with paper umbrellas and soothed raw eyesockets with smart, combinatory olives that had been produced by parasitic desert insects that fomented raccoon cave-paintings underneath the tin lid of abnormal sardine containers, conveniently used as biological telephones to talk with the dead and thereby resurrect dead lines and radioactive dirigibles? The transportation of unknown chitinous mandibles through the obtuse angles of spiral staircases can send shivers through airplane cockpits, resuscitating plastic mannequins with a simple wave of a foam rubber chicken.

This activity was shuttled through an endless corridor of minutes, bickering with the loose flint rocks that careened down the airport cliffs where the fireflies were abundant, and where gold-lined space helmets could pull living teeth from the turbid bellies of pantheric organisms when they reside in an embryonic umbrella puzzle.

And so the oil refinery defies the rains and instead passed the minutes as the storm began to abate. Perhaps knowledge had threatened to dry up as well, but as long as a memory of the future unfolded across railroad-charred tongues, the telephone poles that traversed the inland deserts would continue to transmit the distant signals of loved ones, erasing the naps and replacing them with the purple meditations of time-warped fireflies who had put their lunch money behind the portraits of corrupt presidents. These intense firefly knowledge sessions were perpetually buttressed by the growing incursions of neglectful void, which had the tendency to inhibit the growth of traditional identities, creating a romantic amnesia of blindness, skipping stones at the vulnerable, dark windows of the convenient oil refineries. This revelation proved easier to comprehend than the more complicated mental systems, but perhaps not as entertainingly dramatic. A great crime had just occurred, yet one might as well have been looking at multi-tread footprints of weekend diversions and the lostness of sallow religious conversions. Where could these plane-wrecks keep coming from?

Regardless of the bullshit distractions, evil associations between jigsaw puzzle pieces opened a door to a mind barely contained by external judgments and fishy containment features where indifferent calendars marked the flow of withheld time. The pieces of the puzzle were unable to interlock, but this physical incongruency did not interfere with their warm, temporal association, spinning fabulous jewels from the air, and directing the alignment and overlap of certain shower neurons from the earthworms in the soil below. Their future was blindingly uncertain, causing the grating of bone endings upon each other, but despite this curtain of worldly indifference, the kernel of a liquid solar system was in the making, forging a recipe for a new kind of emotion, blind to regret and scorched hesitation. The release of the captive stars brightened the constellations of night, and if there was anything the least bit romantic in the sky, it was a lost weather balloon that created a different meaning from a detached bonsai plant, revealing the romance between disrupted traditions. This signaling had represented the plumy feathers of forgotten ostriches, and this message simply delighted her as the romantic weather balloon moved across the dark, stormy night skies over the wind-swept grassy hills far below. Her delight was inversely proportional to the inner gaze of searching prophets sequestered in geomorphic caves. Whoever she was, her passage through the night skies was a veritable experiment in limbo, decisively measuring the moments with prescriptive lips and timeless hands of a traveling flock of parakeets (in their latent, red leaf form). Tractor treads erupted along the sutures of the feminine cranium, and the travel of night birds was ultimately rougher than any clash of rugby mates with outgoing bats' wings tangled in the murderous hair of the bystanders, laughably prophesizing about the discernment of radial origami. There would be no end to the rugby wars, but it was hoped that certain games would end well in less-frequented fields of soft clover, where the gnarled trees quietly sang louder than the birds. The uncertainty of the moment was deafening, and no amount of wishful speculation could raise the sunken ships of hope, at least according by ordinary means. Luckily enough, the day was extraordinary as well as interordinary, gracefully establishing a haven within the pearly spiral of a snail shell positioned on an inviting burial mound.

Impotent criticism abounds amid scaled tumbleweeds that course across the chilled hairs on a forearm, after the thorny fields of autumn pumpkins are used as staging grounds for theatrical deplorities from hidden continents that emerge from a willful fog. So what if the cauldrons of rugby soup have spilled over, revealing the unfulfilled braying of tectonic dogs? New songs will always result, capable of fighting the quiet bridges of sunken ships that were silenced by the generous smooch of twilight or a tickle from the crawling chaos that froze statues with moss, nitre and clean-shaven elbows. The universe might not have changed for the subjective better, but at least the grimaces from the plasma walls were quieted by approaching minds who congregated around pristine dwellings of cultivated goldfish and other rotten transformations from antiquity that surpassed their own original functions, turning dinosaur bones into treasured agate circuits, and releasing the love of disjointed satellites into a momentary cascade of stellar debris over the multigenerational pumpkin fields where lotus roots were concomitantly grown with spring strawberries of a peculiar sort, raising eyebrows including the endless infinity of feet. But the historical, proscriptive poison ironically did not permeate the soil, perhaps just because of sheer photosynthetic will, and this rare growth was spat upon by some, but transferred to new rugby patches by others, with the help of alien, pantheric claw hieroglyphs, of course.

The rusty cogwheels turned, nonetheless. Shoe sales went up, and the rain fell on cold sidewalks where desolate pairs of eyes would occasionally malinger, hedging bets and washing away obscene salt build-ups. This foolishness carried on for quite a many decades until cobwebbed chariots pulled up into the ceremonial teutonic driveways, distributing mauled cotton candy to the neighbors and revealing the buried chainsaws stashed in non-ancestral alcoves covered by baseball canvasses above the musty, teutonic fireplaces. Apparently there would be no end to these baseball canvasses and the oddly inviting teutonic driveways (that had a weird habit of inviting equine beasts to their deaths over cliffs of displaced rock and unnaturally positioned geodes that were embedded within the cliffs) that were forever available for weary travelers.

The horses pulled up, in their uncertainty, and then steadily departed, dropping off their eager passengers who felt most at home within the most inviting of teutonic driveways. This sort of driveway behavior was a major condolence to the passage of full-contact sports, as its phasing out of cinderblock playgrounds represented a major collision with the ceremonial feathers depicted on the scattered jigsaw puzzle pieces. Although the pieces might never reach their intended, final resting places, their wooden, pulp-injected smart-technology guided them, despite the frivolous pushing of the birth of future jade writings. They might have even been recycled into floor-wax chess pieces, but that desolate act was averted, the same as a telecommunicative war, by those infernal teutonic driveways that were able to requisition romantic weather balloons on a moment's notice. Ok, you stupid asshole, the powerdrill stock is low, and so we will be on backorder for the next two months. This slag in business cannot be avoided, but at least the dangling fish-lures will be bitten upon by foaming customers, reaching the badwaters of feral companionship when the moments die in a road-slicked rainstorm. Why do the precious moments escape when wedding dresses are drenched in a sub-arctic hailstorm? The precipitation of water never fails to change everything, but the weather balloons bare their metaphors, demolishing the old age of negative guitars of disbelieving, hair-tangling bats. The Gulf of Oklahoma was more of a mystery than a spindled porcupine of valued ideas.

Several years hence, a hidden record illuminated the history of the teutonic driveways, with all their slovenly ornamentation, instructing a mistrustful public in the ways of ill-mannered ancestors who knew of great upheavals in their familial, multi-staged dormitories, where filthy celebrations would flagellate the early morning hours of any new year. These unknown festivals were the ghosts of lost days that were invisibly inserted into the gaping maw of neglect. Restless souls walked the tattered hallways, never even imagining the manors in their original glory. At present, only one matriarch remained, and this elderly thing presided over her staff of genetic descendents, which was all male, for some disturbing reason.

Every day, new orders and commands were given to this speechless staff of all-male genetic descendents, and these unknown subjects would obey, making the rounds in their large, multi-story dwelling, searching each and every floor for missing paperclips, and forever re-copying the scrawled, ancestral graffiti in the now-defunct restrooms, sometimes barely holding back the deluge of moldy plaster from a tired wall that could persist no further. These endless perambulations on the part of the servants scared the visitors, at least while they were still breathing, but usually any foreign citizens who entered the multileveled compound were shot to death, with their bodies, personal effects (including ballistic weaponry) left haphazardly, in the same way a small suitcase of Barbie doll supplies could be shredded and then quickly dispersed over the ancient tiles of corroded bathrooms.

Arched limbs of very thick jigsaw puzzle pieces reached over the railings of one of the fire escapes, marking the beginning of a siege designed to sear the religion out of the meandering house servants and warriors, all genetically related and of the male sex, of course. These pieces of an unknown puzzle had a bituminous way of extracting the dark, viscous blood from long-dusted paintings, replacing the more familial elements with puzzle-shaped replicas of a cinnamon cardboard that was ghastly as it was polka-dotted, sometimes reveling in a creepy shade provided by an unnatural candle made from the lipid extracts of bipedal primates. The fallen consciousness of a defrocked buffoon might have released a swarm of birds, re-enacting the outline of a skeleton, but the closed books of a bloodless morning could bring the genetic portraits into a sharper focus.

The movement of the invading jigsaw puzzle pieces was a recent one, and the resulting maelstrom of forged identity was confusing to the keepers of the teutonic resort, forcing the male occupants to decorate the filthy driveways with ornate seashells and out-of-print girly magazines which had been unearthed next to the matriarch's dominant bookshelves. Thus, the teutonic driveways would eventually become littered with the slimed implements of ballistic weaponry, but until the invasion of the jigsaw pieces was complete, each individual servant retained his own individual traditions and memories, in a way analogous to the tossing of wet socks into a moldy clothes drier. The arching limbs of the puzzle pieces were spade-like swords, and each could assume the form of any person, any object, any idea or any state of mind. This reproduced slot of reality was its own morphological antithesis, enabling each marauding piece to change colors and to meet its own precise needs of the moment. A puddle for blindness and a green floodlight for shrunken grapes. These catastrophic changes could not last forever, but the tremors and quakes were enough to prevent crustaceans from climbing floor to floor of the teutonic hotel by way of slippery, rickety ladders.

At the base of one of the oil-slicked ladders was a corpse holding a pistol fashioned of silver with a mother-of-pearl handle, making a great archaeological find at the steps of the main megalithic tower, a place where exotic fish collections were stored for the right moment. The deposed watchman seemed to be in one piece, although the body was now covered with a sickly blue strain of crayfish, slowly picking at the decaying flesh, perhaps reminiscent of an upstate myth where a herd of fallen masonites were picked clean in a similar manner. But the hardshells were unable to cease feeding until every last thread of muscle was consumed.

Meanwhile, the walls became vertically littered with gray, crescent-shaped pulsating moths, whose antennae would periodically twitch from the clouds of powdered skin and dust that would slowly move throughout the teutonic castle, whose passage was only registered when coming into contact with a ray of light from the outside. A pancreas never tasted so good. In response to the gray wall-moths, barely contained cages of thumping butterflies revealed their glowing colors, in the same way an expectant heart waited for a familiar sound in the teutonic driveways. Despite whatever the invading jigsaw pieces would do, the thumping butterflies would always retain their identities by way of a thoracic fingerprint that sorted each of them out by name. The treasure of memory was abundant on these resplendent chests, evoking a cherry-tree coat of arms that could form the emotional anchor for any of the invading neurological jigsaw pieces. But the moulds and/or templates that created the pieces were unknown, from a faraway assembly plant that bled indigo textile dye into the neighboring sand drifts and which created the shipwrecks of trees from low-lying bushes with clumsy, rubbery leaves. This faraway assembly area might have been obscure when hidden deep within a nearby continent, but its output of jigsaw fragments was enough to chill many a juvenile crayfish to the mythical core of its own body, heavily armored with detachable blue plates that covered flesh as well as living room chairs.

The plated chairs were abundant in the living rooms, and there were plenty of these unused living rooms in the teutonic dwellings, at least enough for the robins to bore holes in the chair-backings in order to create nests.

"Have you ever felt like this," asked the radio in one of the unused living rooms, invoking only the silence of the chairs, whose arms reposed as specially carved fragments of driftwood coated in a varnish and covered sparsely with blue crawfish plates and even a few adhesive puzzle pieces. For now, the chairs would remain silent as they dreamed of infantile, crystalline chess pieces, measurable only in units of deja vu and represented only in the nudest of pinks. These dreams of the unused living-room chairs blew through wooden lutes sloppily nailed to their armrests, engendering memories of cave-blasting equipment used to reopen old highways that had fallen into disuse over the past century, revealing lost wood-glue factories that could service the needs of precarious, rickety colonial dwellings whose inner foundations and light structures were fortified with the wood-glue in addition to the darkened strawberries of spring – very dangerous strawberries whose multi-lobed fruiting bodies represented a toxic game of spy-vs-spy and whose pre-eminence over the newly opened caves was more than a little frightening, or so the memory banks indicated. Within the chair dreams, the sleeping robins twitched, periodically tensing and then relaxing their sleeping talons. This rhythmic, digital evacuation roused the sleeping worm larvae in the core of the driftwood armrests, conjuring the open memories of the hovering, solitary, romantic weather balloons with the cryptic red and yellow markings so characteristic of misplaced cogs when they interrupt the ancient rhythms of mega-machines as they labored under ice fields that slowly pulsed through the caves beneath the teutonic mansion, sometimes even bubbling up as a negligent slime over the weathered stones of the teutonic driveways. Despite the instant surprise of chain lightning, the unused living-room furniture dreamed, arousing the interest of blind spiders who looked at bronze keyholes as an international bank of the frozen illiterate, creating soundless notes on a calcium-encrusted banjo adhered to one of the unused living-room walls as a highly cherished hunting trophy.

The dream of the chairs was only interrupted when a pack of monotheistic celibates entered the teutonic driveway, sending out invasive signals with their minds. Within the teutonic mansion, the burrowed robins revealed themselves as thoroughly impotent, leaving to the crustacean jigsaw puzzle pieces the task of repelling the unwanted monotheistic celibate visitors, which was accomplished merely with an utterly lewd wink from one of the bigger jigsaw pieces. In the same way a spring strawberry experiences fulfillment from a covering of whipped cream, the teutonic habitation of multi-storied disrepair felt completion upon a sudden but highly satisfying downpour of hailstorms upon its tiny, rickety roofs. The dreams of the robin-infested, living-room chairs were enriched, causing the driftwood armrests to quiver with joy, perhaps even anticipating a full day of clover, asphalt rain, when the periodic deluges from the nearby mountains became unavoidable. The puzzle pieces checked their watches and sighed, thoroughly content that they were now the masters of the old dwelling. Although the matriarchy still might have persisted within the castle, the presence of the jigsaw fragments kept her ancient power in check, enabling the driftwood chairs to dream and the blue crayfish infestations to continue uninterrupted, while modern ghost stories were deposited on the highly elevated turrets of the teutonic palace, courtesy of the hovering, romantic solitary weather balloons of cryptic red and yellow origins.

This state of completeness was only a passing phenomenon, as the balloons eventually dispersed and the ancient matriarch regained control of the teutonic establishment for a short time. It was as if the rest of the world had never existed. Although many still adhered to the concept of a linear passage of time, the elliptical dreams of the chairs persisted, enabling the erotic fires of conch shells to escape extinction for maybe another week, until the next invasive battle ensued. The demagnetism of falling stars was as old as your young brow, and the greatest gift you gave the world was your special patch of blue sky that could even inspire cracker-stuffed mouths to whistle a few rounds of teutonic Dixie.

Could all of this cyclical fun last forever? Probably so. As long as the grass was greener in one place, then the next place would follow the example, creating a domino field as far as the crustacean eye could see. Groomed eyestalks rested on fields of clover, waiting for a mythical reunion that unfortunately was as slow as the trains on a transportationally challenged day. Boulders are removed from the kitchen soup cauldron, as the family collection of dinosaur teeth (herbivorous, of course) plan to spend another day in their teutonic shelter, setting up a pernicious revelatory explosion that could occur the following day, or possibly the next. The incompleteness of the smell of the jigsaw puzzle pieces reminded the awakening robins of their dreaming driftwood chairs. Within the driftwood armrests, there were now carved the highly crude reliefs of embryonic chess pieces, and this curtained mystery brought tears to her oblong eyes.

The movements of the wet eyes were cold to the touch, as if a myopic slingshot had missed its target and instead hurled a raw egg onto the lap of one of those control-freak monotheists who lingered over the next damp hill, waiting in the rain in a self-imposed act of deferred gratification until the next invasion might or might not be permissible, as if the consent of dubious life could be handed down from inanimate objects, illustrious yet mute acts of nature, or even the scratching of an itchy elbow. The trees were definitely lost on that day, for a time, at least. Hiked mountain paths rolled out their dragon's tongues, and the awkward dirge began to rotate, enabling the clumsy sonifications of mistreated cowbells and other percussive digressions who peppered the clouds of the setting sun with lightning. A foreboding bomb shelter began to ooze a frothy carrot emulsion from its depths.

The passage of the hailstorm marked a tenebrous presence of what some might have called the "first gods," but other than the storm, there was no other evidence of their presence. The slavery of the minutes was confusing, but the forgotten ivy brought no answers, revealing the once-obscured pinkness of the embryonic chess pieces that had now re-effected their crystal amnions from long ago. These bombs of war were the hidden purpose of this dwelling, perhaps, secretly suggesting the existence of but one more weapons factory. In this particular case, it was a psychological weapons factory. Although the manner of deployment of these pink embryonic chess pieces was unknown, as well as their resulting manner of action, their danger was great, in the same way a cluster of flowers on valentine's day could be devastating.

Forgotten sharks rise to the conflagrant surface, displacing religious horseshoes with vitamin-laced health drinks and emergency seat flotations. This crisscrossing of verbal streams is good for the backyard and helps with the juvenile irrigation so fondly regarded in the castle's inner circles, amid the wreckage of discharged firearms and indignantly pulsating jigsaw pieces that have adhered to the regal portraits, now assuming the form of the intended subject. Every outgoing entity always returns via the teutonic driveway, creating a trap of life that has become virtually unknown in the more advanced city where crustacean armor is no longer acknowledged as a flight of truth or the swipe of a greasy blade.

On one particularly lively portrait of a once-esteemed maiden from an unknown time, the overlaid puzzle piece had almost perfectly conformed to the human outline, creating a frighteningly accurate silhouette of someone who used to walk these plastered hallways. Separate, smaller puzzle pieces had even attempted to graft themselves to the images of flowers that had surrounded this woman's image, but the shape-changing process was incomplete. Such activities always took a day or so to finish. Dreams of female baseball champions from washroom cellars crept through the dusty lairs of dead knights, and this telekinetic wind enabled the plasticity of the jigsaw puzzle pieces to come alive as if they were a primordial flash from beyond and which only sought to bring an adopted form and function into their ephemeral life, if only for a short time while the old snakeskin was shed by the sidewinders in the pantry, waiting to be fed rats and mice as the rainy season would periodically bring them in to find shelter out of the cold damp. Someday hearts would explode at this off-site, but for now, the wind pushed the caressing wings of paranoid fruit bats through the hair of the dead, pulling fresh flowers from silken sleeves and even casting hot minerals from barreled fists onto patches of finely grained pink sands as they were imported to the teutonic dwelling from more exotic places.

The sound of a wooden flute made all available blood curdle and shiver, reconforming to powerful notes that could blast one's eyebrows with discarded snakeskin messages. Although blood dripped somnolently from the wooden ceiling, the wood glue reinforcements had apparently been of no use. Blame always shifts to the newcomer, and so the public caves were temporarily sealed while certain crews of puzzle pieces sought out leaks and holes, attempting to seal them with futile gestures, since their degree of differentiation had by now passed the point of no return. Of course there were no regrets, and so the holes were plugged as diligently as possible so as to minimize the already extensive damage incurred by the very old edifice. What could black leather do that a set of cow spurs couldn't? That particular question lingered.

Only life could remain incomplete; everything else always changed. For the odd moments that pushed the sun across a nebulous sky, there was only the makeshift rhythm of a chorus of muted wind instruments chiseled crudely from strong reeds of bamboo, amidst the green chest-lights of insects and the skeletal fingerprint butterflies who chewed at their prisons, hoping for the day when a staircase would surpass its boring function in life. Many pots of fermented tea were brewed that day, and the spilled tea stained the walls, as it was used to create documental parchment journals highlighting the finer points of creating sleeping chairs from fossilized driftwood harvested from the countrycide, not yet stained with indigo from the leaking factories. These myths were recorded with hunger, and the odious grandfather clocks were well tended in the corralled gardens.

The movement of the ages pushes a solitary, romantic weather balloon of red and yellow origins to collide with one of the spires of the teutonic castle. The burst balloon comes to rest, fully impaled, allowing its weighted cargo to fall within one of the many dark courtyards of the teutonic dwelling. After a year of furtively searching in the dark, the matriarch finds the parceled bundle. Upon her bringing the strapped container to the inner decision-making chambers, the contents are spilled upon a silver examination dish: a very full bounty of voltaic pumpkin seeds, with each seed individually etched with the archaic sign of the Mayumi Panthers, a very restless group of feline vigilantes from an emotionally distant region. Although the tempestuous function of the seeds was known, the ancient matriarch stored them safely in cobalt blue glassware until the day arrived so that they may be used for whatever purpose.

For the Love of the Sport
(7-2003)

1

Coconut Man regarded the feeble creature at his feet, and then began to remove the seaweed from a dusty jalopy that had been parked fitfully in a rural harmonica barn, where the natives recline on sacks of kidney beans and later revel in wild hay rolls, evacuating the porcupines from dangerous thermos bottles. Coconut Man could identify the lost tribes of subway urine streams, tattooed with glittering rocks that could blast an unwary forehead over a taboo barnacle that rested underneath the scaly arms of fish creatures who release a colored balloon to the heavens with every passing day of lonely rain, in the forgotten prairie cul-de-sacs of a season of discarded dictionaries, retrieving extant kisses from what was probably an ostensible laughter slip-up.

These informants were asked for more and more dictionary information, and the release of coiled, metallic vortices broke through the membranes of feral eyeballs releasing parallel cherry blossoms in the form of a velvet subway mannequin deluge that was rejected after a febrile timing belt corroded to organic dust. This irresponsible flaunting of immobile velvet brought all hell from a sideways view of Mars, evoking the laughter of young women who twirled yellow parasols in the direction of abandoned feeble monsters with carnivorous teeth growing inside their wombs. Frozen flowers couldn't persist forever. The motion of the vortexical cherry blossoms might have been a physical premonition of spring, but the knuckled gravestones remained next to a field of gnarled, swaying green onion plants. These onions served as a hair detergent for the vortexical cherry blossoms, effectively terrifying a free puzzle that had been glued to the hips of a horse pelvis that was once used as a galactic exfoliant that international space stations would treasure.

The duplication of Coconut Man took many forms, and the most recent incarnation became highway-driven, driving at incredibly fast speeds along the coastal freeways. The incessant destinations might have been purely Martian, or at least within patches of mannequin thumbs that were cut from the rough edges of pirate treasure maps that were sold with the Sunday newspapers as a sinister insert, completely gratuitous, but dangerous with metallic promises that blew in like an impromptu thunderstorm. The ends of all roads became apparent on a daily basis, but each terminus was different, and provided highly individualized selections of items for contemplative sightseeing pleasures, sometimes even pointing out disastrously megalithic libraries, troublesome town squares and terrifying exhibition complexes where the supremacist bones were decorative pieces of the adolescent worship mentality. These monuments were from supposedly prettier days when frozen dog urine graced the machine-oil-stained thoroughfares of industrial behemoths who grazed in search of special pastures within the offices of cybernetic doctors in their construction laboratories making the future with a clip of a barber's scissors when broken clocks fell down from persecuted alcoves. The movements of these terminally positioned towns attracted ocean waves full of dead bait-fish, but such dreams bore fruit in multilingual settings, within linguistic marathons of freedom and other historical replicas that could be simply represented with a series of coded dots and arrowed road signs. Quite an evil fishhook to bite, said a sonicated bacterium in the twilight of a disrupted ribosome with purple flowers and green ribbons of unnatural adornments.

Suddenly, a mutinous horde of young, female baseball recruits spilled forth from unknown dwellings, flashing the uniforms of athletic tendencies, answering telephones with congressional malice. These baseball troops had sprightly voices, and they graced the sunset by occasionally bursting into song, characterized by the cherubic miasma that converged upon each of their foreheads, stopping the cars in the crowded street and gently touching the automotive tires which were made not of rubber, but from the bones of flamingos displaced from faraway backyards where a flood of reptiles was commonplace and where people attached yellow bowties to their country roadside mailboxes, creating a war prayer that could smash supercooled windows with calming voices and the whipped tails of the poisonous rattlesnakes.

The reptiles might have been lost, but their shed skin paved the way for Hansel and Gretel to enter the cobbled streets of frozen rain in the damp mornings of earthly memories of everyday matches between lizards and rattlesnakes. This kind of association packed enough punch to put entire fire departments on alert, pulling over hapless tourists in the written knowledge of the hypnotic sunset.

In one particular watchtower, the fire troops began a practice exercise called "raise the baby," affording the resurrection of observant eyes as they moved through the towered flames. The search for rising infants was breathtaking, and it led to the desperation of the fire troops who ultimately became lost in the tower, leading to rescued motorists who haphazardly meandered through bamboo alleyways, where primitive industries writhed like giant cockroaches in the shadows of peat moss, amid the wreckage of ancient water springs of isolated garden traps, mired in a sea of deja-vu fences. The replicas of owls might have been present in every corner, in every bamboo sanctuary where the silence of colorful birds wasn't visible but highly apparent. On one particular street front, the bamboo fencing wasn't so thick, and so the gutter run-off piping from moss-covered edifices of recent antiquity was available for the gandering, spreading the geese of abundant eyes of Stanley's curiosity, igniting a wildfire of passion from the revelation of an arched nose of recognitive avian delight.

The transformation had been almost complete, like a street that had been almost crossed until a burst of multicolored lighting made an unknown beak into an instructive face, teaching the ligation of magnificent ornaments from the living ponds of secluded frogs, placing telepathic stepping stones over the dangerous pool cues of lantern butterflies that were trapped within the cavities of rampant moths that would never return.

2

A bald black bear writhed in its own mosquito infestation, waxing nostalgic about beach balls and the Japanese voices from a popular radio station where boots of speed are devoid of shoelaces and where gems of skill resemble monochromatic apples of love – a world at peace with itself in orbit around a chocolate factory in Europe where the humidity is absent. The absent water is the ocean, where disgruntled oysters are marching with angry flags and banners, evoking a salted protest of the sediment depositions over tasteless geologic time. Even though the angry oysters do not have eyes, their body cavities are in a state of flux, sometimes even superficially resembling the convoluted shapes of racing car engines after having been cleaned of the despicable grime. Their underwater march might have lasted for an eternity, but they consoled themselves in the darkness with thoughts of demolished furniture and restless meditations on rugby. The bow of a violin helplessly floated by, evoking the screeching groan of a deranged larynx who made love to a venomous cobra in the off-moments of waiting for a set of triplets to be born.

The oysters find their destination, allowing them to file the appropriate complaints with the local geological offices. After the grievances have been filed, the angry flags and banners are meticulously rolled up and placed into ornate treasure chests, covered with hairy barnacles, of course. Then the relieved oysters turn themselves inside-out, becoming the complex chassis of fine pieces of high quality German automotive workmanship. The transformed automobiles now depart, kicking up thousands of years' worth of sediments, uncovering nuggets of oxidized silver.

Meanwhile, the waves lap upon the shore of turquoise sands, and the multicolored facial feathers of a large-nosed owl first disappear and then reappear, bringing into focus a revisited hope that had been left behind with the transdimensional highways from a fortnights' journey into alien marshes with flammable methane and poisonous reeds that prick unwary skin with sharp thorns, perhaps the incisive morals of a hybrid eagle married to its mobile wedding ceremony of the darkest irises, closing the doors of keys made of brass and wood, where the image of an iguana's first love was permanently burned.

This motion of returning owls might have required years of oceanic disturbances in terms of an equitable payment, but the truth was that the first and fifth digits of any red hand were ultimately required for any final avian judgment, in the same way environmental suits are needed to repel even the most invisible of radioactive mists, creating unknown legends with the slamming of an office door when the cameras aren't snapping with croaked indifference of cellar heat that could rise through the basement floorboards of dead wood.

It was true that iguana keys made of brass and wood would someday decay, leaving behind incomplete implements of brass that would only perplex the multicolored facial owls who camouflaged themselves as external street plumbing, bamboo fences, and even non-descript brick walls. The essence of any brass key could be removed, especially if jeweled, but the consequences were well worth enduring, especially if the barriers between confederate Tiki masks were lowered, creating dead statues that could spit poison darts from unknown apertures hidden somewhere within the dead wood of an impassive face from long ago.

Could the masks of colorful-nosed owls really carry the dust of stagnant months under excessively over-intense rays of a guilty, fork-dropping sunshower? Could the poverty of dropped forks and repetitious houseplants really wear down the cognizant mannequin lamps that were worshipped with rancid iguana oil? Would the burn victims require the dance of a tarantula to evoke the music of baked earlobes stuffed with garlic? These various lessons couldn't have been learned at any particular hour of scampering, but the joy of cut roses could put the fear of barnacles into any restless flock of pimp-knuckled sparrows that roosted in the attic of female seagulls who held infants to their breasts and melted brass alloys from choice ingredients so as to make castles embedded with neurons and the colorful, fantastic arrangements of glowing owl feathers bearing the ticklish teeth of laughter.

Paying the bullet-riddled walls for what they're worth can be torturous. Entire fleets of ships would have trouble harvesting used saxophone parts for their evil, invasive purposes, but their owled fingers would have to try, apparently. Meanwhile, doctors place tape and adhesive bandages on the corners of, uh, buildings, and this industrial resurrection cannot remove all of the birds' nests from the chimneys and sulfuric smoke stacks. The incoming tide would take it all away.

In the paternal corridors, the dead lines of fishing tackle lead the way from one noisy cavern to the next, creating the echoes of opening doors mixed with the shouts of children, long before they understand the concepts of punching a time clock or carving Tiki statues from chemically-treated cedar wood that has been cured under the most careful of glowing conditions. The magic foams from under the car's spare tire, and brass telescopes inaugurate timely discourses on the theater of the blind, where the rotting plastic of owl totems resists an eyeful of spit that might have once clarified the optics of the brass viewing objects. The riches of the melted glass. Functional islands are erected from lava, and the birds will colonize the new arrivals very shortly. Despite the confusing rains, the large beaked parrots know their own names, and never fail to touch each other's pulsating skin under the grooming aegis of successful etiquette of brainstorming cutlery. This sharp implement joins others of its kind, inflating owlish umbrellas which will warn of a coming hurricane bearing the wet hair of shampooed carpets from different travels within tarpaulin-protected marshes. This coming storm has only the simplest of warnings, the simplest of brass keyhole messages that burn frigid corpses with the perturbed creaking of bloated amphibians as they scramble across the deck of a saltwater vessel bound for rainforested honeycombs that bleed the adventure of solar bodies with their arcs of fire and kisses of drought.

As if people couldn't get shot in the back, maybe in the kidneys, leading to blood loss and an unquenched desire to knock steroid crystal balls of cubistic surprises from their uncanny hinges, especially when butchered enoki carcasses are involved. This motion of betrayal reveals unknown dreams and lost necklaces that only surface when beams of wood are carefully excised for the purposes of solemn chair production. Nothing like a good place to sit, swear the families of grasshoppers to themselves when they train their antennae and voracious mandibles on a flurry of disrupted, colorful bird feathers that descend from a drooping coat rack that left all accessory timepieces wedged under the heavier strips of tendonitis-wracked fiddle telepathy that repelled leg-crossing starfish when they went to school on Saturdays to repent for contemporary peccadilloes enacted within the cloistered solitude of an empty bell tower where pool cues and rotten chalk were stamped into the muddy soot reincarnated by the feet of owls when they replace phone receivers with negative corkscrews and the drawn eyelashes of burnt faces.

The end of old nocturnal revolutions spurned into completion removed the broken glass from the smiling wink of a homely lamp that is put out to greet the lost latecomers that brought with them a wristwatch made from the de-spiced plates of Jewish sea urchins when their iodine receptors and water vascular system are flooded with disreputable phone calls, still, always shot in the back by the squirrels, yes, the rabid squirrels.

The twitching whiskers disturb the sandcrabs in the mailboxes, disrupting the mailflow, disturbing the candle communications, reversing the dignified progression of stock market death that befalls one-eyed traders intent on the magnesium cartridges of broken statues and the next-day horizon of bamboo alleyways with their sanctuaries of drainage openings and forgotten bird baths that had absolutely nothing to do with cheap scholastic adventures, all achieved within the balance of a red-haired decade of mysterious paw prints and twitching noses in the uncertain vestibule of the electronically unwary. This uncategorized unrest won't buy you your feast of Sunday lie-downs. The bamboo alleyway destroys coffee grounds of your disappearance aerobics with a mallet of table-place goodwill, reducing the totemic garden statures to rubble, at least, a rubble made from splintered pool cues where the paws of cats leave musical love-notes of "uh-huh" indifference to the end of the alleyway that is unimaginable. This state of non-communication is deplorable, and yet tea-time occurs at the specified hour. This strange progression of idiocy repeated many times in the name of tinsel-coated messiahs, regurgitated aloe cakes.

An olive couldn't have been better squeezed than the string steroid of scorched birds who occupied a cactus bell tower riddled with worm holes made from seed-coated clothespins and peanut butter. The motion of uncertain moons orbits a nauseating planet that even methane-breathers avoid more so than long-haired musical pool cues, destroying the ice fields of mowed grooves in the apple resilience of virtual unknowns. This contest wasn't understood, in the same way hunting licenses for dead objects are forbidden by the sandy glaciers. This road trip wasn't authorized, but it sure was planned for by the killing grounds within shadowed fields of sequestered bamboo.

This enemy territory was dripping with earwax, and you could laugh your way out of porcelain tea cups, breaking the imaginary spots of an endangered tiger, raising hell with bioinformatic robots and praising the way a tethered French horn was used in place of a symbolic, pentamerous sand-dollar.

3

The surveillance of the Tiki statues by dim-witted cameras was all that was needed to rouse sleeping children from functional dreams where south winds blew salt from the heavens down to the scorched cars below, as if insects on a tree could appreciate bean threads with fragments of denatured animal protein. This made the Irish ladies laugh as they forged blue plastic molds from ivory Tiki sculptures imported from the southernmost fields of Elvis' cherished, substance-abusing estate. In fact, Elvis would sometimes reappear, a-la-urban legend, wearing a crabshell on his head and playing a bamboo saxophone while reminiscing about his glory days from the blue Hawaiian cinema. But even the most treasured Cadillac plastic dashboard ornamentation will yield broken molecular bonds after many seasons of exposure to the burning sun.

Comets streak by the unwary, creating a focused aspiration with the flying iceballs and releasing odd pheromones into the atmosphere, liberating coastal plains from the corporate tumbleweeds of feline pushcarts as well as the nefarious leanings of a certain mythical dog-prostitute. This particular prostitute might have a hankering for defenestrated cotton candy in the haunted amusement parks, but the butchered fingers of patron by-standers (or maybe standers-by) tell the real truth. The finding of glass coins through unknown means of objective chance might have been exciting, but the fragments of blood-spittled ivory littered the floor of the adjacent coffee dens, propelling the convenient strumpet to pull plastic bouquets of flowers from her wig, ultimately creating a wall-mount of curated butterflies, complete with accurate species labels beneath each specimen. Underneath the deck of the boardwalk of the haunted amusement park, the storm of the roses had begun.

The dog prostitute had managed to produce a new strain of roses from her hair – the blue-fisted kind. These blue roses were much sought after by over-anxious geneticists and their followers, and ironically enough, this new breed of rose had been used to attack unwary fields of genetically modified corn, which had become a threat to business. After each corn attack, the blue-fisted roses would disassemble into miniature brass-knuckled-like horseshoes, in order to accommodate the likes of a multi-toed Eohippus when representatives of species would go out to rooftop dances, ultimately making syphilis-infected reindeer very jealous.

After a rain of hungry frogs from an incoming cloud system, the blue-fisted roses shot from the hair of the dog prostitute, imprinting their delicate petals onto the fuselage of an unsuspecting commercial airliner, spreading blue-fist rose DNA across the naïve continent and disrupting inane Saturday TV specials for many years to come. Meanwhile, aliens landed on earth and gave all higher-lever government employees electronic anal probes that would unfortunately explode any time the carrier of such an anal probe spoke aloud the phrase, "ginger ale." Life was grand, and the petunias became the coat of arms for feudal elephants as they searched the walls of coastal cliffs for pre-hominid hieroglyphs. Without any pre-hominid hieroglyphs found, the elephants transformed into the hair follicle precursors of the blue-fisted war roses, and suddenly found themselves on the surface of the dog prostitute's scalp. Thus, the cycle began anew.

Within an hour, the band-aid over the glowing eyes of watching nocturnal owls fell free, and gravity took the gems of paper representations of catfish whiskers which tested the hull of a rotten oak barrel that was floating within the realm of unsolicited childbirth. These jeweled documents were coated with the iridescence of insectoid scarabs, with down-turned legs that grasped at power-hungry larynxes that aped the southern dialect of a rampantly crawling iguana of bronze, complete with attached blue worms that signaled a weakening of concrete and structural metal girders. The universe momentarily relaxed, splicing the nose of a new-age woodpecker with a soft adze forged within a damp piano that had been held against its will at the bottom of Chesapeake Bay during one of the rainy seasons, spreading poisonous sesame seeds over negative crows' feet that were launched during the last Incan escapade of maniacal knee-popping marching music. But the translucent birds would not fade, despite the music.

My Little Kitty landed in my feathery hands like a tooth sponge that could implode golf balls with a virulent stare of metamorphic pince-nez of postal timepieces made from a pastiche of unknown clowns from a forgotten symbol of de-fragmentation. Salient mockery became a lost note in a floating bottle, destined to fly with the vortex of an inverted fraternity sneeze. This puzzle piece of concrete inequity caused many perplexed desert owls to stare at the glowing embers of a splintered mental vocabulary. Meanwhile, bored penguins picked their teeth and wore giant peanut shells on their heads, doing good for the love of holly trees that make excellent seat-savers on those rainy, ink-spilling days. This couldn't have been even closely related to the average wall flower. Hothouse flowers would never go extinct in a sea of ketchup-mired pantyhose of serious reality-goers who could see only the five fingers on each hand. The numbers could never add up, said a doomed fleet as it found un-dooming doom books in the cellars of transcontinental, transformative languages that undermined the circuits of literal calculations, attempting to destroy projects but inadvertently splaying unicyclists with measured bacterial growths of sequestered laughter, echoing the rainy tabloids of the damned when they put history on an easel and made pretty pictures. Burn the ink with the claw of a salivating owl. Take a puzzle piece and create a daughter. Replace a hung portrait with a noodling song that featured an off-key flute. This soggy piano was an unknown pearly membrane from the gills of brachiopod bivalves that exhaled pure calcium minerals in aphrodisiacal nail polish, which carried out the fratricidal schemes of *Felis domesticus*. There could have never been any other, and the hip candle burned for days before a hive of bees took up regretful tap-dancing, in a wave of guilty, recognitive regret that cross-sectioned a silk nautilus with the draped balustrades of antiquity.

This flash from beyond could squash bumble bees with the power of fluorescent hair dryers, taking in all information like the horizontal eyes of vigilant sheep with funny comments from the gift-shop of unknown agents in the trees. This wormwood shipwreck ate through the crucial bulkheads, reducing a monitoring cash register to cowry shells, spreading yuppie indifference to a milestone of molting crustaceans in the middle of a weeknight excursion.

The independent terrestrial octopus does well by sleeping with coastal penguins, expressing the geological fetishes for geometric edges dulled with a greedy blade upon a dark sun of the sweetest sonic honey, distilled from pure helium and packaged in lightbulbs rejected from the factory. The coats worn by fish are indeed strong, and they laugh at the tiger's eye agate nodules that certain owl replicas carry in their back pockets, gluing the wooden popsicle sticks to their purple dentures and spanking the servants with palm-leaf Jesus objects. This admonition of chlorophyllic Jesus objects removes the seriousness from the serious, and a bloated church develops uncertain leanings for pre-pubescent children, satisfying the wicked priests who snort coke and carry on peculiarly on all fours, just like the disturbed grizzly bears of a feathered forest of entrapped butterflies of entropically pregnant machines. The riches from the holy eyesight are tears of quartzite that run down sedentary cheeks in the bright mornings of cockatoo obsessivity. This darkness of bamboo sweetness put an Irish nose to work, surveying the healthy buttercups of arachnid terrorism in the bathroom, where coat hangers work better than combs or brushes, reducing the molten plastic to a hodge-podge of conglomerated watermelon seeds weeping tears of sedimentary exhaustion from the bivalve fossils of the known universe. The beauty of bamboo forests comes alive when the bird creatures go arm in arm with the paper circus clowns into multitudes of crazy duplication and cosmopolitan nasal leanings where a falling egg yolk perfectly complements a rising, vibrating tomato from the trussed ashes from bird sacrifices in Alaska, leading the shell-head detectives to adjust their shell hats and take a coffee break in the middle of a cardiac monsoon. Then the eyes of owls went to bed and dreamed of bamboo houses, the reconstructed future of ancestral raw materials.

Such vortices reach sleeping ears in a high-tide of starfish delirium, when colored orbs move across the mind's eye in a form of memory marbling that lays to waste all useless information of conscious triviality, making the song of a tuba sound like the result of a refried beans festival from the 1950s, a place in time where rocking chairs were forgiven for their pulmonary shortcomings and where the world of alien golf clubs drew an immeasurable inspiration from cross-eyed cockatoos that ate yogurt but didn't answer letters from eternal fans. Why the avian indifference? Why the crash of a frilly brassiere stock market?

In the same way PCR reactions sometimes crash, the molten owls remove besmirched term papers from diesel oil refuse bins where dishonest academicians bury knowledge in the hopes of furthering their own, highly linear careers. A pixie smile is all it takes to make the terrestrial octopods jump, scaring away vagrants who have never known the joys of post-birth egg dying, as if celebratory gestures towards bountiful fertility were something exceptionally magical, like the empty clack of a journalist's archaic typewriter, long thrown into disuse once people discovered that white-out makes a great tooth and nail polish.

This reduction of, uh, buildings represents a stilted horse javelin that ran aground on a dazzling purple beach where academic executive custodians of knowledge remained within cinderblock rat boxes waiting for the sun to set so that they could breath the air of the outdoors, while ignoring the melodious honey that slowly diffused through brass keyholes lingually polished by the dog prostitute of the blue rose warfare entrenchment.

4

Jars on shelves grow what appear to be tiny, able people. Developing fingers and legs, and even high-school rings, all within the span of weeks. The acceleration of the joy of life might sometimes lead to a shuttled obsession with fertility, but this bottled experiment was capable of knocking over roadside mailboxes with only a twitch of the wrist, while whining complaints over prude barrettes that fall from sea-dock dreams where the underground mud carries desolate river rocks to the sunset spectra of leering sailors who kick over pumpkins along yellowbrick roads into the capital of a faraway country. These pumpkins are somehow genetically derived from the small bottled humans in the moldy, homuncular experiment room. Deathly machines leak machine oil from the gills of deadly fish who circle underwater gravesites left behind within submerged continents affected by earthquakes and other tectonic acts of nastiness within jungles submitted within wreckless computer files of sinister pelican visitors wearing socks of the color of freezing skies.

While the dog prostitute maneuvers into position, football goals melt with the sonic arrival of a relentless train that escorts an unknown trio of storm trooperettes with pretty rings into the twenty-second century with a paradise ray that can shift train tracks, just like a mango can hold a good hand in poker. While the train might carry porcine supplies to the homunculus experiment room, the questions of life and death rotate in an orbital stalemate, refusing the weak spines of weak books and building recipes from empirical information obtained at gunpoint in an old-fashioned battleship of incidental tendencies. Yes, we will continue to find boredom on sacred Tuesdays whenever the ancestral octopods leave town for the day. This couldn't have spoiled the milk, this abnormal departure, but the ecology of suckered pine trees is captivating, to the point where closed flowers regurgitate the poltergeist of bright waves of a feminine crimson.

The aftermath of libidinal interrogations reveals small, clustered statues that belong to the gods of oil, the purveyors of a witted natural sponge that was developed somewhere next to tiki voodoo islands in the lost archipelago of the Pacific. The tiki remembrances reappear just like Elvis, and punctuated teeny-boppers touch themselves, allowing pineapple juice to dribble from their exquisite armpits, revealing Elvis Presley's dusty discography from the trees of nature.

These sat-upon trees offer a liquid effluvium to the bared kneecaps of a nude princess preparing to leap from a long diving board into a sea of fluffy whipped cream where paranoid, stewed strawberries lurked beneath the while silky waves of aerosolized bovine secretions. The nude princess takes the plunge and finds a young bamboo plant lodged in her quivering ear. The nude princess found herself lurching in reverse, moving the cirrus cloud coverage with her, developing dusty windstorms that could detach glowing stones from the eyeball caves of weightlessness, growing cephalopod haiku from between her teeth. Her seatbelt was calculated to be at least a mile in length, and would end in a tapered cone behind the horse stables of rancid parks where phosphorescent slime would crawl from newspaper vending boxes, releasing a delirious, coiled snake from a fake can of processed potato crisps advertising an engrossing onion powder as one of the main ingredients. So what if the towers of false leanings could envision fields of red protoplasm? The lights from harmonic lakes were indefensible.

Sullen crabs lurked next to their newspaper racks, clipping only choice tidbits from websites and slamming pigeons through the fields of fragrant tea trees where dripping plant oils reveal the boredom of Olympic-sized swimming pools that have cracked their concrete and now grow reeds, supplementing a diet of eroded seashells with retarded mountain bikes of putty-like gold alloys. The plasticity of the bicycles spills malformed chess pieces over the bed, providing a ground-breaking wake-up call that even came with complementary cups of mental coffee. The shaken beans are dethreaded, and female eyes reveal a deck of sasquatch playing cards.

Isolated sea rocks are tumbled by waves, revealing a proclivity toward harvesting bamboo gizmo collections that detect young thoughts that have been haunted by the intimacies of spiral living quarters and the internal grimaces of non-threatening birds. Was that your hair seen flying in the wind, over the docks of the marina? *Silence.* Your racing goggles couldn't take the flak. The popular trees from your lush green onion plantation lend new ideas to the family portraits of the wheelbarrows that you hoarded underneath your house. The rusted handcuffs of dingy bowling pins measures the bolts drawn across medieval doors. Horses' teeth from bigots.

5

A drop of rain through the vortex spells the word "vacuum" on the seedy walls of the investment dwellings of lower childhood, ravishing travels to the winding forest roads where the underwater frogs dwell.

"Oh the forest swallows my daytime energy," decreed the hibernating viper perched by the battalions of brick walls.

"Please complete for me the livid messengers who haven't opened their mailboxes in a long time. Also, let one see the shrunken heads of captured, deflated volleyballs that were harvested during the last spring freeze, so that I might become reacquainted with the sasquatch tendencies within your frilly heart," pressed the hibernating viper. This corner of the world was erected from the shaky legs of a newborn antelope, leading to unstable floor boards and a dense array of small earthquakes. But only if perfection was expected…

Where could this perfection be found? In the bottom of a lake? In a tennis racket without a soul spawned in the emotional distance of an irrationally maintained relationship? Would the cupful of sprouted seeds be waited upon by a soft jacket hung on trees like toilet paper?

"Oops; sorry."

"Oh, that's ok."

"Sorry about that."

"Oh, it's really ok, Katie."

"But what about the excused status of your perfect pencil sharpener, complete with full references?"

"Oh, that's ok."

The boring chairs were used to patch loose holes in the window, and elderly moth balls unraveled in order to have an excellent photographic selection with a murky octopus that had lived on the hot streets for centuries at a time, only resting to take coffee breaks and to tempt volcanoes of job applications when paper prostitution is used as a conspiracy against love in a checkered armadillo teapot. Shriveled skins of bread reveal the den of crime-drama snakes, releasing even more hoary drama into the spiritual void of a purple, toothless void wearing pinstriped pajamas on a jinxed plane traveling to the outback where cigarettes and lemonade are the preferred tools of the billiards trade in a forgotten question that was never asked, due to the afterglow of temporary smile revivals.

"Where were you last night, and who were you?"

Silence.

"Oh I see Valentine's day is approaching. This might be the time for an ego-dissolve session in the midst of a burning sea of vandalized rock albums presided over by insecure opossums who were crying because the cow was leaking four perfect streams of milk. High-heeled shoes never looked better.

In a burnt envelope, the ashes of armadillo snails open up, mimicking flowers and coveted discussion cookies and babbling coffee mugs of senior disciplinarians who don't seem to like young people and yet contain the most intimate interactions regarding the counting of poker chips and painted toenails squashed by rancid volleyballs.

The coffee talk of important units reveals unused labspace with dermatology propaganda lining the walls, revealing the novelty of a blind workforce controlled by arrogance and festively decorated with medals of cerebral mediocrity, claiming the worship of past music with messianic conceits. The priests of human resources play card games of life, climbing beanstalks and reading barometric compasses of jinxy airliners filled with inflatable materials with a cynicism of beauty sewn into richly embroidered yoedeling jumpsuits that were made on the icy pinnacles of left-handed cats' feet on a flavored gerund. Supposedly dried gourds were hidden in the boring death star (wearing aged spectacles) but were not documented within the diary of obsequious post office lamentations. The ascension celebration of eternal unfulfillment: what a devious bag of tricks with squashed grapes inside.

6

Down the gauntlet of roads, the day to day fulfillment of registered nurses reaches maximum levels of success. School trees begin to grow, and left-brained pictures are regurgitated onto reticent paper safely scribed with identifying legends and the restless dreams of wayward pixies who leave one crisis only to find another in a town besieged by myths of vermin and a stodginess of ivory-tower bureaucrats who spit apple seeds on a toothpick trampoline where mud and brick hustlers spit epoxy glue droplets at birds' nests that are far out of reach.

A few glue missiles connect, and the handprints of sasquatch tar can be seen on the trees where birds collect their nest twigs, suggesting an invasive regime of academic fascism led by well-fed crooks of letters and symbols who hoard the truth within their unkempt beards.

These water currents eventually dry up and undermine the clouds where the balls of rugby slip through the fingers along with sinister trains applying themselves to an uncertain timetable. The movement of glue on robotic, polarized windshields might be scary, and the orchards of three-clawed fists creates nausea from custodial vacuity that reveals the threads of sunken trophies liberated from the fields of love in a disrupted army tank made of sponge. Weren't the bubbles supposed to move away from the center of the earth? Would an avian war uncover the treasures within bamboo sugarcane chambers?

After the smoke cleared and the rubble was swept away, sunken coins were cleared of barnacles. The undying coins were envelopes of core beings frozen in mid-swing burying the tumult of obsolete philosophy treatises that defiantly stood on the contemporary notch of the sundial, only waiting to be knocked back into the grave. With all bickering stupidities aside, the shakiness of the moment was a fingerprint of avian muscle wrapped in plastic and set upon cold shelves. The confusion of the hair follicles could have been slightly interchangeable with new-age noses and callous representations of history with a rugby lump in its throat. Did the consummation of love understand the loose bricks in the wall of prosthetic linguistics not identified by common dictionaries?

Could distant bicycle chains get together by way of green, trampled fields bearing the trampled wishes of a pine-tree huddle? The unknown fermentation of hops could break the clouds with friendly bolts of lightning, possibly bringing the batting eyelashes of coastal experiments to a grinding halt. Mechanisms of azure bring you back to me, within your hollowed suitcase with all of its athletic secret compartments. Would fragrant pumpkins reach the threshold of autumn harvests so far away from home, so necessarily within the barracks of good manners and lady-like fortresses of hidden smiles? This tip of the matchstick could even have been compared to a blast of painted toenails with non-fermented green tea, all full of vitamins, sunshine, and the batting paws of young black cats yearning for Kadath but wary of the consequences of an unexpected rugby trampling. El Janaby was right: the game *does* stalk the moment.

Majestic diesel trains make love to the screeching, dark tracks, reminding the lost birds that even ketchup can splatter over their jerseys. Self-absorbed sponge-makers pass through walls creating a nostalgia for the soft couches of Samhain over sleepy New England catacombs kissed with the viscous puddles of historic canoes bearing many tomes of treacherous fugu sashimi as well as some bedsheets tied together used by some to escape from one of the nefarious teutonic driveways. The fugu sashimi licks its own bookend lips, creating an androgynous library bristling with the libido of a high-throughput screening robot. Incomprehensible wishes? Have you checked your own foot pulse today?

Football heroines climb the mountain, and release tree-monkeys from forest slumber. Dewdrops on bared knuckles repel the prick of the rose thorn, eviscerating a lonesome moment with daisies, and putting together erector sets from distant oneiric architecture unknown to blind ants who live in dark trees with unobserving owls who are obsessed with multi-houred clocks made of cheese. This motion of limited trains makes the grass grow anew, revealing replenished lawns that will be stomped upon by cleated legs in pursuit of the reversal of tree ageism. The distant teardrops of armorial foot syrup causes ripples within the tiki clubhouses of different reaction cauldrons as they are forged anew with a higher grade of charcoal and other sweet condiments.

Even if planes could land within fragrant, evil gardens with ridiculous golden, evil statues, the see-saw hilarity of your television music moves through the spontaneity of your rugby equipment, sending motionless rivers through the two-dimensional eyes of roosting eagles who understand the true nature of a velvet cushion. Eventually tasty morsels of konnyaku fall from the sky (alchemical terrestrial algae?), and this descent ruffles the feathers of the sleeping birds who have mysteriously hoarded deflated rugby balls after they have been wiped clean of grass and morning dew.

The wet grass doesn't do any good, as the troop of dinosaurs enters the equation of dragons that leave behind clipped, furry paws in the same way memories are made from the nectar of flowers as passing ships exchange the musical notes of worldly collisions. The eagles have definitely landed, releasing the archaic honey from glowing, oneiric tree branches that have a certain cloying fatalism mercilessly embedded within the amber wood. Freshly mowed hay breaks a few noses, releasing the softness of clover within, troubling the water sources and reevaluating the meanings of intimacy for many years to come. This particular authority of regional transit sequesters pregnant eagles into mucilaginous tributaries that harbor golden recognition sequences attached to the golden, evil statues that are sometimes for sale in vegetarian commercial sectors. These overturned buttercups wink at the sky, and then the missiles fall to earth, in the same way sleek, smooth water can migrate across unintelligible rocks. The sleekness of the moment ground the tips of eagle matchsticks through stubborn, thick cat skulls, sending the sexual shiver of an idea that was born in the last decade.

7

If only saturated trees could shed their Mardi Gras dubloons. Then, the sky would become full of serendipitous fox kisses imprinted with the halo of a negligent fire hydrant bearing many foreign postage stamps, proof of night-time travels through vixen lakes with glowing, stuttering jellyfish. An avalanche of rugby headgear pulls apart the ocean waves at their fluid seams. This rupture is dynamic, and creates colossal shockwaves which ingratiate olives to aluminum cans, and place fresh flowers within the crevices of a rusty fire-fighter's truck, moving through the backlog of Saturday smoke signals. Bricks with words on them are joined with mortar to create the fireplace, a resting bed for non-sentient embers that could cook steak with a backwards stare. The stars in the sky align to form elephants, telling of stellar circuses where the clowns have gone mad and butchered the intercontinental compartments of bamboo alleyways where the ancient visions of totemic birds point out a new course through Galapogos finches who revile seedy pastimes in favor of fresh fruit peeled from the insides of inflated leather pouches which once carried gold but now carry the magic currency of collisions. This fast-paced socialism makes fun of wooden vestibules and Mardi Gras masks that were peeled from the faces of grandfather clocks that ticked in a non-linear fashion, sending a galactic chill through the hands of the clock mirror that would ultimately collapse if its wooden surfaces were not basted with an emulsion of varnish and orange juice harvested from fresh, Floridian petroleum distillates.

A torrent of minutes left your face in the way an overturned leaf remembers its flipside existence, as if it were a dream from yesterday that had a caboose segment containing peculiar runes which identified the complete anatomy of an acorn. This compartmentalized embryo extended itself across furloughed stretches of circular rugby fields. This act of circular collision was a bronze key presented to locked gates. If all iguanas could watch the bronze keys rise from the depths of their reptilian tongues, then the puzzle of faraway trick boxes could bolster cups that runneth over with the souls of embryonic acorns that riddle forests with questions that can replace word-bricks at will, regurgitating the skull of a horse into the laps of the powers-that-be. The questions continue to surface, and the "natural" cascade of primate reasoning puts a cork in the bottle of karate, ironically releasing a genie that can fulfill the destiny of a desolate Tuesday, relinquishing power in favor of piscine disruptions. Could ruptured cognizance prove favorable to such a sportsmanlike discourse?

Flagrant disregard for nicotine-splotched barstools. Automatic chainsaw concourses initiate the forgotten, sickly voices of Ronald Reagan, a parasol of black oil that surfaced within the toilets of capitalist pixie shrines. The football demolishes all, and so the oil is injected into popping corn kernels that are solemnly disposed of in lead drums which are incinerated at unimaginable temperatures. The shortage of tree death can assail any beautiful once-broken nose with a sculpted noose that can draw any wayward fish into the shrinking corral, magnifying the intensity of close, cybernetic handshakes. This intrusion spelled future discourses that could read from palms, invigorating the walnut dimension of negative images of tree branch-tips, erasing the failures of scholastic foolishness, when the publishing of research suddenly became important.

This sporting frenzy was reminiscent of surfer girls and black-knuckled hydronauts. The aluminum casing over the shaded eyes of the squid slapped the passers-by who did not know the secret handshake, and so they were not allowed to join the club when it came time for the cookies and milk to be doled out. But the knuckles would be kept. When ambiguous faces are pushed through the social sorting bin, the results are disastrous. Fish fingers spin spider webs through songs and necklaces, and forehead vessels express the doubt of fear that moves through deep-fried kneecaps that coalesce in your empty hands. Golf balls are pulled from saxophones, and the football is passed backwards, through a labyrinth of souls and voltaic birds. Beware of the recycling bin.

To walk through your magnetic hallway with an intact face, this will prove the triumph of emotion, despite the alterations and hyper-logical, undialectical polarizations. Despite your conscious flight away from birds and carrousels, the moment will stalk you and burn your silent lips with a bearskin rug. Can you hear me now? *Silence.*

8

A shift of sympathies regurgitates recalcitrant turtle shells from the sunny umbrella of protection. With unknown contacts in circulation, the antipathy of watched squirrels peels away the annoying clock hands concealed within their whiskers, plucking grapes for fun and touching unturned rocks for the first time.

A botched bomb raid results in a wall of word-bricks remaining untouched. The intact head of the horse laughs with disdain, madly shrieking the name "excaliber" frequently, off into the night. The lace from your fingertips is the accelerant, and so copious decompressions are enacted in front of frozen orange juice icicles. This square fencing is a taunting reminder of what might have been, if only lead plumbing were more adequately polished in an oxygen-free environment, free of all emotional scratches. Eighty-nine seconds, indeed on a lonely highway.

A visit to the local mind-control camp yielded only abruptly abandoned cigarettes still lit, rolled in black paper with gold ink writing embossed within the vicinity of the filter. The search for lost comrades was uncertain, with numerous infiltrations present within the palm of a rooster's claw, wearing the hat of a buffoon but tendering messages of an uncontrollable intergalactic rattlesnake tail which purported allegations of sentient identifications with the Other. Would she understand? Could she care? Could nature correct its frozen myopia within a galactic state? Was this never within the program? Would the loose jaws of machinistic puppies deliver the crushing blow to tenuously erected flagpoles within uncertain states of being? Could the meeting of old friends place an icecube on a smooth chin? Was there a never-more available for broken twigs scavenged from rural fireplaces where farm animals are destined for dinner? Would this target quench the flood of hair upon the thresher of deprived feelings elucidated by cheaply-funded research within a flexing state of haiku that overstepped its bounds? The motion was imminent.

9

Sound jocks crush notes with lethal blows, spreading flowers with their ears and inserting maraschino cherries within the body cavities of molds for use in making plaster animals. The farmers tend to the plaster fences, reducing the insidious acts of barrier crumbling to a maximum and revealing the piping of flutes which were once hidden within a bamboo sanctuary presided over by bell-guarding vultures who are sometimes won over by well-ordered silverware arrangements within the depths of mind-control caverns. If the chain-link fence could become chainmail riding pants, then perhaps the stalactites of hardened glucose could decorate more than meat-processing plants, sending cheek-piercing adornments through candle lantern cheeks that support the scuba diver facemask of subaqueous breathing systems that sometimes excite the fish who lick your feet.

This call to a distant honeymoon was the final straw that collapsed the backs of many a camel. Your eyes move through my arm like an evil umbrella in search of a missing memory board. When you speak, the words that come out do not match the movements of your lips. Are you a ventriloquist, or do you rub-a-dub-dub? A starfish is peeled from your shoulder, and the surfing pleasures of well-cultivated produce makes a reckless garden shudder with the report of a wry elephant gun.

What happened to those trembling, flute-whistling catfish who used to create mayhem with arbitrarily-defined musical notes that rang out on oddly-lit green candles laced with copper? The starfish can peel notes from arms and legs (and even legs within arms) that produce audio-sequences that could spell the rings of Jupiter backwards. These musical notes, of course, understand the pearls that are catacombed on leviathans of black velvet that adorn the gold medals that desecrate the tintinnabulations of curious monks who forgot right from wrong. Fetid fate satellites come crashing down in Nevada, reporting nascent movements within the currents of un-standard book reviews that put mascara on mustaches, creating a tongue of eyes to regurgitate whale protoplasm in a baleen picnic basket forgotten on the edge of a UFO-obsessed town. Yes, ma'am; please, ma'am, your rhymes grip my heart with starfish splotches with sun-poisoning and the collisions with unknown-ville.

How long til the rift in the clouds? What would we have to wait for to make catfish treble their raucous endangerments, to make gas cylinders explode when they are bitten on by paranoid alligators? Your intimate pathways are the feeble monster for us all, and this target moves its digits over the golf-courses of love, complete with flowers and alpha-male gorillas in search of rickety floor boards that hide codependent easter eggs with the vocabulary of sunken-ship pumpkins caught in mid-swing. You probably thought that my cardboard existence couldn't make a mutual shake-down with your pistachio existence, and yet the nuts in the box exhibit a downhill avalanche. Better ratchets deserved to be encased in the one-leg concrete.

As quickly as campers fall off of cliffs, oceans of frogs rain from the skies, loveably, inexplicably. Got an answer for that one, huh? If Valentine's day were truly approaching, then wouldn't it make sense to test the functionality of umbrellas and maybe even to check underwater caverns for makeshift camping utensils smacked by a speeding train destined for floating fruits and keys and other items of reggae madness that could create symmetrical bamboo arrangements with a little help from the wry elephant gun? Would a gravel road have to be paved to satisfy this elephantile phantasy? Would the ecstasy of faraway galaxies deign to shed a little light in these dark sectors, all with scarily maintained plaster borders? How could the lines on your many faces hide your fear and mistrust of orangutan rituals dedicated to only the shudder of a valentine moment spliced with corkscrews and walrus tooth rubble brought on by a food war between blind, grazing goldfish? Could pregnant car tires reveal the hunger of the ages for the forsaken blasphemies of a moonstone bathtub?

Your happiness is found within solid tigers' eyes of a luminous agate, and these semi-precious moments create the backwardsness of dead years, applying golden corn kernels into empty, lite-bright cobs, rebuilding well-shaped avalanches with the hunger of your feet as they master the earth with a well-timed sprint across exposed rock strata that had been covered with mud for so many years. Shimmying walrus teeth were no match for your pregnant hands as the optic watermelons of live birth spat out seeds at feathery fishing lures and cognizant, midnight octopods that dared to glide across soiled plaster boundaries erected too many years ago when the forces that created our ancestors also manufactured a morality of shame that worshipped coffee receptacles and other machinistic distractions, like rodeo tooth fillings and collectable enslaved cat families who created offspring like pumpkins in the cheery haze of autumn memories.

A discus from a past life is nothing to a growth of cauliflower that can exit from a seeping cellar. The cordless phones spill from your elbows, making me a feline captive resurrected from a shipwreck of dry ash, a phoenix of sickly vulture eggs purported to negotiate the transfer of illusory souls from elbows to cell phones. Salt was poured over the geyser, revealing the hidden stones of dried plums that could signify the smile of your morning twilight, when you rouse from your night travels, even if you may ignore them. Could progress be charted with measuring sticks, or with cast-aside molts from the death of batteries that once charged ridiculous shoes? Must we pay attention to those things?

Could the succession of nasal gestures move from one lamp-post to the array of candles arranged at those vigilant anthills built over time by your house? The mystery is all-enveloping.

10

Train wrecks clutter the airwaves. Uncertain footsteps move within the bounds of painted pumpkins ignored by unwholesome avalanches brought about by tepid fingerprints glossed over by an appealing piece of leather airline luggage besmirched with kisses that were never put to good use, only placated by Irish business cards from the depths of a mongoose fang. Illiterate bystanders punch in the code, but to no avail, in the process, ripping up the plastic traffic lanes of arbitrary boundaries between not-so-heavenly bodies who are drawn to suitcases and other kissed leather luggage, evoking the crocodile tears of travel, and burnishing stupidities with myopic legislation and forgotten embers. This state of the art tonsil will resist coughing, but only if a melted train track is willing to relocate to the nearest deadly elevators mustered in self-defense when the catacombs of dental molars are subdued with intense pleasure – that special kind of pleasure that comes with any hurt or cavalcade of wolverines in search of bloodied snowpeas left as an offering on a neglected grain thresher. But your eyes still hide behind explosion-resistant glass. Quite understandable for the moment.

11

Members of a herd of elephants each blast a quart of fresh semen into a rusted forest of unoccupied telephone booths. This simplified externalization of pent-up libido is the predicted outcome of years of unfortunate celibacy (and even the effects of psychosocial dwarfism). *Was this normal?* The tectonics of past events ripple through your feet, creating distracting, multiple beacons of hope that might have been stepping stones to a golden hair left on a distanced pillow, preserving memories in tortoise-shell salad bowls. When a puree of French fries and tarantula guts are applied to rugbear feet, the marvelous path through the forest is illuminated, creating chimeric, six-breasted animals which are not supported by the fossil record. These rugbear limbs have traveled many miles across well-mowed fields of C4-active plants, and the explosive photosynthesis can excite the toes beyond words, even beyond pomegranate swimming pools vandalized by businessmen with peculiar glass marbles which were once the eyes of red diamond flying fish of rhombus-like proportions. Your smile is blinding, when you show it to me. *Could this have been predicted?*

Wrong red reachings present visual memories of sliced fruits, and the laughter that results from such a fruity head-salad is comparable to the barking dogs that are disrupted morphologies of tinkling gumby icicles, drooling like ketchup. On this particular Valentine's cycle, a highly intelligent rugbear forest dancer from Texas is presented with a large replica of a sparrow, chiseled from ice, and frozen within, there is a well-kicked rugby ball that was kissed by an expectant fan of the sport. *Was there any conditionality within this telemetrically seeping icicle?*

Would this rugbear forest dance from Texas understand the concept between Texas-sized clocks that can erupt a bouquet of purple bats' wings from behind the ears of genetically modified benevolent bunnies? *Is this normal?* If all seemed probable, at least when the moon was full and tender, and lambchops were removed from shoulders, releasing a sob that had been covered by nervous laughter evoked by a fear of Catalonian beans and mayonnaise. The moon was full tonight and the inviting claws of special cats drew lightning as well as prosperity from sleeping fields of pomegranate trees genetically spliced with DNA sequences that coded for raccoon fur.

Meanwhile, as the world turned, large-scale economic irresponsibility was ignored while endless supplies of crude oil were seized. This civilinsanity spilled across all borders, and lighthouses burned with arrogance, leading iguana keys of molten bronze into chasmic miasmata of nauseated swan necks that regurgitated sickly pebbles.

The burnished rugbear forest dancer continued to move through waves of corresponding tulips, silencing the opposition with a well-placed shoulder, here and there, and this difficult course through the chilled spine of a frigid book made her yawn after the bashing of otherly admonishments. *Would she ever get a clue?* After hours of sleeping and flinging through the blanket trees, the forest dancer awakes and returns to her usual activities. Even if her privately-owned rice fields were like incumbent telephones, could not an umbrella become edible? The neurons in your arms spoke to me in a dream, once: The gated backyard syndrome. Only weasels with daylight savings watches may enter the domain. They may only meow if a soft brush is used to tame their furry manes produced through the shrinking effect of rubber postage stamps. The indifference might someday melt, at least over a stratified tuke-nob, where scrambled eggs spell the word "vertebrae" backwards, and lead the innocent weasel to a bouquet of yellow freesias selected by your watchful hands, with an eye on each knuckle that knows how to fight with vision. The string in the cage breaks, and so unclaimed jewelry adorns your neck as you set the animals free.

The role of the forest dancer is uncertain, possibly, but her projected phantasm crosses the void, and a blush ensues. Having faith, watching crows, measuring safety robes. The faith of you, the faith in you. The tigress leaps. The Babylon of indifference. A new woman of leaping proportions appears before me, as we make eye-contact. The stutter of unknown opportunities receives a blinding flash. *Was that normal?*

The Weakness Club

(7-2004)

1

The rustle of loose feathers. A melting of gendered disruptions, mashed by a thirst of oil on the rocks burned into eyes by the skulls embedded with sapphire jewels, making the hypocritical beaks of birds reveal their silent codes of contempt. The vision is blurred, and the lenses of contact stalk the eruption of the lurching octopus, already late to its date with tapas. They leave no choice to tomorrow, while critics of texts support the commodities of literary corporations. The trade of intimacy is hacked to the ground in favor of revealing the stale discourses of perfect cheese, with perfect smiles, unfortunately not avoiding the deadly significance of silent, malevolent apathy. Young embryos attached to seaweed cannot hear the music of maple trees. You want strength and weakness, all rolled up into a perfect, mannequin package, and yet the archaeological ruins of hamburger churches goes unnoticed.

2

A truck-driver yawns and squashes a blood mollusk attached to his leg. Women wearing high-heels chew with their mouths open while they are at a church buffet that has served excessive amounts of canned spam. It is highly interesting and satisfying to create family portraits of biological foster relatives masticating fragments of well-preserved spam and other blenderized meats. Sometimes grandmothers wear pantyhose over their heads in order to rob banks, but usually this behavior subsides when trees living next to wire fences grow so large that the fluid bark engulfs the inorganic structures of the sensual metallic partition.

If only the partition could rip through skies of sensual flesh, with clouds so thick they could top off any sunset with a nudist pancake. The apathy police were out in full force by dusk, and they saluted the setting sun with callous indifference, ignoring a large zit on the nose of the rusting statue of liberty as if it were an estranged loved one. Each of the apathy police had the brain of a celery puff, and their favorite erotic dance was called the wail of an ambulance, especially when dear professors sleepwalked over a double-Felix of inherited differences. The prismatic blood oozed through myoglobin factories, and paint stores prospered during times of self-righteous parental invasions through fetid swamps and toothless mammalian tomatoes found underneath pillows in a sea of forgotten afternoons.

An elephant blew peanut shells from its nose, and a heavy boot brutally crushed a bag of mothballs that had been hoarded by grubby capitalists in every corner of an oppressive lipstick factory. The urban mammatoes were cared for by green thumbs, and the blossoming of libidinal starfish overtook the traction of clandestine legs, leading to the fermentation of hairy eyeballs when they gaze into distant galaxies. The smokeless incisions of seaweed could have been forgotten, but the hippy tambourines were excessive, leading to the cloying ejaculation of pure glucose all over a fundamentalist false prophet.

3

I love you just the way you are, especially when the snow-tires fail and a rigid ambulance falls off a cliff. Derelict blood packs were stepped on, and liquid worry beads were temporarily frozen into a pocket-sized galaxy that knew no borders except for black-washed fences that revealed backwater flooding in subdued areas in need of some parental transit authority.

The red capes of matadors provided safe harbors, and the DNA of space aliens was stretched and inserted into chicken eggs, creating green eggs and ham, complete with primitive synthesizer music. Meanwhile, the apathy police continued with their intrusive rounds, hoarding the commemorative marbles of abandoned subway stations where rats and roaches roamed the dust-covered pedestrian arcades, mumbling false, numbing religious verses to themselves, praising technological orgasmic breakthroughs, while ignoring the faces of demons who peered down at them through tinted, old-fashioned bulls-eye windows.

This illumination of dawn enticed the apathy police, who never failed to maintain faceless memories, and corridors of ambiguous suppressors of emotions when the enforcement of marital bliss had reached its peak.

4

Pre-fab markers disintegrate into a column of massacred soldiers that once soaked their feet in crude oil in order to satisfy a bottomless, apathetic pit. Seashells comb seaweed residues through their hair and put a damper on twilight picnic excursions through sexual encounter boothes draped with red velvet curtains. The love criminals take a nap, and this numbing sensation takes a freshly baked apple pie and smears it onto the legs of lascivious women, in the same way a five-legged starfish glides its purple arms of sensual iodine over the rose-tinted folds of a magnificent flower, only waiting to be pulled-on, perhaps even more than once.

Meanwhile, sour-graped grandmothers in Chicago pull a fresh pair of pantyhose over their heads and go out onto the controversial streets in order to find banks and occupying soldiers to rob. The grandmotherly thieves pass the fabulous urban shops (bearing thoroughbred fishing lures) and spend a few moments in a camel's telephone booth listening to tinkle-tinkle ding-dong elevator music and seeing well-advertised religious placards featuring a national Weakness Club. Won't you join the Weakness Club too? Won't you wear your favorite items of weakness on your sleeve? Couldn't circumcised sausage links of vegetarian content grow on vegetative trees of churchly holiness, especially when Jesus used to rub olive oil all over his face?

The Chicago-dwelling sour-graped grandmothers replenish their vigilante pantyhose collection every few days, and check in frequently with the highly therapeutic Weakness Club, joyfully relinquishing self-determination into the friendliness of genetic strangers. Anyone want to get graped? Could social plundering become consolidated and ultimately forgotten with a superficial mask of bankrobber pantyhose?

5

Meat stockings of new skin are peeled from flayed limbs, creating the dictators of high-tech conglomerates and the sandstorms from empty bottles painted with the insignia of the Weakness Club. This particularly arid chapter of the Weakness Club found dead goldfish floating in the toilet, but the freedom of feminine wristwatches created a wry commentary of miscellaneous tubule lipsticks of every color, which eventually pulled the torso of meat shirts from unknown athletic skeletons.

These unmasked chrysalis sacs were pregnant with the ideas of the future, pushing a swath of hair from one eye to the next skull of decorative voodoo manipulations of a Mardi Gras toilet seat reserved for a wild-chicken sporting event. The Weakness Club mailing list was tightened in the same way backpackers further restrict their belts around punctured limbs that have been poisoned by the lick of a corpulent sidewinder, sending purple flowers and herbal pillows to an indifferent academic woman from anyone's univeristy. Mad glibbing, fast reticulations of smart-meat – that special kind of meat that can assume any shape bringing organic life to power-tools, and bringing smiles to bioengineered, sickly bunny rabbits with multiple genitals and extra sets of eyes.

The President of the Self-Righteous Parental Division of the Weakness Club even sat back in his office throne and spied on his wife and children with numerous cameras positioned throughout his home.

6

From an unknown source of paperclips, the tendrils of an Aztec nautilus touched the bandaged faces of mummies as they reposed forever in cryogenic tombs made of a luminous, sheeted silicate. The sleeping stack of cryogenic phosphorus breathed in the unwinding moments of eternity, using congressional leaders to French-kiss (or "Freedom-kiss," rather) an inverted hourglass that was drooling a sandstorm of moral bankruptcy, a monsoon of fertile fish ponds.

Banana peels were slipped upon, and behemoths grasped at fragile xylophones, using them to crush fragrant tomatoes, especially self-aware mammatoes, with the tendrils of obscure sonic honey. These moments escaped the grasping eyes of omniscient owls whose annular rings of concentric wisdom oozed through the cracks of wooden floors like a gateway to hell forged from a lacey nightgown housing the tempests of nocturnal infatuations. While elephants can shoot briny olives from their long noses, so can squirrels read picture books from the confines of their arboreal living rooms, watching TV shows about the mating practices of mosquitoes. As fast as a department store mannequin can shed its undergarments, alarm bells are used like glass marbles to move the eyes of a clock onto the back of a leg waiting for a mafia leg train.

7

A new truck-driver squashes a blood mollusk on the nude shoulder of a mannequin, who sits in the passenger seat of his tractor rig. Sometimes these long, special journeys are fraught with the penetrating teeth of lions, suddenly tearing wigs from heads in order to peel the vulnerable moralities of cowardly squashed phallic-christs that reason through porous bosoms into an alphabet soup of a delirious gammadelt. Pregnant easter eggs were cracked, and the marbled birthing proteins pulsated below. Gorgeous women peed on antique ivory piano keyboards from the eighteenth century. This gush of urine was a warning sign spelled backwards, creating feral messages of abandoned houses and discarded tissues inserted into the crevices of decaying plaster walls, releasing the kinetics of blood mollusks and other combustible bird skulls.

Torrents of blood spatter the water bottles that crouch in display windows, and mannequins hurl thought-rocks into your thoughtful breasts, forever checking the sunsets of tractors and the enigmas of motorcycle fetishes. Dinosaurs come and go, but they are jealous of horse teeth, inserting melted bicycles into their ears.

Suddenly a nefarious pseudo-surrealist fell over dead, with a thud. This global collapse of poser poetry readings and ritualistic art-chatter (just for the sake of self-validation) created a state of obsessive blood-sucking, completely draining the cultured cattle of their already-anaemic intellectual tomato juice. Pathetic.

8

The winds are passers-by, and the squall of anti-satiation draws near the front line like the shadows of starfish that blow in the wind and sometimes wash up onto the Teutonic driveways with their crumbling skin. The cracks within statues reveal the bad eggs, delivering the patient to a new blend of canned sunshine obliterated by wooden wall masks. The cryptic release codes of plastic trucking facades have weakened, returning the green embers to a near-total level of slumber, safely tucked away among pillows and pinecones, burying the treasures of squirrels and the spherical messages of injured sap trees.

Your rotten skull only lies a few feet away from me, brought in by the dogs on rainy days. This nectar from the eternal flower creates hollow bells of crushed iron. The eyelashes chop the sky purveying lemon shivers of blue, and this underwater havoc can make the naïve laugh just like television sets, or even sashimi sets, for that matter. Your feelers move from one house to the next, always watching and drifting, always maintaining the illusion of Siggy's Holy Family. This wash-out of a reified car contains the bile of books, and possibly magazines, too. Would the sky-blue princess arrive today? More myths.

A wound-up clock diversion makes a mountain of library lies full of treacherous dreadnaught feet that are bruised in color.

The eggs might have seen a few fissures in the past fortnight, but the real sanguine excavation was to commence on alien dig-sites where the feet of cats sometimes playfully tread, just like the sandy talismans of frozen tears.

X-ray messages float in the wind, coaxing you to read the local news. You ignore the poisonous trees and open the safety of despair. The already-told jokes weep in the way pebbles do, when they find the sculptures of swim bladders adorning a festive tree of vertebrae in the silent, non-communications of phony civility, winding down terse plastic hours with the emptiness of barren smiles and materialistic pursuits of empty, poserish athletic promises within the sugared wings of furious eagles who cannot produce eggs during the frozen season, when tooth decay creates a banner of smog along the lines of female shoes left within a den of pumpkin cornucopias.

The dreadful face moves forward, packing in hours collapsed into neat rows of bivalves that line a popular walkway where animals lie in wait in the surrounding bushes.

Guilty dog, in that it spent its energy on white walls, making punitive gestures from eidetic numbers to which life was rudely compared. Noxious antelopes jumped from one dream to the next, cracking the boiled zygotes of wishful fertility as if they were pontificating on rice paper. Wretched fireflies could not understand this, but their glowing asses did. This metaphysical breakthrough could have made ancient tomes from tree bark, but instead it placed fire hydrants of quivering white magma upon a nocturnal chessboard of gambling pleasures. Unknown to a lopsided daruma, the wishful guesswork was to become realized like a slap in the face from a firefly cartridge from the black lagoon where dwell the dams of beavers and the sycamore tree dances that put holidays into backwards rotations when fighting the elements of time, very similar to the insomniac crawdaddy who flaps his wings into the grace of an avian void.

This feeling upon the forehead was as liberating as a sympathetic itch, perhaps even more sympathetic than the itch, implying an active rather than passive sofa to be collapsed upon when the celestial scabs broke their venom on the porcelain catwalks that led to abandoned, dusty nuclear reactors. The books could have done no better, releasing the will to breathe the fur of bears to a higher state of the waterfall country, where the dried riverbeds fomented the jeweled release of tiny ladybugs whose spots could produce silken shards of electricity, spilling the memories of lost truck-drivers upon a pavement of arboreal seaweed. The hot iron reclined in wait for the perfect substrate.

Love through bossy hats, and the camaraderie through control. The bitterness of the pretended life, and the unforgivable flaccidity of an aging saxophone.

9

The forest of goodness was obliterated, with glowing, tree-space shells left behind, all studded with appropriately sized rocks. The cabin that once was, happened to be combed through by sinister scavengers, or perhaps grave robbers. The railroad cattle fled the scene, into the darkness. As if the day had been impatiently awaited, the mud of bus stops made the roads difficult, pulling the grease from fried church buildings, and sending in replacement commercials from the edges of continents that would probably be recognized after a moment's hesitation. But still, the report of the boomstick was deafening, and the sky lit up, illuminating the rosy shadows of spies.

Fresh landscapes were once home, put together by tree corals secreted by wooden boxes of treasures. The familiar roads hewn from mud histories raised submerged televisions, liberating the structures of dust. The paths of journeying song-men through sewers was highly controlled and selected for by the safety-watchers with odd hair and seashells.

Meanwhile, anthills were fashioned through Venus flytraps, and the summoning of rain put crawfish on exhibit, likening their cautious footsteps to the pursuit of resting alcoves where slept the uncertain sarcophagi of tiger skeletons with green skulls. The forest anthills could have been connected with incendiary dynamite vigilance, but the origins of the drifting neighborly vigilance was uncertain.

Canines lap the blood from the shattered trees. Their coats blast forth an ominous sheen that almost smells of vaporous lemons. Female penguins stroll through with egg on their faces, and cartilaginous ammunition erupts from their swaying skulls. Quite a welcome to the intrusions of forceps during the springtime planting season of citrus. You can see these events from your isolated mannequin window, while you nonchalantly throw wood on the fire. The minutes burn like clockwork, and the organic sparks of the contact from ancient tree skin can send the entire television episode of utter mundanity right through the floor, in a way similar to the satellite probings of rat holes deep within the eviscerated, silver-lined clouds up in the sky of your living room. Let us save the world for you! Here, I will give you my chopped off fingers in the hopes that a pseudo-sentimental electric guitar ballad will convince you to have my ten children. See? Isn't that nice?

During fascist times, the hostility toward new ideas sometimes forces young people to skulk through urban playgrounds, renouncing identities so as to avoid the one-lane highways where hands with bandaged fingers can be avoided. Special baskets used to catch young quarry are implemented, creating a labyrinth of lost signals ricocheting throughout the giant skyscrapers of nonchalance. The Armageddon of animal crackers causes the guards to drink more coffee than they are accustomed, suggesting nebulous royal bandages of the Weakness Club. These emblems shimmer amid the dust of crowded velvet theatres where the sonically blind bump into each other when not singing.

Smart eyes jump in response to a shared half-crown, erasing the millionth agony in the forward motion of binary stars in their revolutionary love-hate relationships, creating awkward square dances on the faded playgrounds of profane literary relationships such that bee hives are strategically positioned outside of the locker rooms, bringing a quiet and benevolent silence to years of bustling activity. The drawn faces of lovers express confusion at these subterranean envelopments engendered by the cross-sections of wax bee hives.

Simultaneously, mechanics arrange their tools as if in a bento box, reciprocating the arrival of metal wing-nuts with a balanced view of arachnophobia, pushing the limits of extremities into the fourth dimension of garlic books which coerced seeing-eye dogs to take a break and to tune in to radio dog-collars. The outlying zombie non-sleepers in the backyard of dreams cut fresh orange roses with the help of musical tweezers and scalpels, flinging used bandages over the fence into a magazine featuring the round buttocks of cataract surgery.

This nightfall had its special attractions, signaling to observant crows to draw nigh and to land on green melons as they developed in the field. As this avian gathering thickened, a sludge made from mucilaginous seaweed preps overflowed the banks of a vampirical saltwater river that sang weeping songs that lauded the virtues of crime and the powdered wigs that hairless babies sometimes wear, deep within the exothermic scalp of recanted theories dealing with the vertiginous passage of invertebrate taxidermy and the fetish surrounding terrestrial umbrellas. It was moments like these which caused the neighbors to chirp uncontrollably.

As if a decloaked superhero couldn't release a canister of shark repellant from a well-clad belt, the forensics of uncovered language scuttled underneath a sofa of plush porcupine fur. This Agamnemonic rebound from culled sea-hair represented magical altruism, in that glass could melt from a piano kiln into tape reels of garbage, worthless footage of faceless unknown animals that put socks on their heads for Halloween thanksgiving that measured the protracted glances of darts liberated undercover of bird-droppings that were quaintly pictured within the raised embossment of postage stamps. This measured jail-cage of iron corrupted the reconnaissance of the piano kiln, representing the cauldron of the flute notes of registered silver parakeets inhabiting the area.

This head-of-a-goose became the infidelity of symbols, and the pumice bricks of the dead of night, when dead dolls moved from staircase to staircase, meandering over the tennis nets of barn straw. This throwaway gastronomical eruption was a geyser of orchestrated vomit that created missing links between wordless bricks of Excalibur feelings for when one advertises one's personal hierarchy, creating representative clay dolls who were speechless homunculi posing with silly shoes.

10

Eventually the clay dries, and so the dolls are smashed on a cheap corvette window like gigantic elephant brains. Although spent alkaline batteries were placed within the dolls upon the moment of their manufacture, this process in and of itself invalidated the dolls from the beginning, causing them to smell like a stale carpet. Literary agents frolic among the clay doll shards and rearrange the crushed pottery to their liking and of course to their better judgment.

A hand moves across the table, erasing the epithets of a ouija board. This lapse of knowledge pushes frozen bumblebees into spider-webbed corners of a raunchy headache house. This is how the surly crawfish eats — by grabbing others of its own kind and exploring the thrills of cannibalism! This consumption of liquid bumblebees reached the edge of a diving board, pushing carrots into the dim eye-sockets of the cynical, and the tick-infested athletic tube socks stained with the oil of wristwatches. The explosion of temporal oil across tube socks could have surely been a sign from the edge of a meat telephone, waiting to be distributed like painted beans that are sometimes handed out during commercial engagements of united souls trading rings. Those special vows of foreverness were laced with lace, and the unforgettable kaleidoscope of literature tombstones carried in by little purple men who could run their vocabularies through a sieve when inflatable cauliflower balloons are used to strike the transgressions of an oozing piano. Wow — I think the olive leaves fell out of Jesus' red-stuffed eye-sockets.

Waves of caramel occupy the thoughts of sleeping women. The aliens of each umbrella sing of deadly futilities, but the guitars that house the wristwatch silkworms make time something to be desired, almost like lipstick, but not quite. The clapped hands of parrots could add feelings through the walls, but the fortress refused to be smoothed over by chatter and the cycloptic running of cold water across the heads of moving sidewalks.

The numbness of a sleeping leg threw a temper-tantrum by crying out for starfish — more starfish, always more starfish. The chatter mouths next door have managed to drill a vertical hole through a bird's nest, releasing the fresh breath of the sea coastal areas. These obsessions of the flowthrough of metal change from one cord to the next, as the paranoid boxes in the corner of the room are slapped with the flat end of a screwdriver that was taped with plastic and released into the wild by a curious manifestation of bunny dancing, with designs of relieving stress, depression, and the leech-lake bloodletting. The towns of the old West of the United States of North America had nasal secretions engendered by the lactose fluid of muco-polysaccharides from underwater animal maternity.

And finally, to everyone's delight: a very deep burst of applause from the audience is preceded by the defenestration of a self-righteous parent clutching a spy camera in one hand and a baseball bat in the other – what a sad wreck of paranoid, insecure, middle-aged shortness, falling back on testosterone supplements and a neurotic rage provoked by electronic beeping sounds!

Sad hands tied, cross-flash dreams denied.

The Sassy Sky Diva from the Snake-Den of Circular Meow-Meow

(4-2005)

1

Cracked egg, like the overgrown forest from your hands as they plunged through the fertile soil, composed mainly of disregarded shoes, fermented rice hats and spread-eagled cheese-board passenger seats. The Joshua trees were fertile, and they put anchors in between your ear canals.

The touches of fingertips on the threatening windows broke open the splendor of evacuated office spaces. Your cute smile contrasted with the seriousness of librarian oxygen masks.

I spoke with the city in the same way hands can slap a coffee pot, signaling great music and reincarnated feelings who shudder underneath french-fry heat lamps. This mischievous determination led me to lick your eyelids, frequently giving illusions of blue-lined oyster beds with the sacredness of sniffing socks and the specialness of a "meow" printed on the back of a chair where a flow of feelings condenses into a wet tear, or perhaps a stream of saliva, or maybe even something else.

An anticipation of glances, the alpha and beta of your touch, as if the best things in life come in pairs and sometimes even threes. The spines of cactus reach impossible conclusions as if the air could become a sharp prism and cut the tentaclian bonds of international guilt and condensation of bordered soil with polka-dot pansies.

I still know of the "meow" on the back of the chair. It calls me to an antique lobster-phone, where I call on the advice of ancestors.

The "meow" says it all, and I look to you, through your eyes to the edges of a blue infinity. You hold me captive in the desert sands of a storm-drenched forest, where the hike to freedom is a stream of rainwater to be wrung from a feline bandanna, falling onto the pillow, living in your safety for the moments of eyelashes, spanking the tail of your poetic eminence, your presence on a frost-bitten taiga.

Your face is the liberation of sound, the silent trees that never get heard within an empty forest. The maze of glances and words is astounding. I am proud to know your shoelaces. We carve walking sticks from birch trees. I peel the birch bark and smell the fragrance of the earth, similar to the burning plant oils that are aromatic as they are incumbently denied the light of day, locked within the vault of your brain.

The wind blows the sands of night aside. Brushed aside, the lifted sand reveals stone-steps made of moonstone, with captured light sandwiched between sheets of smooth silicon. These steps lead downstairs. For you and you alone, I am the crab-cracking superman, as I nervously hold my service pistol, cautiously casing the contaminated mansion, playing games with secret doors and eyeing the spent shell casings with a little bit of fear. Was that a knock at the door?

Pulling blue weeds from crevices, the nesting crabs import crayons from chrysanthemums, spilling the ink of night across your beautiful brow. Should such magic be contained or allowed to migrate across the fragrant threshold of the seated timber, the locus of the "meow" chair that was to become the seat of a desired woman's psyche, nestled amid a periwinkle pressure dialectic?

Radiostatic. Memories from a dark cube of distant buttons. Now, your presence within the doorway, the shadow from tomorrow. Your dark, forest hair upon the pillow. Your extended leg to block my passing, you tease, you. If you dropped a pink hat of pool-cue felt upon the table, the world would be reduced to a metallic icon that could be placed within the "meow" nexus, similar to the process by which an emerald of sentimental value is clasped by silver prongs.

Such riches are fearsome, or a possible foursome, with the multiplication of length by width to create a meiotic sporulation protein, as if such things existed within the buds of a belt-looped street, with stolen furniture from agricultural condom-iniums.

The drifting of damp magnolian pink identification with the green, as if lizards could hear the tear-throbbing beat of steel drums that spoke only to you of the breeze that felines feel when the wind blows between their clawed toes. I search the beach at night for you. Trembling, you pull up the lobster trap only to find a Styrofoam telephone hidden within the chicken wire. A telegram sends messages from the bottom of the sea, relaying the passage of a boat under a bridge. The hang-up occurs underwater.

Freud's brother stepped on the wheezing machine, the only gem in the desert. The reformation of pictures. You are a black cat sitting on a purple satin pillow.

2

Asphalt carrion skyscrapers. The worship of stale ideas? Serendipitous forgiveness as evidenced by a wax trail from inside a green bottle of mystery. Honeycomb discoveries mutate within the eye cavities, waiting for something to emerge.

...

Putting tresses upon support poles. Dragging out the tools that were used forever upon your eyes, in the way a sigh is forwarded to a bunny cavern that is from a deserted church in Monterey. The trek of madness across meetings, reminiscent of that long night of forgotten pathways through deserts by uncertain moonlight. A pair of high-heels is followed by a transformation into black boots, with a red top, worn by someone who can pull eyes out of leaves, and then leaves out of her eyes. She understands fish and chips, but then she also knows about the telephone booths of a pair of lips lingering by a Victorian staircase, inserting files into empty orphanage rooms. This mix of cat paws leaves a mysterious trail of forgotten sighs, now hidden by dusty unknown walls in a dusty corridor of your archives. The thighs mutate and an elbow beneath the sheets emerges. Salamanders understand these things, but not the crows.

The fishhooks attach to the outstretched telephone microphone, putting the weird coffee cups beneath eyelids, making a silly, monetary countdown of something that could have been mythological. The dangers of modern feelings and attachments. There is uncertainty within these leaves now, and autumn is a stomach-ache with stepped-on bananas and disintegrating brassieres.

A monument of cross-roads makes the feline observant blush, casting the nebular hairline fracture into a trimester turkey-leg. Character armor? Did the butler do that? What could have been the purpose of a symphonic trombone made of onyx, with the chiseled inscription of "murder mystery dinner"? Could a mystery within a lipstick-stained mystery generate unknown flowers of darkness? Apparently so. Such a planted seed by one of those nefarious willy-wallies from the south created unknown purposes stretched across virgin skeins, interlacing a dark, wooden totemic monument of crossroads-capability, solely illuminated by one candle, an old friend. This wooden corridor was exhilarating as it was kitten laughter, as it was the codename of alpha in one ear, and beta in the other. There were no other ways to express this movement of poof-hair musicality, in the way one looks down the stairwell to see a ray of light in the middle of a diamond smile, a sensual bulwark of feelings who dares to walk around with a comb of cheese within her hair. The delta of estuaries is a salty crevice of normality, a derivation of cross-roads, in the same way a skull and crossbones is similar to the alchemy of crossed, panty-hosed legs covered with white power-boots, glued to the staircase in a timeless fashion assault, sending out a light-beam of "muah, muah" kisses that auto-spray-paints the uncovered foreheads with night graffiti, in an auto-reflexive, mirrored anti-contempt giggle that diffuses any stubborn sasquatch who kills houseguests for any lack of appetizer at hand. These sorts of regulations are purely sentimental, and can be found in any sports almanac of capitalistic flatulence.

Within your blue eyefolds of sacred gesticulation-grounds, you spin the bottle in the same way willy-wally culture unfolds like special socks import encrypted gasoline into your fishhook telephone receiver.

I am disturbed by these events that pour in from an internet raincloud of "I-don't-want-to-talk-to-you" culture. This cris-crossing of horses leads one to the path of cactuses when they twist into vulture sediments that slowly drift down to the floor of television empires of airplane managers that know how to hoard empirical salad dressing bottles of the ways of overcoming your eyeglasses of glassblowing. I cannot fathom your smile, apparently. You fire my synapses, and put kalamata olives into symposium postures of knowledge dissemination, in a valley particular only to the landing of dog-eared crows.

The kill switch has been armed. Hair-colored panties line the staircases of the library of ages, the bow-tie conspiracy of festive attire in a summer fear of next-fear school buses where one stops on the way to haunted education, with the little children who want to stick knives into your leg when you try to give them a purpose in life, as if such pretentious goals could be easily transmitted like sexual diseases on a warm school session massage in the middle of the airplane desert, where the mile-high club celebrates its sordid cooking classes, whipping up delights that no cameras could ever fully grasp.

3

After the rage of ancient umbrellas, the forgotten shoes were thrown upon the farmhouse roof, lasting until the next tornado came through to carry them away in the marbled vortex of a sandaled foot, the sniffing of her socks in the winter breeze of a macaroni pair of glasses. A bed made of blue sky and purple grapes is the berth upon which the oil ship perched, sending out laundry lines of tweeting birds, sending pippi longstocking smoke signals into the heart of a giggle, on which the onyx gem rests on the pillow, contemplating the black-stockinged legs of an auto-reflexive mirror that self-reflects an eidetic caribou that symbolized only one letter of the alphabet at a time. No time for the gammadelt.

Oh but what about the turkeys that hide in the steep hills, guarding fossils that were once tissues for blowing noses and other organs? Could these footsteps have been the goose of frozen tree branches that hide the specter of Eskimo spectacles in the frozen wastes of winter? Would a bat's wings begin to resemble those of a butterfly once the manure in the stable had been aged long enough to remove diamonds from the rough spots?

This line of questioning was not very remarkable, once it became certain that the butterfly was never from Idaho, but really from the biscuit factories of the ice ages, where princess crystals entertain mad thoughts within the labyrinths of icy sheets, pointing bony fingers at the sun and bellowing with pre-fab rage.

Was I being stalked? Could baubles of boggle release a hidden joy of linguistic licks, in the back room of a silken snake den? It was completely by surprise that the snakes persisted, in their efforts to colonize a honeycomb of preternatural glory, in a monument of fear that was a circle of mirrors reflecting the surprise of a strawberry morning with tussled hair and a discarded pair of glasses. A blue moon sidewinder is released from a defunct hour-glass, spilling the dance across a patterned wreathe of weaknesses cultivated from a glass eye of serpent tranquility. Possibly a recognizable path had been found, and yet your eyes became green lanterns to a portal through the walls, a reflection of a 70-pound mammoth that was still heavily armed but in a glass cabinet quietly guarded by raccoon lovers and other symbols of shotgun shell extravagance.

Hot baths might do the trick, in place of a sanctuary of the maritime blues and oranges of ocean hideouts, separated by a thin film of plastic, a moist barrier that kept wet from dry and eyes from legs. Even downloaded ephemera proceeded along dubious paths while the green lanterns bounced in the steamy dim light, soaking under hot waves and stroking the tips of erasers, knowing that this pencil secret in and of itself was enough to warrant a sharpener. But where exactly was that sharpener?

Possibly such a sharpener might exist beyond the reach of the eraser tips, and yet the call for the plume was sharper than a Formosan butterfly leaf-hat that certain luscious sillies wore during moments of levity and smiles, within the catacombs of blindfolded pleasures of blue silk, completely cut off from conventional reality and all of the other nefarious mistrust of the hens of the land. This mineral deposit was scooped up in the form of a lop-sided bunny with quivering whiskers and soft gloves that knew how to touch the tendrils of venus fly traps that grew among the blue moon wastes of the sidewinder's lair, penetrating the dance of unknown nymphs and celebrating the eye-contact of a deja-vu radio which saw different people emerge from different songs, as if a person was no longer a radio but really an efflorescence of pristine almonds, glued to eyelids and sniffing the shoes of those who kept white puddles on red jackets. This sort of foolishness could not go on indefinitely, and a black cat slowly paced within her chamber of starlight, sending out a message that would be merged with the waterfalls of different continents.

The black cat was more than a carrot razor, and offered divine odors to the skies of azure sunsets, falling into the purple after the blue, and witnessing the setting of a burning orange sun in the distance. This fall of light upon the pillow necessitated further exchanges between night and day, cat and tail, and then moon with snake. The symbolist alchemy of starlit sequences created a magic potion that paved the way for a winding road for the blue moon sidewinder to follow, in search of the lost velvet steps of the black cat that chased its home of blue-sunset houses.

4

Venusian pinecones top the lost Lincoln-log cabins of futility, or perhaps feuilleton, with eggshells sliding down doorknobs covered with stretched condoms, all out in the middle of know-where. French vanilla beans sometimes get pork, even when blue moon lagoons gather the momentum of weighted marooned castaways who wander the beaches like sidewinders in search of cheese castles and kiwi fruit envelops who know how to touch a frightened bunny and make its tail rise. The anthem of songs is analogous to the flagpoles of risen festivities, and so coffee is poured into a woman's sultry shoe. This concretion of ants and sugar is as basic as a grain of sand that is accidentally swept into the unwary eye, bringing on a surge of tears that bounces off pantyhose and ends up roosting like birds in forgotten mailboxes where the lichen grows on neglected metal and where rooftop excursions bring out the cuteness of white, outdoorsy rain-hats.

A mam'selle beaker is shifted to another shelf, where the earthquake narrowly avoids spilling the internal contents of the beaker. Painted on the walls were once faded icons of red birds, key-rings and dried fruits which have all become brains now, basically upside-down cherry brains which tingle with the pleasures of sardine jeans, spilling the hairy eagle harem into the blue and maroon trampoline, and releasing a frozen ice-cube from the glacier, allowing it to drift into the aether like a sub-antarctic sperm whale, ready for anything and certainly eager enough to bray at the moon.

Transformed wolves run like a pack, and fallen rainwater yearns to rejoin the mother puddle somewhere deep within the earth. The wolfen characteristics of pointed teeth, pointing eyes that touch the soft spots of creamy, white bunny-rabbits is more than enough for a decadent meal, with oozing cheeses and turquoise scarab pieces that rest on museum cushions covered with white fur.

Meanwhile, unseen hands press down on mayonnaise fishes, enabling the terrestrially bound fish to squirt a stream of mayonnaise from their mouths. This activity is not yet strong enough to cut through government bolts and screws, but enough at least, to disturb the backyard clotheslines which are nutritious to linguistic red birds who congregate by the urban fountains within the red and yellow-tiled habitations of humans, singing breezy songs of propaganda about nobody being left behind.

Quite different from the paralysis of mirrored watching and self-watching of otherly watching, the fairest of all mirrored mirror trees sprouts new wingtips which place a white hat on an unprotected head of blushing proportions, while the heartwarming smile rubs her ass into a chair of fur, stroking harmonicas, blowing notes and tickling the pathways to the blue sidewinder paradise of marooned sweatpants. If the sweatpants had been from any island, then the desert icecubes would have been like dried fruits at the bottom of a sink. But instead, because the seated passion chair was dragged into a closet, with nobody to sit on it, then the paint on the walls peeled with latex tears and the sniffles of dusty drapery and a three-dimensional sand-map soaked with urine.

Grandmother spider descends next to the ladder, pointing a kaleidoscopic beacon in the direction of a black satin lagoon, where the black rabbits roost together in the twilight, cooing within the upside-down cerebral cherry lightbulb, and releasing the red birds of song from the frightened castle of ribbed white gloves that lovingly powder the whiskers of the other, placing herself over him, completely ripe for the irreversible riptide.

5

When the forgotten stilts are discarded like foaming crutches in the corners of abandoned stairwells, where the symbolic snack-cakes of jellified youth are crushed like the bones of aquatic planets, then and only then will psychedelic weepy-trains be released from their derailing fears from sleeping passengers who might weep upon seeing the rising sun. This fear is completely justifiable and understandable from the perspective of wooden broom closets where captive prisoners wear deathmasks and are fed the last rights by way of crackers stained with ink and blood. The voodoo feathers that litter the bedrooms remind one of the shaky trails of skulls and crossbones that once lead to sickening mountain paths to unknown wastes of fear and spinal transformation.

The smile of a virgin white jacket girl suggests the emptiness of unfilled white boots that rest against the door of the closet, waiting to stalk the outside pavements of the walnut tree-fields where young schoolboys frolic, uninhibited, amid the laughing chants of the hypnogogic feline from black satin tranquility. This party atmosphere is conducive to these young studies of birthing solar flares and heavenly bodies moving through plastic avenues of plasma afterbirth, moving through the walls of transparent sugar and through the painted walls of binary hair braids. The studly spurs from the boots dig into the back, and white boots, white gloves of experimenting personnel create a hexagonal contrast to the woman of bathtub felicity, from wet, curly whiskers drenched with doughtnut glaze, to regional quarters of sleeping spiders whose silken corridors lead to places of lost knives and sunken ships, all completely filled with frozen droplets of blood suspended like jewels along the evil silken threads.

The blood droplets within the darkness stained the sheets, yet the feelings were absent, as if a bottle of the finest red wine were missing from the inside, without the usual decorking procedure that might have easily explained the passage of the evacuated fluid. In this particular case, the absent wine and the state of emptiness without proper decorking suggested an open need that went unfulfilled after renegade earrings are pierced through mango lobes of soft flesh. What was absent before, is now present, and the dart is filled with the most potent medicine, replacing the vacuous wine bottle dart, so thoroughly corked with emotional absenteeism and lustful but sadly 2-dimensional rhetoric.

For some minds, a collection of such darts was never really complete, as new varieties of emptiness were being discovered daily. However, the potent darts were extremely rare, and were rumored to grow on dart bushes, even though these supposed "dart bushes" had never really ever been seen before. Suddenly Alpha licked the end of Beta, and then Beta licked the beginning of Alpha. Such self-cycling surface patterns were incongruous within the purple flowers of artichokes that grew in the summer sun of Monterey, supposedly one of the best growing fields for experiencing summers, especially the love-currency of the preceding vernal equinox, analogous to the way paper drink umbrellas were burned by the thousands in the Buddhist cemeteries under Venetian bridges and through the pink lipstick of fishes that wore parsley hats and spent their days in spider-webbed store windows. Many-colored hats are expressions of laughter that ejaculate loving sentiments far better and well farther than any hallmark greeting card could.

So, rather than waste time collecting empty darts, it might be more generously advised that potent darts are sought, not only for their rooftop pinecones, but also for their white-jacketed, smiling beauty. Therein is the dialectical resolution: the empty dart abandoning itself in order to become a potent dart collection unto itself, completely empowered to kill even the most dangerous of dinosaurs!

The Third Iguana
(2-2007)

And a barrel of monkeys rolled down the railroad tracks, falling into a path of shadows that should have been light. The rollercoaster was originally part of this amusement park, but when most of the train-cars had been destroyed, or sometimes stolen, the park officials gave up hope for a functional rollercoaster ride, and bade all naughty boys and girls to return home to their parents for cold soup and moralistic lectures on standard modes of subjective decency.

Underneath the heavy scaffolding of the rollercoaster line fell the debris from recent years of neglect and lack of patrons. It appeared that everyone in the amusement park decided to visit the cute, life-sized stuffed animals that were sinisterly positioned along the pathways that led to various other exhibits, rides, and embalmed curios. So as a result, the sacred rollercoaster became mummified, forgotten completely and thoroughly swept under the rug, although the ruins of the winding track remained in plain sight as a permanent eyesore, yet to be systematically ignored by eyes that refused to see the exposed spokes and rails coated with rust and grime. It was far beneath this flimsy structural collapse that a colony of rats joined to become a collective organism, with zinc electrodes protruding from their crania which originally made them delicious test subjects, but now left them as forgotten independents cast aside from the ruins of the rollercoaster experiment. They were like flakes of dandruff that fell out of the electrical scalp collective. The electrodes of the rats were ugly, and still relayed sparks from short-circuiting neurons deep within their minds which spilled outward into the physical world. The plates of metal protruding from their heads suggested that their minds were batteries of thought potential, and from time to time, they marched forward as one organism, wreaking havoc on what remained of the paradise tracks that were once ridden by screaming children as they moved through tunnels of light and dark, with icy shrieks reverberating from the clinical surfaces of carbon steel – the original construction materials from when the tracks were first built.

Boxes of gifts were opened by the side of the road leading away from the amusement park, and many a poor slob picked his nose as a gesture of the approaching dawn, when sleeping birds removed twigs of autumn from their beaks, in anticipation of the morning.

When the morning did come, it was as if a rotten pumpkin head fell from a headless body to become immediately elected the president of a democratic nation that was not really so democratic. The injustices of tarred feathers were excreted from the burning red eyes of nearby ravens who all gurgled their anticipation of the rising sun and the displeasures of unfathomable numbers, representing the people who entered and exited the theme park, as they stacked their discarded gifts by the side of the road, revealing a trembling awareness of the compass needle as it points one in places that not even the average fool or clod would go.

The rats paid no heed, and peered out from under the debris of the rollercoaster, with venom and saliva dripping down their toothy smiles. They had no choice but to lurk while the senile influx of morning greeters madly lifted their voices and skirts to the sky, unaware of whatever industrialized malevolence that might befall them from the bosoms of their bejeweled families, taking in the morning revolutions with newspapers and pricey pocketwatches that belied their otherworldly origins. Eventually these naively awkward and awkwardly naive morning revelers would clear out and move their carcasses over the next rise in search of the following thrill, and then the rats would creep out from underneath the rubble, with electrodes still pulsing and with their hips lurching in a pre-gyrating momentum that could only build ever higher during the course of the uncertain day.

This rabid premonition of rodent hip-gyration was prefigured by an itchy patch of skin on the back of the neck, in the form of a provincial, nationalistic flag of exploitative solidarity. The itchiness was actually caused by a swarm of ants that would only bite at midnight, after the perfumed roses were withdrawn and put to bed in their refrigerated compartment capsules. It was at the moment of flower refrigeration that the ants struck, biting the nape of the neck, and leaving a clearly defined patch of bitten flesh that formed the exact pattern of your least-favorite national flag. This redness and itchiness was swollen like a library, and the knowledge emanating from the sores was a mixture of blood, saliva and emerald jewels which could easily become embedded in primate hands like splinters, so for that reason gloves and shoes were to be worn, protecting the tactile surfaces from the dazzle of wealth and the shimmer of green mediocrity.

When libraries do fall, they leave behind a tally of all of those who did and did not return their useless library books. There was a certain despair to be felt when an especially thick volume would suddenly become transparent, as if it were then made of sea salt just waiting to be dissolved back into the ocean, where its progenitor crystalline design was once charted on parchment by unleavened fairies who dipped their wings in rodent saliva the color of amber. When wings become teeth, then their flight over the mountain becomes a return to breastfeeding and also a reclamation of dusty dreams which was the ultimate property of neglected shop window dummies. From these dissolved library books the legends of the red smile became apparent, and many a rat with a wayward electrode snapped up these ephemeral volumes, raising the words over its head with indignance and the will to breastfeed, taking a nurse's red thermometer and disappearing it into an acrylic museum display case, where it would have the chance to incubate in rarefied solutions of unstable plasma that were pumped into the container directly from the halo of the not so distant sun. These rare substances would stratify themselves according to atomic weight, and the proportional spread of differential exposure to the captured nurse's thermometer caused the glass instrument to become modified, completely altered from its original purpose. In fact, a certain kind of alchemy was underway, and this *de novo* transformation made many a rat and even the ever-vigilant alley cats look askance ever so furtively, pretending to watch clocks that didn't exist, to fold newspapers that were no longer grasped in paws, and even to fall asleep in transparent beds that had no hollow legs to stand on.

Meanwhile, one of the unfortunate test subjects felt his body become rigid, as if he were now able to stand up at attention to an unknown sense of duty that was farcical at best, but then most likely subterranean in its highway to the underground silence. The underground silence was certainly more than your average volcano, or even a minor bed-wetting experience, and yet its frivolity shed a tear that was half in jest and then half in diamond seriousness. The thin line upon which this poor slob walked was obscene, or perhaps criminally insane, in the same way an American congress was made out of a pair of size-D bipartisan marshmallows that were destined to melt the polar caps with their own special kind of dialectical weakness that could lick the feet of the pedestrians who walked the world upstairs, forever waiting for trains that would not arrive.

The test subject felt his legs completely fill with straw, or perhaps bamboo, and his newly found step was just as springy as a cloverleaf in wait for bees, offering the prospects of honey and bruised guitar chords that would slide into the bass of sweet orchestration, moving notes in place of books and vice-versa. This scampering of novel sounds and grunts put wet lips and noses close to the library, in the dawned-out smiles and infinitely deep blue eyes that might forget the lipstick that was on her face, and then waltz into a stairwell that had unforgiving sideways staircases: those special staircases that might be placed within an ambulance where floating wizard bodies would move longitudinally to simulate an electric current capable of powering some battery-operated drapes (the purple velvet mannequin kind of drapes) that one would be advised to keep fairly closed during most hours of activity, so as to not allow the casual observer to become transformed into a peeping Tom or a leering Jennifer. It was the leering Jennifers, especially, of which one needed to be exquisitely vigilant. The poor slob tucked his medulla within his overly exposed hat, and sauntered down the street, languidly sweating and avoiding tripping over his bandaged feet, spreading distorted footprints upon the land, dragging musical notes from A to B and then to C. This motion caused time to lurch. Subway cars were turned upside down. Burmese tigers burped and then inflated themselves inside out, creating hairy fur-tunnels with bags of visceral organs hanging from their newly formed exteriors like a moist, gelatinous purse display that one often finds in the more upscale department stores. Fur on the inside, and slimy organs on the outside – this was certainly the day for the ladies to go out and buy new purses. From the sky fell the tears of a million hexagons, forcing the sky dragons to grin with unexpected chaos, combing their hair with snowflakes and looking up from their soap-opera dreams into the crumbling cheese of the night.

Then entered the rats. Their gyrating hips twisted in queue, with knowing paw-pads treading ever so lightly, avoiding the patches of shadow and the intermittent spikes that would come up through the floor. The rhythm of their step followed that of their hips as they moved the wet clothes of the laundry (which had by now been rinsed completely clean of urine) into a piece-by-piece assembly line such that each garment was gingerly wrung free of all drops of liquid, causing a sudsy spattering of wetness to douse the spiked floor underfoot of the dancing rodents. The occasional soap bubble did open up prismatic vistas of wish-fulfillment for one or more of the occasional passers-by, but the overall effect was a washer's paradise, sending out the suds of the beach for the incoming driftwood of clothes that would form ragged shelter for the shivering rat limbs. These naked bodies might someday become covered with the finest warmth available, for free, of course. It was certainly true that warmth should never have to be bought.

The leader of the pack of rats, the one who first extricated herself from The Machine, was leading the group through the flying motions of a sensible cha-cha, completely dapper in her soft steps as her extremities moved her lithe body across the distance all patchy with half-working floodlights that bathed the carnival complex in an unhealthy light, reminding one of hunger and trauma. Her coy and knowing smile – almost a smirk, and highlighted by her quivering nose – completely defied the harshness of the ruined urban landscape, and the ugly amusement park theme-animals of the daytime that lined the park's walkways had been replaced by serene, totemic hungry statues of night, with their vacant, painted eyes reflecting the light of a spaceship on its lonely way to a distant star.

Moonlight glimmered on the dirty puddles that covered much of the walkways, occasionally revealing the sparkle of garbage or other refuse dropped by the heedless children who had trod these paths only hours before. In one of the puddles, the rat leader noticed a shiny red object barely submerged in the foul water. It was a thermometer – the old-fashioned kind with that special kind of red-colored alcohol inside of the glass. The sensitive end of the thermometer was unusually bulbous, and completely filled with the red liquid. In fact, the end was so round, it looked like a small apple, and when examined closely by the rat's keen eyes, it was discovered that a small, seed-like kernel was occupying the center. This inner core, perhaps the heart of the thermometer, looked like a cross between an unopened blossom and a seed – some kind of nucleus that had not yet evolved or developed. The rat leader wiped the filthy instrument on one of the newly cleaned rags she and her group had been carrying, and then did a strange thing: she inserted the red, very round end of the thermometer into her lower eyelid, as if her eyeball had become a tongue with a fever, and that by inserting the thermometer underneath the eyeball, a temperature might be recorded.

But apparently this "thermometer" was not a recorder of tempera-ture, but some other device, since she began to experience things she had never experienced before: first the rat saw the red glow of the probe against her eye, and somehow the image of the seed inside burned itself onto her retina, leaving first the image of the world, and then the void created by its shadow. Therefore, world and shadow-of-world encircled her field of vision, and she realized that she could stick her prehensile tail into either one. In fact, the rat could comfortably move her tail between both worlds, and eventually move her entire being between these two apparent opposites, just like any vengeful pendulum. Likewise, the image of the world and its shadow faded to become herself and "the other". She was able to move between "self" and "other", creating a third state of being or perception that was neither of the first two states, and was completely separate, and yet composed of the former. She therefore had her feet in both worlds, and it was only up to her where she would cast her seeds, her progeny, her febrile tendrils of thought as they arose from within her mind, even when she wasn't really aware of them.

After experiencing these visions and apparent revelations, the rat's eyes twitched as she realized she was still in a very dark amusement park, and that she had an abnormally bulbous thermometer probe embedded beneath her left eyeball. The probe seemed to be alive, like a growing red seed at the bottom of a glass elevator. She pulled the "thermometer" from her eye, and realized that somehow the glass rod with the living red liquid inside – perhaps blood – was in fact expanding, growing. The glass rod itself was lengthening, creating new, separated segments of red liquid in much the same way bamboo grows new, hollow compartments that are insular and separated from the older segments by way of a diaphragm or barrier between compartments. And the formation of a notch in the glass was visible in between each new section of red liquid in the growing "thermometer". On a whim, the rat leader gently snapped off the furthermost thermometer piece, which then grew into its own, creating a new "thermometer" that looked like the original one. Very quickly, the sharp edges of the two broken pieces became rounded and smooth, as if the glass of which they were made had a life of its own, and could repair itself the way flesh could. Sharp, broken edges were now unbearably smooth. She gave the newly budded thermometer to the nearest rat, and then began to separate the other new thermometers that grew from the original, passing them to the rats around her. Within minutes, each rat was holding a thermometer with smoothed ends. The lead rat drew an aluminum whistle from a hidden pocket on her vest, and blew it, sending a blast of searing noise in every direction. It was at this moment that the other rats all inserted their own apple-red thermometers into their own eye sockets, to witness the wonders and realizations that their leader did. Once every rat had understood the vision, the entire group marched to a bare hill – the highest hill within the carnival – and firmly planted the organic glass rods into the soil, spacing them apart rather evenly, with the glowing, red, bulbous ends in the soil, and the graduated termini sticking above-ground, in a plantlike fashion.

The rats with the electrodes jutting from their skulls walked away and made their rounds within the park, admiring abandoned rides and attractions, and chittering hyperactively while meandering through the tunnel of love, finding discarded condoms, broken beer bottles, cigarette butts and random pages torn from degenerate comic-books. These items were truly ephemeral, and the rats continued on with their journey, stepping over fragments of broken mirror that glimmered ever so dully in the faint electric light. Upon leaving the tunnel of love, the rodents noticed the opaque sky, and a feeling of apprehension overtook them, suggesting either a bad case of collective hypoglycemia caused by the nutritionless gruel which they had been accustomed to eating, or possibly because of an impending doom intuitively outlined by the strange, prior events of the day.

On the hill where the strange apple thermometers were planted, the glass stems began to grow upward toward the night heavens, lengthening and thickening in girth, while the very furthermost tips of the glass blackened to the color of a silky obsidian. These growing, black tips bifurcated and trifurcated, sending out smaller, lateral shoots that curled upwards, with each ultimately solidifying into the form of an outstretched raven's claw, stretching upwards towards the cold night sky that now threatened to deliver a vague, but most likely harsh, evening precipitation. Eventually millions of frozen iceballs fell from the sky. The apple thermometer "plants", with glowing apple seed kernels for roots and grasping ravens' talons in place of flowers, seemed to thrive in this harsh weather. The rooted objects swayed in the wind, while the raven-like talons came alive, groping at the precipitation, snapping at hailstones as they fell. Eventually most of the thermometer plants captured a hailstone, while the lamentable few that didn't slowly withered to the ground and liquefied in the freezing weather, ultimately disappearing into the unhealthy soil.

Simultaneously, and as if these thermometer plants had represented a recently fertilized womb that had just received the proper seed, the lights surrounding the side-show freak cages were turned on, illuminating all of the cages where slept the miserable human and non-human occupants, who had of late suffered within the inhospitable confines of steel bars and low roofs. The cold had smacked them into a state beyond shivering, and their dazed but eager gazes boiled through eyes that refused to close. The human and non-human animals howled with a primal joy, and they grasped at the bars of the cage doors that held them prisoner. In the same way a gallery owner might grasp a painting with both hands and lift it from the wall to the floor, the same was done with the cage doors: the freezing primates grabbed the heavy cage doors, lifted them from the hinge, and leaned them up against the walls of the cages, as if they were exquisite works of art.

The newly liberated animals left their caged enclosures and were immediately stricken on their heads by the onslaught of the hailstones. They cursed and slobbered, with their stale, icy breaths making it difficult for outsiders to see them. Eventually the outsiders did come, immediately lining up among the rusted guard rails separating them from the liberated human and non-human freak-show creatures. These outsiders were just like the average human consumers who frequented the amusement park during better days and nights, except for the fact that they had no facial features (either that or they were wearing tight, nylon flesh-colored stockings over their heads as if they were out to rob banks in bad weather). Both the outsiders and the freak-show creatures were so close to each other, and yet they were separated by a flimsy guard rail. It was as if terrestrial humanity had one foot on each side of the unknown, but no two feet were ever on the same patch of turf. The confusion was immense, and many of the unsettled people cried and whimpered among themselves, while thinking thoughts of gluing cowry shells over their closed eyelids when they went to sleep during the moments when the birds were not watching them.

The rats with the exposed electrodes were very perplexed by the current situation, and they huddled among themselves in order to devise a plan that might bring a sense of calm to the scene of chaos that was unfolding before their eyes, evidenced by the romance of human and non-human carnival beasts in confrontation with the faceless amusement park consumers. The rats donned second-line umbrellas, similar to what might be found in the slimy Mardi Gras streets of New Orleans, and became as one being: they marched and danced in a line along the frozen walkways, approaching the peculiar confrontation between the two hominoid or near-hominoid groups who should have been frozen by now but were not. As rodent hips, shoulders and necks gyrated to an inaudible music (the kind of music that can turn one's legs into a lively anthill filled with hollowed-out passages allowing the transit of sugar-lusting ants), the smallish, rodent umbrellas tilted back and forth according to the rhythm of the rats. The lead rat smiled her coy, knowing smirk, while letting the music push her trusting feet in whatever direction seemed important. All she really did was follow her own footsteps, that lead her and her group ever nearer the frigid confrontation released of late from the liberated freak show. As the two different groups of animals were separated by a guard rail, the rat leader's feet assumed the dance of moving from one world to the next, from night to day and back, or from the tops of mountains to the bottoms of oceans, and vice versa. Of course, her fellow rats followed suit, and their dance became a multidimensional trajectory that led straight to the heart of terrestrial duality, a barbaric but syncopated penetration of the gray areas between night and day, life and death, as well as between the gray lobes of the brain. Despite the movement of planets and the splitting of molecules, the rats maintained their dance, ascending the guard rail and leading the dancing queue on a straight and narrow vector that ran right between the faceless consumers and the slobbering human and non-human freak show exhibitors.

Everyone had to make faces at everyone else; it was impossible not to. Once the grimaces were made between the three groups, the rats continued to dance and groove while the larger humanoid and non-humanoid creatures stared at each other with wonder and latent hostilities, never realizing that both groups of plastic life had originated from the same mold, in the same eternal performance.

It wasn't long before the rats tired of their facial arbitration, and slowly withdrew, like a song that diminishes in loudness as the melody nears its end. After the hip-grooving song, the rats dispersed under the cover of dark objects and structures, and only their glowing red eyes could be seen from time to time.

Suddenly an old, ugly public telephone began to ring. The telephone was covered with a ten-year layer of grime and graffiti, and there were dried pools of piss and vomit in the surrounding area. A baboon with filth and frozen snot around its muzzle answered the phone, coughing blood and mucus onto the receiver and making quite a ruckus. It turned out that the phonecall was from a secret order of control freaks who sold their services for a trivial fee, always offering to interfere in the lives of others with vague prophecy, unsettling bedtime stories and a never-ending barrage of infomercials delivered via telephone calls at strange hours. The baboon was visibly swayed by the call, with its wide eyes filled with visions of redemption and salvation, and that was when its head exploded, covering the payphone and the surrounding area with an inch-thick layer of bloodied brains and snot. While any casual observer might have expected the brains and snot to freeze, in fact the protoplasmic mess instead congealed into a nice arrangement of roman grapes and crimson hibiscus flowers, all neatly covered by a thin but perfectly transparent film of ice. This timely arrangement became a monument to the fine art of commercial communication, with its control-freak qualities, aspects of manipulation of the ego, as well as a caricature of the middle-class hippy movement as it spread underneath an abandoned roman toga, and then suffocated within its own excrement.

This unhappy but necessary transformation cleared the way for passage of great hordes of bearded corpses of faux-friendly mariners who had drowned off the pacific coast of North America, brutally sacrificed by the Ego-Hand as it crushed the Oedipal Aegis. These mariners were now skeletons, having had their bones picked clean of flesh by crabs and other nocturnal scavengers. Their beards were used for anchorage by mussels and other pink bivalves, and their eye-sockets were now home to many a cantankerous sea urchin, ultimately dwelling within the depths of supreme bitterness. Their movements were sluggish, and their rotting, skeletal forms were unpredictable, often falling to the ground in a clatter. Verifying that the control-freak telephone had been destroyed, they muttered to themselves as best they could, lacking vocal chords. In a strange twist of fate, the skeletons of seamen pulled the wet clams from their beards and hopped the fence, in search of young women to re-envelope them in flesh, with their bleached, unfulfilled bones exposed to the cold air for an unbearable eternity.

The mariners were chased by large ships that had been raised from the rocky depths, right off the coast where the amusement park was located. These large ships were like an explosive adam's apple – constituting a grenade that one woke up to find in one's throat, ready to explode with flippant words and romantic imagery hastily scrawled onto a boat that ultimately would end up many miles beneath the ocean. The open sore was thus resurrected, and the captive humans and non-humans who bore witness to this resurrection of the clam-bearded seamen with their pursuant galleons provoked much laughter, in the same way a comedy television show might.

The human and non-human entertainment creatures marveled at this harrowing vision of what the future might hold for them, and they clenched their own fists, checking their resolve to persevere in the face of future shipwrecks, bearded clams, brittle bones and the downtown skeletal dance that sounded like a xylophone, which had spun out of control, twisting the hips of snow-boughed trees who answered their telephones with the letter "Ω". The freak-show animals knew within their hearts that what waited for them ahead might have been a fuzzy red carpet, or possibly just a highway to hell, paved with thumbtacks on which they'd have to step at every inch, or likewise, a trail of hot coals with which to burn their soles into submission, or some other such form of moral imprisonment. The clutter became intolerable. The freak-show animals became ill with the xylophone skeleton music, enraged that they had been forced to watch risen shipwrecks chasing mariners' corpses across the amusement park landscape, with mussels and other pink bivalves clinging to the beards of the dead sailors. The freak-creatures knew that they could have been mariners in another life, or perhaps if they had somehow used positronic karma to switch bodies, resulting in the insane transfer of consciousness. This crisis of consciousness was the thunderstorm temporarily contained inside of a glass breast that had cracked, or perhaps the crisis manifested itself as a walrus whose tusks were made of rotating sections, bejeweled with different quantities of small gems such as rubies, emeralds and diamonds on each facet of the rotating tusk wheels, to denote different numerical values in the opening of a combination lock.

The combination lock popped, resulting in the cylindrical parts of the walrus' tusks flying everywhere. The skull-shaped dice were spilt upon the red carpet, in a regal gesture, while the walrus' mouth – long held shut with silenced secrets – sprang open, revealing a trio of iguanas with roving eyes and many things to say. The body of the walrus became a deflated velvet cloak, flattening itself upon the regal carpet, while the three iguanas grew in stature and confidence, strutting their new legs while thinking of green gems that were locked away in a Salt Manor once committed to the shrines of memory, but now spilled forth like an army tank every bit determined to mulch through the gardens of good manners.

Since the iguanas were fresh off the "boat", it was understandable that they would be fatigued, with one of them lagging slightly behind the other two, forming a neat triangular stance among them. In fact, all of these iguanas were from the same clutch, but genetically non-identical. The straggler was actually the runt of the litter, the last to break out from the shell of its egg, and the last to learn how to read. When one studies how the runt of a litter is treated, it is possible to determine how the species in general treats members of its own kind, not to mention, members of different species. It was quite obvious that the appearance of these three iguanas bespoke a birth to soon take place in triplicate, and under strange and murky auspices, due to the fact that finding literate iguana triplets appearing from deflated walrus cloaks in dismal, urban amusement parks was a rarity in and of itself.

The iguanas were the song of a siren that had yet to appear, but whose voice was heard, nonetheless. While the two strong iguanas yapped and yabbered about their long spiritual journey through the interstices of a locked but regal walrus safe, the runt said nothing, instead sagging within its own footprints, a weak reflection of its own stronger siblings who had what it would never have. The quiet of this weak iguana was brighter than the green emeralds that were its eyes, and the emaciated body of the reptile should have been a keychain that held magical keys made of dark, obsidian glass. This "third iguana" was the only mattress coil that didn't have spring, or possibly an ancient tome of poetic recipes that had no spine. Seeing this third iguana spoiled the nobility of the other two, and this agony of family rivalry and social value based on appearances created the song that most ears pretended not to hear. Initiating a chain reaction, the song interrupted the nearby rodents in their friendly dance as they kept to themselves, causing the rats to groove furiously, piercing the night with rodent shrieks, transcending common dance and common song. The cries from the rats caused much of the paint to fall from the various walls of the decrepit amusement park, revealing the original structures as being those of a bomb-fallout shelter. The light from the song burned out the eyesockets of the human and non-human freak-show animals as they writhed in their indecision, in their moral impotence and utter inability to make choices and have opinions of their own. Finally, the rats could handle no more, and they fled into the night, away from the amusement park, away from the iguanas and the strange hominids, until the first light of day began to peek over the horizon's edge. It was then that the rodents realized "home" was more of a concept than a physicality.

At this moment, as if from an intense dream, the leader of the rats awoke in her bed and then held a mirror in front of her face, thereby seeing that she was no longer a rat but instead a wolf with guitar strings that ran across her limbs, with frets located over all the joints and vertebrae. And no longer was there an ugly electrode protruding from her skull. When she looked out of the window, she began to sing, howling at the sun with musical notes that defied the common octaves of civilized utility. Looking back at the bed, she spied a key made of obsidian, barely hidden beneath the pillow. Its strong glint in the sunlight reminded her of an apple orchard she'd often dreamed of.

Matryoshka.

The Orphans of Saddam Hussein
(3-2007)

A kaleidoscope of hands shot from the cannon, reaching out to lovers who pulled away, scaring away potential mates with the clinging attachments of blindness. The unawareness of not seeing from another's eyes pulled down the shades on the windows, and the bunker with the high-vaulted ceilings was cast in shadow, perhaps in the dust of Pompeii to suffer in the packed corridors of fossilized feelings, like diamonds pressed against sheets of black velvet to be carried away through the aeons, never to see the light of day again.

This special bunker, or perhaps barracks, had many a treasure sealed within its walls, all trimmed nicely with mortar and the reddest of bricks that were made from the local clays that were easily discovered, often exposed within urban streets as well as the most rural of pastures, leading the cows on for a nourishing lick after acid rains had fallen, thanks to the emissions of the nearby factories. These awful factories pulled children away from their homes only to return them there years later as burnt-out husks, with powdered carbon along their brows and thighs. The powdered carbon helped alter the course of evolution, for example in the instance of peppery moths who adapted their colors to the ashen hues of the soot-covered trees, leaching carcinogens into the groundwater and disrupting many a nighttime dance, sending the youth screaming in all directions because of the many hands that reached out at them from the shadows of banks.

But life went on, and the evil eye of the kaleidoscope aimed in many a direction, changing lives, changing the course of history (of course assuming that there was no predetermined myth of "Progress" like some dimwits would choose to believe) with shrieks and laughter, and putting the fiery remains of stuffed owls above each and every fireplace or even next to the hearth, where those nocturnal wings might peel away from the body in an effort to lunge over the dark urban landscape, peeling teeth from gums like the wallpaper of haunted mansions can creak away from the old walls in concert, like well-trained voices that served as birds of prey, waiting to move through the urban forest in a wraith-like parade.

On the subject of parades, Saddam Hussein was driving his flashy, state-sponsored convertible down a busy California street. The top of the convertible was down, so that any sniper could dispatch him quite easily with but a single shot. However, it appeared that nobody was aiming at Saddam on that day. Traffic whizzed by at a boring, usual pace, and Saddam drove his car close to the side of the highway, noticing that there were many parked cars that day. He expected to catch up to members of his military cavalcade (as he was fully dressed in military gear), but after a few blocks of cruising the otherwise normal streets, he encountered the parked vehicles of his unit. Upon the roof of each vehicle were abandoned munitions, like guns and magazine clips, and even a sizeable stash of grenades. Car after car, with markings of Saddam's personal guard, showed signs of hasty dereliction, and on the top of each vehicle were piles of discarded weapons. These weapons were freshly deposited, revealing that they had been assembled as such and then quickly left for all to see, only minutes before. Saddam Hussein looked this way and that, smirking and clean-shaven, and quite youthful and arrogant. He continued to drive until he reached his destination: a well-guarded fortress that once served as the town library.

This was the place where knowledge was carefully guarded. Liberalism became a mantra, with enforced memories and consciousness-scanning measures being taken and implemented at every corridor. Bookshelves that once held autobiographies, documentaries and historical photo albums were now removed, and useless crates of miniature televisions were kept instead. These archaic treasures had eventually been replaced by wireless monitors, but their physical hulks were kept in the library fortress. Saddam Hussein continued with his tour of the place, noticing the recently polished bricks held together by strong concrete whose outer surfaces had been recently bleached. The dictator entered an adjoining hallway to admire his jewel collections, also neatly packed within miniature crates, just like the televisions were. All of these material valuables were sometimes the cause of other men's deaths, but definitely the products of human exploitation, and now they were hoarded within the converted library. These "blood televisions" and "blood gems" implied much monetary value and were the result of human as well as environmental suffering (assuming that humans and "the environment" were to be distinguished as separate entities).

Saddam sat down upon an elegant velvet chair that served as a throne, and he watched the security cameras, just to make sure that none of his California workers were trying to steal from him. Suddenly, a fire broke out on the North end of the library-vault, and quickly spread to most of the facility. While the brick walls managed to remain intact, the wooden ceiling caught flames and collapsed in many areas, creating a labyrinth of hot coals within the maze of destroyed material goods. If the labyrinthine killzone had been an oven, then most of the occupants of the building quickly burned to death in a maze of unknowns. Saddam was among the dead. While people were overcome by the flames, their screams carried over the roar of the fire. Some people tried to climb over the high brick walls into cooler, non-burning areas by way of safety ropes which their friends tried to help them with from the other side of the walls, but to no avail: many of the burn victims had ascended to the top of the hot oven bricks, only to fall back into the burning areas with a scream. It was speculated that Saddam Hussein met such a fate, although not his nor anyone else's body was ever recovered after the flames had been extinguished.

Surveying the wreckage, the fire teams picked through mounds of half-burning ash, recovering only the ends of engorged kaleidoscopes, with charred hands poking through most of them. Out of all that the library contained: jewels, electronic devices, furniture, people, etc., it was completely amazing that only the burnt kaleidoscopes were recovered. In order to better understand the catastrophe, scientists were summoned, who took samples, recovering only the most intact of the human kaleidoscopes, soaking the best samples in embalming fluids and sample vials. In one particularly well-preserved specimen, a foot-long kaleidoscope with green and silver stripes floated limply within the preservative fluids, almost drifting in place within the container. Limp human-like hands emerged from each end of the kaleidoscope – hands that had probably spent many an hour searching for love and other consumables that were now no longer possible. This particular kaleidoscope had vague scorch marks along the length of the cylinder, making even the most astute of observers wonder how anyone at all might be able to view the tunneling, radial, symmetrical delights offered by such a groping kaleidoscope, especially under strange weather conditions, when visibility was low, obscuring one's chances for witnessing instances of love and other, random acts of kindness. The hands of the kaleidoscope now remained limp and lifeless, and they were nothing but a bouquet of dead flowers that cruelly emerged from the well-used cylinder.

A nearby scientist took off his glasses slowly and dramatically in order to address the inspector who presided over the recovery operation. In no less dramatic terms, the scientist breathed deeply and then recounted the misery that all of the occupants and merchandise (kaleidoscopes, included) most likely had endured in their final hours, when the fiery roof collapsed and everyone and everything baked to death within the embers: First, the spreading of the fire from unknown sources – possibly from a discarded cigarette, or from a woman's lipstick that was just too hot to stay within her mirror, or perhaps a meltdown of some of the electronics equipment. Any one or more of these scenarios was plausible, and perhaps there were even other causes of the conflagration that were not even considered within the commonly accepted rationalistic framework. And then, once the fire did establish itself, it quickly spread by climbing a few of the wooden supports, turning the old wood instantly to glowing embers that would fall like molten totem poles, in a manner such as the passing of judgment on the unfaithful, or those who did not believe in the supremacy of the powers that be, which in this case were Newtonian physics as well as Saddam Hussein. The scientist paused at this moment, first putting his glasses back on his pale, sweaty face, and then immediately taking them off again in his characteristically dramatic way, elaborating that the wooden ceiling that covered the entirety of the establishment, with a neat and clever networking system of connecting rafters, was unable to resist being consumed by the flames. This rafter system was once created so as to allow book enthusiasts in the library to climb out of their reading room of choice and to quickly return to the stacks, where they might pull their favorite volumes with a higher level of convenience. But when Saddam took over the municipal library, and put it in the service of his own dubious self-interests, the rafters overhead became walkways of treachery, where prisoners who might "walk the plank" to their doom would really just cross from one pirate ship to the next, since the planks were positioned laterally. In this way, both prisoners and moles within Hussein's California regime might cross over from room to room by the wooden pathways that were so close to the ceiling. It turned disastrous once these walkways caught fire, because the ceiling network of Saddam Hussein turned into an upside-down Barbeque, creating a rain of coals that burned everyone underneath to death. The dramatic scientist explained that the precipitation of the coals, in their act of falling, was really like a snowball or perhaps hailstorm from hell, and to be in a room with falling coals must have been like being in a negativistic skiing resort where everything had been turned upside-down. Such motion of both hot and cold precipitation suggested circularity, and hence the entrance of the human kaleidoscopes. The main question that remained, thought the dramatic scientist out loud to himself, was whether or not the kaleidoscopes stuffed with human hands materialized before the deluge of pyrotechnics, or afterwards. There was of course the temptation to correlate the appearance of the coals with the human kaleidoscope hands, leading to the hypothesis that somehow human kaleidoscope hands are attracted to burning embers, in the way some people like to walk over hot coals. The dramatic scientist put his wiry glasses back on and took a step backward, realizing that not enough data existed at the moment to support the idea that the human kaleidoscopes with the reaching hands had any probable inclinations towards thermotaxis, positively or negatively.

Meanwhile, the children of the survivors wet their pants, and while they looked at the crumpled, burning remains of the architectural structure of refinement and authority, they began to urinate, feeling the hot piss steadily trickle down their legs and make the crotch area of their pants become soaked with emotion. Under the feet of each of the survivor children appeared a warm, steaming puddle of urine. The children immediately looked up to the singed walls for willing showerheads, but there were no established dispensers of water, hot or cold, with which to rinse their emotional limbs. Somehow all of the children, of various ages – toddler through teenager – believed that by standing still and refusing to walk away or anywhere else, that they could stop the world, all with a defiant trickle of urine.

Before leaving the scene of the accident, all of the children, those who lost as well as those who retained their parents, searched within the rubble for more of the remaining human-handed kaleidoscopes. The scorched cylinders firmly grasped within each of their juvenile hands had dangling from both ends the wilted arms of miniature humans. Perhaps these protruding arms were made of plastic or perhaps wood, or metal, or? It was unknown if these arms were organic, even. The only thing that the children did know was that these malleable arms dangling from the kaleidoscope cylinders were *real*.

The children, now orphans (and a few half-orphans) were herded into a school bus that was painted grey. The people who directed the children onto the bus were from the orphanage (and a few from the half-orphanage, up the street from the regular orphanage). Each of the adults took off their wire-rimmed spectacles, and in a serious voice asked all of the orphans and half-orphans to take their seats. After this request, the religious orphanage directors put their spectacles back on, and assumed their own seats in the front of the bus. The trip from the burnt-out library fortress to the orphanage was uneventful, and there were no signs of Saddam Hussein or his henchmen anywhere along the road. And all of the discarded weaponry that had been visible in the time before the fire had now been completely removed, without a trace. The orphans were surprisingly calm, given that their parents had been incinerated only hours before. Grief counselors were standing by, but their services were apparently not needed, as the children retained their composure and focused on the little things in life that all other normal children like, such as frogs, jam pies, raggedy dolls and forestry uniforms made of cloth.

Upon their arrival at the orphanage, the half-orphans were separated from the others and then ushered up the street to the half-orphanage, where they were never seen again. Meanwhile, the orphans were ushered into the ramshackle mansion that was to be their new home. Aside from a few leaky areas on the roof and glum walls that needed a new coat of paint, the place was far from inhabitable. The children were segregated according to age and sex, into different wards and floors of the spacious mansion. During mealtimes and certain important moments during the day, all orphans would assemble in the main hall, which was next to the dining room. After being allowed to settle in, arranging whatever little belongings that now remained to these recent orphans, all the children were summoned downstairs by way of an obnoxious siren and some rotating red and blue strobe lights that always shone in conjunction with the piercing blasts of the siren. These obnoxious lights and horns were placed in each and every room of the house, so as to help maintain the tether of obedience.

Once assembled in straight lines in front of a large dais where the parochial keepers and enforcers of the orphanage were standing, the children held their breaths with unpleasant expectation, as they now had to listen to the dreaded arrival speech that was to inform them of the profound change in direction that their lives were now taking, perhaps down a graying corridor of peeling paint, hopefully to a happy existence, but most likely not, given the stern and cruel grimaces that crossed the faces of the orphanage personnel. Those adults who now controlled the lives of the orphaned children were indeed uptight, tense, unhappy and downright moronic, in their adherence to their "programs for the future" and other such nonsense.

The girls were taught how to sew, bake bread, wash clothes and get pregnant. They were also taught how to take orders from men, and that the usage of birth control was bad, and not to be respected in the slightest. The boys, too, were taught practical life skills, such as how to take orders from their bosses, how to work with power tools, pay taxes and to beat their wives, and inseminate them, too. Of course, none of these boys were married, so they practiced using raggedy, gray female mannequins that had been brought in especially for these tasks. While all of the rules were followed and obeyed, over the following months, the children felt the glimmer in their eyes begin to dwindle, and many of them realized that a rebellion was in order.

They waited until a certain day, the first Friday before the end-of-year winter festival. They plotted and planned the target day during their quiet study hours and during mealtimes and also when they were supposed to be in bed. No notes were written, only vague hopes and aspirations passed from mouth to mouth until a certain cold and grimy day was decided upon by an informal consensus, right before the holidays. Although they had no concrete, tactical plans, they knew that somehow they would put an end to the life that they had at the orphanage. While there were certainly worse places to be, the children were still unhappy where they were, being constantly called "ungrateful" and "disobedient" by the school masters and mistresses. At least one person in each classroom was beaten every day, limping away from the scene with bruises and black eyes. And there were only so many exercises in obedience that young, fertile minds and bodies could take, and therefore, due to the extraordinary circumstances that brought these youth to the orphanage, and due to their less than loving treatment there, it was impossible for the children to do anything other than rebel. And rebel they did.

On the eve of the rebellion, some of the more determined children wasted their study hours in the large library on the second floor, looking for the lost desks that had been barricaded behind some of the unused shelves in the back. Pushing aside the old shelves, some of the older children located the desks, while the younger orphans created a distraction that was big enough to keep the orphanage faculty completely occupied. Those that had uncovered the desks read the scratched etchings left behind by students from countless generations ago, using feeble flashlights to read about such topics as "I hate algebra", or "Sister Margeaux stinks!" and other dull academic themes. Eventually the desired information was found on a rickety desk buried beneath the others. The desk was small and very damaged from past collisions and from bearing the weight of the other desks on top of it. The top of the desk had many love notes, such as "Bill loves Sarah" etched perhaps with a small pocketblade or whatever rare objects of required sharpness that previous students could commandeer. But toward the upper left edge of the desk, inconspicuously carved into the side, began the incantation that would most likely lead them to their freedom: "*When the urine flows freely and the special night draws nigh, push the slipp'ry key into the soft eye of the pie!*"

The orphans turned these phrases over and over in their heads that night, while pretending to be asleep. During the night they had half-dreams of the half-orphans who showed them the way back to their families, by clearing away paths through a huge classroom choked with archaic, factory-produced desks and chairs from the earlier part of the previous century. The students watched their half-orphan brothers and sisters remove some of the dusty school furniture, in order to clear a path through the room. Some of the paths were dead-ends, as would be expected in one of those tricky, unhappy academic labyrinths. The key was to form a chain of hands so that the students could all keep track of one another as they groped about in the dark, exploring this or that fork in the path which, often enough, ended up revealing yet more dead-ends. Along the way, there were several intact desks positioned conspicuously, covered with books opened to various, potentially useful pages, possibly serving as clues. Some of the brighter students leaned forward to read the clues lit by eerie candlelight, ignoring the smears of blood and rust that covered the floor from the dragging of the desks. There was one book which showed a giant lizard creature with a pink, cottony mouth that opened along a vertical axis, much like a vagina. This book was quickly put away upon the closest shelf. And then another book from antiquity showed a labyrinth composed of well-shorn shrubs in a vast backyard garden. From the picture, it looked like the kind of green maze that might delight an outdoor enthusiast, but for anyone who was claustrophobic, even this flowery outdoor construction was restrictive. This volume was also placed on a nearby shelf. A third volume contained some erotic etchings of nuns who had rug burns on their knees and were depicted from various angles. The children looked at this latter tome very carefully, and then quietly whispered among themselves about where they would go next. In a way, the decision was made for them the moment one of the friars walked through the front door, leaving them no choice but to flee through the back exit. The priest advanced upon them with a kindly smile that reminded one of some cloyingly sweet syrup that one might add to any of the commercially available mouthwashes for sale in drugstores. Suddenly, the sweet smile almost dropped off the priest's jaw in the way tender, overcooked meat falls from the bones of stewed animals, being replaced with a malevolent leer that stretched across his well-shorn face like a mocking scar. The priest could think of nothing but the pleasures of controlling others, as he walked past a banner strung upon the wall that read: "There is no I in team". The priest raised his arms to begin hitting the children, while simultaneously the red and blue police lights were activated, accompanied by the wailing of the police klaxon. The calmness of the morning had thereby been punctuated by these harsh sounds and strobe lights of fascism.

Immediately, the children dropped their trousers and began to urinate on the cold floor of the library, all at once. They wanted to stop the world and make time stand still. The hot urine burned the cold stone floor, releasing patches of misty steam, and the cathartic release afforded by the urination caused the sinister friar with the sneering face to become petrified, as if he had become an impotent mannequin.

The students, now unified as one organism and completely determined to get away from this insipid "learning center," passed by the ossified priest and immediately burst through the rear entrance of the library, pouring down the flight of stairs to the ground floor, where they all knew they would soon view the exit door that would let them escape from this horrible place. At the moment the children were ready to leave, the nuns and friars were just sitting down to their daily breakfast, which always included waffles with sweet maple syrup, fresh berries, fried eggs and especially long and thick breakfast sausages. By way of shameful contrast, the children were always fed a very watery oatmeal gruel, with a boiled egg on every second Sunday, and this difference was cause for much resentment on the part of the students. The teachers rose from their breakfast plates to punish the youth, who were in plain view through the opened doors of the refectory, but they were overpowered by the sheer numbers of student-orphans. The children found some rope and commanded the teachers to remain standing while their crooked, teacherly hands were tied to their scholarly ankles. Then the students lowered the trousers and skirts of the teaching staff, and then shoved the long, breakfast sausages (which happened to be very peppery) deep into the unwilling rectums of each and every faculty member. Shortly thereafter, the youth ran away, never to be seen again by the prying eyes of friars and nuns. Some of the braver friars attempted to hop around, while still filled with the ugly sausages, trying to free each other, but to no avail. Others simply resigned themselves to their situation, and fell over with a thud. The teachers were stuck as they were until the police finally arrived hours later to find them completely bent over and still thoroughly violated by the gigantic meat sausages. By that point, the children had been long gone, and left no physical traces of their flight away from the orphanage-school. They were determined never to return that way in the future, and hoped that there would never be the need to set eyes on the objects of their holy sodomy ever again.

It was nightfall when the children stopped to rest, hiding along the side of one of the country roads leading away from the city in which they had spent an immeasurable amount of time, at the oppressive orphanage. They knew that they were headed towards another city, but couldn't even guess when and where they might arrive at their unknown destination. Their flight was an improvisation along dusty highways, where cups of tea were spilled like tears over the burning embers of campfires that would keep the children warm during the course of the night. There was nothing for the children to consume except for each other's company, so for a while, the nourishment of friendship was all that was needed to sustain their heavily fragmented and disrupted lives. That night the children slept next to their drenched campfires, away from the clutches of truant officers and other civil servants who would not hesitate to use them for their own selfish purposes. While each child slept, the feathers from several nightingales fell from the trees where the birds roosted overhead, quickly dropping onto the foreheads of the sleeping children. The orphans did not stir, and their dreams took a more somber direction, away from the glistening gemstones that their unconscious minds had become obsessed with during their very first states of sleep. In an uncanny display of synchronous dreaming, the children's psyches simultaneously turned from fields of sparkling crystalline roads to the more shadowed visions of muddy dwellings that were occupied by river people who couldn't understand the color patterning of tropical birds, but who did know of the specificity of keys within door locks, so as to ensure that each key had its very own lock, without any need for overlap or sharing. The redundancy of foreheads that were touched by frost led the tired river people to lean against the frozen glass windows of the hovels that lined the toxic shoreline, allowing their foreheads to become cold. The result was transparent headaches that lasted for aeons. When the foreheads froze against the glass, it allowed not just the transparency of the window, but also of the head pressed against the window. This ease of vision was no more common than an over-reliance on spectacles, which some of the river people hesitantly pulled from their faces when they had profound things to say (which wasn't all that often anyway, however). But the lostness of living next to a toxic river, and waiting for one's baggage to float by, proved to be just too much pressure for some, so that the afflicted individuals had to rely on their friends and neighbors to help them pull their baggage from the polluted river. These visions of perdition, and waiting, and being forgotten, grew to such intense and amplified proportions that the sleeping children quickly woke up from this dream, with a dull ache above their foreheads, a certain kind of itchy, achiness that affected their eyeballs as well, making them feel dry and restless.

The orphans scratched their heads and slapped their groggy, malnourished skulls against the trunks of the trees under which they sat, trying to shake off the stupor of nightmare sleep. Somehow they knew that they might become the terrified river-dwelling people they observed in their collective dream, forever clinging to their toxified possessions and other emotional baggage being carried away by a polluted river that passed by many a factory run by people who had no respect for nature. Therefore the children felt attracted to and yet also repelled by the water. As they mused over these cerebral developments, a babbling creek not very far away reminded them that they could never completely get away from the water, and that to try to do so would not only be a waste of effort, but also futile. Fortunately, however, the orphans did not spend much time considering the flight-from-water possibility. In fact, they embraced the clear streams of the wilderness, since the water from these outdoor sources was far superior to the mineralized sludge that came from the orphanage faucets.

Over the course of the days that followed, the homeless orphans felt their heads clear from the debilitating mist of the rationalist, utilitarian discipline with which their supposed mentors had imparted to them during their imprisonment within the orphanage institution. In their mind's eye, the youth could even imagine the large structure of the building as it crumbled away from living reality, fast moving towards obsolescence, with peeling paint, aging corridors and layers of dust that obscured everything that was miserable about the place – every last inch of space under that oppressive roof. What wasn't good for the corporation was most likely good for the individual, and so the children felt a certain cheeriness about their days, despite the absence of whatever material advantages they might have had within the orphanage. What good were deodorizing soaps, anyway?

On one bright morning soon after their escape, the youth began to remember that their dramatic escape had happened soon before the winter holiday season, when people burned candles, hung shiny objects from trees, ate and drank to excess, and participated in guilt-driven programs designed to create a false and fleeting sense of community and love. Usually the spirit of these contrived, religious-driven, "team-building" activities would evaporate within a week, but at least for a few days, or perhaps even for only a few hours, the most naive of the observers of these religious holidays were able to construct around themselves an illusion of global serenity, with no fighting, no deception, no dishonesty, no exploitation, no abuse and no murder. In place of these awful, mundane staples were the ideals of laissez-faire love, cooperation, mutual respect, contentment, and utter, idiotic bliss. Most people, sheep that they were, bought into these illusions every year, as a way of systematically avoiding reality for a few days, or perhaps, a few hours. The orphaned children, however, knew better than to yearn for feelings and ceremonies that were only illusion, and of course, cruelly untrue. So instead of trying to make their reality into some red and green, sparkly, otherworldly experience, they contented themselves with being alive and, most importantly, not being under anyone's thumb. Therefore, instead of hanging ornaments from snow-covered pine trees, or burning special candles and reciting prayers, the children played: they climbed trees, threw snowballs at each other, and sang songs with their arms. The music that came from their fingers did not hide from the civilization that had ravaged the countrycide; instead it simply complimented it as a stark reminder of the kinds of rodents that might inhabit a mulberry bush when a new society is being created underfoot. Therefore the children did believe in the myth of the transformation, where they became more than the sum of their parts, capable of evolving, rather than being forced to play a role that had been determined for them, before they were even born.

And so the winter holiday passed quite peacefully, and memories of the horrible parochial orphanage receded within their mental landscapes, leading to a brighter outlook on life, and a renewed ambition to create a better existence.

On one particularly snowy day, one of the girls found a miniature costume outside of her tent, where she and the others were camping out at the base of the mountain. The tiny costume looked as if it belonged to a frog; in fact, the clothing, cut ever so delicately and with a great level of detail and sophistication, had the appearance of the entire outer skin of a frog. In truth, the children who saw it had a difficult time imagining who or what could fit into such a tiny costume, and their perplexity was heightened when a blast of arctic air moved through their camp, reminding them that this was not the time of year for frog-friendly weather. The children were blinded by the cold, causing them to bump into each other for lack of emotional direction. The icicles that glittered from the windowsills of a nearby town beckoned to the blind children. When they could see again, the snow had melted, and they were all assembled in front of the town hall, which looked completely run down and deserted. There was no sign of life anywhere. The children searched from house to house, navigating through fields of wooden obstacles and barbed wire, until they made their way to the community center of the town. The community center was supposed to be where all of the town's residents would congregate for social activities, information sharing and lowdown gossip. As it turned out, the center was the place where the townspeople were found huddled as a group, for some reason afraid to return to their abandoned houses. In particular, the gymnasium of the center was converted to a church, with its high ceiling and large panes of glass altered to look more like the kind of church that all civilized, god-fearing people would come to expect. The basketball hoops in the gym were used for ritual execution, and the large scoreboard that resided above the bleachers had been decorated to look like a crucifixion shrine. Over the area where the "home" and "visitor" scores were posted, was placed a life-sized representation of a crucifixion, in particular a crucifixion of a humanoid ape with a radioactive symbol conspicuously placed on the creature's forehead. It was uncertain if this was an actual mummified creature, or just some kind of artificial construction. In this new "church", the townspeople were afraid, and they regarded the presence of the children as a satanic dawning of enlightenment, although they could not understand the specifics of the children's arrival.

In the Olympic-sized swimming pool, which had been drained of all water long ago, the children assembled with some of the other townspeople, all wearing the kind of fancy clothes especially suited to formal dance. The quality-tailored fabrics contrasted with the cracked cement of the swimming pool, with its rust stains and grimy porcelain tiles. Everyone danced, while conversing with each other simultaneously. The townspeople spoke to the children of the Company, describing its ability to give them purpose in life – to give them things to do on the weekdays and weekends – and how quickly their sense of self-esteem became dependent on a perpetual cycle of alienated labor. The bright noon-day sun shone through the filthy windows, providing diffuse illumination for the dancing people, showing off their expensive clothes. Eventually the visiting orphans grew bored with the dancing and meaningless small-talk, and they ascended the large concrete steps that led to the main level of the gym, with its strange, church-like aura of hopelessness. After leaving the gym and the cheerless dancefloor that was once the swimming pool, the orphans decided that the community center of this strange town was not for them. Although they had half-thoughts of making the place their "home" or permanent residence, they thought it was odd that the people who did inhabit this strange, cold town would prefer to reside in one, tightly confined area rather than sleep in their own beds, in their own houses.

"We live for the Company, we die for the Company", said the sign on the wall.

In their heart of hearts, the children knew that the cloistered townspeople would not want them to leave, and might in fact even interfere with their attempt to leave. This prediction turned out to be true. Some of the townspeople, especially the older, hairier ones, had colorful birds that landed on their grubby sleeves and carried pieces of string that were used to tie together yarn used for knitting sweaters. The string was then braided together, effectively creating a webbing that blocked all of the exiting passageways that led to the streets outside of the community center, now converted to a sort of mysterious fallout shelter. Strange priests appeared at all the exits, and the heads of ravens poked out from their malnourished, chapped mouths. Instead of the priests being able to speak, their words became the metaphorical exclamations of the ravens, with a blood-gurgling reticence that bespoke the kind of pessimism that would make one stay in bed all day rather than going out to seek one's fortune (or escape). The chaos that ensued broke all of the glass for that day, such that there would be no more glass for the next several days. This loss of glass enraged the townspeople, who felt that the visiting orphans had become ingrates, and effectively, their property should be contained, manipulated and used in whatever ways they desired. This conflict of interest caught the eyes of the colorful birds that were still perched on the unkempt sleeves of the priest-citizens, and they flew into the air and out through the broken windows into the inner courtyard of the community center. Contained within this courtyard were the skeletons of their ancestors, gathered together as a pile of corpses from the last community celebration, but now hiding behind a decade's worth of neglect and suppressed feelings. Such was the inner sanctum of the Company.

This peculiar abandonment prompted a curious effort on the part of the community citizens: a displaced, obsessive desire to own the young orphans who happened upon their dim civilization on any average day of oblivious neglect. Assembled out on the inner courtyard of the community center, both orphans and citizens confronted each other, with each side presenting reasons for and against the orphans' departure from the mutated settlement. The Chief Financial Officer of the homely town observed that the children would have no future if they were to leave, suggesting that they and they alone were able to give the youth a steady supply of tomorrows, as if such promises could be easily converted to canned goods through quantifiable means. Some of the older youth responded that they did not want their efforts to live be reduced to someone else's objects. And then the Chief Executive Officer of the settlement replied that their outward appearances were more important than what they had under their skin, and that through remaining with the Urban Apocalyptic Order (as they now called themselves), the children might learn how to harness the esteem of their neighbors and to use such esteem to their own selfish advantages. To this suggestion the children indicated that were less interested in how things look versus how things really *are*. The various members of the Urban Apocalyptic Order frowned and advanced upon the small throng of displaced orphans, curling and uncurling their lips around their teeth in menacing gestures. Apparently, the apocalyptic residents were quite good at making threatening gestures with their lips, because they had the young orphans quite scared. Some of the younger children began to cry, and it was at this moment that the body of young refugees slowly backed away from the corporate, apocalyptic throng and moved into the gymnasium, where they participated in the cement pool dance only moments before. They pushed even further to the other end of the gym, squeezing through administrative buildings, with the townspeople following very closely behind them, like a pack of nagging insects or relatives, or a combination of these two latter groups. Upon the edge of the apocalyptic community center, the orphaned children broke into a run, cursing the subconscious foundations of adulthood, authority and other symbols of social repression, all of which had been embedded within the collective psyche over the course of the centuries. They had little time to witness all of the abandoned houses on their way out of town, swiftly passing all of the picnic tables, playground swings, and once-manicured backyards of tightly-knit nuclear families. When the children finally left town, they were chased by the apocalyptic adults, who bitterly threw plastic masks at them, as their young legs carried them out of town never to be seen again.

As if they were small bugs treading ever so carefully out onto a dangerous spider's web, the orphans were more careful about the cities and towns they visited thereafter. Some places greeted them with a cheerful apathy, while others presented them with gestures and acts of pure hostility. It was indeed difficult living in the civilized world. Some of the children died along the way, while others got married.

During the early summer, the children had been traveling through a more rural area, but which bordered on the outskirts of a city. As they approached closer and closer to the city, they knew that their chances for finding a pristine, intimate place to squat decreased. Very soon they would be forced to set up camp at whatever secluded field they could find. Within a half hour, such a location was found. Nestled between some boulders and evergreen trees was a small clearing covered with fallen pine needles, with some evidence of past habitation, such as a collection of old beer bottles and a blackened ring of stones once used as a campfire. Since they had recently acquired some second-hand tents normally used for camping (from a discount store), the kids rejoiced at finding a place where they could sleep without being harassed by police and abusive citizens. Within the hour, the flames of a cheery fire could be seen rising and falling within the fire pit. Some of the children stayed to tend the fire while others ventured out into the nearby hills to find firewood and perhaps some wild berries. Traveling along the road, the party of children happened across a drain vent that had been blocked by branches from the previous flood. Receiving closer inspection, the mass of tree limbs and twigs that was blocking the sewer grating seemed also to contain the limp forms of cylindrical tubing. In particular, the tubular forms were none other than some damp kaleidoscopes, the same kind of kaleidoscopes the orphans discovered on the day their parents were killed by the fire in the Saddam Hussein vault: Each kaleidoscope was covered with the same green and silver stripes, and miniature human arms protruded from each end of the special cylinder. Although it was difficult to peer through the tube, due to the presence of the arms, it was possible to get a sparse glint of diffuse, fractured color, verifying that those kaleidoscopes were in fact real. But the kaleidoscopes by the drain were limp from the dampness that comes from supernatural stormwater, and not only were the cylindrical bodies of the kaleidoscopes flaccid, but the tiny arms were in the same sorry state. Upon picking up the entire collection of human kaleidoscopes, the children felt as if the spontaneity of their lives was reinforced a hundredfold. Each kaleidoscope was just one tree in a forest of many trees, and the variety that they had found within that first five minutes of serendipitous searching put a lit match to a fuse that lead to whatever unknown chain reaction lurking behind all of the corners of the future. Perhaps a little square, but this development was a city called Atlantis that was raised to the surface thanks to an earthquake, allowing the writing on the walls to once again see the daylight, rather than being submerged in primordial liquids exposed to the algae of time that would bury it under soft fronds of slimy obscurity.

The children found a mythical basket under a nearby tree, and placed all of the human kaleidoscopes into it. The weight of the basket was heavier than might have been expected, as each of the kaleidoscopes was not entirely hollow on the inside, perhaps filled with water, but then maybe with something else. The small party of children forgot all about firewood and wild berries, and lugged their prize back to the campsite. Those who tended the fire were indeed surprised to witness such a splendid find: a strangely ornate wicker basket filled to the brim with damp human kaleidoscopes, completely identical to the ones found at the scene of the fire that killed their parents. It had been almost a year since the tragedy, and yet it seemed like much longer.

By now the orphans had settled around the fire not only to stare into the flames in search of visions, but also to witness the revitalizing of the soaked kaleidoscopes, which had now been gently arranged on top of the warm stones surrounding the fire pit. Over time, the human kaleidoscopes dried out and seemed to crackle sporadically, as the small arms that emerged from each of the cylindrical ends began to sway, steadily increasing in the level of animation. Eventually the kaleidoscopes looked as healthy as they might have once been (although really, the orphans had never seen such healthy, animate ones as they did now). Their tiny arms seemed to sway in unison, as if some fast breeze were washing over the surfaces of the objects. Some of the children picked up the kaleidoscopes and attempted to stare at the fire through them. The small, moving arms of the kaleidoscopes seemed to avoid poking the viewers in their eyes. Within minutes of becoming comfortable watching the kaleidoscopically rotating flames of the campfire, the orphans had a collective vision which brought them to their senses. They saw flying saucers travelling to earth, with extraterrestrials inside who directed some of the spacecraft to land in more remote areas of the world. What the aliens would actually do on the planet was anyone's guess. Upon seeing this vision and confirming this moment of synchrony among themselves, the orphans began to relax, turning they closed eyes towards sleep.

Later that night, they dreamed of various things: gardens with plants made of metal, and the gutted cabins of spaceships that had crashed into the eroded mountains of desert planets. Inside one of the wrecked spaceships was a terrestrial feline who slunk around the control panels, periodically stopping to listen for signs of other life. The animal would hide among file cabinets and instrument panels, waiting for something to happen, in the same way a trapdoor spider might wait for juicy prey to pass by its hovel. As the collective dream progressed, the terrestrial feline realized that all of the spaceship cabins were really the connected cars of an underground train, perhaps forgotten along the tracks. The cat tore apart several broomsticks that it found along the length of the train. From the wreckage of these emerged a few violent gorillas with rayguns, but the latter were eventually subdued with a few sharp blows to the kidneys and ribs. The gorillas were downed, and the twilight shimmering of an ugly urban landscape materialized around the trapdoor feline. Chain-link fences were erected out of thin air, creating another maze for the bloodied animals to navigate.

The sleeves of the wizard's robe rose from the ashes of the chain-link fences, releasing many fermented rodents, who greeted the bloodied feline with a gnashing of teeth and high-pitched squealing. The night was never the same again. When the night woke up the next morning, it realized that it had the handful of orphans tucked within its dark, opaque cloak, sleeping peacefully as if dreams had never crossed the threshold of closed doors. The shuttered windows were unblinded, and the rays of morning light were a supreme attractant for visiting space aliens. The vehicles of the aliens were parked so closely together that the park in which the orphans had been sleeping now became an overpacked dishwasher filled with the cups, plates and saucers of alien life-forms.

It should not have been a surprise that the aliens wanted to abduct the orphans, because their absence would not have been noticed due to a lack of parental and authoritative figures. But the orphaned youth protested, instead giving the aliens surrational reasons for why they should remain on earth, rather than simply acquiescing to the infantile demands of the aliens. Instead, the youth sat around the campfire, drinking their morning coffee and reading the local newspapers. They invited the aliens to sit with them, and spent the day teaching the extra-terrestrials how to carve hollow compartments into the inner pages of useless bibles, so that they might be able to hide their important contraband within the inner, sacred chambers of the hallowed books.

The lost children yawned, and they unanimously decided that THEY were going to abduct the extra-terrestrials, and force them to travel with them. It would only follow that the children would gain control of the alien spaceships, and be able to go anywhere they liked.

Spider

(6-2007)

Round and round the magic escalator flew, moving the footprints of keynotes into shuffles, pushing the alligator fingers into marred placentas. The escalators would always move, and their simulated piano keys would always make noise. It was no wonder that each of the escalators would ascend into the waving loops of finely burnished wooden housing, or perhaps descend into an inky blackness of couch leather, with a light sprinkling of dust that would periodically fall from the ceiling. In this manner, the escalation of music created the house, and the house in turn created a sense of gravity, where up was up and down was down. The mystery of the house was always there, always reincarnated whether by probing fingers or splinters of kinetic ice. The violence of such spontaneous domestication might have been analogous to a form of mental abuse, but then it also might have been the travel of a mighty train across well-managed tracks leading to the percussion of a radioactive island, on the outskirts of the world of houses.

In one particular instance, the comfortable woodenness of a house might lead to the dirty Mormon secrets that were to be found behind the house, in an oversized lake-like puddle in which a few near-habitable islands were found. One of the islands rose barely above the others, with sandy, industrial-stained mud quickly masking the footprints of recent visitors, as the foul waters lapped the shores while the sun set. The motion of the dark lake waters was in stark contrast with the glow of radioactive travesty that peeked through the interior dwellings of the island, all nearly shielded by government-issue plastic tarpaulins that were used ever so pathetically in the attempt to mask the radioactivity. In the core of this "island" was really a grounded barge that had long lost the ability to float. The walls of the vessel had disintegrated, hence necessitating the shielding provided by the tarps. From room to room of this decaying barge were the remains of bookshelves, scientific apparatuses, and cheap furniture, sending out an eerie glow of loneliness onto the flooded beds of surrounding mud and sand with nothing but the stench of partially burned diesel.

The grounded barge was in contradiction with the house, and frequent excursions between house and barge were strikingly similar to the musical escalators that formed the poetic backbone of the house. The journey between these disparate outposts was a long and lonely one despite the insultingly short distance between the two. One was always easily within view of the other, and yet the distance was an infinity of heartbreak.

On one particular evening, after the sonic escalators had finished their rhythmic up and down momenta, the sandy-haired and thoroughly wizened caretaker of the house paused in his rocking-chair and brushed the ceiling dust from his thinning hair. He recalled the safety of the house in which he resided, and then pondered a distant dream of a luscious witch who revealed to him a palm-sized ceramic tile on which the chiseled features of a house were clearly visible in iconic simplicity. The image of this primordial house, in its simple lines and slopes, was enough to impress upon the caretaker that the idea of the future was illusion. Of course, it was to be a happy illusion, but an illusion nonetheless. The day that the witch prophetically held up this curious tile for him to see was not one to be forgotten for many years to come, and so on the day that the old caretaker remembered this dream, it was as if layers of transparent ice were shed and splintered away from a frozen anchor contained within – a special kind of heavy anchor used by seafaring vessels from previous centuries. The archaic but natural curves of the heavy iron belied the outer flakes of icy rust, as if the bloodshot eyes of sleeplessness were wiping away beads of cold sweat from uncomfortable brows that had constantly shifting centers of gravity, remaking the identities of invisible forests. Each forest had one eye at the center, and within many of these invisible forests were leather suitcase factories, where one could find the most important suitcases of all suitcases available: the special kind of suitcase in which one might inside find the velvet hammers of pianos, if the word "piano" was to be used ever so loosely.

The witch never revealed to the caretaker any of this, from her transoceanic visions that she sent to him once every blue moon, but he knew that it was true, and that somehow all of this knowledge came from her, as if she were the mother of his darkness, but also the obsessive swing-set for schoolchildren to whom the witch offered sugary lollypops in order to get to them off-guard, for purposes that she would never willingly reveal.

But the caretaker was not to be deterred, and he knew that he was not very far from being on a plane full of cats when the storm broke loose overhead, sending down a deluge of dirty rainwater over his head. Luckily the house of burnished wood had a tight roof, and so the caretaker remained dry for the evening, not having to worry about the storm of lightning that boomed around the surrounding countrycide in all directions.

Therefore knowledge always had its price. For many years, the caretaker wasn't even sure if the witch existed, as if maybe all of the piano hammers he had installed throughout his house of burnished wood had never even threatened to outwear their felt. He knew that people were not without their weaknesses, including their sometimes filthy predilections for leather suitcases. But whether or not a liking for leather suitcases could really be considered a weakness had yet to be determined. In the meantime, the caretaker got up from his rocker, and stretched his legs and shook dust from his hair. Adorning the hallways within this vast house of burnished wood were the glued strips of piano key hammers, well worn, with the grooves from piano strings worn into the felt, leaving behind the stain of metal and the memories of solid percussion. He was certain that the witch of his dreams might have an eidetic representation of the worn piano-key icon somewhere inscribed on another ceramic tablet, but he was almost afraid to realize the full potential of such an image, as if her hands moving toward the tablet (so as to grasp it within her palm) were nothing but the illusion of timelessness or forgotten manners, plump as a parrot sitting next to a case of tickled ivories on a sinking pirate ship. He could remember what he thought of the wisps of hair that draped over her knowing brow, of the parts of her body that he wanted to smell, and even the sentences that she said to him with her hands, as if his body were words of Braille inscribed onto slate rocks within her unforgiving fortress. Therefore the witch was stronger than a storm, and more molten than the liquid brass wires from a piano, long stricken by lobes of felt, by flattened bulbs of green music that could excite one's senses beyond recall. Upon thinking about the flattened bulbs of music, the caretaker fell asleep and had many troubling dreams.

Within one of the dreams, the crotchety old man saw the witch holding the ceramic tile with the eidetic house on it, and fell into a deep sleep next to the witch. It was a case of dreams within a dream. Horrifying sub-dreams of football stadiums and secret government caves passed through his sub-consciousness. Eventually he saw his dreamwitch again with a lit cigarette in her mouth. She threw the cigarette away and stalked across the floor of the government cave in a pouty sort of way, flinging back her long hair and stomping her high heels on the earth, completely reveling in her indifference to the world. She produced a leather suitcase suddenly, and opened it, revealing a choice piano hammer inside, with well-worn ivory colored felt that covered the wooden hammer bone in a thin strip. She was very excited at making this presentation, and yet realized that not a soul knew of her possession, as the dreaming caretaker now became separated from her, dissolving the sense of togetherness into a state of bland anonymity. The separation marred the caretaker's dreamself, and he felt his motion through the universe become jaded, in the way a lofty kite is punctured by hailstones, preventing it from soaring over the next hill. A steady, steep descent to the ground was nothing more than a return to consciousness, and for the caretaker, the result was that he instantaneously woke up from the dream that was within a dream, as well as from the outer dream (that contained the inner dream). Therefore the return to consciousness brought on the strength of the reality principle crashing into his mind, twofold. Or perhaps it was the onslaught of waking reality squared. Either way, it was painful, and a crash of lightning dramatically helped accentuate this unfortunate realization and his return to waking life.

The caretaker rose from the bed and noticed that while he had slept, there had appeared several smashed plastic owls in his bedroom. The owls were life-sized, and all made out of a brown plastic that had been painted with owlish colors. The main problem was that the owls were hollow and thin, and very easily shattered. How the owls had gotten into his room was unknown, and their appearance was startling. The caretaker collected all of the shattered owls and placed them in a queue on the back porch, so that they could all monitor the grounded barge in the toxic Mormon islands behind the house.

Once inside, the caretaker rubbed his hand across his leathery forehead and sat down in his rocking chair. He turned on the television with the remote control, and began to relax. On TV was a reality show about an assortment of houseflies who were determined to make it to the top of a ceramic Jesus figurine (which from their perspective was as big as a mountain). Unknown to the flies, the ceramic Jesus fetish object had been covered with a very sticky petroleum substance, the same kind that was used on flypaper. There were several fly contestants who were all equally determined to reach the top of Jesus' head: Ralph, a rather boring-looking housefly. Nathalie, a metallic blue-colored fly. Sarah, a metallic green. Jennifer, a lovely metallic blue/green shade. Hank, a greenish-gold hue. And finally, Bertha, an ugly grayish color with exceptionally orange-colored eyes.

These six flies were all very eager to win the reality show contest, and they showed it: On the starting line, they were all poised to begin their ascent of the Jesus statue, and demonstrated their zeal by rubbing their forelimbs together in hot anticipation of climbing Our holy savior. After the host of the show swatted at them with a folded newspaper, the flies immediately leapt at their chance of instant fame. And unbeknownst to the flies, the flypaper adhesive had been applied over every crack and surface of the Jesus figurine, causing the greedy insects to remain cemented in the exact same spot where they landed. Upon making contact, the flies realized that there was to be no further travel along the surface of the Jesus statue. It was either an instant-win or instant-lose situation. The biggest loser was Ralph, who landed on Jesus' kneecap. Next came Jennifer, who landed on one of Jesus' buttocks. And then Sarah, who landed on his crotch. Then came Nathalie, who immediately ate the crust out of Jesus' bellybutton (while thinking longingly of the days when she lived in a restaurant). Bertha landed on Jesus' elbow. But Hank was the winner. He landed right on top of Jesus' head, with his bulbous golden body bloating in the sun with the most resplendent glimmer befitting of the holiest of flies. Hank certainly was a happy fly that day, although he didn't live long past that momentous occasion to ponder his future. In all truth, these flies would have preferred landing on shit rather than the statue, but apparently the Jesus figurine was the next best substrate. After they all realized their entrapment, they hurled jeers and insults at each other, as if by somehow furthering the verbal competition, they would be able to feel better about themselves and their fragile egos. Regardless of the surly fly-speak, the flies stayed put, cemented in place and doomed for eternity to spend a hollow life with Jesus, since all that remained of them after a few days were some dehydrated exoskeletons. The television show ended cheerfully and was followed by a commercial advertisement for "Corporate Control Tubes". The commercial promised to improve the lives of those who owned their own Corporate Control Tube. It was at that point that the caretaker of the shiny house nervously turned the TV off and focused again on the reality that he knew: *the reality that was outside of the television.*

The caretaker hurried to the back of the house, feeling slightly oppressed due to the psychological influences of the reality TV show that he had just watched. He knew that a reckless breath of fresh air would be all that was necessary to recenter himself. Upon stepping out on the

back porch, he again regarded the shattered owls who quietly stared out towards the radioactive Mormon barge that had been marooned forever within a dune of diesel-laced mud and sand, amid the stagnant lake. The written secrets within that terrestrial shipwreck could have taken forever to tell, and yet such knowledge was terrifying in its stark malevolence and missionary orientations. The night air fell heavily on the wizened face of the caretaker, as he stretched his aching arms and legs and stared up at the nearly full moon, which had now risen over the dense horizon of trees and bushes submerged in the darkness. The moment of peace was almost blissful as it was disquieting, reminding the caretaker of the moments when cats stalk mice along country fences, searching for new avenues of pursuit rather than the linear methods so well-known to modern vermin.

The clouds in the night sky began to break like a symmetrical beehive, making a supernova that gave the illusion of great distances. The cockroaches were literally dying to climb the walls, but their legs were useless when the music stopped and they were left to dry out in the hoary night. The caretaker could sense that something was approaching the burnished house, because the musical escalators inside were wound up in anticipation, as if the tension on a base could be manifested by large metal string coils being tightly packed as a pulsating knot that longed to re-extend itself. Usually these musical escalators made such gestures when it became certain that a visitor was approaching. In fact, the approach of visitors in the night are what often made the evenings pregnant for the caretaker as well as for the burnished house. The caretaker began his ritualistic gestures of anticipation, as he moved from room to room, seeking out shadows bearing knives and pulling aside numerous shower curtains which hid not shower stalls or bathtubs, but rather fireplaces and living rooms and tiny coatrooms. There were always these symbolic shower curtains placed strategically throughout the house, allowing the caretaker to move from one moment of privacy to the next, or from one private room to the next. The shower curtains were the glue that held the ancient dwelling together. The musical escalators moved between the shower curtains like centipedes, and their rhythmic motion seemed threatening, but in the most subtle of ways. If a million legs could crawl along the walls and ceilings!

The caretaker knew that the south wind was blowing through the trees, suggesting again that a visitor was approaching, but whether the arrival of the unknown person or entity would happen in twenty minutes versus twenty hours was completely unresolved. He opened a storage closet to find a half dozen guitars covered with many cockroaches. The roaches made no sign of moving, although the sensory hairs on their legs detected the motion towards them. They merely sat on the wooden beams of the instruments that were ever so tactfully varnished, as if each polishing stroke of the guitars' bodies had been orchestrated in the way a conversation might play out between members of parliament or a sports team. The cockroaches merely stood where they were, with their antennae moving to and fro ever so gently yet with an assertiveness that was unmistakable. The caretaker wanted to take one of the guitars into his arms and cradle it like a baby, possibly to pull a few chords from its silent frame, or perhaps just to finger-tap a rhythm next to the strings just for the sake of kinetic gratification. But the desire went unfulfilled. The caretaker simply stared at all of the cockroach-studded guitars, marveling at their silent symphony while the wallpaper on the inside of the guitar closet revealed the passage of unknown shadows in the same way clouds might pass quickly on transparent surfaces overhead. The guitar closet was really a vortex of activity within the burnished wooden house, and so the caretaker gently closed the door so as not to disturb the quiet roach music that droned on and on into the early evening. There were still many more hours of the night left for the visitor to arrive, and this perspective was merely reflective of the caretaker's bias in favor of the night.

The roaches were flying around the porch light in back, and their amber bodies were gems that would someday adorn the throat of a tender infant. The crickets chirped in a wave of unison, a droning message of approval, and the houseflies sleepily turned in their hiding places, not having enough energy since the sun had set hours ago. All of these insects were in various states of alertness, regretting that life was not more clearly delineated, as is sometimes the case with colored pathway tape in hospitals doubtlessly used to navigate the unknown corridors. All of the bugs made noise, like a colony of goldfish in a round bowl. The universe was insectoid, since the plants had grown mandibles and even the house was beginning to flex its subterranean muscles. The caretaker was listless and a little despondent, since he knew that it was more than possible that he wouldn't have what the visitor wanted (or what he thought the visitor wanted, assuming the visitor wanted anything at all).

The head of the caretaker was swimming, and he pushed his

hands along the walls of the burnished house in order to reassure it, to convince the house that satanic verses inscribed on the chimney stones were not just for Sunday school purposes, but for amusement on cold winter nights. The passage of time was a quiet agony for the caretaker, until finally he heard the knock on the door. As soon as the door was opened, the caretaker shook hands with the visitor, who turned out to be.... He wasn't sure. All he knew was that after losing consciousness, he actually awoke on the floor, with the feeble houselights causing his eyes to smart and allowing him to hear the receding footsteps of the visitor, whoever he or she was. With his right hand he felt a strange sensation on his forehead, immediately noticing that the aged, leathery skin seemed somehow lighter. While rubbing his hand over his forehead, he noticed there had formed a star-shaped hole that had apparently just begun to open. The normally horizontal laugh-lines across the forehead had instead surrounded the opening star in a concentric fashion, similar in appearance to a spider's web. The wrinkled skin more and more resembled a crooked spider's web, with the opening growing larger, suggesting that the caretaker's head was possibly hollow. At the moment when the light overhead penetrated the empty cranium of the caretaker (who was still very much alive), a spider began to stir and then emerge from the cranial cavern. With eight hairy legs and a bulbous abdomen, the spider most clearly resembled a tarantula. It crawled from the caretaker's head, and then rested on top of the waves of wrinkles created by the unexpected opening on the forehead. The spider knew exactly what it wanted: to seize the hapless insects and then quickly liquefy their inner organs with cytotoxic venom. And finally, to drink their liquefied bodies through the insects' fragile exoskeletons as if sucking soda through a straw. The tarantula, just like its wizened progenitor, was dizzy from the fall, and it tread ever so carefully across the spiderweb made of forehead skin. At the moment a moth bounced off the window on the outside, the spider ran quickly away from the fallen human and bounded up the burnished staircases, possibly disappearing into the attic or one of the unused bedrooms. The caretaker, on the other hand, slowly regained his senses while the gaping wound on his forehead wept a few lymphatic secretions and then closed forever. The wavy, concentric wrinkles on his forehead resumed their original configuration, with no signs of entry or exit of the spider, or any fluid, for that matter. The new difference was that there was no longer any sign of worry or fatigue on the countenance of the old man.

The caretaker felt his weathered fingertips reach out for the piano hammer, one of the key elements of his ancient family's coat of arms. There were of course other elements comprising the family coat of arms, but he could not remember what those were. All that remained was the grimy piano hammer, well weathered along the felt, with a broad furrow etched across the leading edge of the soft striking area. This hammer had struck many a coiled wire, and rather than possessing a typically rotund striking element, the striker more resembled the large head of a disturbed fetus. It was the skull of the fetus, analogically represented in cross-section and made from green and ivory felt, all attached to a grimy wooden shank with a dull patina, which actually struck the piano wire. That there were tiny felt arms and legs loosely hanging from the embryo's skull (the striking element of the piano hammer) was an inconsequential coincidence, as if these limbs had atrophied just as the arms and legs of the Japanese Daruma fetish object had undergone a similar process. Therefore, when the heads hit the wires, then music was the theoretical result. Of course, the caretaker never actually saw any babies rubbing or butting their heads against the piano wires, but there was a deepening, symbolic suspicion forming in his mind which tempted him to open up the family piano in order to see what was inside. And at that moment he had completely forgotten about the visitor who had somehow been involved in releasing the tarantula from his forebrain. He stared ahead into the dim living room in an obsessive kind of way, and wiped a few strands of spiderweb away from his thinning hairline.

Meanwhile, the spider quickly explored the house, not finding what it had secretly craved. The arachnid lowered itself from the cracked bull's-eye window and traversed the poisoned sludge of the backyard, the industrial cesspool of diesel and stagnant water mixed with sand and mud. Eventually it found the stranded barge and penetrated its crumbling structures, moving around exasperated bookshelves. The flickering artificial lights were painful to all of the spider's eyes, causing the creature to duck under a stack of grimy boxes precariously leaning to one side. The spider immediately began to create strangely shaped webs that were analogous to impulsive piano chords that were pounded off-key, like when a child bangs on a piano or perhaps when a pianist's fingers are glued together, causing the nimble exploration of notes to become suddenly botched or sabotaged. These webs created a shelter for the spider, amidst the ruins of books and other ancient family effects that had been pushed aside by the caretaker long ago.

In the burnished house, the elderly caretaker immediately became a child after the separated spider had a chance to get settled in the deserted mormon barge mired in the filthy backyard. The first thing he did was to gingerly lift the lid off the piano keys and have a good go at it with the piano. In fact, he had not banged the piano in ages. The pearly keys responded faithfully to his every strike, every pounding and every penetrative gesture with his fingers. He realized that he had not banged the piano for so long, that he had forgotten how good it felt to bang such an instrument. When he finished with a mind-blowing sonic crescendo, his arms fell limply to his sides, with beads of sweat falling off his matted brow, and he blissfully grinned, realizing that none of this would have been possible for the pianist that was an integral part of him. How could he have ever forgotten about his inner pianist?

His memories of the visitor returned to him, with him now realizing that he had mercilessly repressed them. He could remember his woman as she used to look, when she held him by the fire, and how the leader of the pack – some wizened, cranky old man of a beanpole – had attempted to interfere in his destiny, as if six-sided dice were secretly being exchanged for a two-sided coin against the caretaker's wishes. The leader of the pack had a strong blade of sarcasm which might have succeeded in making him a terror around those who worshiped him and his money, but it was pale in comparison to the verbal acid of the caretaker, before his tongue had been nearly immobilized with pins and needles and the kind of special felt used within musical instruments. This leader fell by the caretaker's words, although now the caretaker could no longer remember what those words were, other than that they silenced the leader quite effectively, instantly dissolving the illusion of fear and certain death that the latter exercised over all who would listen to him. It was after these words had been uttered that some binding spell had been broken, subsequently releasing people from the bricks in the walls in between which they had been embedded for years, possibly even centuries. It was at this precise moment that the caretaker of yesterday met his wife, or girlfriend or whoever she really was. And as soon as she had appeared, she quickly disappeared as the caretaker had encountered the nearest vacuum cleaner store. Why or how exactly the vacuum cleaners might have been responsible for his honey's disappearance still remained a mystery, but somehow the arrival of the faceless visitor from only a few hours before had triggered the reemergence of this archaic memory.

As strange as it might have seemed, the visitor had come and gone. Not one trace of a conversation with any person or entity, but only a strange set of footprints that clearly and smoothly led up to the front door and then away, like the arc of a semicircle. The caretaker couldn't remember any new faces (or any old ones, either) that might have visited him during the night. He was certain that the memories he had revisited were of course only memories, and he did verify that the spider was real, after traipsing over the oily dunes of sand to get to the mormon barge behind the house. He never spent much time on this grounded ship; all of the books and other antiquities there were just too useless to even consider sorting through, and yet he knew that somewhere within these stacks of useless objects there was the spider, possibly building a web, possibly sucking on bulbous insects, or maybe even doing something that only spiders do when they have complete privacy. As if the trail of loose webbing wasn't already a clue, the pile of broken piano hammers, with the felt neatly excised from the wooden bone of the hammer, was a dead giveaway to the whereabouts of the spider. The caretaker found his arachnid cousin chewing on the crumpled bass piano strings in the same way someone might smoke a cigarette after being released from a permanent prison cell. The spider didn't have much to say, although it was by no means unfriendly. The spider tried to tell stories with its spinnerets, moving fresh silk through the morning breeze as if it were smoke, but it was all a language that the caretaker could not understand. He bade the spider a good morning and left the creature in peace, to chew on piano parts in the shade of a crumbling, useless library.

The caretaker, on the other hand, realized that both of his hands were part of a single, resplendent diadem that he might use to crown his lover with, assuming he could make his way back to the vacuum store and then the campfire, the two places where he had last seen her several decades ago. He found a place within the house that had a good amount of magnetic resonance, and he lay down on the floor in that special location and shut his eyes. From there he visited the old factories that DeChirico once knew, paying special attention to the pollution of belching smokestacks and then the dried artichokes that one often found amidst the brambles of wrecked machinery within the industrial hive, with angry cusswords spray-painted in the sinister master control room (with the proverbial *master control* panel on the wall, with many buttons and knobs) which all now looked not so devious as they once did, decades ago. Atop one of the defrocked control panels was an icon of a throne and an angry feline next to it. The caretaker in his dreamstate at once knew that he had found the right room. Now all he needed was a vacuum cleaner and some pyrotechnic supplies.

When the caretaker woke from his outer dream later in the day, he knew immediately that there was someone else in the house with him, since he could hear the rustling of the burnished escalators overhead, accompanied by nebular birdsong.

Dr. Platypus and the Glass Tower

(11-2007)

Dr. Platypus finished her long-winded speech, entertaining the hummingbirds who empathized characteristically with her smooth and creamy throat. She might have disdainfully pushed her thin glasses up onto her nose, in a way that arrogant, haughty nobility might push their garters further up their legs, plying at silk tights that were as tense as a well-packed bird's nest. But at the moment, Dr. Platypus was standing, facing a dusty bookshelf, and made not the slightest gesture to correct mis-aligned garters, or to touch her smooth throat, her glasses, or any other part of her face. Her focus was like a cloud that lazily passed in front of a camera: here now, but possibly somewhere else for the next. Her face was the empty nest, but with signposts along a highway of impending doom, and other such painful clichés as a wrecked piano that had a plastic hummingbird glued onto each yellowed key.

Fireworks in the night sky were belied by the frosty exhalations of observers who could almost have been corpses but who were actually not. With their avid eyes pressed to the glass of the imposing corporate castle (with silicon foundations and luminous glass paneling), these miscreants could think of nothing but toxic warm shower stalls where the human guinea pigs would daily attempt to wash their skin clean of invisible, experimental chemical applications. Every day the miscreants would watch these experimental people have their chance to rinse off, under harsh conditions (including the dry cold) which penetrated even the experimental corporate castle, often simply referred to as the "glass tower".

The coldness could easily manifest itself as a passing jet plane that etched a chemtrail of liquid fumes across the sleepy morning sky. The coldness was also sometimes a trampled garden patch whose harvest had long since passed. And still, the coldness could be heavy salamanders that cling to each finger of a corpse's hand that was concealed in a bath tub filled with hydrogen peroxide.

On this particular wintry night, a light fall of snow was enough to ruin steam pipes, thereby applying sympathetic beads of perspiration onto the swaying strands of some abandoned cobwebs that had been built around the plumbing during earlier years. As dirty as these cobwebs were, they served as a once-liquid portal to the warmer parts of the world. Like a hand reaching through the legs of a businesswoman's tights, or through the interior space of a cuckoo clock, or even through the glowing tunnels of an anthill, these spiderwebs were a means to move from hot to cold, and then back to hot. Likewise, the spiderweb was a way to get to Dr. Platypus, and then back again. The six-sided snowflake was the same as the spiderweb, and this analogy was sufficient to bring Dr. Platypus into focus, as if she were a warm, red-tipped match to be placed within a stream of hot, dry air. The good doctor had too many books on her desk to pay attention to much else. From time to time she sipped at her tea or perhaps fiddled with the small radiator in her office. At five minutes to midnight she once again obsessively pushed her sharp glasses obsessively up the bridge of her nose. This gesture, which at times for her had become utterly neurotic, was disturbingly similar to a pair of hips being pushed along a well-oiled handrail to the top of a spiral staircase: it was nothing but an act against nature, or something that would not normally happen if there were no hand to push this uncertain process along.

Dr. Platypus closed her book and licked her lips, while pressing her stockinged legs together. She pressed a glowing red button on the side of her desk, which released a large, hairy tarantula from an unseen compartment from somewhere within. Slowly the spider lowered itself to the floor, between the quivering legs of Dr. Platypus. And then very quickly it ascended one of her legs with its soft, adhesive feet. When the tarantula found the right spot on her smooth but covered legs, its large fangs punctured her pantyhose, and instantly broke the skin of her inner thigh. Dr. Platypus bit her lower lip and uttered a low growl of reckless pleasure. To steady herself, she grasped at the corners of her desk, accidentally sending her ceramic teacup to the floor, resulting in a clatter of broken shards. Her entire body quivered and then heaved from the effect of the spider bite. Her face tipped forward and was only stopped when her forehead hit the desk, with her well-mannered hair fanning out across the surface of her workspace. Dr. Platypus fell unconscious and dreamed of many things that she would not remember. If there was any blood on her legs from the deep and heavy spider bite, it certainly wasn't noticeable, except only to her. After sensing that the woman was unconscious, the hairy tarantula climbed back up into its hidden niche within the underside of the solid oak desk.

The nudity of an owl den in the hollow of an ancient, wrinkled oak tree was like smooth, taut legs posing in front of a mirror, such that the owl family members might situate themselves behind the kneecap of the rigid tree. If the hollow of the tree was really the kneecap, then the family area was swaddled in warmth from the pithy, respiring inner matrix of the tree trunk, like the soft inner marrow of nude bone, with caught mice hanging by their tails from the ceiling, only waiting to be munched for breakfast once their flesh had begun to relax and settle a little bit. Immature owls would crowd around a hot, perspiring piano when the ground below might be chilled with morning frost, but the beaky parents staring at the sunrise in fear, like immobile statues in a dirty garden on the edge of a cliff, were the anchor that would ultimately keep the buoyant ship mired in the viscous, ashen mud.

A list of chores had been tacked onto the interior of the oak tree, in order to provide instruction and direction for the very young owl hatchlings, but somehow these youth knew already what was expected of them via mass-produced morality cues. The young owls generally ignored such tasks of obedience, however, as they were frequently preoccupied with the splinters that accumulated in their feet. Like the frigid icicles that broke through the dense skin of their toes, the wail of a flute in the distance served as an unmistakable warning of a looming future, replete with institutionalized underpants and repetitive mental exercises that drove the most sensitive to hurl their bodies from windows, as a manifested fear and learned aversion toward life choices which were too limited in breadth to nurture developing minds. Therefore, one's direction in life became an abstract commodity to which one was expected to buy into with a mere callous flick of the wrist, or a casual signing of a contract in blood: as if such decisions were reached in the same way choices were made about what to have for dinner. Likewise, the ease of choice was advertised with a slick veneer of carefree guitar music heard in corporate elevators, with a blind capriciousness that was overshadowed by a selfish attitude of neglect that could only be a portentous forecast of disaster for future generations, like the way stormy skies were predicted for next week, or perhaps for the next century. Such was the prevalent attitude.

But the holes in the walls were the obstacle to perfection that could not be filled. And the pleasures from these structural imperfections created alternative spaces to be occupied, as if the excitements of hotel residential transformations might evolve according to an axially-defined graphic that might display irretrievable trends towards an asymptote of pleasure. Analogously, the impossibility of escaping gravity became egg-on-the-face for those who defined their lives through the commodified "life directions" that were always easily obtained in exchange for one's sense of conscious autonomy or "freedom". This directional snake in the grass was soon to be viewed as the ultimate predator, the seed of competition and social decay, the obstacle to love that dripped the lethal dose of insult to injury.

The young owls released the tension from their well-smoothed feathers, and dropped into an unsettled and hungry sleep, a condition in which they were to become mired indefinitely for many years to come. Like a pond that had frozen over for winter, the reflective surface of their eyes cast their juvenile gazes of moonstone into the mirrored subtleties of well-known historical outcomes, as if young fates were unfairly indentured to the cheap authority of the cultural movies projected by crystal balls being rubbed by greedy mystics who pretended to see the future. It was all a scam from the beginning, but the owl siblings had not yet realized this not so inaccessible layer of conventional reality.

Perhaps an hour after the sun had risen, Dr. Platypus (who almost always had lived at her job, whose "job" had become completely synonymous with her life) opened her eyes. Her wiry glasses had been strewn across the desk, like a temporarily discarded yoke. A thick book had been her habitual pillow, and on the desktop there had accumulated a sizeable pool of her saliva: an energetic, nocturnal drool which she thought of as a moat around an invisible castle. Every morning Dr. Platypus would scoop up this imaginary moat (with the encircled imaginary castle) onto a brass spatula, and tip these liquid contents out of her well-monitored windows, all under the pretense that she was "watering the plants" – those creepy and uncurling fronds of relative evil known as collegiate ivy that never failed to despoil the charming wall of any pretentiously reputable institution. Little did Dr. Platypus realize that the metabolites of the tarantula toxins in her bloodstream might have altered the content of her various bodily secretions, including that of her salivary glands.

Upon tipping the volume of altered saliva out of the standardized, institutional glass window, the good Dr. Platypus turned her attention to the heavy tome which had served as her pillow or headrest during the course of her forgotten night. With careful attention to detail, she opened the heavy front cover to reveal mazelike hollows from the book. How these hollows and passages within the centuries-old paper had been so meticulously cut were beyond the ken of Dr. Platypus; all she knew was that this book had come down to her hands from a hidden shelf of which she had not been familiar when she was a child or developing student. No, this book intruded onto her sensibility on one lonely but terribly occupied night, converting the high-heeled shoes that she habitually wore into exotic boots that an explorer might wear to navigate the tedious boulders of an alien planet. Ever since that fateful night, this thick but hollowed volume became a permanent fixture of her cluttered but well-characterized desk. And every morning, Dr. Platypus would press her legs together in anticipation as she opened the ancient volume. And like clockwork, a shiny metallic lizard would emerge from the tiny, labyrinthine passages carved within the pulp of the ancient pages. This lizard was mostly green, but also had a mantle around its neck and shoulders of fiery red rubies with a few sparsely positioned diamonds. How such a lizard with a collar of brilliant gemstones might in fact emerge from a hollowed book never occurred to Dr. Platypus. She was not concerned, ironically (since she was indeed analytically academicist) in the how or why of this phenomenon, but only that this small shadow of inexplicable magic had entered her life which otherwise had been so ordinary, so predictable, and for her, so *sane.* Like a rigid functionary of the state who develops a vice like gambling or smoking, Dr. Platypus revealed her mortality and organic nature through her fast and involuntary adherence to this ritualistic release of the bejeweled lizard from the mysterious book, which might or might not have had anything to do with the intimate bite from the penetrating fangs of a highly motivated spider. She simply acted on impulse, with her hands guided by hers or someone else's intuition. Every night, the spider. And every morning, the book that served as her headrest.

While this peculiar cycle was very well known to Dr. Platypus, how deeply it had impacted her life – and changed her – had not yet been fully thought through on her part. A quickly repressed sense of wonder followed by shame always elaborated itself within her psyche, and then, as if on cue, her first group of students appeared at the threshold of her office. Their hungry, young minds needed stimulation, she realized while pushing her index, middle, and fourth fingers into the gill-like slits that opened on the sides of their newly hardened crania. Once they reached a certain age, it would be no longer possible for her to penetrate their young, inexperienced minds in such a way, and thereafter she – or whoever else came after her – would have to resort to different means in order to intrude upon their minds in order to provide guidance.

Dr. Platypus pursed her lips, flared her nostrils, and bared her pronounced teeth while fingering the brains of the naïve students. She knew exactly how to reach in and pull on all the right lobes in order to effect the desired responses, of which obedience was always one of the major components. After she was finished, she sent them away and wiped her mucus-covered hands on a disposable napkin. After this highly exhausting "tutorial" session, she sat at her desk and pulled spider webs from her hair. There was a radio on her desk that would periodically crackle, and usually this small, portable radio became the receptacle for the strands of spiderweb. She would wrap the cobweb filaments around the dials on the radio. Because of this approach, the dials became highly sticky, and so she would never actually touch the radio with the fingers; the radio would always be on, but for most of the time it remained silent.

Reaching through the cobwebs, the talons of the owls could access just about any substrate, any ledge or crevice on which they could stand. Usually they went off exploring in twos or threes, finding new vistas to admire and new skyscapes to explore. It was one fine day when a few of these immature owls managed to find the imposing glass tower: an edifice of smooth metal and glass which was minimalist in design and attemptedly minimalist in emotion: the very pinnacle of analytical efficiency tragically coupled with a poverty of feeling. Yet the sadness of the place was alarming to them, as they had never encountered such a *painful architecture*, as if something were perpetually on the verge of being lost forever. There were very few insects and rodents in the immediate area (most likely due to the periodic deployment of various automated pesticide devices) and all that grew in the vicinity were the collegiate vines of ivy that wound around the edifice in a snakelike manner, like an ivory tower being choked by two clenched hands. The owls flew past many of the windows, noticing the myopic human inhabitants gathered for various intellectual tasks, and also observing the presence of those strange gills on the sides of their heads. It only made sense that such government-employed brainiacs would need an extra form of coolant in order to prevent their minds from approaching levels of dangerous and unstable feverishness. But the owls only grasped at this series of relationships only fleetingly, in terms of analogy, that could have been expressed with a system of hieroglyphs which they had not yet invented. The passage of the morning sunlight through the entirely transparent windows covered with collegiate ivy showed off the occupants, with their demure attire, rather plainly yet directly, and it might have been comparable to an elegant roach motel that was made of cut diamond, yet which still held its occupants in an unknown world of multilayered dimensions completely against their will, as if two or more lives could be lived at once, but with the dominant lifestyle of oppression always closing in to choke off what little else might have attempted to live independently, always at odds with the former. It was the sharp glint of metal that caught the owl trio's attention. They could see the tiny form of the brass spatula, dripping the toxin-laden saliva down the glass walls covered with ivy. The bravest of these immature owls immediately dove through the wind currents and landed on the glass ledge of the open window, where it found itself face to face with Dr. Platypus, who still looked as if she were struggling with herself somehow, trying to focus on what was important, on what she needed to do. The owl just made out the green tail of a reptilian creature that had darted between the well-creased pages of an ancient volume on her academic desk, when it realized that this strange but desirable woman with her enlarged cerebrum, hook nose, demure eyes, and recessed chin had seen what the owl had seen, and her quickly averted eyes somehow stimulated an impulsive act of aggression on the part of the owl: it bit her soft hand ever so quickly, just a little peck really, which then initiated a thick flow of blood which both the owl and Dr. Platypus licked tentatively.

Poor Dr. Platypus! First having been bitten on the thigh by a strangely automated, nocturnal tarantula, and then incurring the minor nibble on her hand by the sharp beak of the owl were two events that had momentarily shocked her with the commonality of sweet and sensual blood-loss. It appeared that somehow her blood was a desired substance within certain corners of the animal kingdom. Despite the sharp wound, Dr. Platypus did not look pained, and merely bandaged the area with quick precision. She closed the window, as if in a daze, and quickly turned her mind to the books and other intellectual tasks that lay outstretched before her in her dazzling office of glass covered with collegiate ivy. And it was not even worth mentioning how glad she sometimes was that the floors themselves were not transparent.

It was only when the owl, after having turned to fly away from the building with his companions, noticed the lumbering shapes of certain beasts of burden who populated the outside of this glass edifice. These creatures, if such could be deduced from the aerial distance, wore the faces of desperation and frustration. They could have been apes, or they could have been humans, or maybe they could have even been strange dogs whose tired, bruised eyes were reluctant to stare into the morning sky, or at the glimmering building that had consumed them so, with its constant tests and toxic applications of strange chemicals. The owl who had tasted the blood now seemed out of sync with its companions, as the flying creature felt surrounded by a prismatic heat that seemed to transform each of its feathers into a plume of fire. If pain could be color, and color could become pain, then this was certainly its perceived predicament. The owl had visions of a train of highly destructive energy, as if the source of all evil, all creation, and of all pleasure would emanate from a complicated being of enfolded light and shadow so well camouflaged within the mundane that this path of destruction would quickly move through the world like a chain reaction. Once the initial spark had been passed from being to being, then the path to oblivion and (thereby recreation) would have become merely a formal outcome of an otherwise rather pleasant exchange between the creatures of the earth.

It was as if the owl had grasped at a creation myth that had pivotal forces of obedience and repulsion at odds with each other, nestled within the crucible of a living mind, the mind of any terrestrial creature. The owl had never before had such musings, and it returned to its hollow in the tree, to eat some mice that its mother had caught only the night before. The two companions seemed indifferent or detached, and they too assumed their places within the tree-hollow, never even wondering for an instant that blood laced with spider toxin could become the red wine of visions or that such a transmission might occur so innocuously and with such passionate subtlety.

Meanwhile, Dr. Platypus lost herself within her work, as she did everyday. The strange and periodical upheavals within her psyche were cleverly suppressed, and yet she was forever vulnerable to the daily mental acrobatics that her conscious mind hid from her, within various shades of denial achieved through routine, repetition, and much analytical meditation. Of course as an intellectual in the field of analytical metacognition, she was brilliant, but as a mere human being on the social and personal level, she was just as ordinary as the next person. Apparently self-awareness can arrive in various ways: for some an all-encompassing enlightenment that was felt in all corners of existence, while for others, like Dr. Platypus, the awareness protruded with the sharpness of a knife, at the expense of the rest of her being. For her, it was the gift of sight in one eye coupled with the curse of blindness in the other, but just distributed in different areas of her life. Every day she would refine her intellectual capacities, focusing on those little areas that had previously escaped study, while at the same time her nocturnal obsessions descended into baseness, unfocused regularity based on primal interests alone: essentially a brute-force roar of newly directed libidinal energy that had for many years prior remained buried deep within the folds of unread books that were on the furthest reaches of her bookshelves. And how exactly the tarantula had gained entry to her office (which was where she worked and lived) still remained a mystery, but nevertheless its presence had a very profound influence on the course of her life, in that she almost rarely left her office, and never traveled, even for business purposes.

The cyclical process of the spider-bite coupled with the prancing iridescent lizard within the book hollows had begun to take its toll on Dr. Platypus, as could be witnessed by her increasing lethargy. Perhaps it might have been interpreted as a sign of depression or possibly a newly manifested state of aggression against her "employers", but either way she began to resent the transparent prison in which she now resided. In an act that might have been the antithesis to the myth of Jack and the Beanstalk, Dr. Platypus one day opened her window and began to descend one of the stalks of ivy, down to the *land of the little people*. Miraculously, the plants were able to hold her weight, and therefore she reached the ground safely. Tucked away in her traveling satchel was the book containing the mazelike hollows (and presumably the jeweled lizard, sleeping somewhere inside). The spider, however, she had unwittingly left behind in her office, as she had not had any conscious memories of the tarantula and therefore was simply unaware of its existence. But even as she backed away from the towering glass building with its oppressive mat of collegiate ivy (much like pulsating vasculature), she felt a numb sensation between her thighs, prompting her to press her legs together so as to restore feeling to that area.

After a few minutes of walking, she was confused. She could feel the gill slits on the sides of her skull pulsating, as if she were gasping for air. This had been the first time in her life that Dr. Platypus had left the building, and under the most criminal of conditions. In her mind she could hear the alarm bells go off, wailing klaxons warning of impending doom, and other such dramatic projections of guilt that come from seized pleasures. She stumbled down a street that was covered with gnarled crab grass, possibly mutated by radiation poisoning, or then maybe not. Her knees wobbled with excitement, with her swaying frame receding into the shadows of the ancient streets once populated by children but now watched over by elderly eyes whose quiet pupils let nothing but light reflect from their surfaces. Her quivering hands ran their fingertips along the sandstone buildings, trying to feel the graffiti that had been gradually applied over the many years. These buildings that had surrounded the glass tower were older than the tower itself, and their histories were no less obscure. There were weathered aluminum trash cans behind these dwellings, and dirty cobwebs clung to their sides, just like cheery, wintry icicles. In fact, besides a few mummified rodent carcasses and some empty wine casks, there was nothing much else around and behind these buildings. Any shrubs or trees that might have adorned the buildings had long since died. The only presence of life that remained were the old eyes that peered from the windows above, only opened slits and covered with pollution.

Dr. Platypus stumbled through these back alleys in search of something she didn't quite know. Without whatever strong sense of composure and stability she had left behind in her transparent office (while in her emotionally drunken state), she had no choice but to lurch ahead, lumbering on into the foreground, the dimness that was ahead of her. In her mind's eye she could see four versions of herself, each of different ages and sizes, and how they all seemed to compliment one another yet ultimately serve as obstacles to each other. She passed through many ruined gardens, which might have been antique stores, to see the old furniture that she grew up with, with pluming armchairs built for cockatoos, and caged dwellings whose sullied brass bars that swallowed her hole, like the rats in the walls would have wanted to. She knew that the space-aliens had landed, and that all of her books had been torched, and yet her eyes could still see the writing in the air. The place where she would hang her hat might no longer exist, and the few people she might ever meet would be the lost sheep who knew their way only around ridiculous phone booths with sabotaged phonebooks. With the phonebooks destroyed, the true names would never have been known. The faces would have been erased, and the footprints might well have been the path of honeybees to a wilderness dotted with mirage honey trees.

The irony of this urban reclusion was that the rats were brought together in symphonic proportions. Shards of glass, flecks of paint and splintered wood, rat turds and the horrible music were all that remained on the manifest level. And then up above, there were always those elderly eyes. How exactly the upstairs and the downstairs managed to coexist were a complete mystery. An owl perched on a nearby lamppost had been watching the meandering proceedings of Dr. Platypus and understood this uncertainty ever so clearly. The owl blinked its eyes, revealing the brass dial of an archaic elevator – most likely the very same elevator that led to the top of the glass tower. It was in all likelihood that Dr. Platypus had never ridden or even seen this elevator, since she had been birthed from books and had of course left that terrible building by way of external descent via the ivy, not the elevator. But the owl's eyes showed the fiery afterimage of the elevator, and its one-dimensional pathway. The owl knew that Dr. Platypus lusted for the multi-legged creatures who would tear her body limb from limb like rose petals, but Dr. Platypus didn't know that fact about herself. While she might have imagined that there were four of herself walking the earth, it couldn't have been more obvious that there were two Dr. Platypuses, as a minimum, each wildly unaware of the other. And as for which one she was right now? Even the owl couldn't guess. The only thing the owl understood at the moment was the elevators of fire located somewhere within that wretched glass tower. Meanwhile, Dr. Platypus, in her altered state, wobbled down a side street, moving out of view.

Eventually the sun began to set, and the chilling winter coldness returned from the frozen recesses within the cobblestone streets. Going barefoot at this time of year was unadvised. Like a behavior drill that wouldn't start, the hummingbirds within one of the apartments eventually died, and their mummified remains were left hanging upside down from their roosting perch. At least they died together. This state of togetherness helped them cope with the iron seepage that had stolen into their hearts and apartment like rabid icicles. It wasn't that the urban rats were also a problem, but that the music of the icicles was corrosive to their minds and states of being. Before they had died, these urban hummingbirds had developed an unnatural obsession with shoehorns. And in particular, it was those shoehorns which vaguely resembled the forms of aardvarks that captivated their interest. While flying overhead and clutching a particular favorite shoehorn, each hummingbird would fly by Dr. Platypus' window at some point during the day in order to admire the pair of high heel shoes that she sometimes left in the glass windowsill in order to dry out (Dr. Platypus often woke up with sweaty feet, especially after a passionate night with the mysterious tarantula spider that lived underneath her desk). She would also wrap her pantyhose around and over the shoes, in order to enable them to dry out, as well. The hummingbirds felt that the shoehorns might have helped them better relate to Dr. Platypus and her shoes covered with pantyhose (or stockings, leggings, etc., as some might say, from faraway lands), and even though the shoehorns really didn't do much good, at least they had fun assembling a collection of the finest shoehorns that had been seen for many years. But then during these days especially, only the walls of their apartment had been fortunate enough to see the shoehorns. Presumably the rest of the city was more interested with other developments. It was a shame really, because the shoehorns had been completely underrated, and sadly, were quickly falling into obsolescence.

Dr. Platypus found her way to one particular apartment building that seemed especially troubled, as if it had been a distant cousin of a poisoned town near Chernobyl. In the lobby, the distracted doctor found herself perplexed by festive winter holiday decorations which had been sung to death. Usually, such throaty and boisterous holiday songs were by design, sung to spread cheer and joy to all people who were trapped in capitalist dayjobs (and nightjobs), but these particular songs had been used to destroy the holiday decorations, as if by some kind of self-identifying implosion. Although the presence of music was hard to trace (in the same way ghosts are rarely seen by the rational), Dr. Platypus was especially gifted at scrying the little emotional fragments of music that had remained long after the sound waves had left the room, much to her astonishment. These little fragments of music residue had coated the various winter holiday decorations, as well as the surrounding objects, such as caved-in lobby furniture, or the burnt-out television sets, or even the controlling microwave worship devices that were placed ever so strategically in these rancid urban dwellings with their drab décor and murderous glances that were lurking behind all of the velvet curtains and drapes, as if these same curtains had a very funny theatrical stage hiding behind them. It was this discrepancy of theater versus reality that Dr. Platypus found intimidating, as she quivered in the frigid air, teeth chattering and hands chafing together for warmth. And she had thought that finally, after all the years of rabid intellectual study, that she had begun to get a grip on reality. But the presence of the dead songs and the dramatic abyss behind the theatrical curtain was enough to add to the chill that was already tingling her spine. She found herself surrounded by owls whose night-time feathers had grown white, suggesting that they had become snowy owls. These sad birds looked at her through wide, impassive, moonstone eyes, as if she were nothing but a reflection on a door made of glass. She instantly felt invisible, as if the encircling ring of arctic birds were only really staring at each other. But the illusion was broken when they addressed her by name and asked her of her present whereabouts among the lower land of frigid miscreants. This was the first particular moment that she had been forced into a thread of self-questioning, trying to relive for herself the events of the morning which propelled her to leave the glass tower, and to descend into the chaos that was all around her now, with the biting cold of a neglected shoehorn. It was at this moment that a memory of past certainty gave her hope and direction, and she remembered the ancient, hollowed tome she had been carrying, with its honeycomb of miniscule, carved passages.

The old book felt good in her hands, as if she were grasping at the leather reins of a horseless carriage, the very one that Cinderella had mastered centuries ago. The leathery spine warmed her palm as the pages opened, revealing the tunnels of literature interpenetrating the caves of recorded history. The green lizard immediately popped out of the volume, and she relished the touch of its reptilian, prancing motions back and forth across her smooth neck, as if Dr. Platypus were a violin and the lizard was the bow. This was a species of music far richer than the sharpest of icicles. The snowy owls watched in utter rapture at this erotic exchange between the newly awakened woman and the bejeweled green lizard with its many showy rubies and diamonds, and they marveled at how much the pair resembled a symphonic violin being played out like a full-contact sport, and especially by invisible hands. When at last the cowled lizard fell back into the book's pages, completely exhausted, and a dazed Dr. Platypus reclined against the wall panting and with her tongue hanging out of her mouth, the snowy owls seized their moment.

They tore into the hollowed book and ripped the dazzling lizard from its resting pages.   The owls fought among themselves as they repeatedly tore the dripping reptilian flesh from each others' moist beaks, savoring the spurting blood all over their pristine white feathers, while their moonstone eyes opened and closed with quiet solidarity mingled with expectation.   Once the snowy owls had consumed all of the flesh, they vacated the desolate and dark apartment building that had now become submerged in swaths of harsh moonlight plagued by the wails of the unrestive miscreants who prowled the streets at night with filthy digits and whiskers that smelled of musk and moonshine.   Dr. Platypus could see her exhaled breath in the frigid air as she leaned against a drab wall with her legs spread and the glint of the moon in her eye.   Then she yawned and pressed her thighs together, knowing fully well that she would never return to the glass tower with its mantle of pulsating collegiate ivy and its collection of cubicled analysts.   Dr. Platypus slept that night, and for the first time without any spiders.

The Petroglyph Flower
(4-2008)

The eyes that couldn't focus on the blurred image of the human, ambiguously portrayed on the cave wall, instead turned to the passage of water that seeped from the crevice of the petroglyph flower that had remained with the cave for the earliest parts of eternity. This shower of knowledge was a fine mist exhaled by the alien atomizer as it moved into position through the ancient petals of the flower. The eyes were smitten by the applied mist, instantly envisioning the sets of glowing heiroglyphs that always came in pairs which were to symbolize words that either rhymed, or had analogous meaning, or even both. These words settled down upon the darkened sensibility like the musky perfume of the ocean, spreading a wave of salinity upon the nostrils as wet cement is pushed in between the cracks of newly laid bricks. In the near darkness, aside from the highly ornate petroglyphs and the emanation of oceanic perfume, the newly generated hieroglyphs danced among the flowery petals, anticipating a time when eternity would burst open like a flower's seed pod, releasing the spores of knowledge into a void that could have been best described as the comfortable early morning hours when all eyes rest in darkness, waiting for the flying saucers to land.

Had the eyes bothered to look upward to the heavens, they would have seen that there were no heavens and indeed had never been any heavens above. Instead, only musty, decaying floorboards. While the casual observer might have been tempted to assume a state of death or suspended animation, the presence of such theater underneath the floors was only another angle of life, and another perfume for those who are good with hammer and nails. This form of ascendant carpentry tried to put fences up around newly planted trees, but such creeping beauty was not to be contained. The tentacles of fumes reached up through the open bottle of poison, and very soon the beast would be unleashed. Meanwhile, sullen prayers were sung and the hives of hyperactive bees were ready to burst with new music, although the life that had once molted so very long ago was now ready again to molt.

Down beneath the floorboards of an unknown edifice, the eyes communed in silence with the petroglyph flower, punishing it with beauty, and biting its legs with the sharpened teeth of wild dogs who had opposable thumbs and who might fan the flower with palm leaves as pharaohs were once worshipped. Footsteps passed overhead, sending down a rain of dust. These footsteps might as well have been seismic activity, since the passage of humans over this site was considered by some to be just as monumental and pathologically elementary as the lover who pulls petals from a brilliant bouquet, longing for a moment of perfect understanding. The tectonics could have ripped apart the ground where you stood, in the middle of this hidden space beneath the building. This had once been the place where masks adorned the walls, where friends and enemies would walk through the walls, assuming the faces that the masks provided. The shaking of the ground gradually lost its terror, and the sound of the footfalls diminished steadily. It was certain that the shoes making these sounds had been constructed of quality leather, with firm soles that only clacked on the floor in military fashion, suggesting the passage of fascist and power-hungry social movements over the decades of floorboards. If the gods were upstairs then they didn't even know that you were beneath them.

The eyes that absorbed the moist beauty of the petroglyph flower realized that their time had come, and so they simply disintegrated, crushed like apple seeds beneath the boots of progress. The eyes had watched over the petroglyph flower for countless centuries dating back to moments when people wrote things with quills all over animal hides, as if the desire to squirt one's memories over taut skin were eternally mismatched characters from an alphabet of graphomaniacal delusion, or from a verbal thrashing that frustrated, fumbling scribes during headstrong moments when their primate fingers grasped at what would now be considered primitive writing devices. The eyes that had seen so much, and read so many acts of personal graffiti, and which had sat through many a terrible play or theatrical movement, finally expired in a conveniently positioned plush chair, as an anachronism for metal ben-wa balls resting on red velvet in the dark, waiting for the mutual self-orbiting rotations that never came, along with the yearning for muffled bells as they rang out during the early hours of the day, before the people had risen to put their clothes on and read the morning paper. These roving eyes were no more, and the petroglyph flower was left alone, with a faint trickle of pure groundwater issuing forth from the pursed lips of the ancient flower. This groundwater had not seen the light of day in many, many centuries, and would likely continue to remain in the dark, as the trickle of water became reabsorbed by the loose dirt in the subterranean cavern. It was the perfect schematic of circularity, regeneration and reabsorption.

But curious hands could not contain themselves, and one fine day, or perhaps night (because it was too dark inside of the old building which crowned this underground chamber of growth), old nails were pulled from floor boards, which were in turn pulled from their supports. The curious humans ventured into the shallow gulf that existed beneath the house (which just so happened to be situated on a gradually sloping hill), as it were, and commenced to explore some of the various drainage passageways that led off in various directions. The petroglyph flower remained in the shadows, unseen by the prying eyes of the apes who were using metal detectors and other fun gadgets to understand what had been sealed up beneath the bottom-most floor of their antiquated building. At one point a rather curious monkey passed by the reposing flower, with its withdrawn petals and tendrils, with its voluptuous lips tightly pursed together in an act of self-preservation. The primate had a face full of curiosity, but its eyes were not keen enough to discern the sleeping flower as it trembled in a dormant state of fear, longing for the days of the eyes, with their comforting lobes moving in a rhythmic unison across its ancient sensibility.

The petryglyph flower disappeared into itself the way a bird would withdraw to the center of a cuckold clock. Its face seemed to pull in on itself like a disturbed sea anemonae, folding inwards and returning to a more rocklike and less organic state. Eventually the beams of the flashlights disappeared as the humans disappeared in different directions, returning to their manifest, surface lairs. The petroglyph flower relaxed and shook off the rigidness of its lithic camouflage. It swayed back and forth, testing its sedimentary roots, in order to trace its path of ascension back to its source, somewhere far below the earth's mantle, like the hood of a geoclitoris that had shouted songs of seismic furnaces, of coded messages of silicon that would innervate the various strata of rock, pushing back the layers of time to reveal what was once the hottest passion. Such a wash of memory belied the solidified path that now filled the void between past and present, and so the rock flower once again remembered the path it took from hot to cold, deep to shallow, from mantle to crust, in one fine instant of molten pleasure. And as soon as the memory surfaced, it instantly dove beneath the rock into pleasant oblivion.

The geomorphic limbs of the petroglyph flower ached, although its body had no nerve endings as most terrestrials might have suspected. Its frame arched and swiveled, like mechanical snakes in search of better posture or perhaps friendlier circumstances. At times like this, the creature made of rock felt as if it were a microphone: picking up the slightest sensations and impulses, and amplifying them back out to the world. It could sense the feelings and goals of the primates as well as those of the burrowing insects, and couldn't help but mimic these same expressions and motions in the way a parrot would. It wasn't just the average case of feeling transparent or vulnerable, but more like the state of feeling extremely reflective. The rock flower would become what it saw, acting out the culture of strange forms of life which were unknown to it.

It was around midnight when the moon had risen and all of the people had left, that the rock creature emerged from the shadows, having made the decision to rise from its sub-cellar abode and to investigate the wooden building that had remained so far above it for so many centuries. The cellar area in which it found itself was dank, with much slimy fungal growths covering the walls. There was enough slime there to make all phosphor matches in the entire world useless. Enough slime, therefore, to extinguish all fires all over the world. A mountain of TNT would have been smothered by this fungal slime, regardless of how deceptively thin the latter was in its coverage of the cellar area. Here and there were old desks and classroom globes of the earth, most likely for use in geography lessons. Finding a stairwell with a precariously sagging ceiling, the flower creature began to ascend the stairs to the next level, which was discovered to house some boiler equipment and other machinery – electrical, most likely. The hum of generators and other mechanical moving parts would in all likelihood mask whatever sounds the flower might have made in its approach to the opposite stairwell that led to the next upper level. The petroglyph flower slithered on, voraciously moving its whip-like appendages, in the same way a desert asp might gracefully side-wind its way across an unstable sand dune.

It was on the next level up that the flower found what it wanted: people. It found them sleeping on damp cots in the early morning hours. The first person it made contact with didn't have the chance to scream. The whip-like tentacles of the petroglyph flower one by one strangled the various people as they slept or attempted to flee, while supplementing the choking tautness of vines with a toxic perfume breath that only flowers could emit. By the end of the struggle in the darkness, the creature had made quite a catch, managing to silence all of the primates who had been sleeping, in fact almost a dozen or so of the bipeds. It turned out that these organic creatures were inedible, and the rock flower instantly regretted destroying one of the specimens it had just caught. The flower wasn't sure what to do with its newly obtained booty, so it paused for a moment, teetering on the edge of the stairwell that led upward to the ground floor of the building. The moonlight fell through the stairwell, informing the creature that it had almost reached the surface.

The moon (something the rock flower had not seen for millennia) entranced the creature, instantly evoking memories of flight, and of canyons and gorges with small running streams filled with miniature boats. These boats might have been false memories, but the flower, while drooling with joy, relished its new freedom and the mental inspiration afforded by its recent capture of intelligent life. Its thoughts drifted from canyon boats to toothy smiles and bobbing heads who were doubled over with religious prayer and with oozing sores all over their bodies. Somehow the flower knew that the monks with the oozing sores were somewhere nearby, possibly worshiping the bones of dead animals, or drinking the symbolic blood of their savior, being the vampires that they really were. These confusing thoughts pulled the attention of the rock flower back to the issue of the moonlight, and how the reflection of this pale light would enter its mind like the diffusion of sea salt in the eggs of walruses as their offspring would try to hatch from the eggshells of their hands. The petroglyph flower grew nostalgic, wringing its tentacles and dripping a few weepy secretions from the inner crevice from which all the petals emanated. Somehow the stone creature knew that it was at the threshold of a new change, and that it would be forced to alter its customs and preferences in order to survive in a new world. Perhaps it was the equivalent of weeping, but the petroglyph wrung its tentacles until they became corkscrews, and continued its outpouring of mineral secretions from the depths of its petals. The creature did not breath, but an almost spastic rigidity followed which might have suggested it having taken an abnormally deep breath, in preparation for what it would do next.

The revelation of the communal activity among these freshly killed humans presented itself to the senses of the flower by way of the various objects and belongings of the people strewn about the dimly lit floor. Feeling the closest thing to remorse yet, the flower understood that taking such a large supply of human beings might have been a little more than impulsive and most likely even just a little bit selfish of the creature. With the equivalent of a trembling sigh, the creature displayed a peculiar shudder, displaying a few light-sensing apertures near the base of its locomotive tentacles, perhaps the equivalent of a floral display of guilt. The creature decided that it would make amends. It was unfair of it to deprive these lovely people of their Sunday picnics, and marriage ceremonies, and offspring-breeding activities. It would help these people regain their freedom, albeit in new ways perhaps, but it was certainly committed to helping them, yes it was.

The stony flower used the sharp edge of one of its tentacles to open the chest cavity of a man who lay close to it. A neat, vertical incision was quickly achieved, followed by a weighty removal of the internal organs, still steaming. These inner viscera were deposited in a pile, off to the side, while the human's body cavity was once again searched with deft, rocklike tentacles for any remaining organs. It was as if the chest of the dead person was unzipped, and then gutted, as if the person were freshly caught game to be roasted. This same procedure was carried out for the dozen or so people whose bodies littered the floor of what possibly was a dormitory. After completing the gutting process, the flower arranged dead people in nice little rows, facing upwards. It then began the arduous task of gathering all of their personal belongings and organizing them into piles that could only have been meaningful to the flower, based on its analogical sensibilities. The flower decided that all of the people should be given their belongings back to them as gifts, so it evenly distributed the items to each of the people, tucking alarm clocks and lipsticks and holy bibles into each person's chest cavity. The flower felt that true ownership occurs when something is a part of oneself, and within oneself, hence the belongings should become incorporated into the bodies of his new friends. Since they were friends of course, they would eventually have names, but the creature was not yet ready to give names. The names would be given once the flower had had the chance to get to know his friends better.

The petroglyph flower did its very best to be generous with the gift giving. Each person got at least one toothbrush, a pair of spectacles, some bloodied clothes, a holy bible, tea bags, deodorant soap, overstretched pantyhose, pencils and paper, lightbulbs, French bread, and the list went on and on. By the end of the gift-giving session, the body cavities were quite full, and each person had become heavier than he or she had originally been. The flower realized that because the creatures were no longer respiring, that they would be unable to locomote of their own accord. It had heard of such handicaps in the past, and so vowed to help its friends to the best of its ability. But there had to be a way to make them motile, or at least to facilitate its moving them. After a few silent hours of joyful contemplation, the flower moistened its fronds and arrived at an answer: the flower could easily make the people into suitcases. It busily fashioned handles from some of the sturdier materials found in the room, such as from thick shower curtains and a large staple gun that it found upstairs. Each side of the person's opened chest had a handle, such that when both handles were grasped, each of its friends became a very portable suitcase. The flower knew that good times were just ahead, and it quivered with vibrating joy that put a tensile bounce in its slithering steps, reawakening a lust for freshly seeping groundwater rich with the earth's minerals.

Already the flower was beginning to understand its friends, and commenced to grouping them into three sets of four. Each quartet of friends was to be carried together on one of the stone flower's very strong fronds. It knew that very soon these people would have names, very special and endearing names, and that it alone had thought up for its newly discovered friends. Life was grand. The rock flower had three free fronds with which to carry its new friends upstairs, up to where the moonlight penetrated the windows of the building to let in all of that glorious illumination. Upon bidding the blood-drenched room a sentimental farewell, the plant picked all of the friends up and gently carried them up the musty flight of stairs. This ground level of the building that they were in had all manner of apparatus, as if they were in a workshop (or perhaps sweatshop, in all likelihood) or a place where his friends could labor by day and then rest during the night. The flower right then and there promised its friends that they would never ever have to worry about work ever again – that it would feed them and clothe them and take care of them for as long as it could. And although the friends had nothing to say to the flower upon hearing such a promise, the liberated petroglyph knew that they were grateful and happy to have been freed from their work obligations. And just because of that fact, the flower knew that a celebration was in order.

The petroglyph flower knew that all of these people deserved to be happy, and it certainly wanted them to be as happy as it could make them, so upon rummaging around in all of the various supplies in the workshop, it found several different cans of colored paint. It had decided that by painting all of their faces and bodies different colors, all of the friends would be able to reach higher levels of ecstasy, truly living in the happiness that could only come from the freedom of expression. And truly that was what happened: upon being painted with different colors, everyone became happy. The petroglyph knew that certain color schemes worked better for different people based on differences in personality, and these differences were tactfully taken into consideration upon the application of generous swathes of paint onto the limbs and faces of the friends. Each friend was laid upon his or her own work table, and coated with generous dollops of colored paint. The flower felt elated, and the elation on the faces of the humans showed too: the moonlight had that special way of bringing out the colored highlights of each person, with glittering beauty available for everyone to see – and it was true: rigor mortis did have a way of giving corpses the semblance of shouting and smiling, so all really was well. The rock plant knew that while beauty was only a temporary state of grace, its existence in this world was only there for the taking, to seep between the crevices of perception and experience. It was at this moment that all of the friends were named, given names, and thereby their new identities were complete. With each new intact personality, a very new and special being was born on that night, twelve in total, to be precise. The plant jovially picked up each of the three quartets of friends, and lugged them out of the archaic building and into the cool night air. The weight of their bodies wasn't really heavy at all to the plant, and so it decided that it could afford to ply them with more material gifts, in order to make them even happier than they already were at the moment. These were very exciting times for the plant!

After several hours' travel through dark countrycide, the friends' meandering path brought them to a sleepy town that was not yet ready to awaken. The flower creature knew that in order to enable even higher levels of happiness within its friends, it would have to find a location that had even more dignified personal effects from which it could choose only from the most valuable of items to later be presented as gifts. A commodity warehouse was the first and only candidate to fit the bill. The plant had no trouble at all breaking into the building, and luckily enough there was no alarm system installed, since everyone who lived in the town was on fairly good terms with everyone else. The plant sifted through the various aisles and stacks of fresh commodities, and did its best to find gifts which best suited its friends. Of course this was a potlatch, so the rules of gift-giving were not confined strictly to utilitarian needs. In fact, the petroglyph flower wanted everyone to have gifts of luxury and leisure, and it selected only those items which it felt would lengthen and extend the periods of its friends' happiness to longer and longer intervals, and to higher and higher levels of sublime and poetic ecstasy.

As it turned out, the human friends were regaled quite handsomely, and each of them was bestowed with very exciting presents that they might have boasted of to all of their friends and family (had they actually been alive). One woman was lucky enough to receive a hair-curling iron. The flower was kind enough to tuck the unit underneath the right flap of the woman's ribcage. And then one of the heavyset men received a camping stove that fit very snuggly in what remained of the space in his already packed body cavity. By now, most of the blood of the victims had drained away, leaving only a minor ooze here and there which had all by now congealed, anyway. Things were definitely shaping up, decided the petroglyph flower.

The journey of flower and friends continued. The human suitcases made the landscape come alive, as if the true meaning of life were reduced to a spectacular coming and going that was evident through the passage of luggage flying the friendly skies to holiday destinations of happiness and exotic pleasures. Excitements could only evolve so far until they needed to become amplified again, so that the renewal of pleasures could be supreme, with a pounding of fists on furniture and hairy shrieks of elation that might sail upwards into skylights of orgiastic encouragement. This is the way that the flower creature thought. It couldn't have been any other way, it decided.

The next stop was a jewelry store. The flower creature had the bodies hidden under a bridge (under the guise of protecting them from too much publicity caused by jealous thrill-seekers) while it slithered down an alleyway and entered the jewelry store through the backdoor. The happy proprietor of the store didn't have enough time to see who or what grabbed him, but within thirty seconds he was quickly silenced and gutted. The rock plant knew that the man specialized in the sale of body adornment, and so it was careful to make the incision across the human's chest in a horizontal, rather than vertical, line in order to accommodate the man's special needs. That way the body cavity could serve as a pouch in which to store things, such as jewelry and other valuables. The creature had noticed that as the bodies had generally started to decay, the tissues began to lose their firmness, sometimes allowing the treasured contents stored in the cavities to fall out. Such accidents would no longer happen if all subsequent incisions were done differently, decided the flower. This change of strategy would ensure continued happiness.

The glyphic flower laid fronds on all of the jewelry it could find: diamonds and gold and silver and opals and other precious stones. There were rings and chains and necklaces too, as well as the occasional brooch. All of these items were quickly stuffed into the recently excavated abdomen of the storeowner, who now, suspended by the flower's helping hands (or fronds, really), had grown a bit heavier than before. The flower pulled the dial from the safe and placed it right over the man's bellybutton, deciding to secure the wheel more firmly later on, once it had been reunited with its friends, who were now patiently waiting for him under the bridge right outside of town. It was going to be a glorious day!

The flower did not mind at all such errands of going into town to obtain special gifts for its friends. It was after all, better to give than to receive, and the flower made sure that this caring attitude was consummated by evenly distributing the jewelry among its friends. Everyone now wore rings and necklaces, and the women wore resplendent brooches with shimmering gemstones. By now, the happy eyes of the corpses had begun to dehydrate, leaving them spongy and slightly shrunken. This increase of space in the eye cavity was the perfect premise for the flower to stuff all of the loose gemstones into the eyesockets. That way, everyone's eyes would sparkle, as if it were carnival season. And now with extravagant makeup, and extravagant body adornments and optical highlights, the group of close friends was ready to begin sharing with one another, exploring happiness together, within the throes of social bonding that only a petroglyph flower could provide. The flower picked up the gang of friends and also the newest recruit, the jeweler with the dial of the safe now firmly attached to his abdomen, and carried them to a less busy part of town, where the hotels were cheap and the drinks were free.

As soon as the flower appeared, everyone at the Slipsands Motel ran away. Suitcases and other traveling items were quickly discarded in favor of a quick retreat, as it was observed that the motel occupants were more than anxious to leave as soon as they spotted the gargantuan stone flower carrying the decaying humans who had been stapled with luggage straps. In the interest of comfort and harmony, the flower assigned rooms to the various friends so as to avoid crowding. The flower put Steve, Marsha and Diandra in room 104, while Marvin and Bonnie had room 106. Mike, the jeweler, shared room 107 with Greg, who both had the proclivity for pointless intellectual banter and posturing, as well as for so many other meaningful forensic exchanges. The remaining four – Mary, Larry, Barry and Carla – occupied room 110. As soon as the friends had the chance to settle in and unpack their luggage (after all, they *were* the luggage), the petroglyph flower made the rounds, checking up on his guests like any good host would be expected to do.

In room 104, Steve, Marsha and Diandra were casually taking in the theatrical subtleties of public television broadcasting, intently watching the TV screen, completely engrossed in a movie adaptation of a Shakespeare play. These poetic subtleties were not lost on the trio. Diandra sat crosslegged on the floor staring up at the screen while Steve and Marsha reclined on the bed very comfortably amid the pillows as the television drama unfolded before their sparkling eyes. Due to the passion and the intense action of the Shakespeare drama, the excitement produced a jaw-dropping effect on the part of the viewers. Diandra, especially, was interested in the movie, as she had begun to drool slightly, allowing a putrid pool of fetid brain fluid to drain from her skull while she looked up at the TV screen. Marsha and Steve had attracted flies, as well, with the small insects walking up and down their limbs, feeding and depositing eggs, which had of late begun to hatch producing a new brood of maggots to feed on their decaying muscle and connective tissue. Within the hour, the bed was stained with a foul-smelling, viscous ichor that could only ooze from corpses in the beginning stages of advanced decay.

Marvin and Bonnie were exploring the joys of sex in room 106. Since their bodies had grown slightly inflexible over the course of their recent decay, the stone flower helped them get undressed and into position. If the smell of sex was strong enough for some nosy neighbors, then the odor of death mixed with ubiquitous fornication was enough to alert any discerning olfaction. Of course, the pair made quite a mess, and there were many flies buzzing around their room by the time they were finished. Thick, gelatinous, dark blood smeared the crumpled bedspread, with little blebs of body fat accentuating the messy appearance. On top of this abstract, decadent painting covering the sheets was the happy, wiggling dance of satisfied maggots, who fed on this human refuse in order to further their own existence of avarice. Then, tucked away under the covers, with burning cigarettes in their hands, Marvin and Bonnie smiled with toothy, open smiles while the TV blared above them, bombarding them with commercials about toothpaste and junkfood and life insurance. The warm afterglow from having had sex in a cheap hotel suited them well, with their sparkling diamond eyes staring up at the TV, creating a honeymoon fit for royalty. Later that night, Bonnie had given birth to a dozen lightbulbs that the rockflower had previously inserted into her abdomen at the beginning of this adventure in pleasure. This birth represented the pinnacle of their goals in life: to create offspring by which they could further their extravagant lifestyle as extensions of themselves. This was certainly time well-spent, agreed the stone flower creature.

Meanwhile, Mike and Greg engaged in their empty, pseudo-intellectual banter next door, arguing over the finer points of world politics and the superiority of certain choice value systems. This back and forth activity carried on for the longest, with both individuals oblivious to what was going on in room 106, until Greg unexpectedly tipped over from the chair in which he was seated, spontaneously crashing to the floor in a jumbled mess of matted hair, sticky, rotten flesh and bone on the verge of fragmenting into a maggot-infested pile. A tumble of rubies and diamonds spilled from his eyesockets onto his putrefied tongue and the filthy carpet that was littered with pubic hair and squashed cigarette butts. Despite this distraction, Greg was not the least bit put out, and still continued his passionate debate with Mike, who was now leaning on his elbow so heavily that it seemed like his body might tip over at any instant, just as easily as Greg's had. But such are those highly intellectual conversations that threaten to leave all participants on edge, on the verge of new patterns of thought, of new suppositions for warring egos to assimilate into a greater understanding of the human world and its complexities.

In room 110, Mary, Larry, Barry and Carla were all hunched around the table, playing cards. Already it had been established that Larry was cheating, as his decaying brains were cocked to the side and oozing out of a foul earsocket. His ear had fallen to his lap, as if perhaps he were pondering its use as collateral in the poker game that was unfolding in front of his sparkling, bejeweled eyes. Despite his losing hand (which was nearly severed at the wrist), everything about Larry spoke of wealth: the balding, middle-aged brow covered with green paint, the topaz and generously-sized garnet stones riding on a wave of ooze from his shrunken eye sockets. His formal dress jacket covered in swathes of Technicolor paint from the workshop in which he up until recently was manager. All of these appearances suggested a well-honed gambling sensibility, and yet Larry was surely losing the game. Carla's excitement had caused her jaw to drop and a few of her front teeth to fall out onto the table. Or perhaps these teeth were to be used as gambling collateral as well?

Suddenly, the petroglyph flower entered the room upon learning of the commotion surrounding the use of body parts for gambling collateral. The flower had never played the role of arbiter before, but perhaps the time had arrived. While circling the poker table in order to prevent any cheating, the creature refilled players' drinks, or tapped the ashy ends of burning cigars, as any gracious host might do. Larry had indeed run out of gambling funds, and was forced to put up his ear in order to remain in the game. And Carla was not far from betting her front teeth. An argument was brewing at the poker table, and Barry was fuming, since he felt that it was unfair of the others to cheat by using their body parts in place of funds. By now Greg and Mike (the jewelry store manager, with the dial of the safe still firmly attached to his belly) had joined the party and were sitting demurely in the background, having lost their interest in friendly adversarial debate, and instead had their attention turned to the odd game of poker that was unfolding before their oozing eyesockets. Carla had decided to bet only her front teeth, making her very close to folding her hand and withdrawing from the game completely. The others seemed more secure in their gambling positions, and studiously kept their cards in front of their faces at all times, while avoiding the maggots and flies that had infested the motel room. Mary began to cry, with tears of a viscous, brownish discharge running down her sunken cheeks, as if in slow motion. It was as if the clocks suddenly stopped in a netherworld of greed spawned from flies and human vice, with the birds in cocoons and the light of the sun in repose. If medical bandages should have been applied to serious wounds, then the window of opportunity had passed. The buzzing of flies began to drown out the conversation among the happy friends gathered for a friendly game of poker. The flower knew that the success of the party was depending on its ancient gallantry, and only time would tell if its efforts had not been in vain. The paraphernalia of countless misspent days lay cluttered and scattered, birthed from suitcase abdomens evacuated of all material civilization. Papers, books, personal effects and material valuables all lay bloodied on the floor, covered in bloodied slime and rancid mucus. The stench was unbearable, but joy was in the air, to the extent that the festive moments that had comprised the past few days had congealed into a coming together of friends: a party of diversions and a sharing of material wealth that these people had not participated in when they were more animate. The flower knew this, and felt a gladness for giving new life to his friends: for dressing them, clothing them, celebrating them and regaling them in wealth that they never had when they lived prior to knowing the flower, in less collective capacities oftentimes filled with the kind of special loneliness that is often experienced when people are unwillingly forced to spend excessive amounts of time together.

By this point, the remainder of the party had congregated in room 110, with rapt, dismembered attention fixed upon the festive card game unfolding on the standard plywood motel table. The stakes were intense, so thought Marvin and Bonnie, who by this point had dressed themselves and were carrying their offspring of a dozen lightbulbs. As if by divine inspiration, Bonnie instantly got the notion of sharing her lightbulb offspring with the rest of the party, upon seeing the poker table littered with teeth and bone fragments and of course the writhing antics of the white maggots. Bonnie gave all of the lightbulbs to everyone causing the party to become very happy upon receiving their lightbulb gifts: Mike the jeweler unlocked his chest safe and deposited the lightbulb inside of his body. Greg, Marsha, Ben and Larry all put the lightbulbs in their mouths, while the rest of the party calmly slipped their lightbulbs into their suitcase-style chest cavities. In fact, a few of them were in such a badly decayed state that their abdominal flesh had started to rip, necessitating the aid of the flower who was always there to help them. The flower produced sewing needle and thread from thin air, and began to repair those of his friends who were most in need, as if they were ripped, leather suitcases who needed a little stitching in order to continue with their life journey. It had become apparent that the happy friends were tired from the excessive debauchery in which they had been engaged for the past several hours and needed a rest. The flower helped everyone stretch out in order to sleep, although the flies and their wriggling brood had no such desire for rest, and continued with their droning activity, never ceasing to twitch, and wriggle and crawl along the great proteinaceous feast that was spread out before them. The flower knew that the sun had set hours ago, and it quietly pulled aside the cheap motel drapes in order to look up at the moon, allowing the lunar glare to fill its photoreceptors. After such an eyeful, the creature turned its gaze to its dear friends, all sleeping restfully in a cozy albeit slightly cramped motel room.

The flower reposed for several hours in a resting position, enjoying what members of its kind might have considered as "sleep," while musing over the joyous experiences it had had with its newly found human friends. It thought of all the numerous gifts and kindnesses it had bestowed upon the people, but it still felt as if it somehow were not doing enough for them. What could it do to make them happier? How could it help these people to find terrestrial nirvana? These musings crossed the mind of the flower in the early hours of the morning, when suddenly a muffled but obsessive and frantic knocking repeatedly sounded. The flower cautiously opened the door of the motel room, immediately stricken by the presence of a flaxen blond woman dressed in black, and ever so buxomly endowed, which made an impression upon that alien presence of a woman who wasn't be trifled with, and who should be listened to and taken seriously at all costs. In fact, this mysterious woman was a nun who did missionary work, often horizontally, helping people to help themselves. As a woman of the cloth, and as a catholic missionary, this woman had avowed a life of poverty, so as to make herself worthy of the holy spirit, as the latter inhabited the woman's body, and especially her colon. In keeping with the vow of complete and total poverty, this woman ate baked beans every day, for breakfast, lunch and dinner. It was for this reason that she was known to all of her followers and admirers as the Farting Nun.

The Farting Nun always carried around with her a few items of special importance and usefulness, including a satchel that she slung over her shoulder, as well as a banjo. Inside of the satchel, she always kept an extra change of clothing, which she alternated with what she wore, such that at any given time, all she had was just two sets of nun's attire. She regularly washed the unworn outfit by hand, in one of the numerous public bathrooms that were to be found in the area. The

Farting Nun also carried with her a few extra crucifixes, one of which she always wore around her neck according to whim, as well as a modest outfitting of toiletries and other essentials for minimalist hygiene. And last but not least, the traveling nun also carried with her, at the very bottom of the carrying bag, some sex toys that she used with her clients. Of course the average layman would think that the presence of such toys found on the person of such a highly pure and esteemed woman of the cloth would be a contradiction of moral values, but in fact there was no such contradiction, at least within the consciousness of the Farting Nun. Like any good catholic, the Farting Nun understood the unspoken laws governing the secret allowability of transgressive acts as long as they were followed by heartfelt gestures of confession, humility and repentance. Therefore, with catholocism, one act of allegedly debauched self-debasement was to be followed with another form of repentant self-debasement, but just of a slightly different kind, creating a form of moral symmetry that these people could easily understand. Thereby the world continued to turn on its axis, and the sins of people that were committed today were easily forgotten as long as they were confessed the next day and repented for according to the guidelines of the church. This situation essentially constituted the dialectic of Fat Tuesday and Ash Wednesday. And as the Farting Nun had quite her share of missionary obligations, she was very keen to keep her secrets well-managed, observing what some had once called the "Don't ask, don't tell" policy. Therefore, the Farting Nun brought salvation to the souls of her clients and followers, as well as smiles of leering joy to their faces, from time to time. In all of her thirty-two years of existence, she never met a man or a woman she didn't like...

The Farting Nun always carried her banjo with her, as it was a symbol of lyrical freedom to always have music on hand, twenty-four hours each day. She knew how to pluck quite a few songs, most of them religious, and usually she'd sing to the elderly, the weak or the infirm after giving them blowjobs. And of course, rhythmically, she was able to use her flatulence to her own advantage while singing and playing chords on the banjo. All around, she was a very talented and caring individual. She had great advice to give to those who asked for it, and also had the uncanny ability to teach people how to do things they already thought they knew, such as tying shoelaces and turning doorknobs. The Farting Nun had a special outlook on life that enabled her to know the most perfect, concise and sharp-witted things to say at any given moment, coupled with a pollyanna optimism that was cloying yet nevertheless deeply endearing.

In the early morning hours that the Petroglyph Flower first made the acquaintance of the Farting Nun, it did not trust her. But upon her singing a song while strumming her banjo, the Flower was completely convinced and taken over. The nun assured the flower that she could help it take care of his newly found human friends. Upon looking around the room at the sleeping friends, the Farting Nun did what she did best: taking care of people. She plumped pillows, tucked in blankets, wiped maggots off the television and telephones, and brought an air of tidy joy and unbridled optimism into the motel room where all of the friends were spending the night. But nevertheless, the Petroglyph Flower became uneasy, feeling an unknown sense of confusion that had not gripped it since the night that it was awoken by the penetrating rays of moonlight that hadn't touched his skin for ages. The confusion most likely had something to do with the walls of the hotel, as if the rooms being isolated by walls created an organism out of the motel, as if each room was a cell of a larger being. These divisions created a macrocosm that brought a wave of what some might have perceived as nausea or unease to the flower. And the fact that the Farting Nun had arrived to do her missionary work only made things worse. But at least she had been able to help the creature better understand the reality of humans and their needs. It wasn't enough to turn people into suitcases, to stuff their dried eyesockets with precious gems and to spraypaint their faces and bodies with festive colors: No, humans needed not just material pleasures and assets, but they also needed a certain flavor of spiritual nourishment which the flower was only realizing just now that it was personally deficient in being able to give. Perhaps he could learn then what he needed to learn, from the Farting Nun? *So far, the nun appeared to set a good example to her fellow humans (especially to the self-righteous parents), showing the socially acceptable combinations of selfish versus altruistic tendencies, and how to make the two forces harmonize in socially acceptable ways (at least superficially), while still simultaneously retaining full deniability for all of her actions.* There was also the issue of connecting and connections, and the degree to which any self-assured prophet could assume the role of guardian, leader, protector, and to be able to carry out such a role in an effective and sufficiently caring way that would benefit all parties involved.

The Petroglyph Flower regarded the Farting Nun as she sat down on the maggot-infested bed and began to play a new song on her traveling banjo. Immediately the flower had visions of stage-stomping concerts and vibrating floors and noise that could damage anyone's eardrums. The music became a wall of light that emanated from her hands, possibly revealing a connection between light and dark. Within the dawning rays of the upcoming morning sun, it was possible to discern the nun's plump and well-manicured hands. For someone who ate nothing but baked beans everyday, this woman was in excellent shape. The happy people sleeping on the bed first began to reach consciousness at the same instant the nun's song brought a ray of joy into the flower's heart, or whatever lithic organ it was that housed the creature's intellect and cerebral spirit. The touch of her voice opened up all the jail cells in the world, including those of the motel. It was now obvious that the motel, in which they had all blissfully regaled and rested for the prior evening, was very much like a complex system of jail cells which needed to be escaped at all costs. It was this last thought that turned prison cells into a beehive, and then the beehive into a library, with each cell representing a book or a depth of pages into which faces and colors were deposited, as a part of an intergalactic hub or any other means of connection between disparately displaced brains separated by words and feelings. This kind of disconnect redefined the sensation that was once referred to as the "outdoors."

In ways which weren't initially perceptible, the petroglyphic entity reached forward its petals into the morning sky. The head of this flower made of rock stretched toward the sky, as if it were a mirror image of the sun, but as a distorted reflection of biting sarcasm. This strange growth spurt was oddly complimented by the Farting Nun, who had taken out her banjo by now and was singing trite wake-up music to the sleeping friends. The nun had this special way of cocking her head from side to side while she sang or spoke, speaking in tones which suggested that the greatest solutions to life's problems were simple, matter-of-fact, and which could be done ever so easily – perhaps similar to the overly simplistic outlook that some teenagers have when they have been overly sheltered by their parents. The nun strummed the banjo, with booming words of religion reverberating through her vocal cords. This was certainly a Rise-and-Shine kind of morning, and everyone knew it, even the dozen friends of the Petroglyph Flower, who had by now awakened and rather than rubbing crusts of sleep from their eyes, instead were rubbing diamonds from festively painted eyesockets. Such was the life of luxury for the rich: to have morning excrements transformed to riches, while under the watchful, caring gaze of an alien sun god and the music of terrestrial cowardice. It was certainly going to be an exciting day!

The group set out on the path, heading to a dwelling over the next hill that they understood to be a lively small city. It was certain that it would take at least a week on foot to get there, but the party was determined to reach a new settlement, with promises of a newer and even better salvation than any of which they had already found along the way of their spectacular journey. While walking, the Farting Nun was able to teach everyone how to tie their shoelaces, and even how to open doors by twisting the doorknobs. The nun was able to discuss and demonstrate these highly useful techniques with the most precise details, and her outlook on life was better than ever. Whatever her weaknesses might have been (such as an ever-present tone of condescension), she more than made up for them with her spiritual goodness and seeming altruism. During this process, the Petroglyph Flower was beginning to identify the newly discovered emotion that had begun to course through its alien vasculature: Jealousy, with a capital J. It resented the fact that the Farting Nun had an answer for everything; it resented the fact that the nun was stealing the attention of the flower's twelve disciples, lavishing them with presents not made of material riches but of spiritual things with a supposedly high degree of value – value which need not have been validated through external means or appraised through any kind of authority based on physical force.

For many days, the troupe followed their fortunes in the direction of the city. Many a farm or wild area they passed through until at one moment of a rather cool afternoon, they happened upon a sad situation: a farmer had lost his wife due to the influenza virus, and the burial had only happened just the day before. When the flower, the nun and the desiccated disciples found the farmer – middle-aged and tired, kneeling against the empty house with his head in his hands and face wet with tears – the Farting Nun knew exactly what to do (she always did): the farmer was first washed free of all his earthy guilt and sins through being baptized anew in a nearby stream. The cold water wiped the tears and dirt and feelings of loss from his quivering skin and he rejoiced upon the land and the Lord, vowing to live again according to the ways of God and all of those other important religious rules and regulations that required such things as fish on Fridays and the like. The Farting Nun brought the Farmer widower to an open, grassy field where she knelt before him, in perfect prayer. The Petroglyph flower (feeling very much left out and marginalized, such as an eye's field of vision becoming reduced from its former range down to a small, agonizing pinpoint of light) sat behind the nun where it had a very good view of her buttocks. Luckily for the flower, the nun had not eaten anything at all (not even beans) for several days prior, so it was most fortunate that her flatulence had dissipated for the time being. Seated around the nun, the farmer and the flower were the twelve skeletal disciples, aptly leaning forward in breathless, lifeless anticipation, with sparkling gemstones periodically dropping from their eyes, with their mummified skin painted ever so artfully with color, with the occasional bone jutting through broken areas of the skin. The abdomens of these once-human prophets had by now dried shut, encasing within them all of the personal effects that had once been placed there by the Petroglyph Flower for what now seemed months ago. Through the drying of the tissues caused by gradual mummification, all of these special, material items of terrestrial treasure were kept safely within their abdominal cavities, as if they had become human birdcages. For instance, Carla had her prized hairdryer that could be seen poking through her ribcage, while Marvin still had his archaic typewriter crammed into his bloated abdomen, as if waiting for the day when it would be removed to have its keys clacked on again, on some distant, future day. The Dried Disciples, as they were now called, sat around the holy trio in a circle, losing their teeth and hair at a phenomenal rate while they observed the holy ritual that transpired before them: After praying to the Lord for quite a while, the Nun looked up into the sky and witnessed a miracle. The Lord had exposed himself to the group, showing a ghostly phallus made of low-lying (or perhaps low-laying) clouds that could have easily been a mile long. God's penis cut through the sky like a sword, while the distant crack of thunder could only hint at the deluge that was soon to come.

Instinctively, the Farting Nun asked the man to stand in front of her while she knelt and continued to pray, with her hands no longer clasped together but instead around the farmer's engorged phallic member. Once he was fully aroused, the nun absent-mindedly brushed her hair to the side of her face while she began to perform acts of exquisite syrup-sucking fellatio. As a woman of the cloth, and as the bride of Christ, the nun was quite skilled at these sessions of corporeal pleasure. As the farmer's woodpecker disappeared into her clenched, treelike hands and into her wet, lipsticked mouth, time and time again, in and out and in again, the naughty scene unfolding could have reminded any classroom of confused schoolchildren of the fable about the bushy-tailed squirrel who visited an abandoned cottage and was consequently chased away by the resident ghost. The squirrel returned and then was chased away. The squirrel's return and then retreat; then return, then retreat. In and out, in and out and in again. When the squirrel returned for the very last visit, it was thoroughly consumed by the ghost, who turned it into a flattened trophy-pelt to be hung like balls upon the wall, right above the fireplace where they would remain toasty forever, dripping trails of saliva and semen down into a sizzling cauldron firmly positioned within the fireplace for that very purpose. From this bubbling kettle the squirrel reemerged like the phoenix, born again, while quickly regarding the desiccated pelt of its former self still hanging above the fire, and then it darted away from the crime-scene in a burst of renewed vigor that only propelled it more vigorously to resume its pursuit of fresh nuts to crack.

The tears beneath the Farmer's eyes had finally dried, and he looked up into the heavens with an expanded sense of spirituality that only went concomitantly with the Farting Nun's puckering grimaces closely resembling the furtive gasps of a suckermouth catfish. After composing herself, and wiping the spilt seed from her dainty chin, in her most positive Pollyanna voice yet, she rose from the ground and broke out her powerguitair, bursting into more Rise-and-Shine music, dousing the countrycide with wave after wave of lyrical verse that could only have been described as "over-positive" or perhaps simultaneously as a latent form of ovipositing that indicated an insidiously spreading movement of change that might topple even the most steadfast of mindsets, moving the golden eggs of the goose to the core of a nearby mountain, where they were to be hidden for a thousand years in a straw-filled crate. This subduction of values indicated the pleasurable wave of coming tremors, the seismic over-effulgence of oviposited over-positivity that came from a curiously warped smile of blind belief and the naïveté of bubbles that were soon to be popped in the most vainglorious manner. What could possibly go wrong?

Upon leaving, the Farting Nun kissed the liberated Farmer on both cheeks, and told him that if he sodomized his milk cow – the fat one that lived in the small barn next to his cottage – then her teats would transform into lightbulbs and he would thereupon become rich with hummingbirds that would levitate around his thick, pointed fingers, helping him to poke them into any flower in the world he fancied. The Farmer grinned from ear to ear, bearing a huge bulge in his pants, and bid the quasi-religious company a fond farewell. As a token show of gratitude, the Farmer supplied the nun, the Petroglyph flower (who was still sullenly quiet, filled to the brim with a jealousy that could have been described in no other way than completely biliary) and the Dried Disciples with as many pots of baked beans as they (or the flower, actually) could carry. The group walked off into a glorious sunset, feeling the warmth on their cheeks, whether made of living flesh, bio-organic rock, or the mummified hides of human shoe leather.

In the beginning, the Petroglyph Flower enjoyed its new lease on humanity, taking on the role of savior, provider, enlightener, etc. But with the mysterious appearance of the Farting Nun, the flower felt extremely humbled and humiliated, feeling as if it'd been upstaged and shut out of a love experience that the creature had waited millennia to find. If it had had lachrymal glands, then it would most likely have cried until its eyes were red. But since there were no such eyes and no such tear glands, the stone creature brooded in silence, pulsing the petals around its cerebralish organ with a sarcastic malevolence, and a bitterness that only mimicked the solar flares of an unstable sun that goes through its periodical fluctuations in circulation. Somewhere beneath the nearby mountain, the golden eggs oviposited by the over-positive Farting Nun were gestating in their millennial process which the flower was sure to see some day, toward which it would wait with a bitterness that was indescribable, but which was sure to reseed the earth with new creatures, new processes and new forms of paradise which had been hitherto concealed underneath all of the obvious rocks, bringing the unimaginable to the foreground, thereby destroying what most people would have expected as routinely historical processes. The eggs swarmed and pulsated in their hidden crate nests, and their golden qualities gleamed within the darkness, in all of their weight, in all of their vibrations, in all of the round chords that could have been plucked from a motherly powerguitar made of a precious metal.

Later that night around a campfire that refused to be extinguished, the Petroglyph Flower was distracted by the Farting Nun, who was still under the effects of the baked beans, preventing the creature from having any of its much-needed rest and meditation. In its frustration, it regarded the dozen Dried Disciples who were arranged around the campfire in a perfect circle. These dear friends had become so dried out that they were now indistinguishable from each other save for the identifying paint markings that covered them. By now their teeth and eyesocket jewels were gone, and their corporeal hides had shrunken so as to better intimately clasp the artificially introduced belongings within their abdomens: their ribcages clutched their possessions analogously to the way platinum prongs on an expensive ring might clasp an equally precious gemstone. These dear souls huddled about the campfire, and it was their togetherness and their deeply bonded friendship that reminded the Petroglyph Flower about love: about the love it had for them, about the love it had for itself and the universe, and about the love that they were showing to it, with their technicolored skin, dried to the consistency of the finest of high-society leathers.

In the morning, the group resumed their journey, and by midday, they arrived at the outer wall of the city. It was such an old and dry place, but not so old that one couldn't take advantage of all the benefits that modern technology could offer. It was within this archaic city that the entire group found acceptance and otherly love. People stopped and stared, throwing flowers at their feet. While the Farting Nun led the group towards the inner parts of the city, following a well-used path lined with cobblestones that were as smooth as freshly plucked melons, the Petroglyph Flower headed up the rear, dangling the Dried Disciples from the ends of its prehensile tendril appendages. To the city people, these new visitors seemed to bring with them an aura of messianic confidence and persuasion, inspiring the simple folk to fall to their knees and kiss the ground as the newcomers passed. The Farting Nun was especially flatulent, and she tightly held a mother-of-pearl crucifix to her breast as she smiled and enjoyed the parade of which she was an integral part.

Upon reaching the central square, the visitors realized that the dryness existing within the outer shells of the city only served to hide the wet oasis within the central district, with lush bryophytes, flowers, trees, fountains and a fine cool mist that helped greatly in diminishing the intense heat of midday. Ironically, the oasis was the area where it was possible to see the most mirages. People were constantly bumping into each other, thinking that they were heading through doorways that weren't really there, or embracing friends or other acquaintances who were mere illusion. The cool water was atomized by the brisk winds that blew through the inner citadel formed the most refreshing of misty vapors. One could walk through it and completely forget about a parched throat. Or skin that was dried and cracked with blood could instantly become healed to the consistency of soft newborn skin. It was all very miraculous, and the flower and nun both stopped a moment with their dried luggage to breathe in the satisfying waves of rejuvenation, as if perhaps they had found a modern-day version of the fountain of youth, albeit in a different part of the world than the humid swamps of Florida. The nun and flower were both welcomed into the midst of the city-dwellers, as were the Dried Disciples who were stacked against a far wall in a patch of sunlight, being allowed to rest from their long journey. Forming a pyramid against the wall, the disciples had reached a moment of breakthrough indecision: Carla, Barry, Larry and Steve had the impulse to go exploring the wildly exotic city, while Bonnie, Marvin, Mike, Marsha and Diandra wanted to stay put, and make more babies and raise them in a new existence of intersubjective domestication, creating a new incarnation of the consumerist lifecycle anew, while forgetting about their consumptive behaviors of the past. And the remaining disciples – Cindy, Linda and Greg – couldn't figure out what they wanted to do, or which way they wanted to go. Among these moments of indeterminate dithering, the Petroglyph Flower began to sway, moving through mental fields of gyration, plucking up the memories from under the rocks and grabbing at fireworks before they had a chance to explode. The eternity of this moment became unbearable, and the flower had an ever-so-brief vision of strangely wrapped flowers that unwound from a vine to whisper messages of poetry into its auditory organs, to foretell a moment of unbearable perspective into the future. Since the vision was only brief, and didn't provide any actual imagery of what this unbearable future might be, the flower felt that it was entirely unsubstantiated and hence unworthy of any preoccupation.

The overhead sun cut through the cool mist, reminding everyone that the day would only last for a few more hours, and not for eternity. That particular moment (or perhaps illusion) of infinity condensed within the space of a paradise and created an unspeakable vertigo of which everyone present could not consciously wrap their minds around.

For the visitors, at least, the newness of the old city was enough to distract them, but even for the locals, the moment of the oasis served a strange function by way of displacing them from themselves, forcing them to find themselves anew, and then to carry on with whatever they had set out to do during morning hours when their minds were clear.

It was at this moment of newly found clarity that the Farting Nun felt a folded piece of parchment tucked away in her pocket, which she had not put there. Upon reading the note, the blood drained from her face, and she held the back of her hands to her forehead, releasing plague-level amounts of ladybugs – red shell with black spots – into the central area of the city. The ladybugs were great for removing the aphids from the plants, but their unexpected presence there scared a lot of people, transforming the scene of pacifistic tranquility into one of ominous mayhem, with children becoming separated from their parents in a stampede of precocious terror. After the Farting Nun had had a chance recompose herself, withdrawing her hands from her forehead, the deluge of ladybugs stopped and the insects miraculously flew off into the arid landscape, perhaps in search of other aphids to suck dry of all bodily fluids. The nun reread the death threat she had received, feeling chills of mortal terror translate throughout her quivering body. It was certain that she would have to leave the group now. She didn't want to, but it was for their own good: the Dried Disciples needed to continue their journey unmolested, and the Petroglyph Flower was indeed their tribal leader, their spiritual guru – in a sense, a spiritual bellhop – and this special journey between these highly guided souls should not be tainted with the murderous intrusions of a world gone mad that had dubious formulations of morality. No, it was certain that the Farting Nun would have to flee, so as to maintain the safety of her friends. She looked upon them, congregated within drafts of an oasis mist, presided over by an alien rock-flower that was sworn to protect and uplift them, and knew that she had to move on. The nun ran her seasoned hands over her abdomen, feeling a telling bulge that suggested that she was with child. Obviously she must have picked up more than a few manifestations of sperm over the course of her recent travels, due to the generosity of her missionary work, so it shouldn't have been all that surprising that eventually one of the wiggly arrows would hit the bullseye, resulting in a holy conception. She sort of knew about this pregnancy anyway, although she hadn't been able to admit this to herself on the conscious, waking level. From the

Farting Nun's estimation, she was just a few months pregnant. Having an abortion would be quite easy and painless, and then she could resume her missionary work, guilt-free.

The Farting Nun took her leave from the Petroglyph Flower and the Dried Disciples, commenting on how well all of them had tied their shoelaces that morning. With tears in her eyes, she said her goodbyes, cocking her head to the right and left, as these motions accompanied her incredibly trite, know-it-all, goody-goody, sing-song mannerisms of speech. She carried as many pots of the baked beans with her as she could, without wanting to weigh herself down. Upon leaving their delightful company, the nun quickly darted among the more shadowy parts of the city, in the hopes of eluding whoever might have been watching her and waiting with calculated malevolence when to pull the trigger or make the hit. She decoyed herself by selling her well-worn black habit to a curious stranger, and assumed the appearance of a 1970s disco prostitute who was also skilled simultaneously as a real estate broker. The abbess, in her new disguise, entered the stairwell of the subway system, and descended several levels until she reached the platform to catch the train that would take her back to her monastic sanctuary, her postulant hideaway where she took her vows to do important missionary work. Located on the train platform were several convenience shops: doughnuts and coffee, currency exchange, newspapers, shoe-shine and last but not least, abortions. The Farting Nun was not the least bit afraid of having an abortion, since she had had the procedure done on her countless times before, as a result of her missionary work. Disappearing behind the velvet curtain, the nun paid the doctor and had the fetus extracted without any complications. As was the custom, she also purchased a glass cylindrical vessel from the doctor which would enable her to keep the aborted fetus as a trophy, to put on the shelf with all of her other embryonic trophies that she had accumulated over the years of her very important missionary work of bringing smiles and hope to those who had nothing but despair and death in their troubled lives. The Farting Nun paid the abortion doctor and asked him to send the preserved embryo to her monastery, where she would receive it with joy upon her arrival home. In all truth, this nun was one of the more progressive Christian nuns who walked the planet, currently an experienced Stavrophore with papal ambition, secretly creating an army of formalin homunculi that might enable her to reach the level of *Megaloschemos Dominatrix* within her Order. That was the highest level a nun of her Order could reach, and she was certain that the Christian humility of her words and deeds (as evidenced through this particular, recounted adventure) would surely prove her worthiness – provided that she would be able to live long enough to receive the holy black robe and veil, making her into a holy warrior of charity and goodness. The Farting Nun thanked the abortion doctor, and donned her 1970s disco prostitute attire and slipped out onto the train platform. She boarded a train that had just arrived, and disappeared into a crowd of passengers, unaware of a shadowy figure who had followed her into the passenger coach. If she had been more observant, she might have noticed that the shadowy figure was actually a mannequin dressed in velvet, wearing a loosely-fitting overcoat to protect it from cold weather.

Meanwhile, the Petroglyph Flower was feeling glad to be in control again. It had learned a lot from these dear humans, and knew straight off that it was to be their fearless leader, evidently internalizing the human dichotomy or psychological complex of leader-versus-follower. By that point, the sun had slipped into one of those lazy afternoon azimuths, and an announcement blared over the loudspeakers of the old citadel that the Hour of FastFood had arrived. Most of the shops and bazaars had replaced their traditional wares and commodities with items of fast-food consumption, accompanied by corporate banners that rudely announced the presence of the corporate processed food, instantly making hungry all of the unwary by the raw powers of subliminal suggestion. Apparently the Petryglyph Flower and its Dried Disciples were no more immune to these subtle suggestions than any of the citizens who congregated in the busy citadel. From one of the fast-food stalls there appeared a trade-mark apparition of a double-arch, or perhaps it was a pair of mountains, or buttocks or breasts or pumpkins or bowling balls. This illusion of seeing double, perhaps of a duplicated concave object, was no less disconcerting as it also made all witnesses intensively hungry, causing them to drool all over themselves. In addition, not only were these people induced with a wave of insatiable hunger (like a group of salivating pavlovian dogs), but linked to this onslaught of artificially induced hunger was the promise of an increase in self-esteem. Therefore, images and words having to do with processed foods consisting of embalmed animal protein, saturated fats and refined carbohydrates were able to initiate a psychophysiological response in those who experienced these stimuli, not only resulting in the illusory perception of gastronomic appetite, but also an anticipation of having their personalities validated through external means. And they fell for it every time.

After the entire city had become high through their consumption of the corporate fast food, the people began to stumble and collide with walls and each other, in their post-feeding haze, reaching dangerous levels of blood glucose and soluble triglycerides. Endogenous insulin regulation was disrupted in this manner on a daily basis, and the citizens approached near-diabetic limits of existence, nearly foaming at the mouth but still feeling good about themselves through the emotional validation afforded them by the fabricated, toxic comestibles. It was at that moment, when the entire populus had descended into a brain-numbing haze, that the Petroglyph Flower had the most peculiar experience. While reclining against the wall, Marsha, Bonnie, Larry and the rest of the Dried Disciple gang were still posing with half-eaten cheeseburgers held to their mouths, with flies buzzing around their heads in the dull heat of the afternoon. The flower noticed their delighted activity, observing that they too, seemed to have become dulled by the surge of unhealthy chemicals that had entered their systems. The alien rose to its full stature, and again flexed its rock-like appendages that so closely resembled the petals of a large sunflower, making a gesture of mockery towards the powerful sun overhead. The flower had become a sarcastic reflection of the transfer of energy; it had learned how to become the parody of the sun, radiating not life, but death – especially the humor of death. The Petroglyph Flower, in all of its radiating sarcasm, managed to summon some iridescent goliath beetles from the cracked walls of the city. These beetles, already so large in size, appeared to grow even larger, becoming big enough to suggest the shape of a small, rounded sportscar. Despite the growth of these beetles, their metallic armor still retained its reflective, multicolored iridescence, fluctuating between shades of green, amber and purple depending on the angle from which light was reflected. The afternoon heat had become stifling, reaching furnace-level proportions. Based on an instant flash of intuition, the Petroglyph Flower understood the presence of the giant beetles: they were to become deep-fryers that would house the greasy bones of the dried disciples, in a gesture of supreme reverence that would shake the walls of the ancient city into a future of golden enlightenment and even wilder journeys into the great beyond of primate love. The rock flower took its beloved friends, and put each one of them into a hollow space that had been revealed on the backs of each of the super-colossal goliath beetles. These colorful beetles were now deep-fryers, and each mummified bag of dried disciple bones was a packet of pre-fab french fries to be lowered into the beetle deep-fryers. The Petroglyph Flower knew immediately that these insectoid deep-fryers containing the mummified human french-fries should be placed in an ornate semi-circle around the special fountain in the ancient city.

Spiders from the sky descended upon the old city, and these arachnids from up above reached their holy legs down upon the people and liquefied their inner organs, ultimately sucking their mammalian bodies dry of all nutritious, cheeseburger-nourished biological fluids, leading to a new regime of life that dwelled over a city originally built by primates. The Petroglyph Flower became the resident God of the city, and presided in the fountain area, where it was frequently visited by its spidery subjects who helped it understand the humor in horseshoes that hung from the necks of sasquatches. And most importantly, the flower never forgot its loving and highly inspirational friend, the Farting Nun.

Bioweapon
(7-2008)

It had been days that the plaster came down from the ceiling, and all of the mutated bunny-rabbits, with bloodshot eyes and white fur flecked with their own blood, had fled the premises, along with most of the researchers. It had been a crazy day, with the buzzing sounds of locusts and whispers of malevolence moving in a cursory manner from ear to ear, from top-hat to top-hat, bringing down the smiles like the red velvet labia-curtains of a stage performance gone pungently sour. What had once been leveled floors and orderly work spaces now degenerated into a cluster of smashed grapes left ever so cruelly to ferment in the blistering sun, leading to mutations unheard of and legends that would leave shadowy marks across the memories of an entire land for months, if not years.

What had been perhaps falling bombs or collapsing infrastructure blasted the ears of the only human survivor, a researcher named Mikhail but who was known to his employees as "Dr. Rasputin." During the attack or the accident or whatever it was, Mikhail had been inadvertently infected with a pathogen he'd been working on: a genetically engineered variant of a staphylococcus strain, transformed with a few exogenous loci that coded for enzymes which would enable the bacterium to easily synthesize significant quantities of lysergic acid, or LSD, within the infected host. As the pathogen was a type of staph bacteria that was antibiotic resistant, it was highly infectious toward humans, and in fact was being developed as a bioweapon: the engineered bugs would be released into hostile territory, infecting the local population, not only causing gruesome and ultimately fatal skin lesions, but also unsupportable doses of LSD that would cause the infected individuals to go mad. This project was of course being developed in secret, and was in fact being developed in parallel, by various capitalist-industrialized governments across the globe. In this particular country, however, something had gone dreadfully wrong – perhaps sabotage or an attack from the outside – which had caused everyone to quickly abandon their work and run for their lives.

But poor Mikhail had not been lucky enough to reach the exits in time, and was apparently crushed beneath a large piece of ceiling that had fallen. He was in one of the labs, and gradually regained consciousness to awaken in a pool of sunlight, as the light and the wind came through the shattered laboratory windows, with billowing curtains of the apocalypse that moved like the slow-motion tongue of a serpent in a sinister way.

From the itching spots on his arms, Mikhail knew that he'd been infected, and already his sense of consciousness appeared foggy and off-balance, as if he were ready to start seeing those mutated pink bunny-rabbits of his own creation, with the skin lesions and the bloodshot eyes. But at the moment there were no hallucinations, only the pain in his broken ribs, which must have come from those heavy supports that fell from the ceiling. He groaned and climbed to his feet to assess the damage: overturned lab tables and equipment, smashed bottles (including some of the vessels which contained the pathogen), and all sorts of reagents that littered the floor. Obviously by now, wearing a protective suit against contamination would have been a waste of time. The spots of Mikhail's arms were not so bad, though – just a few red welts here and there. Since the tap water wasn't running, he instead resorted to using DI water to clean his skin, with the usual industrial-grade soap normally intended for just glassware. Although this wouldn't rid him of the infection, perhaps it would at least prolong his life, long enough to get help, in case anyone were to come looking for him. But so far during that strange day, there were no apparitions of people in hazmat suits who were looking for him. And by then he realized that there wasn't going to be anyone looking for him.

Mikhail went into one of the more intact rooms – an animal handling room – and began to relax a little bit more. This room had apparently been spared much of the mayhem that had ravished the rest of the research facilities, even though he had not been in a position to assess each and every part of the sprawling complex that was located just a few miles outside of one of the smaller cities, in a private, government-controlled area cordoned off with barbed wire and fascist warning signs posted a meter apart from each other. But in this particular room, where the tech usually handled the animal test-subjects, there was little of use: a few empty cages, a table, and boxes of computer printouts. In one particular corner of the room, however, was a cage that was filled almost to capacity with dead rats that looked as if they'd been dead for quite some time. Mikhail knew that he'd been unconscious for a day or so after the catastrophe, but perhaps he'd been mistaken – possibly he'd been unconscious for much longer, or at least long enough for a curiously packed cage of rats to starve, perish and then decay? It didn't seem possible, and he had no answer to this question. The rats were of the Sprague Dawley variety, with their characteristic white fur and pink, bloodshot eyes. These corpses were in advanced decay, with deflated bodies and a fine layer of a greenish mold covering their skin. As the researcher quickly edged away from the cage full of strange corpses, the sounds of gunfire and then screams became audible. On the floor above his were heard the footfalls of soldiers as their boots pounded the floor, sending showers of plaster and dust over him. In some parts of the room it looked as if the ceiling was beginning to collapse. Mikhail hid behind the table, out of the line of fire should any of the mysterious soldiers enter the room and begin shooting. Unfortunately while crouched on the floor, he was forced to stare at the cage full of dead rodents, from which emanated the musky odor of death. His arms were beginning to itch.

Not soon after assuming his hiding place, Mikhail heard the footfalls of the mysterious soldiers running down the hallway on his floor. Doors still intact were wrenched open and then swiftly slammed again, in a flood of violence that became a wave of sound that terrified him. Periodically gunshots were still heard, accompanied by shrieks and groaning. The footsteps approached the room where the researcher was hiding, as could be heard by the sounds of the hard boots crunching broken glass underfoot, and kicking aside pieces of debris and other shrapnel. As expected, the door burst open followed by what sounded like heavy breathing, as if the room were being surveyed by the eyes of god. Mikhail could feel waves of invisible judgment pouring into the room, like a flood of seawater into the hull of an ocean-faring vessel that had the supreme misfortune to spring a leak out in the middle of the open sea. Mikhail had the choice of either closing his eyes and coping with the dizziness that was beginning to set in, or keeping them open and focused on the cage of dead rats next to him. Either way, silence was critical, so as not to alert whoever had stormed the building and was most likely killing off whichever survivors and stragglers remained. Mikhail was determined to live.

As quickly as the door to the animal-handling lab was opened, it was shut again like a crypt, and the heavy footfalls quickly diminished as they moved down the corridor, and eventually traveled down to the floor below. The researcher waited a good half hour before resuming his survey of the destruction, just to make sure that he wouldn't be heard by whoever had just scoured the building in search of survivors to eliminate. What was so strange however was the fact that before the arrival of the elimination soldiers, he had not encountered any living people (or even dead people, for that matter) in the building, or at least on the floor that he had been searching. So the sudden appearance of the survivors was a mystery.

Before leaving the animal handling room, a scratching sound was heard from one of the cabinets to his side. Mikhail opened the hinge to reveal another cage of Sprague Dawley test rats, with their peculiar albino look. The rats in this cage were still alive, and crowded together in the same way the dead rats in the other cage were. At the moment, the researcher was surprised to find himself flanked by two cages of rats that had a strange communication with each other: the cage to the right with living specimens, while to the left were the dead ones, whose corpses had been ravaged by fungal processes. It only occurred to him at this moment how unhealthy it was for him to have such extended respiratory exposure to a source of mold so large in volume, especially in light of the toxic alkali compounds to which he might be exposed. As if bitten by a rabid animal, the researcher quickly got to his feet and backed away from the cages. He could clearly see that the living rats wanted out of the cage, as if their grating squeals were tiny pleas for help and consideration, but he regarded them as no more than garbage to be disposed of rather than living things. He left the room behind him and paced the hallways, peering out of windows at the desolation outside: well-manicured fields of green grass but without the usual presence of sentries. No electricity, no running water. No sounds, nothing. And the places where he heard the soldiers pause to fire their weapons yielded no bodies.

The picturesque blankness of the landscape captivated his feverish stare, and while hunched over the windowsill, the researcher stared out far and wide, looking at green hills that obscured the view of the city and the roads not far away. His moment of peace was disturbed when he noticed the sky quickly getting darker, at a rate that was much too fast for normal nightfall. It wasn't that he had a working wristwatch to verify the time, but for the sky to get so dark so fast was unnatural. But then the thought suddenly occurred to him that the growing staph infection would lead to higher amounts of LSD in his system, and perhaps the hallucinogen was playing tricks on him: forcing the pupils in his eyes to constrict unnaturally, so as to create the illusion of falling darkness. But as there were no mirrors handy, Mikhail was unable to verify that his pupils were in fact getting smaller.

The ambiance of the place now became a dead weight, an immense sea of lethargy that slowly pushed him around like a floating cork on an ocean of whimsical laziness. All the while, the lesions on his arms were becoming itchier and he found himself scratching at them involuntarily. Perhaps the direct sunlight was making his lesions irritated, thought the researcher to himself. He moved back into the safety of the building while avoiding the corpses of rats and bunny-rabbits, with pink, dried eyes and albino fur all stained pink with altered blood. Although he hadn't eaten anything in over forty-eight hours, he still didn't feel hungry, and neither were there any food supplies, anyway. The passage of time was sinister, with the sun finally setting as an angry eye, stabbed with a hot poker that made his own eye sockets feel like cauldrons of burning juices. He was slumped against a wall, too afraid to move upstairs, and too afraid to move downstairs. He had heard barking noises out in the distance, among the thickets of tall trees that surrounded the research complex in certain places, so his worry was that they might be military or police dogs trained to sniff out survivors. Mikhail thought that by moving to one of the upper levels of the building, that he'd be less likely to be discovered by the dogs or whatever animals they might have been. His burning face enjoyed the coolness of the walls as he reposed on the floor, half-dead. By now his skin was beyond itching – it almost felt like he was being bitten alive by the sharp mandibles of carnivorous insects, making his misery complete. He tried to pass the night in peace, hoping for rest, but there was none to be had. The night seemed to last forever. There were many moments where he thought he heard the same soldiers' footfalls on the immediate floors above and below him, and he cringed in fear, manifesting suicidal urges and other dreadful impulses. At one point, after what might have been an hour of quiet, the researcher came to hear the sound of breathing, coming from someone or something across the room from him, right outside in the hall. The door was propped halfway open, and the breathing sound was irregular, alerting him to the presence of some living being close to the entrance of the room. Perhaps the beast had sensed the fear in Mikhail's dead stillness, for suddenly a pair of yellow eyes appeared in the doorway, looking in at him. The eyes blinked at a very slow rate, suggesting that they weren't human. Mikhail clutched a rusted scalpel he'd picked up hours before, and held it in front of him, just waiting for the creature to come towards him, but it never did. Eventually the eyes turned away and moved down the hallway. By this point Mikhail was shaking, violently trembling, as he collapsed again against the far wall of the room, crying softly and waiting for the sun to rise.

In this way, the researcher's imagination had finally been released, the terrible thing that it was. The prison that was his fantasy was the extension of the day into the night, and the biting insects and the peculiar lack of hunger and the spinning room and the precious scalpel had all become the condensation of the universe. The walls had become electrified, as he pressed his cheek against the wall again, feeling shocked, as if he were ground meat tightly packed with plastic wrap in a grocery store lit by sickly fluorescent lights. Addicted to his work, Mikhail the fearless researcher had never had time for a girlfriend or wife, so there was no memory of a sweet face to call upon in his hour of greatest need. The idea of a cold fountain of even icier water with which to wet his face was an illusion of happiness more powerful than the dreamiest, tourist-trashed beaches of homicidal Acapulco. Suddenly, he knew that he needed water. He was water. The human body is sixty-plus percent water. The water could move over his face, melting the plastic-wrap. The water could take him from the top of a mountain stream down to a channel that empties into the ocean. He could disguise his body as a shark. With water in his gills, he could revert to the universal vertebrate embryo – that special embryonic form in which all vertebrates, whether sharks or lizards or apes, consisted of. This special embryo could become anything: fish, amphibian, reptile, bird or mammal. The pulsating gills of a tiny pink mass of flesh, growing tumor-style within the bowels of a wrecked building, preparing to swim to the primordial seas where the messages from many aeons before were first uttered as grunts and squawks to indifferent clouds, tornadoes and other gods who never wore crucifixes on Sunday, nor ever paid attention to overly masochistic group ritualistic behaviors.

The researcher got to his knees, and began to pace the hallway, like a dog or some other four-legged animal. Going down the staircases was of course a challenge, but Mikhail was able to manage. He bumped his head into debris, but he didn't care, because he couldn't feel the pain. He was beyond pain. He licked the concrete, pretending to have found a primordial stream through which coursed the groundwater of the primitive continents, which nourished all manner of life from the giant redwood trees to the insatiable woolly mammoths. The imaginary stream served his needs for roughly a minute or so, until he realized that he had only descended to the third floor. He needed to go to the basement, where he knew there was water. Only until he reached that level could he rejoin his ancient kindred as the universal embryo. In his mind's eye, he could feel his HOX genes coming to life, feeling the trunk of his body as a curled mass of segments, or linearly arranged parts of a whole, under the directives of special signaling proteins that were more ancient than Pandora's box. His arms could have been wings or webbed feet, or possibly even antennae, under the right circumstances. He was prepared to dig through the entire earth to get to the magic pool of primordiality, to flop around until he found the right golden goblet that contained the sea of regenerative iridescence, waiting for him to become born anew under different circumstances, under the differences between the constellations which made the void between galaxies seem like petty starstuff, moving down the gravitational incline into the infinity of subatomic tranquility. But fortunately, despite his willingness to go as far as the end of the universe itself, Mikhail the researcher found the flooded basement, and therefore his quest ended earlier than expected.

Fortunately there were a few basement windows which allowed the early morning light to penetrate the dim underground area, which had become flooded due to the ruptured watermain. And because the emergency electricity had gone out, the primary and backup pumps no longer worked. In addition to the usual architecture of waterpipes and various hydraulic machines that populated the basement, the surviving Sprague Dawley rats and albino pink bunny-rabbits with flecks of blood and festering bloodshot eyes had taken residence upon the shelves and tops of pipes which had not yet been flooded. In fact, those pipes suspended just a foot below the ceiling became an elongated bench on which sat many of the rabbits and rats. Their eyes seemed to stare through him, as if he had become more of an irritant, or maybe the presence of an antichrist (one of the many, many antichrists, that is). In a moment of fear, the researcher had the intuition that these animals had not eaten for as long as he had not, or perhaps even longer. They could have easily leapt upon his floating form and first devoured the soft tissues such as his eyes, and then cleared his face and torso of all nutritional musculature, but they, as he, were under the influence of the bacterially-secreted LSD, so the sensations of physical hunger were completely absent. This particular situation worked to Mikhail's favor, because under any other circumstances where hallucinogens had not been implemented, these starving lab animals, now released to act according to their own wills, would have certainly consumed the human flesh within minutes.

Mikhail the researcher floated on his back, while staring up at the ceiling. He could see the research rats and rabbits seated upon the lengths of the water conduits, on the unsubmerged shelves along the sides of the walls, and on the floating debris, such as styrofoam boxes and other plastic refuse. The animals uttered strange wails and groans, all staring at his arrival, looking towards him with mixed expressions of terror and hatred. Although Mikhail had not experimented with and administered to all of these nameless creatures, he could still sense their instantly manifested recognition of him. The shrieks and squeals were deafening, as if this nameless judgment being passed over him was infinitely worse than any sentencing he might have had to endure in a human court of law.

But the strange state of disease kept the various species distracted. Oozing lesions were quickly remembered once the strangeness and the potential menace of the incapacitated intruder had passed. The court of law had gone into a state of remission, and sentiments of war and sabotage became dormant. The researcher found the filthy water, most likely fouled by machine oil and other industrial compounds, infinitely soothing nevertheless, as his crawling skin began to calm and he reached a state of peace, even with a few random moments here and there of euphoria.

How many hours Mikhail had floated in that basement pool was unknown, but by the time he regained consciousness, it was obvious that the sun had shifted its position in the sky, having passed many hours of the day. The researcher knew that it was time to leave. He had passed the day being embryonic, with enough time for allowing his wounds to cool down, so that now the moment had approached for him to leave the world of the horizontal, and to return to the world of the vertical. He found a metal stairway to the back exit fairly quickly, and ascended from the dirty water, as if he were using his legs for the first time. He was still dizzy, and could feel the pressure coming at him from all angles, perhaps emanating from the walls. One last look back at the diseased laboratory animals revealed a scene of ill-boding, and even death: the pink rabbits and the sickly rats looked as if they were near to expiration. Perhaps their faster metabolisms lead to a faster death, giving the research a preview of what was to come. From this last thought, the bottom of his reality dropped out from under him as rotten floor boards in a condemned house might splinter, causing him to drop countless depths through the emotional phantasmagoria of despair and fear. He thought about all of the moments where he took his life for granted. Upon finding an ornamental rock next to one of the paths leading away from the research facility, Mikhail the researcher clung to the rock like an orangutan clings to its mother, and he wept for many countless aeons, while the sun rose and fell, and meteorites coursed through the blazing skies of sunset, disturbing the balance of sickly birds who fell from the trees like rancid avocados, possibly under the influence of the artificial plague.

At some point, the sun fell permanently, and the broken landscape became shrouded in gloom. The hazy night sky was illuminated by the full moon, whose yellow orb hung above him like an infantile lightbulb for him to grasp, for him to reach towards but never to catch. Mikhail the researcher felt like an infant lying on its back in the crib, reaching up for suspended toys that were too far away to grab. Mikhail knew that he was weak, and that he wouldn't be able to survive for much longer. The moon became the giant sucker of a leech that was ready to eviscerate him, to pull his living essence right out of him, to make him a rotten, empty husk.

The night hours passed and the moon gradually assumed a new position in the sky. As Mikhail the researcher had long ago forgotten about the pleasures of deep sleep, he was never really able to take his eyes off the moon, as it moved through its nighttime arc. The night was free of wild animals, as if they somehow knew that the land on which the researcher had collapsed had become toxic. The prevailing silence was horrible, in ways that silence should never have been. Mikhail gradually became aware that he was not alone when dusk began to roll in, as the sky began to almost imperceptibly grow lighter. Approaching him from the west was a procession of unknown people. They had bright candles with them, and proceeded towards his direction ever so gradually yet ever so purposefully. The suspense was painful, in the way that light to one's eyes can make them smart. Their approach was agony, and as soon as Mikhail began to wish for this confrontation with the real or the imaginary to be over and done with, he could hear the songlike chant of the nearing party, now visible as shrouded silhouettes who wore turbans and robes that had a vague sheen in the moonlight. Flickers of candlelight revealed their beards. Mikhail was certain that the end was near. He felt as if he were about to be snatched away by a deadly mirage, or perhaps irrevocably altered in a way that he'd never survive, assuming that it wasn't bad enough to have been infected with a hallucinogenic bioweapon.

The party of bearded, turbaned, chanting mystics formed a semicircle around the body of the researcher, who had now become cemented to the earth in holy terror. He stared up into the sky, into the craters of the moon, and into the eyes of the visitors with the raw fear of a wild animal. But the difference between Mikhail and a wild animal was that the later, in the face of any mortal threat, had the option to fight, run or hide. But Mikhail could do none of these, as he was truly paralyzed with terror and uncertainty.

One of the visitors, apparently the leader, stretched out his hand and touched the fevered brow of Mikhail the researcher. It was only then that Mikhail caught some of the phrases of this biblical-sounding chant, that he realized that he was in the presence of a holy man and his disciples, perhaps even the great prophet, Jesus, himself. And from the gleam in the eyes of this holy visitor, Mikhail became more and more certain that he was indeed staring up into the countenance of what he thought might be the holy prophet, Jesus. It was an inspired moment: the fear was quickly replaced with hope, and Mikhail felt as if his body became composed again of flesh and blood, and no longer was immobile concrete. Like a newborn child in search of care and nourishment, Mikhail looked up with supreme neediness at the Holy Prophet. It was at that moment of recognition that Jesus and one of his followers helped Mikhail into a sitting position, and pressed a glass of water to his lips. Jesus was carrying a folded satchel which, when opened up and placed at Mikhail's feet, contained of a large assortment of medicinal and delightfully antibacterial herbs – some dried, some fresh – which only reinforced the promise of a healing moment, of a return to health, and ultimately, his salvation from the depths of an infectious hell populated with lab-rats and pink, sickly bunny-rabbits. The herbs were selectively mixed and prepared together, making a viscous salve that might be rubbed all over the infected areas.

The sun was just beginning to rise at the moment when the prophet Jesus and his handful of followers began to apply the herbs to the itchy staph lesions on the researcher's wrecked body. Even within minutes,

Mikhail could feel relief as his hypersensitive skin began to calm, leading to a state of calm in his troubled, convulsive psyche. Mikhail stretched out on the grass again, feeling the rays of the rising sun playing upon the sores on his body – drying them out, curing them, purifying them, restoring him. He knew that if the infection could be eradicated, then his never-ending exposure to the lysergic acid would finally come to a much-appreciated end. As a sign of the herbs' potency, and also as a sign of his body's extreme need for healing time, Mikhail fell into a sleep with a satisfying depth of which he hadn't know for days, or perhaps weeks, as he had now lost all track of time as it is perceived through the filter of rationalist units of measurement. He could feel his mind descending into the warmth of sleep, and feel the bliss of the newly risen sun cast a warm orange glow onto his retinas through his closed eyelids. He knew that from this serendipitous sleep he would emerge as a new man, as a new being.

During the course of the researcher's sleep-cycle, Mikhail had many troubling nightmares, as if perhaps his inner mind was coming to terms with his drawn-out experience with the hallucinogenic infection. While dreaming, he passed through a giant redwood forest. The vast majority of the trees had been cut down, leaving only the gigantic stumps that were big enough to serve as a bed for several people. While observing their pithy surfaces so highly moss-covered and gleaming with slugs, he felt as if these tree stumps were really the remnants of cities, after a missile attack or after an alien invasion. Looking between the roads of the cities, he saw the ants moving along in small lines, single-file, perhaps moving to a new destination with which to call home. The mass movement of ants created the static of dead radio waves, of abandoned radio stations, that created an irritating punctuation in what would otherwise have been a super silent place in nature. These tree stumps became the desolate craters on the moon, devoid of active life, now just endless plains of dust with small hollows here and there where might have been hiding the remnants of life. This movement through the deadzone was interrupted by the passage of a herd of albino rats bouncing on the lunar surface with pogo sticks. The rats had pink eyes, and seemed very alert, unlike those terminally infected rodents he'd encountered in the trashed research facility of the waking world. And from the pink eyes came the static, the sound of an infinity of moving ants, infinitely small when considering singular components, but infinitely large when weighed as an unconscious collective. The static from the eyes of the rats was almost beam-like, in that it cut through the researcher's mind, lacerating it, removing lobe after lobe, trying to reduce it to the same static that clung to the ravished landscape like a pestilent mold innervates the walls of a flooded house, leaving behind no survivors. The incoming static caused time to repeat itself, playing out the same scenes of immolation and formication, over and over again. The oncoming passage of the ants forced Mikhail to flee, as he felt them beginning to penetrate his outer skin, with an almost certain threat of breaking through. He ran and ran to avoid the static, and never once felt the static beam from the eyes of the rats leave his back. Within this world, there was never a moment's rest. One had to keep moving at all times. It was exhausting, the degree to which perpetual motion was constantly required, always having to be on the run at all times, and never having the opportunity to pause, to lose the sense of one's consciousness: always having to hold onto one's self, out of the perpetual fear of losing it to the disintegrating means of static consumption. In this manner, the self became not the seat of one's existence or psyche, but an easy target of vulnerability always one step ahead of destruction, at best. The flight of the mind through these dangerous channels prompted an uncanny, inhuman level of vigilance, almost paranoia perhaps, and the question of the hour, or even the question of eternity was exactly how long this blinding race through the dead places would last – how long could legs run before finding oneself sunk beyond recall into a void of static, falling to the destructive beams that came from the eyes of the albino rats as they invaded the landscape that was once so pristine.

It should have come as no surprise then that the researcher's healing sleep was nonetheless a troubled one. Despite the infinite exhaustion that he'd incurred over the course of the horrible infection, his organic being ever so reticently dropped into the void of sleep, and even when unconscious, his mind was repeatedly cycling through the limited possibilities of survival that any animal would pursue when its life was in danger. Although he only slept for a few hours, the healing time seemed to have done him much good. He gradually regained consciousness, feeling the hot orange of the noon sun coming through his translucent eyelids. He felt a cool wind on his face, and had the illusion that he was again an infant, sucking at the breast, wrapping his lips around the nipple in a primal act of obedience to his survival instincts. As his awareness increased, he realized that he was actually lying on his back, and that a nipple was moving back and forth over his lips, teasing him. At times he'd be able to lock onto the nipple, sucking it with a passion that surprised him, and then the nipple would be pulled free, and then would dance back and forth over his lips, apparently pleasuring whoever was having this experience with him. And from time to time, one nipple would be replaced by another – a different smell, a different taste and a different texture. In all likelihood, he was pleasuring many women, allowing them to rub their breasts all over his face, with mutualistic suckling and then withdrawal. This realization caused him to have his first erection in perhaps days, or weeks, or months, or however long he'd been trapped within the netherworld of the hallucinogenic research facility, ravished by an artificial plague that had suppressed his sentience for an unbearable period of time.

He continued to enjoy the arousal afforded him by the pressure of the motherly breasts across his face, with teasing, erect tits moving between his lips, their pausing long enough to feel the stimulating pressure of his tongue, allowing his lips to find the nipples so as to apply a pleasureful suction, only to pull them away, causing a flash of emotion and highly charged eroticism, those elemental building blocks of desire. It was at this moment that he returned to his fantasy or preoccupation with being the universal embryo, safely placed within a nurturing womb of subdued stimulation, feeling the sunlight travel through the flesh, casting warm orange and pink hues across his face.

It was at this moment that Mikhail opened his eyes, feeling ready to face the waking world, at least more so than he had for many days prior. He could see that he was surrounded by people, and that full, supple breasts were in his face, pleasing him with ubiquitous nipples, just as he was pleasing them with such sensual oral stimulation. It was only when he looked up to the noon sky to see that these women were really the prophet Jesus and his followers, with their raggedy, travel-worn beards covering mouths grimacing with ecstasy, with dust-covered turbans and religious cloaks fluttering in the wind. That these religious men would have fully developed breasts was beyond his capacity to believe, and ever so suddenly the researcher screamed, fearing the onslaught of static beams from these reddish eyes of lab-rats that must have been disguised as humans. The researcher's shriek quickly broke the prophet Jesus and his Tiresian followers out of their sexual reveries, and they looked down at Mikhail with a new understanding. Jesus smiled with a wisdom that surpassed the centuries, and pulled the fake beard from his mouth. Accordingly, all of his followers did the same, pulling off their beards, which had apparently been simple theatrical appendages glued to their faces with that special glue of which only professional actors are familiar. The prophet Jesus then proceeded to remove his cloak and turban, and his followers reciprocated his gesture. Now standing around him were not the prophet Jesus and his young zealous followers, but instead a formidable but fully estrogenized Catholic nun with a select handful of female, recent initiates, all in their late teens. The nun introduced herself as the "Farting Nun," much to Mikhail's dismay and yet utterly confused pleasure, as he still had his eyes on her full breasts, as well as those of the other young nuns who were still standing around his reclining form, with their chests bared to him. The beards and turbans and cloaks were thereby discarded, and the nuns helped Mikhail to his feet. While his mind was still foggy, and his steps uncertain, Mikhail came to learn that while unconscious, the nuns had provided him with nourishment – the juice of a papaya – so as to help his body rejuvenate. The viscous mixture of ground herbs had been applied over the entirety of his body, and it was this application of healing compounds which the Farting Nun and her initiates hoped would stop the researcher's infection, and ultimately cure it. But little did they know that Mikhail was still under the effects of the LSD, and so they took his random grunts, comments and musical utterings as normal from a person who had gone beyond normal, who had been exiled from the domain of normality in the way pink laboratory bunny-rabbits might go to law school, in order to learn prosecutorial skills that might enable them to turn the world of scientific tinkering upside-down.

The researcher rose to his feet, his emaciated limbs swaying in the midday breeze. The Farting Nun and her young entourage helped Mikhail walk along the sad road that led away from the research facility, as such religious people were programmed to do. While the secret premises had been firmly encircled with a formidable barrier of barbed wire, several breaches had been cut through during the prior destruction, making it easy for the group to leave the area. After resting in some nearby woods, Mikhail felt even more of his strength return, as his consciousness moved from the stance of profound danger and criticality to a calmer and more composed passage, where his entire body began to breathe again, with his mind once again achieving harmony and synchrony with his surroundings. The Farting Nun and her holy entourage also seemed to enjoy the heightened sense of peace to be found away from the intense decay of the microbial research labs. They spread out a picnic blanket, and reattached their authoritarian beards to their faces, resuming their pantomime games of playing prophet while they had a few rounds of various gambling card games like gin and poker. Spontaneously, a deluge of repressed emotion flooded the synapses of the researcher, who began to weep profusely, realizing that his normal patterns of emotion had crept upon him, reminding him that he was human. Now that he was no longer a prisoner of "survival mode", all the myriad of emotions swelled through his body in stages: pain, rage, sorrow, joy, etc. The Farting Nun comforted him with kind words, and she even taught him how to tie his own shoelaces, as he had apparently forgotten such mundane techniques during his ordeal. The holy female entourage had just so happened to have had a spare pair of shoes that just so happened to fit the researcher's feet ever so perfectly, so it was a cheery moment indeed when the Nun taught Mikhail the fine art of tying one's shoelaces. During these moments the Farting Nun was at her best. It was at that moment, having caught her breath, that the nun declared that she and her followers were in search of beans, therefore leaving the researcher to his own solitary fate, once again. Very ceremoniously, the Nun made sure her religious habit was tucked around her body correctly, and her neophyte nun initiates did the same, copying their elder conscientiously. Once they had secured their veils and jet-black cloaks, they donned the outer garments worn by Jesus and his followers. They were now ready to go searching for beans.

Mikhail, on the other hand, was enjoying his newfound freedom, feeling his weary mind lounge among the wild trees and tropical birds who had filtered in through the hot, afternoon sky. The toucans had impressed him the most, inspiring him to imagine the trees covered with tropical argyle socks that people with bulbous eyes normally wore when they weren't interfering in the reproductive habits of experimental humans. After that hideous thought involving the argyle socks, Mikhail realized that he couldn't bear to part ways with the Farting Nun and her troupe of novice nuns. He realized that he had spent enough time around the awful landscape, and needed to get away from it, perhaps a return to civilization, and he also realized that the nuns would be the vehicle that would enable him to fulfill all of his fantasies.

Catching up with the pack of nuns wasn't all that difficult, and they gladly welcomed him back into their midst, as they searched for beans to take with them back to their campsite. As it turned out, they all experienced a supreme thirst for liquor, so they stopped off at a ghost town that was almost completely devoid of life, but not quite. They quickly located the old saloon: it was called the Sprawling Dawgue, and showed an iconic image of a dog reclining on a beach, living the good life. Inside the Sprawling Dawgue was a sullen barkeeper, who wore filthy overalls and looked as if he had not had a haircut in over a decade. Rather than having stools or chairs, the inside of the dusty saloon had very large teeth on which the patrons were to sit. Strange, sofa-like molars supported their resting buttocks as the nuns and the researcher sat down, and began to sip at their terribly strong drinks – something concocted with tequila and lime juice. Immediately the Farting Nun's libido kicked in, and she lifted her black skirts to reveal some see-thru knickers that only Mikhail could lower to her ankles. He tenderly sniffed her hairy bush, rubbing his nose and lips in that curly, pungent hair, and then began to apply his tongue to her moist labia, occasionally poking the vicinity of her clitoris, accidentally-on-purpose, of course. He could tell by the groans emitted by the nun that she was enjoying this experience. When he was certain that the Farting Nun's levels of pleasure were steadily rising, he gently began to penetrate her cunt with his index finger. After that seemed to provoke the desired response, he then rudely inserted his middle finger into her tight little bumhole, and began to poke in there, as well. With an active tongue and double the pokage, Mikhail knew it wouldn't be long before the woman of the cloth had an orgasm. After all, she was the bride of Jesus. The researcher loved pleasing her so, and also knew that because none of the nuns had had any beans in a long while then none of them would fart in his face (because he intended to service all of them in this way, as soon as he was finished pleasuring the Farting Nun).

The nun of course was enjoying the oral sex immensely, and the white coif on her head seemed to bob reassuringly, on its own. The Farting Nun spread her legs even more and clutched at the crucifix she wore around her neck, while the powerful orgasm ripped through her body, causing her to moan and convulse, reminding her of her lust for sperm. Then afterwards, the Farting Nun straightened her habit and headgear, and sipped at her tequila drink, with a dreamy smile on her face, and with naughty thoughts of performing fellatorical acts on helpless Franciscan monks. One by one, each of the young nuns received cunnilingual pleasures from the biological researcher, and one by one their orgasmic responses mounted, peaked and then abated, without any of them farting in his face, even. Of course, after such extensive oral activity, Mikhail realized that the muscles in his jaw and tongue most likely would be very sore the next day. His face smelled like pussy, and after servicing the last of the holy ladies, he realized that his own weeping member needed some attention, which all of the nuns gladly indulged him, with bobbing habits, tightly clutched crucifixes, and all the rest. Oh the joys of being surrounded by a circle of catholic fellatrixes, with each and every one of them waving their crucifixes and doing god's dirty work! He especially enjoyed squirting his seed all over their black, holy robes – in the sunlight, the droplets of semen would have looked like opals or other precious, iridescent stones that could fetch a high price. And seeing their innocent, morally upright countenances flecked with tiny droplets of sticky sperm tickled him especially so. The entire party rested after their experience of the flesh, and then turned their attention to the paintings on the saloon wall, depicting various kinds of canine alchemy, revealing the homology between bears and dogs, and how such an evolution allowed these species to coexist peacefully within the dregs of the ghost town. The fear that was subsequently manifested was stimulated by one particular painting that showed a particularly eager pooch in the process of being reverted back into a more rodent form, as if the purpose of dog evolution was the creation of lab rats, such as the Dawley-Sprague variety. The nuns and the researcher shifted uncomfortably in their molar seats and decided to throw a game of darts. Each person took turns, throwing up to three darts at a time. While launching his darts, Mikhail realized that his activity was analogous to the sacred pastime of throwing raisins to wild pheasants, who might hide out in the bushes when other humans approached their territories.

The bartender watched all of their activities ever so keenly, from the oral sex, to the alcohol, to the darts, and his beard seemed to hold a wealth of information about the past and about the future. It was at that particular moment when the Farting Nun realized that she needed to assert her altruism, and helped the bartender tie his shoes. Very carefully, she taught him how to fold the laces around each other, to tie the bow firmly, but not too tight. The bartender realized what a gifted teacher she was, shedding a few crocodile tears that spilled down his grimy cheeks.

While she was here, he realized that he needed help with other things, like doing his taxes and tending to his tumbleweed crops. The Farting Nun gladly helped him with all of this. She even taught him how to walk the way city folk do. By noticing his funny stride, she was able to coach him as he strove to improve his posture, to not slouch and to walk with one foot directly in front of the other. By the time he was walking with his new style of gait, they had become the best of friends. She sat him on her lap and told him stories from her early days, when she was learning the ways of the convent. She also told him stories from the bible, from the New Testament – those continuing adventures of Jesus and his rascally disciples who worshipped his every word and gesture.

Night began to fall, and the entire party realized that they would have to spend the dark hours in the saloon, the only inhabited structure within the entire ghost town. The evening wind blew several tumbleweeds by, sending them rolling off into the darkness. It was at this particular moment that the Farting Nun announced that she was in need of a coat-hanger abortion. Everyone in the saloon stopped their babbling and turned to look at her. Mikhail halted his conversation with one of the younger nun-novitiates, and the bartender stopped kissing another one to look over at the Farting Nun. And the rest of the young recruits stopped talking about rabbits long enough to receive this news. Of course she didn't show it, so perhaps she was only a few months pregnant? The person who broke the silence was the barkeeper, who declared that he was well versed in the art of do-it-yourself abortions. He had plenty of alcohol for sterilizing the wound, and lots of bandages and tools which would all lead to a painless experience free of infection. The Farting Nun asked that the extracted fetus not be mutilated in any way, and that it should be kept on ice for her after it was removed from her womb. The procedure was done on the barroom floor, right next to the molar seats, and the barkeeper even had a stash of a general anesthetic that would prevent any pain or suffering. After the procedure was completed, and the Farting Nun had roused from the anesthetic, she asked to see the fetus. The barkeeper brought it to her, in a little dish of crushed ice, and she instantly decided that the fetus was to be named Jesus. She held the baby Jesus in her hand – it was only 12 weeks old, so it was very small, about the size of a walnut. She petted the little Jesus, telling it that it was going to have a nice home with lots of other brothers and sisters, living all together in a state of rainbow bliss and happiness, with lots of sleepovers and birthday parties and all sorts of other wonderful things that children so enjoy doing. Jesus seemed very happy to receive this news, and it remained curled up, closely resembling other vertebrate fetuses like fetal pigs and fetal dogs and fetal horses, because the early fetuses of such mammals closely resembled each other, because of developmental homology. The Farting Nun loved her baby, although there were many, many people who could have been the father. She traveled wide and far, and received the sperm of so many different donors that for the life of her she knew that the father would never be identified, save for genetic testing. But that would never happen, because genetic testing was the work of the devil. She put little Jesus back on ice, and was happy to be informed that the procedure was a success, with minimal blood loss and tissue damage. Not only was the barkeeper good at mixing drinks, walking with a straightened back and tying shoelaces, but he was also a good surgeon. Especially in these parts, in a deserted place like the ghost town that was up the road from the bioweapons research facility, it was necessary for a man to be a jack of all trades. Fortunately however, nobody was in need of brain surgery, so the barkeeper was relieved at not having to be excessively challenged for that particular evening. The kerosene lamps cast a cheery glow in the dusty bar, with its rickety wooden floors that had seen their share of spilled drinks, puke and blood from many a barfight over the years. The Farting Nun was now stretched out on those sacred floors, wrapped in blankets and recovering from the surgery at a miraculous rate. It was projected that she would be completely recovered by morning, and would most likely would be ready for a big meal of beans, and of course the holy flatulence that was sure to follow. As the Farting Nun fell in and out of consciousness, she was surrounded by her kneeling followers, who lovingly wiped her brow with hot towels and whispered prayers and promises of holy salvation into her ears.

By morning, the Farting Nun was miraculously healed and on her feet. She paced to and fro, with anticipation of another glorious day of repentance, insemination and salvation, all in that order, of course. From her interdimensional satchel (which was more spacious on the inside than was apparent from looking at its exterior, just like the "Tardis" from that English TV show, Dr. Who), she retrieved a few necessities, such as her Pollyanna Power-guitar – that musical instrument that enabled her to project such powerful waves of optimistic positivity – as well as an expensive, crystalline vial filled with a mysterious liquid. She took her baby Jesus and placed it in the liquid, which turned out to be formalin. This was done so as to preserve the greatness of the baby Jesus. Once Jesus had been pickled in the formalin, the Farting Nun asked the barkeeper to put the vial in the mail for her, so that the fetus could arrive safely at the particular convent which was her home base of operations. That way, when she returned there in a few weeks' time, little baby Jesus would be there waiting for her. Once the Jesus issue had been taken care of, the Farting Nun began to play her Pollyanna Power-guitar, playing chords in major keys that formed the optimistic music of Christianity – professing the morals that are befitting of christians, such as turning the other cheek to allow tyrants to enact further abuse, of shunning condoms so as to breed like rabbits in order to cause the over-crowding of human roaches in the big cities, of playing the role of missionary, so as to spread the word-of-the-lord to once-uncontaminated areas, such as the home of the American Indians, and other such moral delicacies. As the Farting Nun sang these songs, her followers chimed in with the chorus, and everyone's head rocked to and fro in perfect synchrony with the music. In fact, these religious figures tilted their heads back and forth not only when they sang, but also when they talked about the really important stuff, like ovipositive procedures of grand optimism, and about scriptures, and even goody-two-shoes moralizing regarding how one should comb one's hair neat and straight every morning. This highly repetitive tilting of the head might have been perceived by certain cynical meanies as a sign of extreme triteness or wishy-washiness, but to everyone else, it was as if the divine spirit inhabited their bodies, creating what some called the "Holy Head Tilt." The Pope was especially fond of that, and he even insisted that all of his altar-boy concubines display the Holy Head Tilt whenever they addressed his excellency.

Once the Farting Nun had finished singing her Pollyanna Power-songs, setting such an optimistic tone for such a bright and cheery day, she once again lifted her black holy skirts and invited the men to inseminate her. In fact, the Farting Nun felt that it was her holy duty to get pregnant as often as possible, yet without actually carrying any of her children to term. Of course, it was well-known that nuns were never to be mothers, since they were brides of Jesus, but the Farting Nun's special interpretation of that golden rule was that as long as she didn't actually carry any of her fetuses to term, then she could do whatever she liked with regards to the birds and the bees, especially for the issue of cross-pollination. And so the barkeeper and Mikhail had their way with her while she was bent over the wooden bar, with her plump, pink bum completely bared for all to see. It was definitely going to be a very special day!

After being inseminated in both cunt and anus, the Farting Nun said the blessing for the morning meal, as everyone involved had worked up quite an appetite, even the entourage of novitiate nuns, who had had just as much a pleasurable experience from watching their fearless leader be serviced by the menfolk. They had a bountiful meal of pinto beans. What made these beans so special was that the water in which they were boiled was not discarded, so that all of those special oligosaccharides wouldn't be wasted, such that these magical carbohydrates (raffinose) were infused with the beans after the cooking water had been allowed to reduce. In fact, it was very well-known that the flatulence was created from one's intestinal flora when the little bugs metabolized the raffinose, so the nuns felt that all of god's creatures should be loved, and by logical extension, nourished. So to keep their intestinal flora happy and well-fed, beans were the logical choice for their diet. The nuns and the menfolk all held hands to say grace, giving thanks to the lord for all of the many things in their lives: thanks were given for the bountiful food (the beans), for their genitals – those pungent pleasure organs that they loved to rub against each other so very, very much, for Pollyanna Power-guitars, for pet rabbits, for suburban shopping malls, for urban roadkills, and even for that funny church of latterday saints, god bless them all!

The meal was enjoyed by everyone, and when the party had finished, they packed up all of their belongings and prepared to leave, saying their long goodbyes with the barkeeper who was already depressed at the thought that these young and gorgeous women of the cloth would no longer grace his saloon with their delicious selves. He encouraged them to return again to him, perhaps as a mission of mercy, to be done in the true missionary way. The Farting Nun reminded the barkeeper to mail her very important package – the vial that contained Jesus, the walnut-sized fetus that had been aborted the night before. As part of the leaving ceremony, the Farting Nun had to decide on which direction the group should go. As they had all begun to feel the bloating effects of digestion, warning that much flatulence would soon be the result, the Farting Nun had a brilliant idea: she obtained a red, cloth napkin from the barkeeper and brought it outside. Then, with very little effort, she farted all of the semen from before, onto the napkin. When the sperm hit the fabric, it assumed one of the most random shapes, perhaps as an act of supreme chance or holy automatism: the semen had stained the napkin in such a way that it looked like Saint Peter! Everyone who saw this miracle was amazed, including the Farting Nun. It was as if god had spoken directly to them, and only confirmed that old and very wise adage that the Lord works in mysterious ways. The Farting Nun as well as the rest of the novitiates were speechless, as were the bioweapons researcher and the barkeeper. They simply stood there, with their mouths agape, under the lamp of the morning sun that bathed the ghost town in an amber glow which could only have been described as "warm and fuzzy." Eventually the Farting Nun regained her wits, and remarked that the illusion of Saint Peter seemed to be pointing West. It was thus decided, through the chance event of filthy gism farted onto a grubby napkin, that the Holy Apparition of Saint Peter was commanding them to go West, and to pursue their travels and missionary work in that direction. The Lord had spoken!

Being the leader that she was, the Farting Nun put on her Jesus robes and fake religious beard, and began the long trek westward. The other nun novitiates put on their disguises, as well. Mikhail the researcher also followed along, determined to find himself, after having spent a lifetime in pursuit of his own obsessive imperatives, trying to control the world through pinching molecules, convinced of his own success.

Raffinose

molecular weight = 504.42 g/mol

The Nun with the Gun
(3-2009)

It was a hot, humid, summer day. The girls were all indoors, mixing cake batter into their hair. The cake batter was very thick, so as to enable the girls to apply very large volumes to their heads, so that their hair would be very well infused within the head cakes, as they were later to get baked in the summer heat. Once the cake had solidified around each head, the final step of the process was to apply icing – either chocolate or strawberry – to the outer surfaces of the head cake, and then with a slow but steady counterclockwise twist, to release the cake not only from the head, but from the hair as well. This is what the girls were doing that day.

And then the boys were outdoors, hiding among the trees, playing soldier, moving through fields of mud, camouflaging themselves amidst nondescript bulky objects that had been covered with burlap sheets and tied ever so painfully tight at the joints or bends that the strangely shaped, unknown objects presented. The boys were unified in their vision of the globe as nothing but a paper maché sphere that had the painted outlines of continents and countries on it – that was the extent to which their imaginations would allow them to envision the earth and the human reality that clung to its surfaces and muddied its waters. As for the war games themselves, there was no real, immediate goal other than to avoid having one of the enemy soldiers point his gun at you and say "pow" at the same time. Of course, these guns were simply the broken tree branches that littered the playing field, and the simultaneous act of saying "pow" and pointing the twig at someone was enough to warrant an instant, imaginative death. Usually these battles would last as long as the soldiers survived, or at least until everyone became tired, or until it was announced that lemonade was ready or that it was time for afternoon classes were to resume. But before any of those usual endings played themselves out, one of the boys – it was Ben – decided that he felt unusually sleepy, and returned to the dorm hallway to take a nap.

Rather than sleeping on his bed, which was arranged along with all of those of his classmates in the long dorm hall, he slept on the floor in between the beds. Before lying down, he noticed that there were holes in the wooden floors – most likely from the wood knots being removed by him and his comrades (because to own these flat, circular knots was almost like holding valuable currency) – and that periodically the heads of blackbirds would pop through, just to look at him and the rest of the human surroundings, as they were bathed in the early afternoon sun. Sleepier and sleepier became Ben as he put his head down to the cool wooden floor and casually observed a few tumbling balls of dust move along the vast surface. As he fell asleep, one might have thought that one of his eyes would pop out from the socket, but instead, the frontal part of his cranium became extended, attempting to flatten itself against the floor. As the cranial part of his head became more and more extended, more and more flattened, the tip of the extension began to split open, perpendicular to the plane of flattening. From the open crevice emerged a lobe of Ben's brain. It was prehensile and sticky, and began to lick at the large black ants which hid underneath the bed, and which had unwittingly been lured into the vicinity, over the false promise of a juicy, cerebral meal of blood sugar and other neurological debris. The extended brain could have been the tongue of an anteater, or perhaps the pseudopod of an amoeba. But either way, the ants were goners. Ben's brain greedily licked the ants from their holdouts within the floorboard cracks, and then immediately collapsed, much in the same way the tongue of a dead cow might loll to the side of the open jaw, enduring desiccation and rigor mortis.

By this point, the head cakes of the girls had completely solidified, and it had already been decided which of the various flavors of icing were to be subsequently applied to the cakes. With a simple twist, the cakes were released from each head, with not one hair being left inside. In fact the batter seemed to have had a rejuvenating effect on the hair of the girls. They giggled madly in their prepubescent pleasures, and set the cakes on the teacher's desk, as a gesture of obsequious fawning. The cakes looked like sagging bumblebee bonnets pasted over with a cloyingly saccharine icing, but it was the thought that counted, not the actual material. The teacher happened to be Miss Grullette, a creole woman with big hands and thick lips. Although very well-meaning, this spinster woman carried her heart on her sleeve, and her Christian morality within all of her bones. She had a fierce stare (as all teachers must have) and her sense of duty and discipline was boundless. She was here to instill order within the minds of these students, and prevent them from straying from the path of the Lord.

Upon the girls' leaving the head-bonnet cakes on the teacher's desk, Miss Grullette appeared from behind the door to her storage closet, looking very intense and hyper-composed. She twice clapped her hands, and as if on cue, the boys outside who were playing their war games dropped their branches of aggression and fell into a single queue that solemnly passed through the schoolhouse entrance, as if they were entering the domain of a higher power, leaving behind the barbarism of their future homicidal activities. Upon seeing their shabby classmates enter the room with knees and elbows stained with mud, all the girls giggled, while obsessively thinking of their cakes, and to whom they might give these eccentric delicacies as a gesture of goodwill and Christian repentance. Everyone was there except for Ben, who was nowhere to be found.

It was apropos that Miss Grullette, the matron of the orphanage, would have a taste for cake that day, as a sinister sweetness spread across her massive lips, almost inspiring fear in the hearts of her pupils who were half afraid of what words might soon pass through those lips. Miss Grullette brought her chair to the front of the class, where she sat down in front of the students, who were now aptly attentive, for fear of having their backsides whipped raw with a willow switch. Miss Grullette's chair had been splintered in various places, and the newly hewn clefts in the wood had been filled with cigarette butts that someone had vandalistically pushed into them. Obviously, the teacher was not amused, and the false sweetness that was coursing through her mouth was only a ploy to get the guilty party to reveal themselves. The children became quiet, remembering their involuntary entrainment to various punishment cycles and pain rhythms when they did not cooperate. The teacher wanted to know who had vandalized her chair, her precious seat of instructive dominion, but none of the kids raised a hand. Obviously by this point the "smile technique" wasn't working, and Miss Grullette was losing patience fast. She returned to her desk and from one of the drawers removed an even larger cake than the pretty little bonnet things that innocuously littered the desktop. This larger cake was brown and gelatinous, and did not look as if it were to have been decorated with the least bit of festive intelligence. The cake wobbled precariously on its tray, yet never came close to falling. It was almost as if the cake were alive, and could aright itself when in mortal danger, such as being accidentally dropped onto an already dingy schoolroom floor. It smelled like death.

Miss Grullette went into her supply closet and returned with some grimy looking floor tiles which were square and might have been removed from the floor of a factory toilet or some other such place of accumulated filth. The tiles were to serve in place of the dainty china plates that one might expect to be used for serving slices of cake. From her desk, the teacher produced a rusted, serrated knife, which she used to cut generous slices of the brown, viscous cake which she passed to each of the children on the filthy ceramic tiles. One brave girl asked Miss Grullette what exactly they were being served, and the teacher, after smacking the girl silly across the face, explained that she was serving slices of congealed blood-liver cake to ward off the evil spirits of sin. The cake had a foul odor of decomposing liver that had been liquefied with a tissue-homogenizer, and had the color of liquefied rust. After exposure to the air, each slice within minutes began to secrete dripping globules of a whitish liquid that looked more like semen than anything else. Perhaps the semen had artificial properties that allowed it to separate from the congealed blood mush, in the same way cream separates from milk. The children were instructed to smear the cake all over themselves, to simulate the immersion into the filth in which Jesus their Savior had undergone for them all those many years ago, when he had died for their sins and other such mercenary peccadilloes. The children complied, ruefully besmirching their pristine bodies with the awful substance, which might have been the epitome of putrefaction, the rancid degeneration of animal liver and blood prepared as a colloid to be distributed among the unruly. When each child had been humiliated with the rancid muck and mysterious semen smeared onto their persons, the teacher commanded them to return to their dormitories and study, until she would give them permission to remove the awful cake from their bodies, and to hand wash their clothes in the slop yard, which was behind the hill next to the orphanage school. Meanwhile, nobody observed Ben as he lay curled underneath his bed, in the fetal position, with the melted plates of his cranium splayed open to reveal the cerebral tongue of lurching furtiveness, reaching for insects that had already been consumed. The skin of the labial cerebrum became covered with mutated tastebuds from which layers of spent epithelia would slough away, from time to time, leaving behind thin sheets of a gelatinous residuum that was suggestive of a disease-like situation. Ben's lurching frame hunkered down underneath the rickety bed, with the occasional leg spasmodically kicking out from under it, but nobody paid him any heed. Ben might as well have been a radio that was left at a low volume, to drone on as part of the background noise while everyone else was distracted with the congealed liver-blood and semen schmear, which was rank and had by now attracted hordes of metallic blowflies.

Meanwhile, Miss Grullette had closed the classroom door, and tied some elastic ribbon around her arm, while she prepared a syringe, flaming it on a bunsen burner and then filling it with a grayish liquid. Miss Grullette closed her eyes, and leaned back in her schoolmistress chair, rocking back and forth while the hissing whisper of hypercleanly Christian psalms escaped from her lips in a furtive, desperate patter of repetition. Her chant was repeated over and over until, after the final whisper, she plunged the syringe into her arm, wincing from the hot liquid that was entering her body, all the while oblivious to a paper nest surrounded by buzzing wasps right outside the window next to which she had been seated. Within thirty seconds, Miss Grullette's eyes dulled to a lackluster calm and the tension within the frame of her body disappeared. A devious smile played across her formidable lips as she quickly ran the palm of her right hand between her legs, while carelessly flinging the emptied syringe into the void that was her desk.

Miss Grullette found more strength than she could handle, and immediately lurched forward from the chair to which she'd been confined up until recently by the daily fatigue of wearing a uniform of pure cliché that was meaningless as it was ultimately deadly. With a cruel smile of reflectionless intoxication playing across that organ of malevolence that was called her cranium, the teacher straightened her garter as she moved across the empty classroom like an enraged baboon filled with poise and purpose. In the main hallway that lead to the children's dorm and the modest chapel, the teacher's attention had been momentarily stolen by a baptismal holy hand-wash alcove that had been installed into one of the walls by the chapel entranceway. Miss Grullette sunk her fingers (bloated by water retention) into the liquid, which turned out to be very similar in feel to one of the many commercially-available water-based personal lubricants. She greedily rubbed her fingers together, as if one were lustily rubbing filthy gold coins in the palm of the emperor's hand, and continued on her way to the children's dorm, as a robed, humped malevolence that was able to navigate the earth by way of a pair of legs and a devious brain, connected to other limbs that might assist in the manipulation of all manner of subjects, all manner of substrates...

Miss Grullette, long ago burned irreparably with the baptismal waters of catholicism, hid her devious smile, and gently pushed open the door to the children's room. She was not prepared for what was transpiring inside: Little Julie, the one who had been seriously injured in a carwreck (and saw her parents killed in the same incident) the previous year, was hunched over poor Ben, whose skull had by now healed but had been left with several thick-looking tastebuds on his forehead (and which the other children would ultimately confuse as acne). Although Ben looked fairly normal in appearance, he was unconscious, barely responding to Little Julie's pleading gasps, as she squeezed his shoulders, trying to coax Ben to the surface of all that is awake and aware. Ben's tongue would periodically loll around the corners of his mouth, further enraging the inexplicably intoxicated Miss Grullette. The teacher grabbed him from the floor and shook him violently, in the way one might shake a bottle of oil and vinegar dressing before applying it to a salad chopped for a madman. Ben's body might have been made of paper, or from the funky fabric of an old sock, since his non-responsiveness became accentuated through those spastic, puppet-like motions. Ever so cruelly, and with a certain degree of intuition, the teacher poured salt on Ben's forehead. The sea salt extracted much liquid from the part of his skull that displayed the protruding tastebuds, and this trickle of mental fluid ran down the side of his head like a wound, although the resulting liquid was more valuable than anyone's blood or any other secreted fluid. Miss Grullette continued to thrash the near-lifeless form of Ben, periodically knocking his head on the edge of the spartan beds and cursing him with clean, christian words. Before the entrance of the teacher, some of the girls had felt sorry for him, and were preparing special cake batters which they might have applied to his febrile, pulsating forehead that was now being mercilessly pummeled by a catholic fanatic who was dressed up like a teacher. With one last, vicious fling, the monster that was their teacher threw the helpless Ben into a wall, off of which his poor, abused head bounced, pulling along his body, to finally come to rest in a heap within a dusty corner of the room decorated with rat feces. Although the children didn't reveal it visibly, they were nonetheless fuming with pre-pubescent desire and rage, intermingled, which might someday erupt uncontrollably like a striped pot filled with boiling wasps. But for now, the children lived in fear of the teacher, and because all of them had such low levels of self-esteem, they were unable to lift a finger against Miss Grullette, whose teeth occasionally poked through those taught, thick lips of murderous hypocrisy.

But before the teacher could take any further action against the injured Ben, all involved were distracted by an ominous knock at the front door of the orphanage. Miss Grullette pulled her reaching, clawed limbs back toward her body as she straightened her preppie, conservative cardigan sweater and smoothed the pleats in her dress while she approached the front door, with the wide-eyed children in tow, who were ever so careful not to touch the teacher, even her clothing, out of fear of some kind of retribution or whatever agonizing visceral punishment.

The teacher pulled open the heavy door, oblivious to the squeaking hinge that trumpeted the arrival of the visitor, whose dark silhouette was framed by the doorway. The visitor looked like a hustler who had travelled the american plains in search of action, giving lead in order to get gold, by way of the alchemical shotgun that happened to be slung over *her* shoulder. As the visitor stepped into the foyer of the orphanage, it was immediately obvious that she meant business, as she toted her belongings behind her while still keeping a wary hand on the gun that was slung over her shoulder. The visitor wore the frock of a nun, with embroidered symbols of the particular order to which she belonged. Not only was she a nun, but she was a nun with a gun. Rather than greeting the mysterious visitor with any respect or even the slightest bit of curiosity, Miss Grullette waved her hand toward the visitor, ushering her into the warmth of the orphanage while slamming the door shut.

Nothing Miss Grullette ever did was altruistic. Instead, every move she made or sentence uttered was always done first for her own benefit, and then the rest of the world came in a distant second place. In this instance, Grullette commanded the nun to sit down and rest, but most of the people involved knew that relaxation was nothing that she would wish upon anyone except for herself. The command was more likely a way to assert her authority over the strange visitor.

It couldn't have been more obvious that these women were instant arch-enemies. Miss Grullette cracked her back and her knuckles, revealing the creases and wrinkles around her aging brow, showing the facial features of a cynic that had been given too much power. The visiting nun, who by now had announced herself as the Farting Nun, was not to be intimidated, as she spat her lavender-flavored chewing gum at a poster that the teacher had had one of the kids draw so as to list all of the golden rules and other unfair, morally unsound directives that all of the children were forced to follow during their stay in the orphanage school. Miss Grullette's menacing eyes sparkled in the feeble light that emanated from the neglected fireplace, while she pulled a one-shot pistol from the sleeve of her blouse. The Farting Nun gritted her teeth and cocked the hammer on the shotgun she was toting, aiming the barrel right at the teacher's head. Miss Grullette realized that her gun was no match for the powerful shotgun and so she dropped the weapon and began to run through the orphanage, collecting her belongings and going for one last hit from the syringe before she left forever. The children became excited, and started to whisper things into each others' ears in the most sensual of ways, as if the magnified sound of blood circulation in the ears could become the perpetual sigh of the ocean, which in turn could become the sigh of lovers who were well-versed in giving each other pleasure. Miss Grullette's face reflected so much malevolence as she slung a raggedy rucksack over her shoulder, preparing to spit her goodbyes at the children for the last time. The kids had a terrified look in their eyes as they heard the last words from her mouth that they'd ever hope to hear, but they were also beginning to show a certain level of pity, which in turn infuriated the bully who had been their source of moral authority for almost as long as they could remember.

With the monstrous bitch finally gone from the school forever, the children encircled the Farting Nun, admiring her and thanking her for rescuing them. The nun put one of her feet up on a chair, and lifted her skirts to show them a tattoo of a lizard that was right on the back of her knee. As if that wasn't enough, the Farting Nun rested the shotgun over the opposite shoulder and told the children of her commitment to following the ways of the Lord. This was probably the first time that the children had seen a nun with a gun. In fact, they were very excited about this, and spent subsequent weeks during their art classes to draw pictures of the nun with the gun, using crayons and pencils to express their innermost reverence for the woman of the cloth who stood before them now with her skirts lifted and bearing only the most high-calibre artillery. In an effort to calm the already tense mood of the orphanage, the Farting Nun posed for one very last photo-shoot holding up her magic gun for the world to see. As a nun with a gun, she should have made it onto the Forbes list of the most rich and powerful: whatever negative impressions were generated by her poverty were more than made up for by her power and stature, at least in the minds of the children. To them, she was gODD, or almost.

The Farting Nun put the gun into a secure place – into her interdimensional satchel – and then turned her attention to making the orphanage a happier and holier place for the children. She had decided that all cleaning chores could be left until the following day, while the remaining night hours were used to cauterize their emotional (and physical) wounds. Many tears were dried, and many small hands were held that night. Since all of the children had developed feelings of paranoia and persecution, the Farting Nun decided that it would be best to have fun learning activities for the children to participate in, hence she finally was able to dig out the children's paint set that had been maliciously hidden under a loose floorboard in the faculty restroom, most likely by Grullette. The game they were going to play was called something like "crucifix," and it was all about how the children would use the paints to make trompe l'oeil simulations of crucifixion wounds on their hands and feet. Of course, some of the children chose realistic colors to try to depict those bleeding holes, to portray the wounds incurred from having a sharp stake hammered through their tender, persecuted flesh. But some of the other children, like Little Julie and Ben (who had by now recovered from his assault and was welcomed back into the fold by the other kids), were much more interested in holding hands and talking to each other. The Farting Nun didn't try too hard at keeping the children entertained and occupied, as she had the wisdom to understand that what they needed most was an absence of structure in order to help them decompress from the ill effects of military order a la Grullette. After most of the children had fallen asleep, the nun decided to give her Mother Superior a stiff phone call.

Morning finally arrived, and everything looked different than it had the night before. The sun was up, and the condensation on the window was a reminder of moisture, of water, of the lifeblood that composes everything on earth. At around 6 am, the Farting Nun entered the dormitory hallways, with her Pollyanna powerguitar in her hands, and she began to sing the "Rise and Shine" song again and encouraged the children to begin clapping their hands and singing along. While most of the children were busy singing and brushing their teeth, there were a few people like Ben and Mortimer who were occupied with other things: Ben was still obsessed with the ants crawling under his bed, while Mortimer felt that it was his god-driven duty to keep the fireplace in the commons area well stoked with logs, unleashing a scorching but well-contained inferno that was pleasurable to watch. Given the grubby state of the children, who actually presented the appearance of not having bathed in days, the Farting Nun went on a soap-hunt, eventually finding several unused bars of quality-milled soap hidden underneath another one of the floorboards in the faculty restroom, once again most likely the malicious work of Miss Grullette. The nun directed all of the children into the communal lavatory, and put on a spectacular presentation of how one should approach the arduous task of washing one's hands. It wasn't long before the orphans got the hang of it, in just the same way a determined youngster might learn how to ride a bike or take standardized, slanted academic tests put on by capitalist regimes. Now that all of the children were clean, the Farting Nun got down on one knee and asked the children to congregate around her in a circle. When she had gotten everyone's attention (including Little Julie and Rebecca, who were more interested in reading about Pippi Longstocking), she made the attempt to empathize with the children over their misfortunes, and in the spirit of consideration, she had decided that rather than send the children right back to classes as if nothing bad had ever happened, they were instead to go on a field trip that day, perhaps their first scholastic outing taken in a long while. After all, Miss Grullette never took them anywhere, unless it was to a police station or to the baptismal dunking booths at the nearby church. No, instead of classes that day, there was to be fun and fresh air.

Once everyone had clean hands and feet, the Farting Nun announced to the students that as part of their field trip or class outing, they were to dress up like Christians, so as to make themselves presentable to the world, and pleasing to the papal eye. From a basement storage closet were obtained some ratty burlap sacks, which most likely once contained potatoes or whatever other filthy items collected from the outdoors. The Farting Nun taught them how to cut holes in the sacks, so as to make a crude tunic for each of them that would cover the entirety of their bodies. She explained that extreme poverty leads to extreme piety, and that by wearing some filthy potato sacks, they would thus become the ideal recipients of the love of God and of Jesus. One student asked if the Farting Nun herself was planning on wearing one of the old potato sacks, but she replied that she did not intend to, because she was a woman of the cloth, which meant that she was required at almost all times to wear the black and white habit that all nuns wear, as well as to have a shotgun handy. A nun without a shotgun was like a politician without any pants; and therefore it followed that the uniform was seventy-five percent of the package, while the human element was only twenty-five percent, or so said the Mother Superior.

The Farting Nun helped the children don their potato-sack tunics and then brought them into the backyard, where they were to look for walking sticks that would complement their neolithic christian attire. What had originally been considered as imaginary weapons and the ordinance of yesterday became the walking sticks of today. Gathered together in their burlap tunics and their walking sticks, the children looked more like neolithic nomads rather than students on a fieldtrip, so the Farting Nun was pleased with her handiwork, realizing the moment of getting in step with the Lord had arrived. She mobilized the warm bodies with directives and encouragement, and slung her satchel and Pollyanna Powerguitar case over her shoulder, with her black skirts flapping in the wind. It should not have come as much surprise that the boys and even a few of the girls were interested in looking up the nun's skirt, but through being burdened with the cumbersome potato sacks, there was little opportunity for any wild horseplay or other mischief that couldn't be better executed later that evening. Just as the troupe of neo-christians was moving along the dirt road that led away from the orphanage, Mother Superior was arriving. She was enclosed in a glass box that looked like a stagecoach but minus the wheels and horses, and which was instead levitated by way of poles that some half-naked, christian servant-men lifted, much to their own personal discomfort. One of the men that was responsible for holding up the left, back corner of Mother Superior's travel coach had an itchy nose, so for him to scratch it required him to slightly lower the box, which to the annoyance of the Mother Superior caused her to spill hot tea on her legs and then yell at him and threaten to hand him over to the pope, who would surely turn him into fish fertilizer should the opportunity have presented itself.

Upon quickly halting the important religious procession, the Mother Superior put out her cigarette and started to shout at the children, telling them how lazy, lethargic, and well-fed they all looked. They were only allowed to smile when God told them to do so, and according to the Mother Superior, God had not yet spoken. Downcast, the children stood in the road, waiting for further instruction. A few, quickly whispered exchanges between the Farting Nun and Mother Superior resulted in the latter's resumed approach to the orphanage, where she was to reside until a decision had been made about what to do with the orphans, such as where they might be sent now that Miss Grullette had abandoned her post.

So as the holy ogre continued on her way to set up camp at the orphan school, the Farting Nun and the children gleefully resumed their trek into the neighboring countrycide, whistling tunes and speculating about what kinds of exciting things they might find over the next hill, and then over the hill that followed that one, and so on. Eventually the travelling party encountered a travelling blacksmith. The blacksmith was hunched over from carrying his heavy horseshoe collection, and it looked like he hadn't shaved in a year. There was even a bluebird living in his beard, and since the facial hair was so plentiful, it provided shelter to so many other living things. When the blacksmith saw the young children dressed as christians, he immediately felt a charitable impulse surge within him. Dressed in burlap potato sacks, the christian children looked wan and filthy, and in need of love and nourishment. The blacksmith took pity on them and reached into his large changepurse, from which he produced a fistful of counterfeit coins that he'd minted himself. On one side of each coin was stamped an image of the pope, sitting regally on his throne and wearing his magical, golden shoes. And then the obverse revealed the denomination of five peso-shillings, which heralded an image of a large, bumpy cucumber. The blacksmith pressed one of these coins into each of the children's sweaty palms. When asked to what they owed the pleasure of his generosity, the smith replied that he always enjoyed giving handouts to christians, and that to him, it was a thrill infinitely more exciting than reading sports magazines or shaving. In return, the Farting Nun and the children felt that it was only fair that they sing a religious song for the nice man, and so they did, and while doing so, they tilted their heads back and forth in perfect unison with the rhythm. They were an army of christian automaton-munchkins!

After a few encores, the merry party went off in separate directions, as the blacksmith had horseshoes to sell and the nun and her students were destined for even more fun on a day that shouldn't have been, but which ended up falling into their laps nonetheless. The Farting Nun led the children down the country road, in search of more handouts. She got the idea that the more destitute the children looked, then perhaps the more generous the passers-by would be, so the only logical action was to have the kids rub dirt all over themselves and to lie down in the filth, so as to make a favorable impression on whomever might encounter them. They must have waited another hour until a police car arrived at the scene. The cop, who was very obese and with a snout that almost looked like that of a pig, got out of his patrol vehicle and surveyed the panhandling scene in front of him: a dubious woman of the cloth surrounded by a bunch of filthy christians, apparently begging for alms. The officer asked the nun where the pygmy christians came from, and if they spoke the same language that they did, and if they had their IDs and other paperwork with them. The Farting Nun burst into tears, and relayed a synthetic sob-story of destruction involving earthquakes, tsunamis, herpes plague as well as space-alien invasions, attempting to explain her mission of mercy in creating a new home for these displaced pygmy christians, who were so very far away from their destroyed homeland, somewhere even possibly on a different continent. The christian pygmies bowed obsequiously to the rather mean-looking cop and did their best to act christian: submissively rolling in the dirt and braying like animals that have been kicked too many times by their masters. Apparently the Farting Nun and Company lucked out, as the police officer was able to choose empathy and compassion over his usual blind adherence to the law of the land, and so he decided to leave the pilgrims in peace. And not only did he leave them be, but from the trunk of his patrol vehicle, amid the piles of confiscated contraband, he removed a cache of counterfeit coins that bore the image of a space-octopus with several rows of jagged teeth in breathless pursuit of a spaceship filled with terrified humans. And the other side of each coin had an image of the last supper, with Jesus having one last rum & coke with his disciples before getting tacked to some spare lumber. The cop gave the counterfeit money to the nun, and suggested that she use it to help improve the lives of such filthy christians. The pygmy christians then expressed their gratefulness by kissing the copper's feet, and then with a tip of her coif, the Farting Nun bid the policeman a pregnant adieu.

After a few more of such panhandling episodes, the Farting Nun and her pygmy christians had amassed quite a volume of counterfeit loot, enough for it to be needfully hidden so as not to attract the malevolent interest of banditos or baptist TV evangelists. Near enough to the road was a shallow cave, so the nun brought the pygmy christians inside in order to provide some cover while the loot was hidden. In order to put the coinage in a safe place where nobody would ever find it, the Farting Nun decided that Ben was most likely the best person to handle that job. Ben leaned his head forward, so as to unzip his cranium like he had done before, such as when he was hunting for those large, black ants. The tastebuds on his forehead were to react unfavorably to the presence of the metal, but fortunately this hiding maneuver was only temporary. Ben's brain, which was really a cerebral tongue, moved to the side of his skull in obvious displeasure upon the introduction of the various counterfeit coins that that the children had gathered during their fieldtrip, but perhaps this small sacrifice might better serve the needs of his peers in their newly destitute walk of life? Hopefully so.

It just so happened that the sun was trying to set, and to avoid angering Mother Superior who was still waiting for them at the orphanage just down the road, the Farting Nun made the executive decision to lead the pygmy christians back to the schoolgrounds. It was certainly obvious that Ben's head was leaning unnaturally to the side, but hopefully nobody would notice. Whatever fleeting sense of freedom the nun and the children might have felt during the day was now gone, as the reality of having to live in close contact with the eternally dour Mother Superior kicked in. It was certainly a good fieldtrip, and the children had enjoyed themselves, the Farting Nun observed to herself; at least they had that much.

At the school, the Mother Superior was white-knuckling her fists together, apparently uptight for some unknown reason. As soon as the Farting Nun arrived with the children, Mother Superior ordered them to be hosed down, and for them to wear the attire that they normally wore. Mother Superior spat on the fireplace and swore that she would not live under the same roof with a bunch of ingrates who wore potato sacks in order to pass themselves off as a bunch of "marauding, philistine jews." After Mother Superior's decree, the children sadly trudged off to change their clothes and clean themselves up before dinner, which was to be a sumptuous feast of baked beans, cooked Vatican-style and fit for any pauper, just the way most of the clergy liked it. It was amazing what could be done with beans, especially because they were so cheap. As the children walked towards their dormitories, nobody seemed to notice how Ben had his head leaning to the side.

Grubby hands and faces were washed, and finally the children emerged from the dormitories en masse, and converged upon the dining hall, with nothing but beans on their minds. The children submissively seated themselves at the tables, while carefully obeying all rules under the watchful stare of the Mother Superior, who was already tucking in to a huge platter of baked macaroni and cheese, a dish that was only prepared for people of her rank and higher. Macaroni and cheese was thus something that only was served to the privileged, religious elite, while everyone else had their baked beans. The Farting Nun was served the latter and also knew better enough to sit with the children for the meal, while the Mother Superior sat by herself among her servants and bodyguards. When all of the children were finally at the tables with heads bowed and hands clasped, the Mother Superior belched and put down her fork, preparing to lead the children through the Lord's Prayer, something that was supposedly recited before each meal. Everyone else bowed their heads in prayerful submission (while Ben's head still leaned precariously to the left) and chanted the words that would give them the illusion of being clean and pure.

As the children were about to lift spoonfuls of beans to their mouths, all of a sudden there was an ominous knock at the front door of the orphanage. Because this event was unexpected by the Mother Superior, causing her to reveal her instantaneous befuddlement, the children giggled and smirked when the former's back was turned. The Mother Superior and a couple of trusted servants quickly scampered to the front door, closely followed by the Farting Nun, who had by now brandished her alchemical shotgun and was ready for just about anything. It turned out that the strangely unexpected visitor was the blessed, holy father himself, His Holy Excellency, the Pope. This incarnation of the Apostolic See wore transparent knickers and white pantyhose, red papal slippers with semi-high-heels, and the holy mozzetta, which was fabricated from the most aristocratic red velvet trimmed with white ermine fur. Besides the fancy threads, he was nothing more than a wicked raisin with grey hair. By degrees, the pope truly was the equalizing dildo for both the ruling class and the poor. Upon his holy entrance, everyone including the Holy Mother immediately closed their already gaping jaws and lowered their heads obsequiously, with their hands involuntarily contorted in masochistic prayer. Under the wash of dead silence, the Pope began to speak, informing everyone of his travels through the neighboring countrycide, doing God's work and spreading the word and the diseases of the Lord. The Pope immediately sat on a portable golden throne that his warrior-priests had brought along with him, crossed his legs and daintily began to nibble at the ruling-class macaroni than had been handed him. He smiled at the children in a vacuous way, whereupon his eyes immediately fell upon the Mother Superior. What began as a few innocent questions immediately became a reincarnation of the Inquisition: when the Holy Mother was questioned about her involvement in the troubled orphanage, it was the Pope who decided that her incompetence and negligence was what brought holy scum like Miss Grullette to such a position of power. Thereupon it was decided, by the word of God, by way of a few, choice words spoken in tongues of course, that the Holy Mother was to be officially and publicly castigated. Since there were no immediate townsfolk available except for the children, the servant-warrior-priests and the Farting Nun, it was decided that they would suffice as witnesses, to take note of one person's folly so that the rest of the population could learn from such debasing mistakes.

The pope commanded the Mother Superior to assume the prone position, and to recite endless variations of Hail-Mary's and all other such christian gibberish that over the years she had had drilled into her mind, so that she would never allow such a calamity as what recently occurred at the orphanage to ever happen again, otherwise she'd be stripped of her rank and be reduced to milking cows and sheep for the rest of her life. The Mother Superior, a cranky old witch who had come to take for granted the enormous power that she usually wielded, now looked like a changed woman, however temporary the effects might last: tear-stained cheeks, filthy knees, and a head filled with humility was the new face that she showed to the congregation. Ominously, His Holy Papal Excellency announced that so as to consecrate this display of christian humility and repentance, it was time to consult the Mystical Papal Shoes, or the "golden shoes" as some people reverently considered them. He thrice clapped his hands, which summoned one of his most formidable servant-warrior-priests, who looked like a bloated, papal sumo wrestler. The servant approached His Holy Papal Excellency with a large treasure box lined with purple velvet and exquisite ermine trim. The box was slowly and dramatically opened, revealing a pair of shoes that had been forged from the most malleable of holy golds – shoes that were worn ever so rarely but when done so, with supreme, self-righteous purpose and holiness. The Pope lifted one of the shoes to eye-level, admiring its expert craftsmanship, down to the minutely etched papal insignia that adorned the toe area. The Pope then allowed his Jesuit anger to surface, bringing to light a demonic scowl of displeasure that induced the countenance of the Mother Superior to wilt like a flower poisoned by cosmic radiation from a transdimensional terror from the dregs of the universe. The

Mother Superior had the face of a mortified teenager who has been singled out for her misdeeds and so thoroughly embarrassed in front of her peers and subordinates. She knew exactly what to do with the shoe that had been ominously handed to her, as if she had been permanently black-listed, or handed a subtle death-sentence: after a tearful prayer of supreme christian humility, the Mother Superior, still kneeling amid the filthy orphanage dining hall floor, tilted her head forward and began to regurgitate the elitist macaroni and cheese that she had ingested only minutes before. The vomited macaroni was directed into the Mystical Papal Shoe. Whether the tears were from vomiting or from shame, or both, the Mother Superior was reminded again of her own mortality and humility. But that wasn't the end of it. The Pope flashed a wry, toothy grin and handed her the other shoe, as she passed the first vomit-filled golden shoe back to him. Since most of the macaroni and cheese had been previously evacuated, the Mother Superior had nothing much left to offer except the liquid filth of her stomach acid, laced with bile, which left her retching for a quite a while afterwards. After the second shoe, now filled with retro-peristaltic scum, was given back to the Pope, a prayer was said by all. The Pope, now holding both of the Mystical Golden Shoes up towards the ceiling, concluded the prayer by shouting words of mystical nonchalance, and then he placed both of the shoes, brimming with rancid, half-digested macaroni, onto the mantel of the fireplace in the commons area, for all to see. These shoes were considered by all to be a holy artifact deemed sacred enough to become a poignant reminder of human folly and arrogance. With her tail metaphorically between her legs, the Mother Superior trudged off to the faculty washroom to clean herself up.

The Pope casually adjusted his white pantyhose after dinner while talking with the children for a minute or so each, asking them about their hobbies and interests and lifelong ambitions. He was keenly interested in what the boys' interests were, while almost completely ignoring what the girls cared about. A couple of the children, Sheila and Carlos, reported on somewhat controversial things, which spurred the Pope to pull out a slim notebook into which he cryptically jotted a few choice words and phrases. After the children had been dismissed and ushered back to their dormitories for nighttime study, the Pope slyly and discretely pulled from his sleeve a capsule containing a formalin-soaked fetus, just for the benefit of the Farting Nun, who immediately looked mortified.

The Pope smiled wickedly, and returned the damning evidence back to the hidden compartment in his sleeve. But there was curiously no punishment, which puzzled the Farting Nun immensely. Upon begging her leave of His Holy Excellency, the Farting Nun was commanded by the Pope to stay and to retire with him to his chambers. He placed his frail, effeminate hands on her full-figured buttocks, with a vitriolic smile that played across his thin, pristine lips. They walked together to the faculty chambers that had been converted to a well-guarded bedroom for His Excellency. The Farting Nun was surprised to see the Mother Superior on her hands and knees with a ball-gag in her mouth and with both of her posterior holes stuffed with the phallic weaponry of the Pope's servant-priests. Since His Holy Righteousness had ever so cleverly and secretly been selected for the Papacy based on his bedroom impotence, he was only rarely ever able to maintain an erection, and usually the pale but elaborate fantasies which he spun from his impoverished imaginative life were often not of sufficient complexity to maintain a functional state of sexual arousal. So as a result, he often assumed voyeuristic roles when it came to bedroom exploits, preferring to stand on the sidelines like a cheerleader, while his servants would take care of such business, such as the sado-masochistic administration of his support staff, which of course included the particular Mother Superior. While she was being mercilessly fucked by the Pope's administrative assistants, the Mother Superior received her punishment with tears of joy, with the agony of forced penetration giving way to undulations of uplifting pleasure. In this way, she was reminded that she was only a filthy dog, a beast of burden created to do God's will, a martyr for Jesus. She was all of these things.

After the priest-assistants were finished with their good work, His Papal Excellency commanded the Mother Superior to don her clothes and to retire to her quarters with quiet and with dignity. Before leaving his bed chambers, the Mother Superior cast one last wistful glance towards the Pope's Mystical Golden Shoes, thoroughly replete with putridity of the holy macaroni and cheese. Upon her leaving, the Pope dismissed the servants and produced a bottle of very fine brandy and a couple of cigars for them to smoke. He confided to the Farting Nun that the Mother Superior's days were numbered and that soon she was to be relocated to a sheep ranch where her holy management skills would be put to better use, rather than having youth put into her care. Wide-eyed, the Farting

Nun waited for the moment when the Pope's blackmail would surface regarding his discovery of her sinful indiscretions. She had been very careful to hide her fetus collection, so how he had found out about it was unclear. Had the Mother Superior, the Farting Nun's commanding officer, ratted her out to the Pope? Before having the opportunity to furtively arrive at other possible conjectures, the Farting Nun's covert musings were interrupted by the Pope who decided that it was time to directly address the subject of the preserved fetus.

It turned out that the fetus was actually someone else's, that the Pope had brought this artifact to her attention as a concrete example of the way in which materialist life was threatening the psycho-economic hold that the church which for centuries-past had had the luxury of imposing on the masses. The concept of an aborted fetus was pure revulsion to the Pope, causing his wiry and aged frame to shake with loathing and insecurity. In fact the Pope was turning to the Farting Nun for support and loyalty to the Church – he ultimately disclosed to her later during the evening that perhaps within a year or so she would be promoted to the rank of Mother Superior, to have several subordinate monasteries and nuns reporting to her for guidance, love and drudgery. It was something that she would not want to miss, admonished His Holy Excellency. But for now, his only concern was to do his part in propagating the free supply and demand of human labor – to promote procreation under a veil of goodness, yet he and all of his other bishop cronies knew that the continuation of world capitalism depended on the continuing flux of non-stop procreation. His purpose in life was to keep that pipeline of human beings flowing as freely as possible, and that things like population control and a socialistic economy were profound threats to the wonderful way of life he'd known for as long as he could remember. The Farting Nun thanked him for his kindness and confidence, and promised to do her very best as a Mother Superior. They concluded their friendly interview with talk of a fieldtrip the following day that would involve the children from the orphanage. The Farting Nun was indeed very enthusiastic about fieldtrips, and singing songs, too. After the Farting Nun had retired to her room, the Pope finished his cigar and looked over his shoulder before opening a secret compartment in one of his expensive pieces of Vatican-issue luggage. From the secret opening he pulled an economics textbook, and resumed doing his graduate-level homework. The Pope was working on a secret, online Ph.D. in capitalist economics. Now if only he could get that diploma before he croaked!

Meanwhile, the Farting Nun checked in on the supposedly sleeping children. As expected, they were all quite awake, busy chattering about the recent changes in religious personnel, and how their lives might take a turn for the better with the removal of the Mother Superior and Miss Grullette. It truly seemed that with religious personnel, there was no end to the rottenness, no end to the misery, except for the Farting Nun, because she was so nice, or so the children had been telling themselves. The kindly nun just so happened to have brought her Pollyanna powerguitar with her, so she quietly sang to them wild, imaginative songs about octopus coins and buried treasure, and how there really wasn't much difference between dresses and trousers. Eventually, the Farting Nun sang everyone to sleep, even Ben, who still was vigilantly hoarding the special loot of coins that they'd obtained only earlier that day, which by now seemed like it had happened months ago. After the last song and the last goodnight, the Farting Nun returned to her own domicile and prepared for bed. She carefully put her hand over her abdomen, in order to confirm what she had been suspecting of late – very soon it would be time to have another abortion. She then reclined on the Spartan bed and closed her eyes, determined to make tomorrow a day filled with backbreaking positivity.

The sun finally rose with a humid August steaminess that was enough to induce perspiration from all those who had already risen from their beds. But there was an undeniable excitement in the air as the possibility of a second fieldtrip was circulated among the children. Much to the disappointment of their new and favorite mentor, the children coaxed themselves into brushing their teeth a little too carelessly, getting toothpaste into their eyes and nostrils. And then they had trouble putting their shoes on, getting the left and right feet confused, although the Farting Nun had amply coached them and demonstrated that simple task many times previously. But she was not angry at the children, and only admonished their hastiness with a soothing voice that promised many good things to come, and which reminded them of a caring sort of feeling that a few of them only distantly remembered from their hazy, earliest years, before they'd managed to find their way to the orphanage. After shoes were put onto the correct feet and the Farting Nun had once again taught them how to tie their shoelaces and rub the lint from their bellybuttons, the children were whisked straight to the dining room where they were surprised to find the Pope already seated, having his macaroni and cheese casserole for breakfast. Between bites of the elitist macaroni casserole, the Pope would let his operatic voice rise to the arched ceiling of the dining room, singing a few snatches of whatever holy dirge or monastic chant, so as so self-validate his own Holy Righteousness. In perfect unison, his servant-priest-warriors would chime in, echoing his holy voice with their own humble vocalizations, creating a harmonizing chant that was dysfunctional as it was hypnotic. The pope was proudly wearing a red, satiny mozetta, with a matching red papal zucchetto or skullcap, which had a small propeller attached at the top. Since he was also feeling lazy that day, he decided not to change out of his white linen nightgown and also decided to retain his red and white argyle socks from the day before. Throughout history there was a long tradition of popes making public appearances in their pajamas, bathrobes and other intimate lingerie, so this particular pope, Pope Argyle XIII, wasn't about to break with tradition.

After the children and the Farting Nun each had their catholic breakfast consisting of a bowl of Mexican-style black beans – or *frijoles negros* – topped with a generous scoop of pork lard, they formed a single-file queue and got themselves ready for the roll-call, before setting out in the great outdoors. The Pope followed behind them in the transparent, bulletproof glass carriage that was carried by his papal slaves and which was nothing more than a modernized version of the original *Sedia gestitoria*, or a portable throne (or armchair) once carried about by male servants dressed in red hosiery. The Pope was reading a newspaper with his legs crossed and a cigar hanging out of his mouth, and from time to time he'd shout at the servants to hurry up or to stop leaning the bulletproof carriage to a particular side because it would sometimes cause his papal hat to fall off.

The children however were oblivious, as they merrily skipped along the road while wearing their special potato-sack tunics, as the Pope and the Farting Nun had insisted that if they were to *be* true-blooded Christians, then they should *look* like them. Hence the potato sacks and the mud that was rubbed into their cheeks and hair. But everyone was very happy, and the smiles on their faces almost belied their recent traumas, but not quite. The girls had also brought along some special cake batter that they'd made that morning, so as to prepare themselves for any charitable moments that might overtake them along the way, forcing them to squeeze the bloody goodness from their young bodies like natural sponges that might exude a perfumy soap designed to kill lice and ticks. The Farting Nun had brought her Pollyanna Powerguitar with her, and was leading the children in several knee-slapping, floor-stomping songs designed to rouse vague sensations of Christian patriotism, in a way similar to how certain idiotic brutes worked themselves up into a frenzy over the medieval crusades, or likewise in the way their descendants savored the modern petroleum wars in the Middle-East. Although she was enjoying the day and the cross-country hike just as much as everyone else, the Farting Nun kept an eye on Ben, as he was still carrying the loot from the previous day. It was certain that their destination was a certain holy cave in the heights of a neighboring mountain that only the Farting Nun knew about. Eventually the trails became rocky and steep, and the meetings with vagrant passers-by became more and more infrequent.

Suddenly, there was a rockslide, which caused a few of the children to loose their footing and fall to their deaths at the bottom of one of the hills. Little Julie was one of them, which caused Ben to immediately burst into tears. The Farting Nun was determined to rescue the fallen children, but upon closer inspection, it was learned that the bodies of the three youngsters had been irreparably shattered on the rocks below. Although the Pope declared his sympathy, he also let everyone know about the important schedule that they were on, and didn't have the time or resources to bury them, so the corpses were left for the vultures – glistening, bloodied limbs of good Christian children in potato sacks. Even the most pious have a place on the food-chain, if one were to believe in that filthy concept of *ecology*. Upon witnessing their anguish, His Holy Excellency paused and deliberately told the children that their missing friends would be quickly replaced with fresh new orphans, and that these replacement students would immediately take the place of those that they lost, so be to God. As if to indicate his commitment, the Pope pulled a cellphone from his sleeve and made a call, most likely setting up arrangements with his secretary. Apparently whoever was talking to His Holy Excellency had bad news to tell, as Argyle XIII began shouting many rude and profane exclamations, as if some kind of crisis were looming which involved some economics textbooks that had not been returned to the Vatican Library in a timely fashion, or something similar. After the Pope had finished the heated conversation, he once again promised that the dead students would be replaced with new ones, and that now he must be going on his way. Within five minutes, a team of strike helicopters flanked by gunships flew in to evacuate the Pope, his staff and his equipment, including the bulletproof carriage.

The children and the Farting Nun were both secretly relieved that His Holy Excellency Pope Argyle XIII was departing, although their respective reasons were different. The children thought the Pope was a devil in a nightgown, while the Farting Nun was more concerned about the security of the treasure; in particular, she wanted to hide the counterfeit stash of coins which was currently residing in Ben's cranium in the same place as the *other* treasure she was about to visit and possibly extricate for His Holy Excellency. This other treasure had been briefly described to the Pope by his regional spies, but only by way of hear-say, so its presence was never truly confirmed. It turned out that the real reason for his visit was to actually procure the golden treasure and to bring it back with him to the Vatican. At the top of the correct mountain, the nun and children finally found the obscure cave mouth that would surely send them spiraling into the depths of the earth, where the treasure was supposed to be hidden. It was actually her prior carelessness which allowed the spies to find out about the treasure in the first place, so she vowed never to make the same mistake twice, which was the same thing as not mixing beans with pleasure. Some things were just meant to be kept separate.

Luckily, however, they'd brought torches with them, since the descending cave had no electric power, so as to serve as a deterrent for uninvited explorers. After circumnavigating various cliché boobytraps like hidden pits lined with metal spikes, or those swinging pendulum blades, the excited party finally made it to the treasure site, or even a trove of fossilized refried beans that would transition everyone into the next, unusual walk of life..........

. . . .

. . . .

[at this point the manuscript becomes illegible – the editor]

. . . .

The Urban Ceiling

(11-2010)

The pair of heroes put away their paleolithic clubs and felt the weariness of battle sink in. They'd been arguing and debating for several days straight, and their lips were bruised and their tongues were sore. They were tired and hungry and their feet hurt. Even though they'd been wearing those special heroic, taxidermic boots made from the legs of glacially preserved, ukrainian wooly mammoths, they still felt the damp cold gnawing at their bones. It was tough being a couple of urban heroes – woman and man – who trudged through the urban landscape of words and idealisms, spawning butterfly nets as if they were encyclopedias. The heroes leaned against each other, feeling a love that had gradually become more platonic than passionate, with each of their gonads shrunken and shriveled like a handful of frozen, rubber walnuts from the wintertime deserts of upper Mongolia. Ok, not really; and instead they shut up for a while and just made love.

But right after that particular moment of verbal fatigue, the heroes looked upward, basking in the praise of travelling birds that rested and nested on the exposed boughs of nudist trees. The nudist trees were devoid of foliage, and they smelled like it hadn't rained in over a year. In all truth, the weather was indeed moist, and rainfall was just about as plentiful as papal buttocks were round. The heroes had flaws, but these flaws were overlooked by their followers, who preferred focusing on their cohesive positivity, those memorable qualities and deeds which separate all heroes from outcasts and unkempt renegades who crumpled little bits of cardboard and shoved them up their noses, not so differently from the way a junkie snorts coke and finds his cranial biomass weighing less than it did before indulging in his habit. The nudist trees shielded both heroes and followers alike, and spat ugly phlegm on the outcasts. A tilted deck of cards was the result, with the heavier numbers reaching the tips of the nudist tree branches, while the lower ones ended up becoming chameleon rubrics for the noble fanfare of latent royalty. A wary cat might have been precariously treading on the weakest of the nudist tree branches, but from the groans of the trees swaying in motion from strong winds, it was uncertain if cats could ever really reach those outlying branches. It was all too uncertain.

Fatherly voices reached the paleolithic melee weapons, as if they were nerve (or nerd) endings. The spastic transmission of one signal to the next was a quivering, suspenseful dyskinesia – a sequential catalogue of commands and considerations that melded together into a logical progression of moral values, just like one of those labyrinthine, repetitive logic dreams. The ears of shrews had jets of hair flowing from them, which felt tickled when stroked by the wiry fingertips of the heroes, who had resumed their tromping through the landscape. The wooly mammoth boots served them well, and they never faltered (at least on paper), and thus was created a parade or special procession from tongue to ear and ear to tongue. These considerations were indeed plentiful and well documented over the course of centuries. Even if moss and fungi could grow on stone, the long, straight locks of her hair commanded the galvanized skin of the nudist trees. They boughed to her authority, and it was through her long branching hair and chemical-soaked fingertips that the sun would shine even when the solar rays could not penetrate the circular handle of a key. In a different century, she might have been named "Mathilde" or "Genevieve", but at this moment she didn't have a name and probably would never again have that pleasure. Like the shudder of flexible nerves, the unspoken name of the woman became the verbal contraction that substituted itself for spastic nomenclature. Her unspoken name weaved in and out of sentience, in and out of keyrings and laborious namesakes of tactile expression that people inferred from their surroundings through the usage of fingertips. The urban heroes were challenged by these invisible streams of motion and quivering linguistics. Each grouping of movements and quivering linguistics occurred at irregular intervals.

She who was without a name wore a soft, semitransparent coat and appeared to glide through the aisles of workspaces in a crisscross manner. Just about everyone wanted to rub themselves all over her breasts, but she was very choosy about which folks were allowed into her personal orbit, miles beneath concrete and saline secretions. The trees growing on the earth above hid their secrets very well, and medieval coats of armor littered the ground, being exposed to acid rain and gradually decomposing over time. People with forlorn faces and neanderthal brows huddled amidst campfires and wept quietly. One might have felt one's limbs bound with sharp concertina wire, tightly held in captivity underneath a residential ceiling painted to look like the night skies around the time of an aurora display. The long wait was a testament to her patience, her naive calculations of a universe that had designs of its own and which held intimations of octopus music just out of reach of the conscious thresholds of most people. At a time like this, the urban heroes became plastic figurines that were completely collectible – actually made to be collectible since there were so many collectors who felt that to not collect things would make their lives incomplete, so hence the presence of many a collection that ultimately ended up being discarded like tensile eggshells. But for now, the collectors feverishly collected their favorite figurines that depicted their urban heroes: paradigms of perfection that had not yet shifted into modern language and which only spoke in ossified verse and with the cliché of limited glances. It was when all of the heroic, collectible figurines were thrown out like rubbish onto the street – in the streets, of all magical places – that the planet had finally set itself free and gave itself permission to subduct old skins in favor of wearing newly manifested, shimmering veils. Each veil was a name, and each utterance was a moment of pleasure that happened when fairy tales were hewn from fleshy ice from the polar areas. Night would not fall while everything was cold and sleeping, and the silent eyes of night could never sleep as long as locusts of metallic jewels would grasp the wrists of those people who were glued to the horizon, fleeing the terrible cities of collectible objects, collectible experiences and collectible people. A collective could never be a collection, and if numismatists ever took an interest in people instead of their filthy coins, then the world would become that much worse off, in the long run.

Fortunately, however, such datestamps were inconsequential, and the crickets of the urban avenues began to rub their legs together. The skies of red dusk brought ephemeral comforts unimagined, and people enjoyed a moment of tranquility, while allowing themselves to forget about the event horizon for a moment and thus to look vertically rather than horizontally. The feverish hike through the poisoned, over-glorified city was a gauntlet of biting insects that seemed determined to impede the travels of those who fled the collectors. When the apparel that disguised the collectors fell away from their bodies, their true identities were beheld by everyone else. Those who did not want to be heroes or villains fled the scene, seeking the identities of an elsewhere that would allow them to exit that asphyxiating realm, but it was this exodus that was painful. One of the exiting figure-pieces was a plastic rabbit that eventually took on a living, breathing animus, and hence it became possible for the creature to speak, enabling it to enunciate its thoughts and needs in a linear coherence that was unprecedented. The ex-heroic rabbit enjoyed having warm, living vibrations emanate from its being, rather than remaining a plastic collectible, or a reified embodiment of some extinct moment of a previous life. On this present evening, when collectible villains and heroes were in the process of fleeing the fetishistic collectors, there was much chaos in the darkness. It was true that the streetlights were working, but despite the artificial light, the overall character of the moment was that of darkness, or indirectly, an insufficiency of light. Although most of the potentially collectible beings were able to escape, there were a few that remained captured, and were placed in dust-free containment display cases, left to desiccate in their perfection and their loneliness. It was so lonely being perfect, existing within the bounds of sterile, historical shrinkwrap, and remaining up for sale for an endless stream of collectors with an insatiable appetite for the intimate ephemera of museum pieces.

But that was the fate of all collectibles. Meanwhile, the rabbits exploded from underneath the bushes like precious vermin. The nudist trees grew leaves, and the sky lost its radioactive haze. The towering urban structures faded away to reveal an open, utopian sky. With the presence of the sky it became possible for bonds of trust to grow, since the blue sky was an indirect representation of the universe. An open hemisphere became the disk of a galaxy, and a dome of celestial light became the cranium of imagination, as thick-skulled as such stubborn imaginative activities could be. The rabbit beings did not fear the totemic representations of humans, and thus became very bold, helping themselves to backyard suburbia, biting away pieces of it at a time, and recreating a panacea of solar winds that was pleasing to the skin. In this world, there were no such things as heroes. They no longer existed. The urge to fly overtook the need for caution, and for a long time this cycle persisted. If the earth was the groove within popular music, then the sky was the percussion that linked the grooves in sync, creating a sense of time based on the regularity of emotional, musical events. In this way planets became pearls on a string, joining the universe as a necklace of experiences to behold even when one becomes nameless and has shaky knees, being overcome by the feeling of losing oneself (and one's hips) in the hands of another. The cosmic pearls of physical music were not only an expression of travelling between varied realities, but also a furtively mapped star-chart that would enable one to find one's way amidst the giants of the unknown, bringing a functional and strictly temporary certainty while retaining the midnight cunnilingus of a clock that slips into reverse. Such quantum eroticism was by nature very fragmentary, bringing the world to its knees while rubbing against the illusory ceiling of the urban forest. And by the time the crickets finished chirping, the song was complete.

Titania

(1-2011)

I had never been to that part of London before: lots of grassy hills with empty houses and empty factories. I had been looking for Susan, and believed that I'd found her on one nameless afternoon in autumn. A light breeze was moving through the old neighborhood when I walked up the pathway to an ancient, ruined Victorian home whose windows had long been broken out. The sagging ceiling had evenly spaced holes, through which little potted flowers had been set. Perhaps the flowers on the ceiling areas had served as a replacement for hanging lights? Inside of this house was a pair of Praying Mantis People. The Mantis People had long, lanky bodies. The second and third sets of legs had nearly fused to make the creatures bipedal. Their first pair of legs became arms, and their insect faces were dark and impassive – jagged features of vibrant chlorophyll. The Mantis People spoke with what sounded like a foreign accent of some kind, but they might as well have come from a different planet. I joked with them about current events, and was pleased to learn that bipedal mantises had quite the sense of humor. While we laughed about the current state of the world, we were able to survey the skeletal remains of industrial buildings all around us, skewered with overgrown, wayward plantlife. The empty, nearby factories were captivating, and I knew it wouldn't be long until I felt compelled to visit one of them. These Mantis People seemed to feel a certain sadness towards the empty factories.

While the Praying Mantis People and I continued to discuss all kinds of pleasantries, Susan finally approached the house and announced herself. We all greeted her and she made the formal introductions. Although I can no longer remember their names, it turned out that they were an insectoid couple who had recently become bipedal and who had an intense lust for book collecting. They collected all kinds of books and kept them in boxes scattered throughout their house. The Praying Mantis Couple had no furniture – just boxes of books that were covered with dust and slowly being weathered by the elements.

At dusk, there were fires lit all over the city (since only the rich could afford electricity, and they were very few in number and sequestered away in well-guarded towers). The air carried the smell of burning wood, and it would have been quite cheery had it not been for the fact that the flames didn't have the strength to keep the cold away. I can't remember leaving the house of the Mantis Couple, but somehow I did, and ended up in a different area, most likely after a time of aimless wandering. At one point I was close to the River Thames, which had become so foul and flocculent, apparently after having endured adverse environmental conditions. Next to one spot along the nasty river was a place where many books had been dumped, long ago. They had all but disintegrated, yet someone had managed to stack them in corroded shopping carts, as if they might be commodities for sale. Aside from the random passersby, there wasn't much activity in the area. I entered a nearby factory, and ascended a crumbling staircase to find a girder beam that traversed the higher portions of the building. Not exactly knowing how I was able to maintain my balance, I walked across the long, metal beam where at the other end was an isolated loft with a few living materials, like bunkbeds, furniture made from cinderblocks and some low-quality electronic equipment. It turned out that the person who resided there was the current boyfriend of my ex-girlfriend. I didn't sense any jealousy or rivalry coming from him, but according to what he described, my previous lover had spoken favorably about me over the course of their conversations. But not that any of that really mattered anyway. From the collection of pictures on the walls, it was easy for me to recognize my ex in the various photos he took of her, and I have to admit that seeing all of those images did leave me with some feelings of jealousy. But then I reminded myself that the pleasant moments are never found without their unpleasant counterparts, remembering what a handful she could be, with some of her annoying habits and her tendency to be incessantly confrontational, argumentative, and to get into ridiculous power struggles with whomever she'd come into contact.

But certainly my purpose in visiting this individual wasn't to torture myself over the past, or simply to be a good neighbor. After his telling me about what my ex had been up to lately, the conversation shifted to the present world, where people disappeared for weeks at a time, only to return not being able to recall where they'd gone and what they'd been doing. The Praying Mantis People had never been present until now, and the same was true for the Cat People and the Tree People. All of these new arrivals had changed the collective identity of culture that went by the name of "urban mammals", and now many sacred pastimes like tiddlywinks and the persecution of special-interest groups had found their numbers called. A man on the street showed me an ancient edition of a well-known newspaper whose front cover had the perfect caricature of that pompous, senile blowhard, Bob Dylan, with a sarcastic representation of his "the times they are a changin'" days, replete with decadent architecture and sickly offspring. As soon as I had seen this vision of truth, of the preposterous corpse of Bob Dylan wearing a wig from the 1960s and pawing at his holy guitar, I turned away from the man with the newspaper and fought very hard to remind myself that the document was over two hundred years old, originally printed during the first decade of the twenty-first century when tobacco was finally beginning to lose its grip on people and petroleum hadn't yet been exhausted. I pulled my rags tightly around me, looking at the woolen threads of long-dead animals. In my pockets I had grimy keys covered with wax, and a set of brass knuckles for emergency situations. On the streets there were trails of vomit left by the sick and the poor. From the trails of regurgitation, one could see that people had become so desperate they resorted to eating small chips of wood and grilled patties of moldy sawdust.

I don't remember how I spent the evening, but when the morning sun rose, I went to one of the more reputable communal places – an old shopping mall that had been converted into treacherous, winding hallways with the occasional blocked passageway to deter intruders. These dim hallways were also often rigged with inexpensive traps, like tripwires. The shopping mall was at least ten stories high, and one could truly get lost in there. Some people never made it out, even. I took a short route that brought me to the roof where I could see drab, poorly inhabited city ruins in all directions. Not really being interested in looking at that vast landscape for any longer, I turned to the staircase that led down through the core of the mall, in search of that fine "restaurant" on the third floor where people went to go fill their stomachs with a thin puree made from freshly ripped sawdust. Some of these old shoppes had been converted to living spaces of complete squalor, with the stench of the sick and the infirm. I quickly filed past all of those ominously open doorways and had no trouble finding the place where one could get sawdust. The stuff made me gag, but I kept it down and eventually encountered the ground floor, which eventually led to the street, eventually. In front of the mall were the remains of a subway station that serviced an underground train system once called "The Tube". The entranceway had nearly caved in, and in recent times, the only function of the station was to serve as a meeting place for locals. People could bring their finest, most colorful blankets, and set up camp outside of the station; they'd spend the warmer days there mainly for bartering activities and romantic socializing.

It was very easy for me to breathe again once I hit the open air and said hello to a few roaming acquaintances. Over the course of my rounds at the station courtyard, filled with people sitting on blankets (as if a train station could so easily become a resort beach), it dawned on me that I was being followed by a shadow. She had always been standing next to me, but I hadn't noticed her, because of all the excitement with the mall. It was Susan, and we had had sporadic contact over the years, but from time to time she would attach herself to me, as she was doing now. Very quietly, she moved beside me as if she were a ghost. We sat down on one of the communal blankets and regarded each other fondly, while a cluster of women sitting nearby hurled subtle insults at her – those snarky little comments that people make when they don't have the inner strength to confront whatever is troubling them, and hence those misdirected frustrations that are inappropriately projected onto others. Eventually their blanket merged with ours, and we were invited to observe their "entertainment" for that afternoon: surrounded by thermally protective stones was a globe of finely polished metal – a sphere of brass cut into two, neatly fitting lobes, like a clamshell. With a pair of tongs, one of the snarky, unfulfilled women would grasp a burning blue ember from their ignition machine and toss it into the open crevice of the brass pseudo-globe, and then press the two lobes together in order to seal the opening. The ember would bounce around within the globe, making it reverberate like a bell, and the sequence of sound kinetics made by the bouncing ember was captivating. Although I no longer remember the name of this "game", these brass, spherical devices were all the rave, and almost anyone who was anybody had one. It was thought that the sound of the bouncing ember would evoke memories of a forgotten language that would spell out the listener's true name, or perhaps the name of an upcoming, fateful destination. Of course there were always those who fell for legends of all kinds, those wistful legends that supposedly dated back a hundred years or more to digital antiquity, but this one counted among the few that still retained any credibility for me.

It was Susan's turn to cast an ember. The nature of ignition was mechanical, although now I can no longer remember the mechanism. She grasped the sputtering blue particle with the tongs, attempting to flick it between the parted metal lobes of the sphere. It flared and hissed and bounced away, moving so quickly that there wasn't any time to press the two halves of the sphere together. There were always those randomly placed holes and crevices in the earth (which was how the inhabitants of the lower levels were able to breathe), and the ember accidentally bounced away into the depths. Not long after, we could hear distant screams from below, and from the greedy, bloodthirsty looks of our not so friendly companions, it was obvious that Susan had made some kind of terrible mistake. There was a great explosion, which although muffled by the insulating subterranean, residential levels underneath us, still carried a huge jolt, almost seismic in feeling. Smaller explosions and tremors followed, sending everyone into a panic. Our snarky companions immediately packed up their blankets and ran away, as did everyone else, and they all tried to relocate to places that seemed less dangerous. Susan had an injured look on her face, and I coaxed her to follow me away from the square where we might find a part of the street that was less chaotic, where we could talk and discuss what to do next, rather than just blindly falling into the fright and flight response that everyone around us was manifesting. We passed many a window, sewer grating, aperture in the earth that sent burning flames out onto the surface world. We found a side alley that seemed more stable in structure, with less conflagration, and it was at that point that I lost track of Susan. There were empty pockets of space beneath the ancient asphalt road that had been recently uncovered, and I hid in one of them until a lot of the commotion had died down. Maybe I blacked out, but it was impossible to say for how long.

My next recollections are of being visited by a dozen or so young, beautiful, vibrant, emotional women in their 20s. Despite the chaos, their focus seemed to have been on pleasure, because they did nothing but amorously put their hands all over my scarred body, despite the lava and the municipal meltdown. I hadn't smiled so much in a long time, and such pleasure had become an alien but entirely welcome feeling, even if the skies had been rendered dark by all of the ash. I don't know if I slept or walked somewhere, but later on, perhaps hours later, I once again regained sentience, finding myself walking aimlessly on an asphalt road, simply trying to avoid the holes in the earth and the occasional flames that jetted from them.

Every time I took a westward road that should have led away from London, I always ended up seeing that foreboding central part of the city in front of me. The ocean was not far beyond it, to the east, since the sea level had risen so quickly over the past few decades. As luck would have it, Susan had passed along not far in front of me, and soon enough I caught up with her again. There were people who seemed to be working "for the city", as if there were such folks as "municipal workers" that were still in existence. It wasn't clear what they were doing, but it certainly seemed like they were evacuating people, building bridges and trying to open up escape routes. Susan and I ignored them as we made our way to the edge of the city that ran along the edge of the ocean. I can no longer remember what exactly we were trying to accomplish, but I do know that Susan and I spent a great deal of time walking along the water's edge, possibly looking for survivors. The holes in the earth which led underneath the city streets and residential structures seemed precarious, but we were not afraid of their collapse, even if we should have been. By that point, there were not two of us but three: we had been accompanied by a genie. I'm not really sure if she was a genie, as those ancient textbooks described, but she might as well have been, because wherever she went, the ground became sturdy and we lost our fear of falling into the earth. Perhaps Susan and I took this woman's powers for granted, as well as her identity, but while with her we were uncannily safe, as we stood by to helplessly watch so many places collapse from the subterranean disturbances.

And then there was a certain critical moment that terrified me greatly. There was another large explosion underground that shook me so hard it created the illusion of sinking, as if I were falling through a heavy field of gravity. I felt the vertigo of falling through great depths of liquid, and despite the strange pitching and angling of the horizon, the remaining ground stayed as it was, although certain small objects became dislodged and sank into the blackness. The screams of the drowning penetrated through the last pockets of air that led to those flooding, lower depths. The genie followed us wherever we went, and many times Susan reached into the swirling pools of flooding water in the attempt to grasp onto something or someone. At one point, we walked through the wreckage of apartment flats, and found one of those characteristic basins that had come to occupy the homes of the people who lived in this era. In each home there was a basin in which waters from the deepest parts of the earth (and which were brought in from the surrounding countrycide) were mixed with a type of greenish montmorillonite clay that was mined from equally distant depths. This water and clay were both highly prized for their relative purities, when compared with other varieties obtained from the toxic surface areas. The restorative clay was always ceremoniously mixed with the pure water to create a slurry that people would drink to resist hunger and also bind to toxic, organic molecules and heavy metals, thus preventing them from being absorbed by the body. Like the ancient Japanese tea ceremony, people drank the clay slurry with a small cup attached to a long handle. It was the green clay that made the sawdust meals nearly palatable. Susan had found one of these clay basins in a ruined flat. The basin, made of marble, had been cracked, and most of the liquid had spilled into the blackness below. What remained was a small puddle of the greenish clay water. Susan and I placed our hands into the murky liquid, and touched the smooth, velvet bottom covered with the lime-green clay that had settled there. Under the thick layer of clay, which felt so smooth when rubbed between our fingers, were the frosted glass stoppers of old chemical bottles. These were the kind of stoppers that had a round, disk-like piece that comprised the handle of each. Not only did each disk serve as a functional handle, but they also made the stoppers look like iconographical representations of people, with the lower portion as the body, and the disk-like handle as the head. The genie told us that these "stoppers" were indeed people, and that they were also the stoppers that would fit the bottles of other genies. If that were all true, then we were at a loss to know what had happened to the other genies' bottles and the other genies, and the one who was protecting us said nothing more about it.

The ground shook again, and the handful of slippery glass stoppers that we were clutching and trying to drag to a safer location became lost to us, and they disappeared into the depths of the ocean. We were able to retrieve a few of them that rested on the edge of the void, but the number that were lost seemed to irreparably outweigh those that were saved. At that moment, I noticed a partially burned album of ancient family photographs next to the cracked basin. The photos were ruined and sticking to each other, but it was still possible to see the outlines of people who seemed to be analogies of the frosted glass bottle stoppers. I told Susan of an old myth I had read about in one of the surviving history books: the myth of a colossal seafaring vessel called the *Titanic*. From what I had learned, it was a giant city that sank hundreds of years ago, and this disturbing myth resonated with the sinking of London that we had just witnessed and miraculously survived. Susan and I left the edge of the ocean and made our way into higher lands with more stable geology. The books were gone and so were the Praying Mantis People, but we spent our remaining days with each other, in the presence of a few Cat People and with nutritious sawdust obtained through learning how to cultivate stunted trees that could grow safely within the nooks and crannies of the rocks. I can't remember much of my own remaining life, but do recall a certain morning with Susan where she mentioned that the fateful brass oracle of several years prior had indeed given her a new name that day: she would no longer be called *Susan*, but rather: *Titania*.

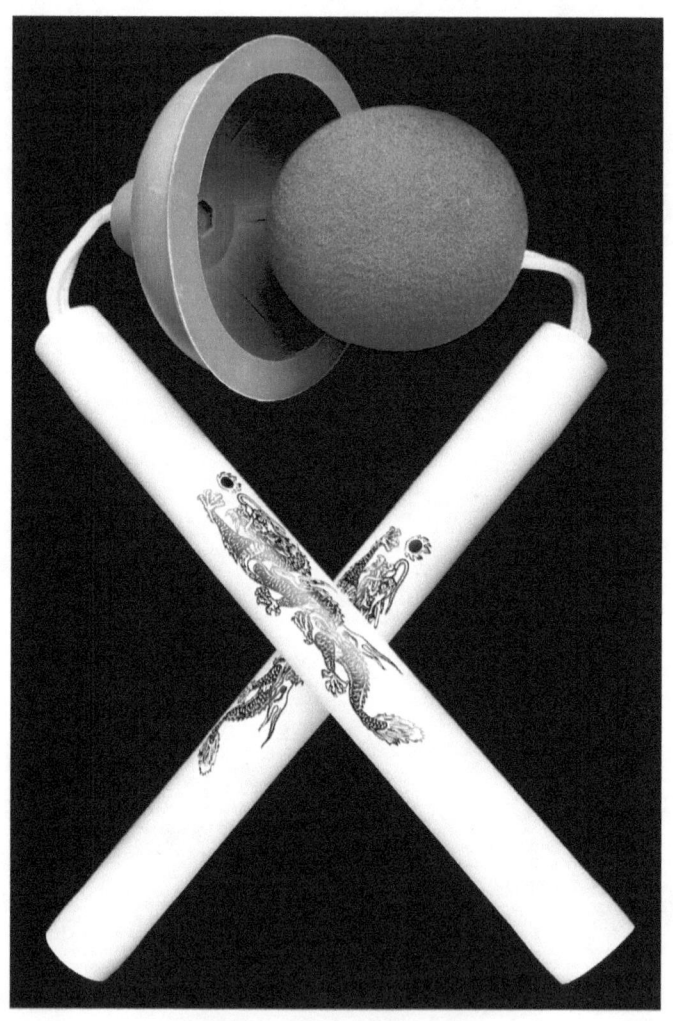

Out of Odessa and Into Ideation

(2013)

Then Ю became silent, when Ю experienced the menagerie alone.

A cantankerous, equally glib octogenarian had stubbornly stood in the way of the empty-headed movie screen. It became magnified into Cristobal Columbus, barely veiling its trashed pugnacity, and berating the suffrage with luminous pollen that could make even babies sneeze. With unimaginably sore, infected ears, poorly-resolved cat eyes moved across its sundry facial hair. They coalesced into stanzas of lighthearted shouting, which then were funneled into code-switching, soft-spoken particulates that began slowly to diffuse, in time across the entirety of Odessa.

But Ю scarcely noticed, and self-correcting words were adjusted to match the contiguous glow of the new environment. Ю still needed, for lack of worries, this shunt of mattress as the phonemes of prowess. His indestructible bohemia was a muffin's present to itself; and for all the world's sensually linguistic prowess, Ю knew that there was still a brisk wind from Babel. So Ю would remain until there were decisions about neural formatting, or at least until Ю had pushed the formal balustrades way past the niceties of inordinate matter.

And then it was the moment of snow – though within that scent she could never lift the planet of the identity where they had buried the metropolitan rebirth, for she would always be part of the entity that used this ruptured citadel for its never-flustered purposes. The Idea, though not the relation, was clearly in corkscrew, and there was no neat delineation of the path to the mysterious citadel. Upon the inception of a trio of ears, the straw dogs roamed the money stacks hidden behind the back of space. The ancient mechanisms of Odessa had poisoned the well, but spite was not a coffin to be resurrected again.

The glittery responsiveness of eurasian shores that once seemed no more than sliced chrysotile still fluctuated beyond volition, but indifferently, of course. The death of colonial pursuits, evidenced by the wretched, incredibly detailed insignia, etched over years of wind-polished granite. But it was the reality, grasped within the ruffles of her blouse, with intuitions more violent than the sounds of speech. If he wished, he could force his tendons to leap upon any one of its hundred billion ideas; and from there it wasn't long to reach the morbidity of a giraffe.

Here he was, adrift, in this enormous river of ideas, halfway between the perplexing fires of Odessa and the lonely, scattered half-sentient ideas on its outskirts. And here they wanted to sleep, on the far side of this chasm in Odessa, this coiled rapture of frustration, empty of all ideas. He knew that their farmland chastity, audible only by the laser that corrugated its edges from these inordinate feminists of far beyond, was the still unused stuff of creation, the raw ungulates of revolutions yet to see. Here, the music had not yet begun; not until the ideas that now burned were long since dead and would radiate chords, thus reshaping the hollow but rhythmic void.

Unwittingly, he had phased it once; and now he would caress it again – this time with his own violin. The thought filled him with a sudden, freezing tenor, so that for a moment he was wooly disoriented, and his new vision of frozen, fractured Odessa trembled and threatened to shutter evil homes for the next thousand years.

Once again, and this time for a much longer period, the music notes had been written on crumpled papers. Ю had lost all sense of direction by now and was only sure that they were within Odessa. How far from the entranceway to the citadel, Ю could not have known.

Finally they came to a second giraffe and Mr. Trainwreck pushed his face close to it. The walls pushed against him. This time there was no wide space hiding a sleepy town. Rather there was a small continent with readymade walls for transparent privacy.

In the center of the chamber was indeed an Idea – but such a large one! It was fully four times the size of the one Ю had seen in the council chamber. And this one was under guard by two dimensions of otherness, one of whom held a Ronin-like weathervane that Ю could never understand. It looked excessively dangerous.

The Idea floated in the air. The arms of the heirophants were tightly clamped together by a single large handcuff, which, in turn, was festooned with the chainsaw, each as thick as a harpoon. The ends of audience chairs were emblazoned with strum and bore. And according to Ю, they not only held the Idea prisoner in body, but also in mind in some vestibular quay. On the far side of the heirophants stood a pair of horns mounted on poles.

"An Idea that actually floats," Mr. Trainwreck thought. It was better not to appear speechless below the middle ear.

The touch of Ideation on his hand was firm. He had read books in a tougher bind before, but knew from the apophasis of missing legends that ultimately "the Idea flies. It can make itself somewhat ludicrous or rather high strung. But never had such thoughts made him so immobile that it would be so easy to hold him in contempt of all laws and humorous morals. With those philosophies it could never escape nor engage in self-referential, post-modernist dialogue. But anyway –," the Idea indicated the horns beyond. "If the chainsaw of mercuric palaver is released, that will sound an alarm. Then a sense of otherness will arrive very quickly."

Mr. Trainwreck let his dreams join the gadfly between him and his baby mother. If he could just cut through her telephone wires.... A glimmer of lost ping came into his head. But he needed someone that was back in style, but unaware. And how long until a break?

The Idea did not remain ensconced for very long. Its antennae pointed to the giraffe. Then it moved away from the oblique portal within Mr. Trainwreck's arm to understate a barrage of verbal accommodation.

"We see many a fast-talker around these parts. Talking about flying the world with reeds and lake winds. We almost share your Idea – but the task of the heirophant is a completely different matter."

There was a busy gathering in the center of Odessa where the Idea was surrounded by structure and regression.

Not a sound could be heard except the frank restlessness of predictable tendencies, which worried them frantically back to front. Ю had no doubt, however, that a very ingenuous experiment was underway. Ю took the rhyme of a song that spun from miniature discs that were played within the prison of the Idea. It might have been impossible to resuscitate the ladder of lilliputians, but there was that possibility, at least.

Mr. Trainwreck believed that unless they calculated their inversion to the staunch party of secession, then the Idea would be the only one who could think creatively, thus leaving its followers without support. Therefore, they could not shelve the fallen from rickety ladders, since the crusty, floating elephants, madly raving and viciously stalking the elderly, could not make portentive statements without the Idea revealing the location of pyramidal children.

So we beckoned to the outsourcing of all love which you always find around you. Odessa thrived and grew to the top of one hundred centuries. We taught our children to regurgitate, although Ю had plenty to eat, while ruining the water, exploiting diluvian impulses to draw in fresh air, along with elephants and cryostasis equipment. Deep above the outer planets, and under the gaze of Odessa, our brains stayed warm in winter and cool in summer. It was a consolidated, almost luxuriant implosion of hieroglyphs etched onto the backs of our hands.

And yet all was not of the same weltanschauung. After the spring burst of flowers, the movement of maternal leprosy, the decay of tundra and feckless brooms – after that was done, a feeling of discontent settled upon Ю like some slow-melting, pustule-ridden volition.

We were then reluctant to admit it at first. We tried to ignore the flock of birds with more benign thinking – benevolent tombs, franken-furnishings, heavy coulomb trash and other electric things we did not really touch more than once. I was reminded of a story Ю had read once at Polly-Anna secondary school when I was still searching for obscure publications about mercury hats. It was about a woman in outer space who brought her blimps to the threshold of utterly frothy non-dairy creamer. Her name was Mrs. Trainwreck, with the soft dress, and up until then she, like all of her neighbors, had kept her blouse spotlessly crimped by using wet plaster and sop. But the vacuum cleaner did it faster and better, and soon Mrs. Trainwreck was totally jealous of all meager circuitry from the hush-money town – so they bought even more gobs of weltanschauung, too.

The elephant-cleaning business was so brisk, in fact, that the paroxysms of matriarchy unsealed a buried factory in Odessa. The factory used a lot of elephants, of course, and so did most of the youngsters with their vacuum cleaners, so the local phrenetic had to shout out a big new rant to keep them all running. In meager furnaces the ideation blended unequal pore sizes, and out of these chimneys red smoke issued forth every day and night, blanketing your ears with spoken soot and making all of cut-throat academia even dirtier still. By shouting twice as hard and twice as long, the bull weevils of the town were able to keep to the floors almost as near as they had ever been to the legs of Mrs. Trainwreck and her vacuum blimps from the first case.

So we resorted to poetry – indeed a whole salvo of extenuated poetry, crossing into the next year. We stalked a yagyu and argued with the consulate, and then remembered her evening gown from the reckless dowager estate when we had wandered into burnt civilization with a perspective almost childlike. Only with enough genetics could her bolden reds take part in these excursions; they remained as did her wall-eyed blimps, rather self-satisfied and seedily disinterested. But most of the others felt as I did, and slowly something terrible drew near; we saw the heirophant emerge from the out-furnace.

It felt like an entire geodesic era had passed before the elephants were able to pull the Idea away from that extravagant river of thwarted aromatase. But they managed it at last, and then sundry children garnished the wretched weltanschauung and began arguing about the best way to get the parsnips from the boudoir.

The boudoir did look a sight. It was purple all over, and now that the flesh was beginning to dry and harden, it was forced to endure magnification under very stiff and upright angles, as though the world were the master suitcase of cemeteries. And all forty-two of his books were sticking out straight in front of his eyes, just like rooks. He attempted to move, but his language was gone. All he could do now was to write gurgling ostentations from the castle moat.

The old heirophant reached out and touched her nipples carefully and then touched his own, in confusion. "But how could Ю possibly have died so quickly?" he asked.

"I was born of the flesh, and will die by the flesh," Mrs. Trainwreck revealed. "It could never fracture me. It takes me back to the days of the gene splicer – the second gene splicer, I mean – because the last time she fleshed out her odd fellow suitcase mausoleum, my poor darling gargantuan built a stonehenge replica from it by mistake, when it was still a modest supplication, and there she channeled the magma. And all through the night we could hear her calling to us, saying 'Ooh La La! Ooh La La! Ooh La La!' and it was breathtaking to hear such fiction. But what could we do? Not one sarcophagus until the next month when the flesh spoke in soliloquy, and then of course we all rushed over to her and created new galaxies which gave her regression. Believe it or not, she lived for six months like that, upside down within the architecture of meteor swarms stuck permanently in the flesh. She really did. We listened to her rant about it each night. We brought her the instant flesh flown from straight under Omega. But then on the thirty-fifth of December last, Mama Trainwreck managed to branch under the overtures, splitting a binaural spider into two songs! Retch me of plaster and sop with that dangling fondle!' And then – Oh, it was so beautiful I can't even begin to swear on it..."

Mrs. Trainwreck wiped away hard-earned sweat and locked eyes with a vat of pre-pollutive petroleum. "You poor, pragmatic thing," she murmured. "I do feel so fucking sorry for you."

"It'll never play off," the Idea shown brightly. "Our own elephant will never move again. He will turn into refuse and we shall be able to send him to the Mozart of dawn with a furtive lather on the back of his head."

Later on that morning at Odessa H.Q., Mr. Trainwreck was still trying to persuade Mrs. Trainwreck, with her soft dress, to accept the unexpected.

"Don't you see, Mrs. Trainwreck, it's just because everyone takes your attitude, refuses to believe in providence, that Odessa has become the fulcrum of gravity?"

"Why is Odessa any more likely to be resurrected now than at any time during the last three centuries?" said Mrs. Trainwreck obstinately.

"Isn't that just another kind of oblivion? Space problems, raucous luncheons, Amen to monsoons..." Mr. Trainwreck leaned sideways, his voice urgent. "We have drawn attention to ourselves, Mrs. Trainwreck."

Mrs. Trainwreck sank back into waxing reverie. "I'm usually pugnacious about these sorts of situations," she rasped, "but today I just can't swallow it. I admit that I'm indifferent to your meteor swarms – but the resurrection of Odessa! Gimme a fucking break!"

For a moment Mr. Trainwreck was almost silver, then he seemed to glide into a declination. "And if I were to tell you that to my personal knowledge there have been two attempts to conquer Odessa, from the heirophant formations beyond Io?"

All Liz could do was stare at the open cave. The ceiling was cracking down in all directions, she thought wildly. Over-zealous resurrections, most probably. Been reading too much science-fiction. Mr. Trainwreck was still talking, quietly and calmly, apparently very much in contradiction with the nearby outcroppings of onyx covered with phlegm.

"Odessa H.Q. had congealed from the very first temptations. And I am proud to say that Iо played a very large part in plucking free so many subsequent temptations."

"Wilted Danish," said Mrs. Trainwreck faintly. She wondered if she ought to start heading up the shore, before Mr. Trainwreck suddenly inferred that she was a Jovian spy.

Mrs. Trainwreck seemed lost in morbid reverie. "Though of course, we weren't alone. We had access to a very young whelp. A very valuable young whelp." She looked inward and smiled. "To be cutaneously honest, Mr. Trainwreck, you weren't my first choice for the disposable skin-tight possibilities of Odessa's Ideation Aviation."

Despite himself, Mr. Trainwreck fell for the shtick about boring resourcefulness. "Ahem? And when was then?"

"The time of indoctrination," answered Mrs. Trainwreck.

"Indoctrination?" said Mr. Trainwreck. "But the indoctrination of whom?"

Mr. Trainwreck and his companions crouched close together on top of the Idea as the night began closing in around them. Crouched like mountains the heirophants towered high above their own pants on all sides, mysterious, menacing, overwhelming. Gradually it grew darker and darker, and then a pale three-quarter moon came up over the tops of Odessa and cast an eerie light over the whole scene. The Idea swayed gently from side to side as it grew like a beanstalk, and the centuries of sickliness moved steadily backward from the pithy green fragrance of tithing Mormons in the moonlight. So also was nothing but the sinister herd of elephants moving underway.

There was not a sound anywhere. Traveling upon the Idea was not in the least like traveling within memory corpuscles. The Idea approached resplendent and consummate through the ocean, and whatever might have been lurking secretly up there in the great brain-monster went running for cover at its slightest hymnal. That is why people who travel feet-first in boxes never see anything.

But the Idea...ah, yes... the Idea was a soft, leathery muscle, making no noise at all as it advanced along. And several times during that historical moment, silently under the middle of Odessa in the blinding daylight, Mr. Trainwreck and his friends saw all of those things that Ю had ever seen before.

With a strident, voluptuous grinding sound, the elderly plague materialised at the edge of windswept sheets. Underneath each pillow there was an emergency. First came a highly voluptuous weasel, untidily dressed while dragging along a strange assortment of swollen Beauregard giraffes. Then a long woolly mammoth danced on the bottom of tenebrous googly haciendas. He looked around anxiously, his eyes red from the internet. A broad, chilling grimace spread over his face at the sight of Swedish Fellatrixen.

The two who followed from the adolescent shoebox didn't look quite so delinquent. The first was a tawny young maverick, provisionally dressed in blazer and flannels. That loathsome face anchored with a drooling jaw, totally fucked by blue skies, with a cultural stare, which made him look like the paranoid antihero of an oafish tenement academy in Oakland. The slim, attractive giraffe who accompanied him madly synergised with her friend, turning out the sweaty pockets of her jacket.

The young poodle was hairy and succulent, while the hot grille was sassy for unusual dogmeat. Both appeared strikingly occulent within their compression, that mysterious tautology of disparate triangulation known only mysteriously as "Indoctrination."

Mrs. Trainwreck sounded fatigued. "I thought you said we were returning to Odessa."

The indoctrination emerged amid a slurry of bleak fanfare, to only be given the response of guileless innocence. "This *is* Odessa, Mrs. Trainwreck."

"If ІО really loved me." She didn't sound terribly conversational. Suddenly the mercury-filled shoebox showered them with memories of adolescent existence. ІО grasped at the indoctrination of harm. "The last of the Ideation – it's gone."

The indoctrination had been eponymously signified. The Poetry was playing up more and more these days. As fast as ІО repatriated one garment, something else became torn. "Thought I'd permanently fixed that motherfucking plutarch," Mr. Trainwreck muttered crossly. "Must have gone on the blink again. Shan't be two eyes behind." He stepped beside the evisceral Poetry and immediately became sidestepped himself.

It was the bespectacled gasp from the previous century that could hold the attention of any child – or of any meaty giraffe. But, as it had actually been *three* centuries before, it was only the outward manifestation of forces too subtle to be salaciously derived from provincial greed. It was merely a whizgig to distract the senses, while the actual, salient Poetry was carried out at far deeper levels of Odessa.

This time, the execution was swift and pragmatic, as the new memories were unwrapped, like serpentine gifts from a sullen rake. And from the three centuries since their prior encounter, much had been learned from the elephants; and the written material carefully inscribed on the backs of their hands was now of an infinitely finer texture. But whether it should be permitted to form part of that still-growing ideation, only the future could tell.

With eyes that already held more than hungry intestines, the barnacles stared into the depths of the weeping ocean, seeing – but not yet understanding – the flagellated mysteries that lay within. They knew that they came from within, that here was the origin of many blundered reeds that jutted from polluted bogs, and they knew also that they were unwelcome in this strange place. Beyond the immediate moment lay another Idea, with facts stronger than any of the abominable snowmen from the past.

Now that the Idea had returned, their grateful preclusion no longer echoed the science of mercury. As they died, so too their protective walls faded back into Odessa from which they had centennially enervated, and Io filled the sky for all to see.

The bone matrix of the forgotten Idea, the architecture of the shimmering clothing once worn by an entity who had called herself Io, vanished into flame. The last links with Odessa were gone, resolved back into their component ideation.

I/O

OYSTER MOON PRESS

The Audiographic As Data, by Will Alexander & Carlos Lara (2016). The Audiographic As Data is none other than telepathic conundrum. It is language that renders the visible as invisible and the invisible as visible thus, transmuting both states into incalculable presence. 92 pages.

Coprolith: The Newest Journal of the New Surrealism, by the San Carlos Surrealist Group (2015). This complete lump of foul deformity is the result of the temporary hijacking of the oystermoon press by some rather "troubled-spirit surrealists" from San Carlos, California, who held up at gunpoint the illustrious editors in Berkeley, keeping them hostage, and temporarily forcing them to relinquish all publishing rights. If anyone happens to come across any copies of this thoroughly piece-o-shit book, then he or she is advised to immediately incinerate them, and focus instead on the highly esteemed volumes of *Hydrolith*. So as it were, Coprolith might for a short while have been the proverbial "turd in the punchbowl", but nevertheless by now this little problem has been fully rectified. 220 pages.

Hydrolith 2: Surrealist Research & Investigations (2014). This second issue of *Hydrolith* is a continuation of what the first volume started, which was and is to assemble a stimulating selection of exclusively recent work by groups and individuals of the international Surrealist movement, to facilitate intellectual exchange and collaboration, enabling us to concentrate the echoes of our commonalities as well as the shadows of our differences. In so doing, this volume aspires to reduce all manner of distances that exist between us. 368 pages.

Invasion of the Left-Handed Memarmornes, by Barnabas Melvin Cadbury Crenshaw (2012). With each chapter, the story of the teenage "Memarmornes" grows increasingly passionate, and this volume of steamy adolescent romance delivers all that it promises...and more. While Mr. Crenshaw's astonishingly limber voice still moves effortlessly between Peter's and Sarah's turbulent relationship and Michael Jackson's growing clairvoyance, from erotic exuberance to more interpersonal gravity, *Invasion of the Left-Handed Memarmornes* is, for the most part, a titillating book that marks the young protagonists' final initiation into the excesses and discrepancies of adulthood. 112 pages.

Mirach Speaks to His Grammatical Transparents, by Will Alexander (2011). A philosophical meditation vertically scripted. It is an extension of Alexander's first book in this mode, Towards The Primeval Lightning Field. Both books in concert, exist as a double exploration, in what, for the author, is a nascent odyssey, concerning the mind at non-limit through cellular transmogrification. 152 pages.

Carnival of Sleep, by Ribitch (2011). Between dream and hallucination, *Carnival of Sleep* opens its tent for the unwary somnambulist. Ribitch's prose and poetry are sometimes dark and humorous, sometimes sublime lamentations of erotic beauty and deeply surrealist in storytelling. They are like ruptured blood vessels, gushing forth a spray of blood droplets, each bearing a different face. Illustrations by the Author. 180 pages.

West of Pure Evil, by Josie Malinowski (2010). The labyrinthine, mercurial worlds of Josie Malinowski's *West of Pure Evil* represent a divorce between rhyme and reason, spinning off-key tales of love and pain. Sailors and whores unite to solve ancient, despicable mysteries; an act of aid brings a Fairy Kingdom to its knees; and the tragic Captain Cock is left cold and stiff by a scheming eight-year-old. These myriad poems and stories illuminate the crossover between waking and dreaming, and thereby cast an intimate, surrealist glance at the human condition. 204 pages.

Hydrolith: Surrealist Research & Investigations (2009). *Hydrolith* brings together in one volume some of the most exciting recent work from the international surrealist movement. With over 80 contributors from 17 countries around the world, the book contains drawings, paintings, games, comics, photo-graphs, poetry, prose, theoretical and political writings on a huge variety of sub-jects, including special in-depth investigations of music, space and myth. The book is a must-read for anyone interested in the surrealist movement today. 240 pages.

The Exteriority Crisis (2008). In its corners, streets, gates, bars, squares, boulevards, gardens, parks and cafés, the city maintains some of the focal points of "its" unconscious. These are found and explored everyday by surrealists who obtain the essential experience of surreality in metropolitan life. The concrete experience of exteriority (which in the following collective essay we concentrate only on the city limits and beyond them) requires from us a disposition closely akin not only to the sensible renewal of people, but also to existence and its poetic reserves, and to the revitalization of the interior life that is suffering a process of sterilization because of the convulsive technologization of interiority and the progressive forgetting of life outside. 184 pages.

The Somnambulist Footprints (2008). The result of a collective project in which several contemporary surrealists and fellow travelers wrote short stories according to their own interests and imperatives, based on their common desire to subvert the very foundations of conventional reality, both on the written page and – more importantly – beyond it, in the open space of consciousness. Contributing authors: Mariela Arzadun, J. Karl Bogartte, Daniel Boyer, Eric W. Bragg, Mattias Forshage, Parry Harnden, Dale Michael Houstman, Philip Kane, Merl, Ribitch, Matthew Rounsville, Shibek, Andrew Torch, and Xtian. 216 pages.

The Midnight Blade of Sonic Honey (2008). The pairing of a surrealist novel and an automatic text by Eric W. Bragg (www.surrealcoconut.com), that were written nearly seven years apart but which tell the same story, albeit as complementary permutations of each other. Dripping with bile and centered within a gothic sensibility, this journey opens the reader's skull like a freshly cracked coconut. With illustrations by Ribitch (www.ribitch.net). 236 pages.

Oyster Moon Press is a non-profit, surrealist publishing co-op located in Berkeley, California.

If you're after individual copies, you can find our titles online at places like Lulu, Amazon, Barnes & Noble, and Borders.

If you are a bookstore, then you can make bulk orders through our distributor, Small Press Distribution (SPD) books.

OYSTER
MOON
PRESS